Contents

PART ONE

What Began It

Spenlove in Arcady

OTHER BOOKS BY WILLIAM McFEE

A Six Hour Shift—Aliens—An Ocean Tramp

Captain Macedoine's Daughter

Casuals of the Sea—Command—Derelicts

Harbours of Memory—More Harbours of Memory

No Castle in Spain—North of Suez

Pilgrims of Adversity—A Port Said Miscellany

Race—Sailors of Fortune

Sunlight in New Granada—Swallowing the Anchor

The Beachcomber—The Harbourmaster

The Life of Sir Martin Frobisher

Watch Below

WILLIAM McFEE

Spenlove in Arcady

RANDOM HOUSE · NEW YORK

SECOND PRINTING

ALL OF THE CHARACTERS AND EVENTS DESCRIBED IN THIS BOOK ARE PURELY FICTIONAL.

Published simultaneously in Canada by the Macmillan Company of Canada Limited

Manufactured in the U. S. A. by H. Wolff, New York

To

Dudley Nichols

and

Esta Nichols

with love

i

At last it was done, and he was free of his lifelong bondage to the sea.

Was he glad as the train, passing under the city in a darkness barred by sunlit openings, carried him away from that bondage? Did his soul leap at the prospect of an endless anchorage?

"An old hulk, a non-fighting Temeraire, being towed to his last berth" was his version of this performance. It was of no importance to any one in the world, apparently. At long last, he had made room for another man. He had given the whole long line of aspiring juniors below him a chance to move up one rung of the crowded ladder toward the top. It was part of their professional theology that any change of personnel was not to have any effect on the ship. So there would be no change, technically.

He repressed a smile as he thought of his successor. He knew well enough that there would be no change of policy for a long time. On the contrary, his own records would be religiously followed and quoted as gospels. The Company's Rules and Regulations had been based, in large measure, on those records. He did not consider them in the light of gospels himself, or even as commandments. They were, to him, Apocrypha, with a chapter or two from Revelations. Ah, yes!

Well, he was done with them now! He had ascended into the heaven of seafaring men and had retired to what old Captain Wensley called "a bit of a farm." There had been a dinner at a downtown club near the Battery when that magnificent old monument had retired, a dinner attended by newspapermen, cameramen and officials of the Line. Captain Wensley had sailed on a Cunarder for England, to settle on his bit of a farm—in Westmorland was it?—an imposing John Bull to the last, seeing the shores of Long Island vanish without a quiver of regret, without any emotion at all!

Mr. Spenlove, not being a commander, had had no dinner of farewell. He had, in fact, merely left, unspectacularly, telling no one save his immediate superior in the office that he was through. He had been scheduled to retire a year earlier, according to the rules; but the rules were elastic in such cases. He had carried on until sailing-day and then had taken his belongings ashore. Not through the gate into the city streets, however. One of the customs men, who had been on that dock ever since Mr. Spenlove had been coming in and going out himself, had taken charge of that old duffle bag, that long, black, officer's trunk with the name and rank in the Reserve painted on it, and the two old cowhide suitcases. Had put them in the customs lock-up shed for the time being, as a favor to an old acquaintance. So his juniors, seeing him go out with his raincoat and his overnight bag, had no suspicion that Mr. Spenlove was at last leaving his employment, after thirty years of service.

Yet so it was, and as the train emerged into the country, carrying him toward the oblivion that enfolds the superannuated, he made a conscious effort to see the day as a great event in his history, the beginning of a new era. He was, he told himself, entering upon the last of the Seven Ages of Man. Infancy, Childhood, Puberty, Romance and Socialism—he had survived them all and was able to regard with benignity and compassion the fierceness of the young and the bigotry of the New Liberals. He had "weathered Cape Horn as well as the Cape of Good Hope," as he liked to say, by which he meant the Thirties and the "Roaring Forties." He was now in the fifth decade as he entered what he called Dry Dock. This was the end of his professional career.

It was characteristic of those people in the office of the Afro-Iberian Line that they should have all silently assumed that he was headed eventually, like Wensley and the rest of his surviving contemporaries, for England and "a bit of a farm" over there. He had let them assume anything they wanted; but he was not going, nevertheless. It gave him, of course, a queer feeling of complacence that they should be thinking of him shortly (if they ever did think of him) as having returned to "the Old Country." Like an Indian nabob, or Roman proconsul, going into retirement.

That was what they all intended to do themselves, of course. Like Old Captain Wensley, they had drawn their sustenance from the United States year after year and had banked their surplus capital at home in London or Liverpool, buying building-society shares or Burma Oil Fields or Savings Certificates, so that when the time came they could follow Wensley into retirement, keep a few chickens and go fishing.

They preserved in their hearts a romantic England that no longer had any existence. They called Mr. Spenlove "an old crab" when he pointed out that they had been away from England a long time and the present generation at home had other things to think about. What did that matter, his colleagues, chief engineers and commanders, wanted to know, if you had a bit put by?

He found that he could not explain. All his life he had been aware of an incandescent core in his mind which fused the gross delusions of his shipmates into fantastic shapes. All his life he had watched those shipmates. He had seen them at sea and on shore, drunk and sober, married and single, covered with glory and occasionally with dishonor. He had bade them farewell, some of them, when they retired, or merely ran off home to England because they cherished the crazy fancy that they would be happier there. They had never failed to provide him with proof of his theory that they were bewitched, that they never knew when they were well off. Only old Romaine, his crony of many years, who had built up a restaurant business over on Second Avenue, of all places, had made a success of life on shore. He had done it by the simple process of accepting Mr. Spenlove's ironical suggestions in a serious spirit. "Why not make your customers feel they're on Park Avenue?" the latter had said. "You pay a Second Avenue rent, so you can afford to give them something special in the way of grub."

Romaine, a frustrated epicure and gastronome, who had cherished during his years as chief steward the ambition to cook an ideal dinner, had seen nothing bizarre in this advice. Many times, while at sea, he had experienced shame and indignation when his carefully planned and fastidiously cooked meals had been ignored by passengers who descended, dizzy with liquor, at nine o'clock, to be boisterous and uncivilized before tired waiters.

Spenlove had great wisdom, in Mr. Romaine's opinion, as proved more than once in the past. And now Romaine's business was prosperous; he had made the change from sea to land. It did not occur to him that his own temperament was largely responsible for his success.

But with Mr. Spenlove himself—whose restless curiosity and undisciplined imagination had been fed for years by the amazing kaleidoscope of Americans at play, Americans in love or in lust, Americans in search of culture—how would he fare, now that he was superannuated, placed on the shelf, condemned to be forever an obscure civilian in nondescript clothes, a gray shadow of his former magnificence?

These were the thoughts that engaged him as the train bore him away into the Connecticut hills. He was much too intelligent to miss the difference between a few days or weeks in his retreat just beyond the Norbury town line, and a permanent seclusion, with no pleasant resumption of his authority on the ship. So, in his imagination, he was now setting out on an uncharted ocean. There might be occasional landfalls and anchorages, and he might meet with friendly natives; but of these he was not so sure. He had never fooled himself into believing that he was, in the American sense, gregarious. He could not fool himself now by forgetting that he had exploited his position on the ship to evade the professional good fellowship demanded of captains, doctors and pursers. Now that he was a private person, without a uniform, he might miss the prestige and the attention he had accepted so carelessly for so many years.

These were some of his thoughts, not to be sweetened by the reflection that, after all, he was now independent of all passengers and their peculiarities. Independent, unless the financial structure of the Western world collapsed, of shipowners too. He could now, as the port engineer phrased it, "keep chickens and go fishing."

Mr. Spenlove was not so sure about the chickens. The widespread delusion that a seaman cherished a frustrated passion for farm life had never fooled him. He had other plans for the future. The hickory copse in which his shack, as he called his cottage, was built was screened from the side road that ran down to the long arm of the sea below Norbury by junipers and hemlocks, with a more distant line of enormous white oaks that made a tunnel in summer, through which the road passed to a humped "down," very much prized by Mr. Spenlove because it was the nearest thing to Hampshire he had ever seen in America. Along the back of that long hill he would trudge to where it fell away to the wide flat shore of the estuary. This was peaceful and invigorating, and save for several large estates, uninhabited. On the land side, a half mile walk toward Norbury took him to Sutton Corners, where there was a general store, a grain, feed, and hardware emporium, a drugstore, and a gas station with two bright pumps. It gave Mr. Spenlove a peculiar satisfaction to see, on the store's shelves, homely cans of malt for home brewing. Strings of dried apples were festooned with onions and hams from the ceiling. There was a large wood stove with an oak bench flanked by an apple barrel and a cask half full of dog biscuit broken small, in which a tortoise-shell cat often slept.

Brewing his own ale was one scheme he had in view, storing it in a barrel in his dark cool cellar, where monolithic columns of rough-hewn granite supported the floors above. Now that he could be sure of physical activity without the strain of the eternal vigilance which his position had imposed, he felt he could relax his asceticism as regards food and drink. The tendency to dyspepsia could be defied on shore, he believed, by wood-chopping and the carpentry he thought he could do about the place.

He had stumbled upon this seven-acre plot some years before, as it were by accident, through a passenger who was in the trustee department of a New York bank. A man like himself, in sight of retirement after many years in the same service, Mr. Merry had been at Mr. Spenlove's table for the cruise, and they had enjoyed each other's society. Mr. Merry lived in Manhattan, and there had been some further acquaintance, between voyages.

Mr. Spenlove had acquired a number of contacts of this sort during his years in the Line. He found Americans of that type congenial, and when a matter of a stock transfer came up, he had called on Mr. Merry at the bank. Mr. Merry had at once settled his business with the suave dexterity of his kind, and the conversation had turned to general investments. The banker, with a smile, had inquired mildly, "You don't want a first mortgage on a bit of real estate, do you?"

Mr. Spenlove had cautiously asked how much was involved, and where was the land?

"It's near Norbury in Connecticut," Mr. Merry said. "Six thousand dollars. The mortgage was part of a minor's estate. He isn't a minor any more, and we have orders to pay him his inheritance, in cash. The people who own this farm can't pay up. It's a six percent mortgage, due in two years. We don't handle farm properties out of New York State. Want to buy it?"

"I might buy the place itself," Mr. Spenlove suggested, scenting a bargain.

"Oh, I wouldn't advise you to do that," Mr. Merry said. "Not till you've seen it, anyhow. There's a lot of depreciation in those things. But the place is assessed ten thousand, so your little investment would be all right. We see to that."

Mr. Spenlove followed this sage advice and continued to go to sea awhile. Then he went up to investigate for himself while his ship lay in New York over a week end. He was always impressed by the casual way Americans spoke of sums that to him were far from casual. It had taken him several careful years to save six thousand dollars. To Mr. Merry it was a trivial transaction, by heavens! Well, it wasn't to Mr. Fred Spenlove. He had been thinking quite a lot about his new interest, a farm mortgage.

It was the beginning of his new life. Hitherto he had cherished the usual dreams of going back to England, an adventure that his intelligence told him would end in a dreary disillusion. England today was quite different from the England he dreamed about occasionally. It had been his favorite method of tormenting his colleagues, to point this out.

So the idea of the farm mortgage grew in his mind. He was now an investing capitalist. Along with his stock in the Afro-Iberian Mail Steamship Company, Limited, his maturing life insurance policy, his assorted bonds, the list of which Mr. Merry had contemplated with his nose all screwed up, and his pension, which was his reward for loyalty to capitalism, he had a farm mortgage. His curiosity had been aroused by Mr. Merry's story of the "minor" whose estate had owned the mortgage and who had now achieved what Mr. Merry called liquidity, and who was patronizing night clubs and the people who sold sport cars and twin-screw cruisers. That was democratic capitalism, Mr. Spenlove supposed. Some old hunks had left a fortune after a life of furious industry, and now the nephew was righting the balance, pouring out the cash into the coffers of entertainers, chorus girls and the vendors of expensive equipment. Some of that money Mr. Spenlove himself had supplied, and in return he had a first mortgage.

He had taken the train from Grand Central, as he had done this very day, and went out to Norbury. The taxi-man, when asked if he knew the Mudge place, started his aged Cadillac without replying and set off. Evidently the Mudge place was well known.

As they came up the road through the oaks (it had been early summer) the taxi-man flung out his left arm and slowed down.

"Want me to drive ye right up?" he said.

"What's the objection?" Mr. Spenlove inquired. "I'll want you to wait for me."

The taxi-man was looking up the hill through the hemlocks to where the hickory and chestnut trees guarded the old weathered shingles of the house. A single thin brick chimney, slightly out of line, poked up above the curved spine of the roof. In the foreground a gaunt barn, dark red and black, was closed save for a round hole in one of the doors, through which a black tomcat darted as the car approached.

Mr. Spenlove waited attentively. It was his habit to wait when he did not comprehend. He followed the line of the driver's arm with his eye and then he understood. From a horizontal branch of a large tree in the yard hung two swings. An old man and an old woman were seated facing the long fall of the land toward the sea. They were swinging, ever so slowly, in unison. They were not conversing. They were just swinging. A bird in a wicker cage against the back porch was shrilling. The bucket stood by a well, screened with a green lattice, and a small yellow cat was trying to drink from it.

Mr. Spenlove said nothing at all. He presumed that the taxi-man, whose delicacy had prevented him from intruding, would have some solution for this extraordinary piece of Americanism. Mr. Spenlove's experience with Americans was necessarily limited to the well-to-do, who came on board as passengers, and those efficient executives or artisans with whom he did his business. Apart from their restlessness, they were not so very different from the same types in England.

But this sudden glimpse of the America that lay behind the Glamor Cruise, behind the vast marble and concrete temple in which Mr. Merry worked, behind the crash and blare of Manhattan, was intoxicating to Mr. Spenlove. He had no idea that it was still in existence. He had imagined that it had vanished after the 1907 panic. He had been in Southern cotton ports where they had had no money at all and had to make shift with bills they printed and circulated among themselves, like children gravely playing at keeping shop with pieces of paper for money. He had seen the real America then, in the streets, in the cigar and drugstores, chewing straws and gum, red-necked and keen-visaged, and speaking an incomprehensible dialect.

Here it was again.

They were old, those two people. Not old like Mr. Spenlove, who was a vigorous fifty-odd, but really old, with the introspective blank gaze of those who can see over the edge of time. As they swung, twin human pendulums, back and forth, the sun caught their faces and illumined them like wrinkled parchment. They were startling; they were perplexing, and they reminded Mr. Spenlove of nothing so much as of some gray monkeys he had once seen in a foreign zoo, swinging in their cage, their arms around each other, bemused by their own motion.

The taxi-man turned around and released a grin. Mr. Spenlove got out.

"Sound the horn a little bit," he said. "I'll walk up."

At the toot, the swings slowly came to rest. The old woman, in elastic-sided boots, vanished indoors. The old man got off his swing and made his way down through the trees. When he saw a bearded stranger in city clothes and carrying a cane he stopped, his head lowered, as though he contemplated a charge.

"You Mr. Mudge?" said Mr. Spenlove. "Hope I'm not intruding."

"What you sellin'?" said Mr. Mudge, in the faint, faded voice of the old. Mr. Spenlove explained who he was. Mr. Mudge regarded him uncertainly.

"I only want to look around," said his visitor. "Nice little place you've got."

"It's the way it allus was," said Mr. Mudge. "We don' want any improvements."

"I see that," said Mr. Spenlove pleasantly. "Neither do I. It's all right the way it is."

There was the well, and in the yard he could see the immemorial symbol of rural America. There was a cord of stove wood stacked in a lean-to and another pile of logs. There was a five-gallon can of kerosene. A ten-year-old Ford touring car with a patched top seemed to have bolted behind the barn, as if to hide.

"You ain't goin' to foreclose now?" said Mr. Mudge.

"No. I was thinking I might buy this place, if you want to sell."

"Buy?" Mr. Mudge was nonplused. It had evidently never entered his head that anybody would want to buy his place. He scratched his chin and seemed uneasily balanced on his old limbs. "You want to buy? I'll see what she says." He ambled toward the back porch.

What she said became audible but not intelligible. It was evident, Mr. Spenlove reflected, strolling to and fro, that the front porch was hermetically sealed and out of use. The steps were in bad repair and the stone buttress wall, on which rambler roses were making a romantic pink parade, was falling down. The putty of the windowpanes was miss-

ing in many places, and whateve
spare time, it was not painting, Mr.

The conversation indoors gave him
unpretentiousness of this neglected
him. The great country places on the So
velously equipped guesthouses, stables, k
and swimming pools, their immense garag
their servants' quarters, had always struck
to the American scene. He couldn't afford th
sense, anyhow, even if he had wanted it. He di
nor did he desire too much suburban modern
neither an invalid nor a voluptuary. This was
week-end or vacation spot, where he could, as h
phrase it, experiment with time.

Mr. Mudge came out on the back porch looking a
conversation with Mrs. Mudge had added years to hi
He moved more slowly and he came down the step
weak and worn as himself, sideways, holding to the rick
rail. Mr. Spenlove approached with a tactful smile. M
Mudge, who must have been born during the Buchanan
administration, did not respond. He seemed to become ever so slightly smaller. He looked hard in the direction of the narrow lane that led to the taxi, which was being turned around by backing into the lane. Mr. Spenlove was conscious of the old man's embarrassment. He said,

"There's no hurry, you know. Take it easy!"

"She won't sell," Mr. Mudge said in his thin, faded voice.

"Well, of course . . ." Mr. Spenlove said, nodding. "Don't bother," he added. "You've got a nice place here. Nice and quiet." He glanced at the two swings and smiled. Then he touched his hat with his cane, saying, "Good day to you," and walked down to the car.

After all, he had argued in the train going back to town after a dinner at the Tide End Tavern at Norbury, where would those two old people go? They were probably as much part of the place as the well and the barn. The taxi-

ad given him a look when he inquired about the
and then had shaken his head slowly. Mr. Spenlove
o intention of deriding Mr. and Mrs. Mudge. "End-
rocking," he recalled, was a national tradition, from
cradle to the grave. He had watched wealthy Mudges
board ship swaying their bodies in anguished longing
that sort of motion. But he was curious as well as sym-
thetic, and he discovered from the taxi-man, who joined
n in a drink near the station, that the Mudge children
ere in the West and South and didn't come home much
ince the Depression. The old folks cranked up that old
jalopy of theirs a couple of times a month and drove into
town to get groceries and kerosene and feed. Yeah, they had
turkeys one time. Now they'd only got a few chickens. Didn't
need much cash the way they lived, he figured. There was
a lot of them about, people who didn't move with the times.
Go to bed with a candle, maybe, or maybe go to bed in the
dark. Why, old Pa Mudge, for years he came into town with
an old rig with a hurricane lamp hung on the back axle.
Hoss died, so he got him that Model T for twenty dollars.

There was a train due in from Stamford, so the taxi-man
took himself off to work. Mr. Spenlove dined at the Tide
End Tavern, among antiques, in a low-beamed room that
had a concealed and crooning radio behind a model of a
New England whale ship. He was exhilarated by his visit;
but he had no intention of evicting those two old people.
It would be, he suspected, equivalent to amputation and
death, quite apart from the fact that he had no use just yet
for a place in the country. His usual stay in New York was
now less than a week. The passion of Americans for ocean
travel had become so overwhelming that everybody was
being speeded up. Only a dry-dock job had held Mr. Spenlove's ship over the week end.

When he studied the list of his staff with a view to giving
the married men a chance to stay on shore over night, he was
glad he had no such ties. Strange to note how those whose

families were in England were less restless than those who had brought them over, or who had married in America! The exiles were resigned. They waited until they got leave, and made off on a fast Cunarder to the old country.

But sometimes he was tired, and then the notion of a small place of his own, where boiler-cleaners, machinists, and all the office underlings with chits to sign and messages to deliver, could not find him, appealed very strongly indeed. It was a popular superstition on ships that an unmarried man had no cares. Mr. Spenlove had once had to point out to a group of his colleagues, masters and chief engineers, that it was purely an assumption on their part.

"You mean you've been married all this time and held out on us?" said one, indignantly.

"For all you know," Mr. Spenlove had gone on patiently, "I may have not only a wife but half a dozen mistresses."

He stood by his bed place, reaching for a fresh bottle of whiskey, and he listened smilingly to the hilarious snorts of unbelief.

"He might keep quiet about a wife, but a man always lets it out about mistresses," said one skipper. Mr. Spenlove agreed. He was only trying to get them to see that we really never know, in such cases, how a man is situated. It was immaterial too, because what business was it of the rest of us?

One of his visitors nudged his neighbor.

"Old Spenlove's preparing an alibi," he said. "It must be that show girl he had at his table last trip. That mezzo-soprano. She went down to Cuba with me. Some baby!"

Another captain, a Prince Edward Islander with a weathered, wrinkled, nutcracker visage, croaked, "Only half a dozen mistresses?"

Mr. Spenlove smiled when he recalled their pleasure in imagining him with a seraglio. They were forever declaring that he couldn't possibly have anything to worry about, with no family to think of. Some of them, he reflected, allowed their marital responsibilities to weigh them down precious little. There was Captain Ellicott, who had a beautiful photograph in his cabin of a wife and four kids, who kept a cantina girl in Panama City. There was the chief of another ship, living comfortably at each end of the trip, in New York and Buenos Aires, in apartments, on Madison and the Avenida de Mayo, with what he called a water-tight bulkhead between the two.

What disappointed Mr. Spenlove about these exploits was their inconclusiveness. They guttered out like candles in the winds of circumstance. They had no real bearing on the lives of those men. Men of vast professional integrity, but emotionally, especially since the war, with no guts. Even the young men were more like dogs and cats nowadays. They had reduced love to a physiological function and knew more about prophylaxis than passion. More than once they had destroyed themselves, but not for love. They had not died nobly. They had got caught by blackmail, or disease, or the law invoked by an angry wife, and they had lost their nerves. They had gone over the side, or had shot themselves in their locked cabins, and had caused a brief annoyance to their survivors. But after that it had been no more than if they had gone ashore and failed to return. The sea had closed over them, as it were, and everybody on the ships tried to forget them as quickly as possible, knowing there must have been that canker of modernity in their characters.

It was because Mr. Spenlove had never accepted that easy gospel, because he had kept his own counsel in matters of principle, that he had built up his own peculiar reputation. He had, some of them said, a bitter tongue, and his inability to endure fools was almost as well known as his cunning in keeping up with the dishonest. The legend that he knew too much about the heads of the Line for them ever to fire him was a caricature of his reputation invented by those who were aware of his real character without being able to appreciate it. As he himself remarked, when a naive junior repeated the tale told him by a disgruntled official: "What he means is, I know too much about *him.*" And he added, "He's right, of course, but the other way round. The people in the office know too much about me." His cryptic answer confused the younger man, which was Mr. Spenlove's intention. He might talk for hours to an intelligent passenger, spinning yarns of the men and women he had known, but he discouraged conversations with his staff as leading to tale-bearing and wool-gathering; and he was not, he insisted to himself, a good shepherd. He had none of the qualifications of a father-confessor either.

To his contemporaries, whom he was now leaving forever, Mr. Spenlove's evasion of the usual affiliations of his class, membership in Freemasons, Elks, Buffaloes and Moose, or in the various knightly orders whereby men achieved unity and courage and mutual assistance, was a grave defect in an otherwise impeccable professional conduct. It was not, as one talkative skipper put it, as if Spenlove was religious. He wasn't even Episcopalian! So why didn't he belong to the Order, like every other white man in the Company? The only conclusions the talkative skipper could imagine were that "either Spenlove is an atheist, or he has influence upstairs we don't know about." All of which reached Mr. Spenlove in due course, but without evoking any comment from him save that "All sensible men have the same religion, but not the same ability to keep quiet about it."

Now that this pressure, as it were, was gone, and he could float at his own intellectual level, Mr. Spenlove had a sensation of lightness of spirits entirely unexpected. It heightened his excitement, which he kept secret, as he approached the Mudge place. It was still known as the Mudge place, supposing anybody at Sutton Corners had occasion to mention it. The Mudges were now, in the local phrase, "in Maplebrook," that being the Norbury cemetery. They had swung themselves, ever so gently, into the next world, a year or two after Mr. Spenlove's first visit. With the precision of reflex action Mr. Mudge, after burying Mrs. Mudge, began to die himself. It had been like a mechanism coming slowly to rest.

Mr. Spenlove was then in possession of a mortgage note immediately due and payable on an estate which seemed to consist of nothing very tangible except the Mudge Place itself. The heir was a son in Chattanooga who was not doing very well, and who certainly could not pay six hundred dollars, to say nothing of six thousand.

Mr. Merry had given a word of advice at this point. Turning from an analysis of Central American Utilities, involving a terrifying number of millions, he had done some telephoning into Connecticut to a brother wizard, and had at once suggested that Mr. Spenlove, instead of foreclosing, which would hold everything up for a year at least, make a cash offer of two thousand plus the mortgage note.

The gentleman in Chattanooga, who had numerous obligations owing to his increasing family and decreasing income, was in a pitiable state when he heard of Mr. Spenlove's desire to own the place. Mr. Mudge, Jr., like most of his kind, had no resistance when spot cash was dangled in front of him. He had, it transpired, to put a son through college. Once he comprehended that he would immediately receive the whole two thousand, all at once, without deductions, and that the new owner assumed all responsibility for the place, he nearly broke a blood vessel in his hurry to accept. He came up by bus, with an artificial leather suitcase, to sign the papers. His hands, roughened by work in a stove foundry, trembled as they received Mr. Spenlove's check.

Mr. Spenlove, sitting on a hard chair, part of a semicircle in the rear office of the local law office, watched the performance with pursed lips and smiling eyes. Probate, a word which had been ringing in his ears for months, had been granted to this nervous person from Chattanooga, and the leisurely, solemn processes of the law were grinding toward a climax. Mr. Spenlove had brought his certified check from town. Stamps were affixed, and a few local creditors of the late Mr. Mudge signed quit-claim receipts. The lawyer, Mr. Spenlove noted, was addressed as "Judge." This, he reflected, was a definite invasion, on his own part, into American life.

He went back to the ship on that occasion with a feeling that he would certainly stay a while in Norbury when he retired. He took, too, a new and more cautious interest in the passengers. They were now only more elaborately-caparisoned versions of those toothpick chewing folks sitting on chairs in that dusty law parlor, standing outside the drugstore, driving cars in the Norbury Main Street, or using the train to town. More than once he found himself remembering Mr. Mudge, Jr. and detecting a resemblance of some cruise passengers, with subtle marks of former indigence still about them, to the anxious gentleman from Chattanooga who was putting a son through college.

Mr. Spenlove thought he saw the replica of that son too, on the cruises, and he was not enchanted. He wondered, but without excitement or bitterness, at this preoccupation with college among humble folk whose capacities for learning were almost pathetically non-existent. He had had experience of juniors in the engine room who, as they expressed it, earned while they learned, by correspondence, to write advertising and electrical therapy. One was even studying for a ministry; but none had ever served an apprenticeship to what he was doing on the ship.

They were all, however, alive, and old Mr. Mudge was dead. Mr. Spenlove recognized, now that he was retired, that he stood somewhere between these two states. He was under no illusion as to that. If he was to continue to exist on a higher scale than those human mollusks that cling to the body of society by suction, he had to adjust his philosophy to living on shore. He had to have a new motive for existence, now his work was gone. He had studied, more than once, retired businessmen who had failed to effect this transfer of emotional forces, and he had noted their dull apathy when away from the financial pages. What did they want? he used to ask himself querulously. They spoke of sums in six figures, yet they never seemed to enjoy what they had. Their rancor toward labor grew shriller as they grew richer. Their faces set in the same savage folds and ridges he had seen in those of the stevedores and mine-foremen who drive coolies. The right word to describe their expression was exasperation. They had done well in this life; they gave to charitable institutions, and often they were decidedly churchy at home. But they became purple with anger and almost apoplectic at the thought of the proletariat which their capitalism had created. And sometimes, as they divulged to Mr. Spenlove the rascality of that proletariat, they would find his reaction not sufficiently enraged, and steal a glance at him, as if they thought he was perhaps, after all, a traitor in the beleaguered City of the Plain.

Mr. Spenlove had a number of vigorous resolutions, arrived at as he listened to passengers or regaled them with his tales of adventurous years. One of those resolutions was to avoid ever becoming like those old men. It was impossible, to him, to believe that retirement necessarily involved him in any such erosion of morals and petrification of faculties as he discovered almost every voyage in some costly suite or other.

Another resolution was to keep a record. The word he used in thinking of it was "scrap log." Of his life on shore, his "daily-run" (by which he meant what he had accomplished), and also "wind and sea."

This last phrase concealed his real object in keeping a log. He had the notion of recording what might go on in his own mind. The adventures of his soul among masterpieces were not so important, in his opinion, as his escapades with personalities. The only reality, as he had grown older, was thought, and the whole apparatus of modern living was elaborately contrived to prevent thought, to bring about an abortion every time a thought was born, or at any rate a miscarriage.

The scrap log, then, was to be a means rather than an end. His thoughts, he had observed, had always been, in his own words, vaporous and intangible. Perhaps, he believed, a scrap log might condense them, or even reduce a tiny residue to solid form. He dismissed the idea of distillation as ridiculous. There was occasionally something explosive in his thoughts, but they were not intoxicating.

But on the platform at Norbury Mr. Spenlove, watching the procession of cars and station wagons moving off as the train gathered speed and thundered away behind him, felt suddenly shy and forlorn. Both taxis had been seized and had rolled away before his heavy baggage appeared on the station barrow. The place seemed suddenly abandoned and unfriendly. A solitary station wagon, with the unusual name Church Yard in small black letters on the panel, stood solitary with its stern jutting over the platform, engine idling, door flung wide.

Mr. Spenlove's timidity, having achieved its object, retreated into the dark hole of his mind where it had dwelt ever since he went to sea, and he took a walk along the platform. That object, he knew, was to restore his humility. The owner of the station wagon was walking up and down in an agitated manner. He was not humble. He was, apparently, angry. Someone, Mr. Spenlove suspected, someone had missed the train.

He walked on toward the man, who was now staring at the station barrow trundling toward him with Mr. Spenlove's baggage. Why had he called his place by that peculiar name of Church Yard? Why, for that matter, did he wear a green eye shade, a well-worn pullover, light yellow corduroy slacks and tennis sneaks? Mr. Spenlove's curiosity, which had been the life-long enemy of his timidity, became active at once. The baggage man, who logically associated his load of travel-stained leather bags and their many labels with the station wagon, came to a halt. Mr. Spenlove advanced to meet him.

"No," said the man in the eye shade. "Not for me." He leaned forward and examined the labels.

"Spenlove is the name," said that gentleman. "At your service."

"And R.N.R. eh?" said the man in the eye shade. He looked hard at Mr. Spenlove and once again at the name painted in white on the end of a japan-black cabin trunk. "A man of rank, I see." He laid a finger soiled by typewriter ribbon on the words "*Eng. Lt. Com.*"

"One of the mugs," Mr. Spenlove explained. "I was looking for a taxi."

"Were you? Which way do you want to go?"

Mr. Spenlove told him.

"Mudge Place? I didn't know anybody lived there. There's never any light at night. No signs of habitation."

Mr. Spenlove told him. The man in the eye shade motioned to the baggage man and opened the rear door.

"In that case I'll run you along. I'm going that way. I live just past there. No. No trouble. There's no train for two hours now." He seemed to be saying this to himself. His eyes were troubled even if Mr. Spenlove was no trouble. Suddenly he smiled. "Get in," he said, and Mr. Spenlove was gently impelled into the front seat.

The baggage man slid the japanned tin trunk into the rear, dumped the leather bags on it, slammed the door, accepted a quarter with a gracious yet independent gesture and resumed his progress along the platform.

The man in the eye shade, which thrust up his sparse hair and overhung somewhat tired, humorous eyes, got in and the station wagon went off with a jerk that set Mr. Spenlove back on his spine and caused a shifting of the cargo, as he expressed it. The seats at the back had been removed, so his baggage went sprawling into the corners.

He held on. They swept around in a wide arc and flew up the street to the intersection where a red light made Mr. Spenlove wonder whether he would suffer a fresh concussion when they stopped. But his host knew all about that particular light. It changed as he charged across and took the road to Sutton Corners. Mr. Spenlove remarked conversationally that he was in no hurry.

They slowed down and the driver lit a cigarette.

"That's right," he said. "I'm just in a nervous mood. You aren't scared, are you?"

"Oh, not at all. But don't hurry on my account."

"You going to stay up here?"

"If I survive."

The man driving laughed. He patted Mr. Spenlove's thigh and seemed suddenly more cheerful.

"I know! I get thinkin', and the old foot goes down on the gas. That's all. Just a habit. Did I understand you to say you owned the Mudge Place? I thought they'd foreclosed on the old couple. I live just up the road." He made a quick gesture toward the road ahead. "On the shore."

Mr. Spenlove could see that his companion was merely making conversation. He could sense the preoccupation of the man's mind with some private problem. So he made only a brief allusion to the Mudge Place.

"But you don't live there, do you?" said the man with the eye shade. "Got a place in town? I mean, I haven't seen you around these parts."

"I come up for occasional week ends," Mr. Spenlove said. They were rolling along quickly but quietly now, the station wagon making the rattling noise Mr. Spenlove had learned to associate with station wagons. "From covered wagon to station wagon takes three generations," he had once told a passenger, who had replied crisply that "It was only one generation, very often, from station wagon to patrol wagon."

"I see. My name's Ducroy. Elliot Ducroy. Ever heard of Elliot Ducroy?"

Mr. Spenlove had heard of him. At first he was not sure how or where. He was not a devoted reader of popular fiction, but his senses had been exposed for years to the impact of names and faces in magazines, on magazine covers, in newspaper advertising. These superficial impressions, the result of advertising storms, hurricanes and steady downpours of newsprint, floated on the surface of his mind, or just below that surface, like masses of floating weed in the Gulf Stream.

Now, with an effort, he fished up, as in a bucket, the name "Elliot Ducroy." Ah! *"A new series by Elliot Ducroy."* He remembered seeing that, in stentorian type, on a magazine cover. But a new series of what? That was the worst of not being a reading man in the modern sense. His mind struggled with the problem. Yes, he had seen a story in a magazine. There had been an illustration of a man with a gun and a half-naked girl in a penthouse roof garden, sprawled violently athwart a page. There had been a story written around this picture, the type flowing into the irregular vacant spaces of the drawing. In small fat black type above it had been the reminder that it would take eleven minutes seven seconds to read it. He had remembered the exact time.

"Oh, yes," Mr. Spenlove said. "Now I remember. *Reading time eleven minutes seven seconds!*"

Elliot Ducroy, his eyes on the road, nodded. Then he laughed.

"Read it?" he said. Mr. Spenlove shook his head.

"I was short of the seven seconds," he said drily.

Elliot Ducroy twisted his face into what he would have described in his fiction as an impish grin. For a moment he forgot his own private problems. He nodded again amiably.

"You don't have to read those things," he said. "Sometimes I wish to God I didn't have to write 'em! But they're good! My stuff's always good. It has to be, to make the grade."

Mr. Spenlove saw that they were approaching Sutton Cor-

ners, where they would have to turn left. H
theme of Mr. Ducroy's professional excellenc
ment. He was happy in the company of a fresh
but he was a shade nervous as he approached t
a new and untried existence. There were mome
which the whole scheme struck him as hideously o
acter and partially insane. What, after all, did he,
seaman, know of the real lives of those astonishin
among whom his lot was now cast? He felt at such m
that he was nearer in spirit to Mr. Mudge, Jr., who
at stove-making in Chattanooga and who felt dizzy whe
thousand dollars fell into his lap.

Those moments were only moments, but they were ver
tense and made him apprehensive about the future. He co
manage old Mr. and Mrs. Mudge because they were ve
much like conservative old people in England. They we
more conspicuous because their background of wealthy shor
residents was more violent than the English countryside. He could manage the shore residents when they were passengers on his ship. But now he was here he realized what he had always known in theory—that America was no more a classless society than England was, that he would have to classify himself if he wished to live ashore; if he desired, in Mr. Ducroy's vigorous phrase, to make the grade.

"That way," he said, pointing left. "And about a mile along, on the left-hand side."

"Okay, big boy!" The station wagon swerved and came to a jerky stop in front of the general store. "Just a few smokes," Mr. Ducroy added, and Mr. Spenlove smiled with the benign tolerance of the cigar smoker for the cigarette addict.

So this, he reflected, was Elliot Ducroy, whose name, he now recalled, was large in the contents of national weeklies. Mr. Spenlove was one of those cantankerous customers whose nerves go back on them when they attempt the mental acrobatics of hunting for the needle of reading matter in a haystack of advertising. It was a comfort to note that Elliot

Ducroy, the human being, had no delusions of grandeur about Elliot Ducroy, the author, but a quaint professional vanity only. Evidently something had gone wrong with him when he raced to the station and found nobody there save a stranger. Evidently celebrated authors had their personal problems. Mr. Spenlove wondered what this one might be. He also wished he could remember what the devil the man wrote about. Hm-m.

Elliot Ducroy was approaching fifty, Mr. Spenlove figured. He was lean, plain, save for those unusually keen, humorous eyes under the visor, and with a manner that was a confusing blend of humility and arrogance. You can tell nothing of a man's personal character or position nowadays, Mr. Spenlove reflected, by looking at him. Everybody is disguised as anybody. He had once had an admiral at table who propped large national weeklies against the flower vase and read all through the meals. He had had a swindler whose manners were those of an old-world diplomat. Elliot Ducroy did not have to watch either a clock or a superior. That was about all one could gather in a general way.

The subject of his thoughts could be seen just inside the screen door of the store, engaged in conversation with Mrs. Dooling. Mr. Spenlove knew Mrs. Dooling slightly. She was large and imperturbable. She was not quite certain of the new owner of the Mudge Place and was pleasant but reserved with Mr. Spenlove. Mrs. Dooling's knowledge of local history included the dossiers of numerous underworld characters who had glided inconspicuously into Norbury from New York and set up temporary quarters. But Mr. Ducroy was obviously on her private list of acceptable neighbors. Mr. Spenlove heard her laugh, a deep-bosomed chuckle. Mr. Ducroy, he thought, was probably a good customer. Suddenly the man emerged.

It was now four-thirty. The screen door smacked shut, Mr. Ducroy got in and started off at what apparently was his customary pace. Now they were on the dirt road that led over the

hills to the shore, the hills on the slope of which was the Mudge Place. Cars shot past them, driven by chauffeurs, or by hatless young women who smoked incessantly. Mr. Ducroy looked at his wrist watch and frowned.

"Am I keeping you?" Mr. Spenlove inquired. "You know, I appreciate this lift, but don't let me keep you."

The machine rolled swiftly along the familiar winding road.

"That's quite all right," said Elliot Ducroy gloomily. "We'll be there in two twos. Are you a Britisher?"

"I've been told it sticks out all over," said Mr. Spenlove.

"Yeah, I guess it does; but I was thinking of something."

"That sticks out all over too," Mr. Spenlove remarked. "That was why I didn't want to take up your time. We go up this narrow lane. And when I say narrow I mean narrow. Mind the big stones."

"Well, here we are," said Ducroy. He had scuffed one fender against a large boulder. "Anybody at home?"

"Nobody but me." Mr. Spenlove got out and walked up the steep stone path to the now-repaired front porch.

"Well, who feeds that thing?" Ducroy indicated a large black tomcat that was vanishing through the round hole in the barn door.

Mr. Spenlove, busy with keys, was heard to say the cat was probably able to take care of himself. Seemed to belong there.

Elliot Ducroy followed his passenger into the house. Mr. Spenlove pointed to a chair by the brick fireplace.

"How much time have you?" he inquired. He was becoming more cheerful. He held up his hand toward a corner cupboard. Opening it, he revealed a row of bottles. "How about wetting our acquaintanceship, Mr. Ducroy? The well water is very good!"

"The next train . . ." The wrist watch was again examined. "I ought to get back and do a few licks before I go to the station."

"But now you're here, eh? I would regard it as a favor. I'll get some water."

"Hey, wait a minute. You see, I'm expecting somebody and I don't want to miss them, you understand. There's a special reason I must meet them myself."

"You don't need to apologize, explain or anything," Mr. Spenlove said. "I'll tell you why when I get the water. You will find that unblended malt in the stone crock very smooth."

Elliot Ducroy watched the newly hung swing door leading into the kitchen sway to and fro. Then he went over and examined the stone crock of Highland whiskey.

"Yeah," he said to himself. "Smooth as a rubber truncheon and nearly as quick in the kayo." He put it back on the shelf and carried a bottle of gin to the table.

"It's a bit early for unblended malts," he said in explanation. "I'll take a small spot of this. And a dash of angostura. Well"—he held it up—"here's mud in your eye, Mr.——. I've forgotten your name. After readin' it on the labels too! Now I remember, R.N.R."

"Spenlove. One of the mugs," added that gentleman, holding up a glass. "Where is your house?"

Mr. Ducroy waved his arm.

"End of the street and turn left. Back of here. Faces the Sound."

"You must think this is a pretty dingy dwelling," Mr. Spenlove said.

Elliot Ducroy looked around.

"It's all right. You aren't married, are you? You don't look married."

"Don't I? I'm not sure that's a compliment."

"I'm married," Mr. Ducroy said.

Mr. Spenlove said nothing. He had never known any good come of interrupting a self-revelation.

Mr. Ducroy drank off his half glass of gin and bitters, filled the glass with water from the pitcher and drank that off and set the glass down.

"You don't know what you're missing!" he said quietly. He seemed lost in thought for a moment.

In the ensuing silence he lit a fresh cigarette. Then he rose.

"Here, I'll give you a hand with your stuff. Luggage you call it, don't you?"

"Traps will describe it," Mr. Spenlove said mildly. "Don't bother. Just dump it."

"I ought to have had more sense," Ducroy said at the door. "No use bothering a stranger with your own troubles. Forget it."

Mr. Spenlove waved this to one side.

"You've been acting as if you had something on your mind ever since I set eyes on you," he said.

"Have I? I guess I have. I told you I was expecting somebody."

"And she has missed the train. All right. Mussolini made the Italian trains run on time, they say. But twenty Mussolinis couldn't make women run on time. So why not be philosophical?"

"I'll look you up some time," Elliot Ducroy said. He held out his hand. "Are you sticking around now?"

Mr. Spenlove nodded.

"I've retired," he said. "After thirty years in the Afro-Iberian Mail Line and its predecessors, I am on the beach."

"I was in the naval reserve over there," Elliot Ducroy said. "This is a funny place to hide away in. All the same, I'm glad. Thanks for the drink. I'll be seeing you."

He backed his wagon to the barn and spun off down the narrow track to the road.

ii

IT MAY be so," Mr. Spenlove said peaceably, "but I like it all right. I know what you mean, of course, but it's an expensive hobby."

She was the first visitor from the outside world who had not come to sell him something. On the contrary, she was looking for old furniture to buy. She sat on his porch, rocking steadily in the chair of the late Mrs. Mudge but, unlike Mrs. Mudge, she was smoking a cigarette. She was about forty, Mr. Spenlove thought, very robust, with the solidity of figure and clear, shallow blue eyes of many middle-aged virgins, and her weatherbeaten features were handsome and indicated character. The expression on those features, as she had glanced around Mr. Spenlove's shack, sizing up the furnishings, was humorously regretful. It was, from her point of view, terrible, she assured him. And she accepted a cup of the coffee he had just made.

Miss Penge—she had thrust her card toward him when he opened his screen door—had introduced herself as a neighbor. She was looking for New England pieces. Primitives she called them.

Yes, she had visited the Mudges quite a long while ago, and had drawn blank. She had been disappointed. If they had ever had any old stuff, she said, it had all been broken up and thrown away years ago. Or possibly they had sold it to a New York dealer. Their own stuff had been golden oak, mostly, ordered from a mail-order catalogue. And the most awful linoleum rugs.

Mr. Spenlove's additions, his substitutes for the golden oak, had been selected for utility and comfort, he reminded her. The lady's professional eye ranged over them again without further comment.

"You been up in the attic?" she inquired. "You'd be surprised what I've found in old attics. This house is over a hundred years old. You'll need to put in heat if you stay here winters," she added, nodding.

"What do you find in attics, for instance?" he said, not very enthusiastically. He himself had found an old leather riding boot, a broken crate full of preserving jars, a saddle and some portions of harness.

"Antiques," she said gravely. "Chairs, tables, lowboys, glass. And silver, maybe. Colonial."

Mr. Spenlove said he had read somewhere that the regicides had hid in the hills behind Norbury. They had what was called "plate" with them. Silver tankards, dishes and candlesticks.

Miss Penge nodded. She had heard about the regicides. But she suspected he was teasing her a little, not taking antiques seriously.

"Jacobean!" she said. "Why, if I thought you had any of that!" She shook her head slowly. "Regicides!" she exclaimed, smiling at her own audacity of thought and dismissing the idea. "You don't find much of that nowadays. Not around here."

Miss Penge's car, an enormous Locomobile of ancient vintage, filled the yard beneath Mr. Spenlove's screened porch like a megatherium in a prehistoric wallow. She had bought it second-hand for a song, she said, and it suited her business. Lashed to the back of it was a pine table with a drawer and a stretcher missing. A large green glass carboy sat, like a corpulent, transparent matron, on the front seat. Mr. Spenlove glanced out at this equipage.

"Jacobean silver, eh?" he said. "What do you do with this stuff? Sell it?"

"I work on commission," Miss Penge said briskly. "And of course I'm a collector. Glass."

"Well, I doubt if there's anything here of any value," Mr. Spenlove remarked. He glanced around. "I saw the place when the owners were alive, and they didn't strike me as having much interest in those things. Why don't you try down the road?"

"Down the road? You mean the big places on the shore? They give me commissions sometimes. They visit my store. What houses do you mean? They're all new dwellings."

"Mr. Ducroy's isn't. He told me the original structure was seventeen-sixty. You might find a Jacobean spoon in the attic at Mr. Ducroy's."

Miss Penge made a gesture of good-humored impatience. "He told you that, did he? He's right, in a way. The original structure was seventeen-sixty. But the original structure was burned down in eighteen-fifty-one. There's no Jacobean spoons there now! I ought to know."

"You don't mean you burned it down in eighteen-fifty-one?"

"No, smartie!" Miss Penge finished her coffee, lifted the cup in a half-hearted way to look at the mark, and gathered her belongings. "No, it was the Penge place in Colonial times. My great-grandfather, who fought the British in eighteen-twelve, he built it. The first house was built in seventeen-sixty—that's right enough. But the place before this one was built on the site of a house my folks sold to go to California. That was burned down and another house built and that was the one Mr. Ducroy bought and had altered to suit himself a year or two ago."

"That's very interesting, Miss Penge. He could almost make a story out of that."

"You know Mr. Ducroy?"

"Slightly. I've met him. He's a writer, I understand."

"You know Mrs. Ducroy?"

"I haven't had that pleasure so far."

"It may be a pleasure. Maybe not," Miss Penge said, smiling. "Mr. Ducroy, he's all right. I like him all right. As for her, well . . ."

"Why don't you like Mrs. Ducroy?"

"I didn't say I didn't like her. She's English, I've heard, and she's a very beautiful person. He met her in Hollywood, they tell me. I heard she was in silent pictures. You know, she . . ."

Miss Penge stopped suddenly, her pocketbook open in her hands, and laughed again.

"I'd better run along," she said, "or you'll think I'm just a gossip, talkin' scandal. Thanks for the coffee. Maybe you'll come out on Route Eleven and see my stock. Sorry you haven't any antiques."

"Well, you found me, Miss Penge. I suppose I'm late Victorian, not Jacobean. Plate, of course, not Sterling! Come again and stop longer. And tell me more about Mrs. Ducroy. Met her in Hollywood, you say?"

"Mr. Ducroy was in Hollywood, doin' stories for the screen," Miss Penge said. "He did *Gentleman Church Rides Out*. I saw it in Norbury."

"He's had a wide experience. He was in the war, he told me. I suppose it's all material for his writing. Writers have to use their own experiences for their stories, I expect."

"I wouldn't know about that," Miss Penge said cheerfully. She seemed to think her adventure in calling on a strange man very amusing. She gave a short laugh, and held out her hand suddenly.

"If I can't buy from you I can sell you some time, maybe. You *ought* to have some decent pieces here."

"I'm too poor to take up that religion," Mr. Spenlove said with decision. "I mean antiques."

Miss Penge looked indignant, as though the comparison of antiques with religion were a blasphemy—against antiques.

"Religion! Don't you like beautiful things?" She smiled. Mr. Spenlove seemed to be thinking it over.

"Come and see my stock," she went on. "It's on Route Eleven, the other side of Norbury. You got a car?"

Mr. Spenlove nodded toward the barn.

"I took over the Model T," he said. "The old man used to drive it occasionally. But I think it's seen its best days. I may get a bicycle. What does the T stand for? Terrificus?"

Miss Penge waved her hand derisively, and walked on.

"You might be interested in buying it." Mr. Spenlove pursued. "It's a genuine antique. No? Well, I'll get a bicycle. I suppose you know that story? By the way, why don't I see Mrs. Ducroy? Weren't you going to tell me something? I'm sure you were on the point of telling me something about Mrs. Ducroy! Of course I'm aware, h'm, in a vague way, that there's something over there . . . Yes. Something I wouldn't be told?"

"I didn't say anything about Mrs. Ducroy," Miss Penge protested.

"You said meeting her wasn't, in your view, a pleasure. Come, come! I've a good memory, especially for intonations. The way you said it!" Mr. Spenlove pulled his iron-gray beard and sharpened his bushy eyebrows at the lady.

Miss Penge laid her hand on the latch of the new screen door. Her pocketbook and driving gloves were clamped under her left upper arm.

"If you're so smart, you'll find out about Mrs. Ducroy for yourself," she said, and opened the door.

"Probably I will. When I get the bicycle I shall be discovering lots of things about my neighbors. Route Eleven, you said?"

"It's on that card I gave you. You can't miss it. The Spinning Wheel, it's called. Pity you don't have a telephone."

"It's coming. It takes time. The Mudges never had one. They'll get around to fixing the line in here soon."

"I'll give you a ring, then."

He stood watching her as she got in and started the engine. He pointed to the antiques she was carrying.

"I see you had better luck elsewhere," he said.

"Junk shop in Bridgefield," she explained briefly.

"What do you do with a thing like that, for instance?" He indicated the green glass carboy.

"Glass! I collect glass. But that's for a customer. She wants it to put on her lawn, with a light inside it. It's very decorative. You ought to collect something, now you're retired. Gives you an occupation."

"Well, at present I'm collecting impressions," he said. "They take up less room than antiques. Not so expensive either, I imagine."

"Think so? That depends. Some impressions . . ." She hesitated. "You're English, aren't you?"

"I give you three guesses . . ."

"Seems funny, you comin' to live here."

"I'm giving the natives a treat."

"Oh, is that so?" She made a derisive gesture and let in the clutch.

He watched her maneuver her car back and forth, struggling with the large steering wheel in a determined manner and coming perilously near to knocking a corner off his well-curb. The green glass carboy nodded to the jerks of the car as if alive. The decrepit pine table vanished among the bushes and emerged wreathed in vines. Mr. Spenlove wondered why a lady so devoted to the past did not have a horse and rig.

At last she was in the fairway. He waved. She proceeded down the narrow track, entirely filling the space between the walls of foliage, the pine table trailing a torn vine.

Mr. Spenlove dusted his hands and, relighting his cigar, walked across to his barn.

There was a lot more within those dusky red walls now than the ancient Model T he had mentioned to Miss Penge. That vehicle stood on its thin, flat old tires where the rig and buggy had once been. It was like a complicated scare-crow on wheels. Beyond this cobwebby chamber were the stable and the hayloft, and there, by an eastern window, Mr. Spenlove had cleared away the debris of two generations and had installed a bench and some power-driven tools. This had meant new electric cables from the house and a new floor. The old planks were rotten with age and manure.

Nobody, save the workmen, so far, knew anything of this transformation. Mr. Spenlove, engaged in getting his bearings in a new life, had been assailed by several fears. One of them was occasioned by the difficulty of making his actions comprehensible to shore people. He had no intention, for instance, of degenerating into a pipe-smoking maker of ship models. The average shore person, like Miss Penge, for instance, would be quite unable to understand Mr. Spenlove's dislike of model fanciers. Miss Penge, in fact, as she had sat studying him, had been suspected by him of liking models of whale ships and New England clippers. She probably took a loving interest in that last futility of the nincompoop, the ship in a bottle. Mr. Spenlove, in his years at sea, had been at close quarters with the seamy side of model-making. He held heretical views on its morality, and classed it with the culture of tropical fish and philately. The motives of most model addicts had nothing to do with naval architecture as an art, and nearly all the models they admired were wrong in detail or grotesquely out of proportion. It was, really, in his jaundiced opinion, which he had expressed to Mrs. Colwell on her estate at St. James, Long Island, a bigoted sect of the new religion. The Chinese worshipped their ancestors, he pointed out, but not even the Chinese worshipped the cradles and cupboards of their ancestors. Mrs. Colwell, whose gun room had a number of expensive ship models made by experts, listened with amusement as Mr. Spenlove expounded his theory of totemism indigenous in America.

So he was not making models. In fact, just the reverse, he reflected, surveying the keel and stem of the eighteen-foot hard-chine power boat he was building. The local express man had roared up one day and delivered a confusing consignment of heavy lumber very much weathered, massive packing cases, and a lot of sacks containing lumpy metal fittings. He had backed up close to the open end of the barn and had tumbled it all out in a heap, where it had lain until Mr. Spenlove had found time to unpack it.

Now he had started work. A local contractor had put in a large window, had laid a concrete floor, and had built a long, heavy bench, under Mr. Spenlove's personal supervision. The space scooped out of the cobwebbed gloom of the stables was limewashed a dazzling white, for it was Mr. Spenlove's strict doctrine that you got twice as much light that way. It was dramatic, too, because the rest of the barn, with a small door at the back leading to the stall of the derelict Model T was left untouched, dark, festooned with cobwebs, defunct onions and fragments of harness, the lower beams crowded with crates and crocks. The rusty bars of the mangers contained ancient fodder fallen to dust and foul offal. Old farm implements had been piled in a corner.

There was an opening into the hay loft at the top of this place and Mr. Spenlove, at work in his bright new workshop, could sometimes make out a pair of green eyes watching him. Invisible in the darkness up there, the old black tomcat would watch the invader of his fortress. There were squirrels in the eaves and an owl somewhere, and mice could be heard on occasion.

Mr. Spenlove enjoyed the perspective of agricultural decrepitude. It gave him an agreeable sensation to contemplate the broken disc-harrow in the corner, with its beautifully moulded cast-iron seat, which resembled, he thought, an iron petal fallen from an enormous and obscene metal flower. On its fluted curves the posteriors of long-dead bucolic Americans had rocked and trundled sweatingly across the boulder-strewn fields of New England.

He enjoyed also the pictures in the garage, cut from the glossy, heavy-coated catalogues of long ago, of early automobiles, and nailed to the garage walls. The younger Mudge, when he had come up from the deep South to get his money, had glanced at them with an abashed and mocking air. Yes, he had put them up when he was a kid. They were, Mr.

Spenlove divined, the shapers of his boyish dreams. They were astonishing enough now, the Merry Oldsmobile, the Chalmers Six, the Stanley Steamer and the two-cylinder Cadillac. Their fabulously colored tonneaus, their brilliant yellow brass gas lamps and incredible fenders, were part of the American Dream, which was to go as fast as possible from where you were to some other place, in which you had no intention of remaining.

Only a Model T had materialized in the Mudge family, which accounted for the heir's quick-glancing expression of good-humored shame as he passed through the barn with the new owner. It *was* shame, of course, Mr. Spenlove told himself, because there was no other test of virtue in the country but horsepower on wheels; and the Model T didn't count in that race.

He himself, he reflected, as he carefully affixed a thumbtack to a frayed corner of one of those pathetic antique pictures, didn't count even that much so long as he had no car!

Prowling now through the barn, he discovered that he was already looking at things with the eyes of Miss Penge. That tin contraption on a nail was probably a candle mould! How often did one look at physical objects with one's own, one's very own eyes? On land, he meant, of course. At sea one had to take the responsibility; no other eyes would serve but one's own. On shore, and retired, it was beginning to dawn on Mr. Spenlove that, so far from being a revered member of society, he would be beginning all over again. "In my second childhood!" he said to himself, pondering. It was certainly curious that Miss Penge, by calling and imposing her forceful native personality upon him, should be able to deflect his thoughts from what he was doing, should make him wonder how that savage-looking mole trap of ancient vintage was regarded by connoisseurs, and whether the elderly turnip-slicer, which resembled an abandoned guillotine, had a market value among the *cognoscenti* of Americana.

It would be only a short step, he suspected, between estimating their value and becoming enamored of them. Which he certainly did not desire. His philosophy had become worn down by time to the austere simplicity of self-denial of material things and the acquisition of impressions, which he attempted to arrange in some sort of spiritual pattern. Collecting material things was therefore not merely "bad form," to use a phrase which had been corrupted from its original intention. It was a sin against the spirit of man. He suspected that the things Miss Penge and Mrs. Colwell collected had had a totally different significance for their makers and original owners. He also suspected, by a clairvoyance that surprised himself, that the cult was a compensation for some defect in the present age of western civilization. Though of course in the case of the wealthy it was something else again. It was tribute, possibly. He recalled Miss Penge in her enormous car, the damaged pine table, with its legs in the air, strapped to the rear, as if it had been carried off, kicking, from its hiding place, and the corpulent, fragile carboy a safe prisoner within. They were to be sold to members of the wealthy equestrian order to adorn their triumph over the proletariat . . .

Well, he thought, in self-defense, one never sees the working classes at that game. The swarms of cheap cars that whirled through Norbury during week ends had impressed Mr. Spenlove profoundly as he had stood in the late afternoon sunlight watching them. No, it was a cult, and a very important clue to what he was looking for, a key to the national soul; but it was only one clue. It only applied to a section of the mature well-to-do, and seemed to consist largely of middle-aged women. Ah! Was that another clue he wondered. Did Mrs. Ducroy, for instance, collect Duncan Phyfe tables or Pennsylvania walnut?

He stood at the entrance of his new workshop and contemplated the scene with satisfaction. The smell of oak sawdust, even if it was American and lacked the strong, almost ammoniacal quality of British oak, was delicious! So was the turpentine reek of pitch pine and the lighter bouquet of chestnut. These blended beautifully with the smoke of his Havana cigar, which for many years had become a necessary luxury.

At present his handiwork faintly resembled one of those Viking ship skeletons unearthed by archeologists. Only the keel, the chine, and some ribs were in position. This was a month's work; but of course these were the crucial days. Also of course, he took his time about it.

He turned to the smudged and much-revised drawing pinned to the wall. It was Mr. Spenlove's idea to build a hard-chine boat without glamor and regardless of what sailing men might think. His sufferings with motor boats supplied with liners during the last twenty years had inspired him with the notion that the builder of a power boat for use should proceed on his course uninfluenced by the traditions of canvas or steam. Motor cars and railroad trains had had to emancipate themselves from the tyranny of the horse-driven vehicle. Of course this had been done by men who designed racing craft; but they were simply hulls crammed with engines. The noise was frightful, the cost of fuel only to be borne by millionaires, and the pleasure, in Mr. Spenlove's opinion, nil. What he himself was after was stability, moderate speed, weatherliness and no frills. It was amazing how much thought he had found necessary for those simple requirements!

He stood now, enjoying his cigar and also that subtle sense of near panic, which assails the craftsman in the midst of his toils, when he wonders if he might not with advantage change a scantling. Mr. Spenlove had already played the devil with some of the formulas of hull design most revered by conservatives. He wondered what some of his old cronies would say when they found the thrust block in the fore hold, for instance! And that was only a minor detail, by Jove!

He smiled to himself happily. It was very good to be alone for a while, he thought. His staff was now extremely small. Old Jim, who was "in back" as he called it, worked to his own slow rhythm clearing the Mudge land of undergrowth and dead timber, and was eventually to tidy up the yard, piling the kindling and firewood in neat stacks. And Mrs. Sankey came in during the forenoons to clean the house.

He was about to take up a chisel, to work on the frame held fast in the bench-vise, when he heard a dog bark, and he stood listening. There was no dog on the place at present. He heard a soft scurry and the sound of claws on wood. The old black tom had flashed through his private hole and had leapt into the upper gloom. The barks, the quick, senseless, vapid yappings of a young and conceited terrier, continued diminuendo outside the barn and a girl's thin clear voice, very peremptory, after the fashion of girls with dogs, could be heard more distinctly.

"Hector! Will you come here, Hector?"

Yap-yap-yap-yap-yap . . . yap!

"Hector! Come here, sir!"

Yap-yap!

A scrabble of paws on gravel and a throttled bark. Mr. Spenlove made a face. He had often wondered why young ladies who adored dogs were invariably born with a complete incapacity for the training of dogs.

He waited. Puss crouched in the gloom of the rafters of the barn, listening to the fracas outside. To arrive on the scene with dignity Mr. Spenlove had to go out by a door he had cut in the south end of the barn, and stroll around through the shrubbery to the porch.

"Hector! Oh, *will* you be quiet!"

When Mr. Spenlove reached the corner of the barn he had a clear view of a brindled terrier of undoubted pedigree being dragged away by a girl of twelve or thirteen.

She was bent low over the animal and her tawny bob had fallen over her face. She was bare armed, and her shorts were rucked up her smooth round limbs by her struggles with Hector. On her wrist were bangles and a watch strap. She wore a beret the color of blood. Her belt and her short woolen socks were blood color too, contrasting with the brief blue garment that covered her body.

Mr. Spenlove stepped out from the bushes.

"What's this?" he said mildly. The girl raised herself so that the dog was held suspended on his hind legs. She had a blunt, freckled nose and eyes of such unusual color Mr. Spenlove could make no decision. She was no more than thirteen, yet she was all there, he observed, and she was unembarrassed.

"It's all right," she said, continuing to drag the dog toward the driveway. She unwound a leash from a diminutive pocketbook she carried and hooked it to Hector's collar.

"What's all right?" said Mr. Spenlove in a slightly harder tone. "Trespassing? Private property?"

The girl stopped hauling the dog and her entire personality seemed to change. She stood up and looked directly at him. Mr. Spenlove smiled. He knew that his old corduroys and mess tunic had led her astray. She had believed him to be some sort of servant, like Old Jim, who was chopping away behind the house.

"I'm sorry," she said. "He—he ran after a cat."

"My cat," said Mr. Spenlove, though this was a lie, he reflected. Old Tom was nobody's cat but his own. "Our cat?"

"I'm sorry," the girl said again. She was standing erect, sturdily beautiful in first youth. "Hector will dash after cats."

"Hector! And what's your name? Andromache?"

The curiously colored eyes—were they brown, green or yellow?—seemed to be veiled for an instant. Mr. Spenlove's study of mankind led him to believe that sex was perceptible in all females of the species from the age of two to eighty-two. Here was proof.

"I'm Sonia," she said.

He nodded gravely. Yes, he thought, there was a wave of Sonias around 1925. Post-war mothers fell in love in droves with names like Sonia and Natalia and Dagmar.

"How do you do, Sonia?" he said. "My name's Spenlove. I live here." He waved his hand toward the house.

"Is that your wife? Is that Mrs. Spenlove?" Sonia pointed toward the broad-beamed figure and fiery, untidy coiffeur of Mrs. Sankey, who came in by the day and who was hanging up some dish-clouts on a line at the back.

"No," said Mr. Spenlove, and was amused in spite of himself. "Mrs. Spenlove is not visible just now. And where do you spring from, may I ask? Are you sure you aren't Andromache? She was Hector's girl friend, you know. Or Diana ranging through my woods? Perhaps you've come to pay a call."

The girl's expression changed rapidly several times.

"I—I'm Sonia Pagett," she said. "I live over there." She held her slender arm, with the absurd little pocketbook clutched in the fingers, on which were cheap rings, toward the south. "We came through the plantation, and then Hector saw your cat and I had to come after him."

"Well, Sonia Pagett, I'm glad to see you. Let's sit on the porch and you can tell me more about yourself."

"Oh, I think I'd better go home, thank you," she said. "I'm sorry to have intruded," she added politely.

"It's no intrusion," he said gently. "Where do you live, if I may be so bold?"

"Over there." She made the same wide gesture with her sweet youthful arm.

"On the shore?" She nodded.

"My father's a writer," she said. "He writes the Gentleman Church stories."

"Does he? I thought that writer's name was Elliot Ducroy."

She nodded and looked slightly confused.

"My mother is Mrs. Ducroy," she said. "Mr. Ducroy married my mummy."

"Ah. So that's it. I know him," Mr. Spenlove said, nodding. "He's been here. I've been there. Where were you?"

"At school," she said. "I'm home now. We closed for the summer. I'm at Harris."

Mr. Spenlove nodded gravely. He knew nothing of Harris,

but he divined from the tone that it comprised her present existence and was important. There was, to him, something pathetic and magnificent about American youth, even though he suspected both the pathos and the magnificence to be pagan.

"I see," he said. "It is a pleasure to make your acquaintance, Miss Pagett. Come on in. And bring Hector."

She dragged the dog after her toward the porch steps. Mr. Spenlove had the delightful and revivifying sensation that invariably came over him when he found someone who was not repelled by his manner. That manner was assumed, had been assumed a long while ago, to conceal his own fear of humanity; or rather his fear of a too-close contact with them. So long as they remained on the outside, mere decorative figures on a promenade deck, fenced by the formal rules of the social game, he could enjoy watching them. But if they wanted to pass the turnstile and enter his private world they had to submit to the ordeal of his manner, sly, caustic, confusingly humorous and dominated by his eyebrows and beard, as though he were trying to disconcert them. Those who ignored the manner, who instinctively perceived the sort of man he was inside his protective shell, had no difficulties. They knew him for what he was, a shy, lonely person, who had become so accustomed to spiritual solitude that he enjoyed it as a rule, but who was always being betrayed into conversation by his philosophical curiosity about humanity and his passion for telling stories.

Hector was another victim of curiosity, it appeared, for he at once attempted to get under the porch.

"I expect his sense of smell must be a perfect torture to him here," Mr. Spenlove said confidentially. He opened the door for his young visitors. "Think of it! I've only been here two months and I've seen a deer, a woodchuck, about a dozen rabbits, several chipmunks, assorted squirrels, a skunk, and an opossum in this yard. Each with a special smell! And of course there's Tobermory."

"Tobermory?"

"That's what I call the cat your dog was after. He isn't really my cat. I mean he's on his own. He likes Old Jim, the man I have here to work, much better. He likes Mrs. Sankey, who cleans for me, because she brings him a piece of liver sometimes. He sits in my barn and watches me at work. Well, think of all of those animals leaving their scent, and poor Hector plunging into a sort of maelstrom of smells! With an olfactory apparatus like Hector's it's a wonder he doesn't have hysterics."

They sat on the porch. Mr. Spenlove lay back in a cane seat and Sonia began to swing sensuously in the rocking chair. He relit his cigar and contemplated her beautiful and innocently revealed person, the flat-soled childish canvas shoes, the bright baby-socks, the smooth contours of her limbs and the girlish nipples thrusting out from her young bosom. He watched with pleasure the curious change of color in her eyes, her nice little snub nose with its freckles, and the tender mouth. He wondered swiftly about Mrs. Ducroy, and then returned to Sonia.

"Is that his name, Tobermory? Does he answer to it?"

"They say all cats have three names," Mr. Spenlove mused. "I can't answer for this one. He was here before me. He really owns this place, you know."

"I thought you were Mr. Mudge's brother or something," said Sonia, rocking. "When you first came."

"No. I expect the cat is a reincarnation of Mr. Mudge's brother, if he ever had a brother. I bought this place from his son. I call the cat Tobermory after a famous cat who learned to talk."

"A cat talk?" said Sonia. She leaned forward, forgetting to rock and thrust her bare arms down between her thighs. She scented a story. She adored stories.

"You can imagine the sensation it caused in the family," said Mr. Spenlove calmly. "It was a house like yours, only in England. There was a large party for the week end, and the family cat suddenly began to make, well, rather catty remarks, you may say, about the behavior of the guests."

"Oh! Oof!" Sonia gave a delighted gasp, almost a grunt. She put her knuckles to her mouth and shivered with excitement.

"Go on!" she said in a stifled voice. "Please go on!"

"It's in a book," he said smiling. "I'll lend it to you if you like. He's one of my favorite characters in modern literature, Tobermory."

Hector had subsided, his highly bred head on his exaggerated front paws, a gloomy expression on his face.

"We'll have to change the subject," Mr. Spenlove said, pointing to Hector. "They're psychic, you know, dogs are. They know what you say, to a certain extent. I suppose you are too. You look as if you might be."

"I've never been psyched," Sonia said, suddenly grave. "Mother thinks there's something in it. I don't like it."

"I don't either," Mr. Spenlove agreed. "I didn't mean that. I said psychic, not psyched. You're sensitive to influences from . . ." He made a vague comprehensive gesture. "You got the idea of Tobermory at once. Girls, and boys too sometimes, are like radio tubes. They pick up things we miss, from the ether."

"I don't quite know what you mean," she said looking down at Hector and rubbing his head. "Are you a doctor?"

"A doctor? Oh, I suppose you think the beard goes with the idea of a doctor. No, I'm just living here, retiring from the world. The country's good for my health, you know. You might say I was in hiding! I want to be quiet. But I met your stepfather when I came down here to live and I went to your house once. Lot of people there that time. But I didn't meet your mother. How was that?"

"I don't know," she said slowly, as though she were thinking of something else. "Were they tight, the people at our house?"

"Tight? Oh, I suppose some of them were. It was a party, and there was plenty to drink, I remember."

"Do you have people tight at your house?" she inquired casually.

He blew out a great cloud of cigar smoke that drove away suddenly as he laughed.

"Well!" He laughed again. She was so earnest about this that he was forced to revise his somewhat shadowy conception of Mrs. Ducroy. "Not many. I don't have parties, you know. Not yet. Don't you like people to get tight?"

She gave a shrug of her shoulders and shook her head, making a faint grimace, a subtle gesture of repulsion.

"Eh?" he said, and after a long pause, "You mustn't be too intolerant, you know. When people get on in life they haven't *your* resources for amusing themselves. They take a few drinks to jolly themselves up. By the way, you and I ought to drink to our better acquaintance. There's some ginger ale and Coca-Cola, and there's my tipple, ginger beer. Like to try it? It's very popular with kids in England."

"You're English, aren't you? Elliot said he thought you were English. We have English girls at Harris. Their families are in Washington."

"Are they? Elliot? Who's Elliot? Oh, your stepfather. You use his given name? That's the new style, I suppose. Or is it just a very old style come back into circulation? Yes, I suppose you can say England is my country of origin. It's a long while since I lived there, though. I can assure you I would be much more of a stranger there than here. I've been at sea for nearly thirty years, you see. On ships, you know."

"Elliot said you were a naval officer."

"Something like that. Now I'm on the beach. I'm like a boat hauled up out of the sea for good."

He smiled and got up to go into the house. He took two glasses from the corner cupboard, and put a finger of gin in one of them for himself. He opened a stone bottle of ginger beer. On the back porch he extracted a piece of ice from the old-fashioned icebox.

"Try this," he said. "Here's luck."

She took a sip of the ginger beer, and then several more sips. He was not sure whether she was going to like it or not.

"I suppose you have ginger ale as a rule," he said. "I usually have tea in the afternoon. What does Elliot drink?"

"He says tea in the morning and whiskey and soda in the afternoon. But he really prefers coffee. He has something the matter with his heart."

"Not heart disease?"

"No, but sometimes he has been very sick, so he doesn't drink very much."

"Not like his guests."

The girl said nothing. She sat taking sips from the glass and looking out into the sun-drenched yard. Mr. Spenlove contemplated her and thought of the flight of time. He was reminded by this drinking of gin-and-ginger beer of his days on the old *Sycorax* in the Aegean during the last war. Everybody in the ward-room used to order gin-and-ginger beer, or sherry and bitters. They had had only one souse on that ship, and he generally had the tact to get drunk on shore. That was twenty-one years ago, he thought. Where were they all now? It was probable that he had survived all of them. Sitting under his own roof-tree, in an alien land, he was entertaining a fairy child who had come suddenly out of the woodland!

She was a strangely attractive person, half child and half nymph. Mr. Spenlove delighted in her beautiful and charming poise, her completely American acceptance of him as a social contemporary. But her manner had also a delicate shyness, like a garment of light from another world.

"I'm English," she said suddenly, as though she had been thinking about this fact for some moments. "I mean, Mother's English."

"Father too?" Mr. Spenlove said casually. For some absurd

reason he was eager about this, though he did not want to let her know.

She nodded. She was wishing she had a straw. She was certain this stuff would be even better taken through a straw.

"Is he in England?"

Sonia shook her head gravely.

"Mother got a divorce," she said in her clear, candid voice. Mr. Spenlove nodded in return with what he hoped was sympathy and intelligence. This sort of thing made him cautious in claiming knowledge of his adopted country. Or perhaps it was merely his knowledge of the new generation that was not too good.

"I see. And now you've got a stepfather. And he's got a nice daughter."

She laughed, and seeming to think of something she said, "Have you any daughters?"

Mr. Spenlove laughed, and after a pause, laughed again, much louder.

"That," he said, "as they say, is a new one on me. When I was on a ship the passengers used to ask me all kinds of questions, but they never hit on that one. No, I haven't any family, Sonia. I am not married. Your stepfather said I didn't know what I was missing. I'm beginning to see what he meant. I am beginning to think he was right."

Sonia smiled and drank some more of her ginger beer.

"Elliot said you were funny to talk to," she said. "I think so too."

"Very handsome of you both."

Sonia suddenly seemed to become shy. She put her glass down and examined her knees. Her tawny bob fell over her face like a shutter. Mr. Spenlove wondered if there was anything more beautiful than the young female body. Or the young body, possibly. There was something almost painful in the contemplation of its tender immaturity. And if you kept sentiment, the cheap sentiment of the market place, out of your thoughts, that pain made one understand what the old religious artists were trying to express.

For a moment he sat silent, seeking to capture that elusive idea.

"Well, I hope you'll come and see me again," he said gently, adding, "now you know the way."

She took another swig at her drink and finished it and looked at her tiny wrist watch. Hector, who had given up hope that anything would ever happen again of any interest, strove to drag her out to the door.

"I must go," she said. "I promised Mother I would go to Norbury in the car."

"Don't let me keep you. I'll come and have tea with you one of these days."

"Tea?" she said. "All right. But at our house tea is always drinks. Elliot says that's what they come for! I'll ask Louis to have some tea."

"Who's Louis?"

"He's our houseman. I like him very much. He was with us in Hollywood when we lived there. Louis makes the drinks for Elliot. Elliot calls him his mascot."

"I remember Louis. He has a very lugubrious physiognomy for a mascot."

Sonia clapped her hands softly. Like most adolescents she had a delight in reverberating polysyllables. They delighted her as a rattle delights an infant. Mr. Spenlove smiled, and wondered what it was he had intended to do. It was a delightful sensation, just wondering without remembering. Young people were charming.

"Yes, that's Louis," Sonia said. "I have breakfast in the breakfast nook, with Louis. Mother and Elliot have theirs upstairs. Louis takes it up. I'm going to camp soon, though, with my friend Shiela Boldwin. She's at Harris too. She's at their apartment, in New York, now. They live near the lighthouse." She made a vague movement of her arm to indicate the Sound.

"That big place near the yacht club?"

"Yes, it's just after you pass the lighthouse. Shiela's mother is getting a divorce too."

"Well, I suppose living near a lighthouse results in illumination."

Sonia smiled a small tight smile. It was almost a twinge, as though a memory had clouded her understanding of his allusion to lighthouses. She was poised to go now, holding her absurd pocketbook and hauling the dog close to her side.

Hector's delight in descending the steps was theatrical. Sonia was now a young animal suddenly scrambling in a panic back to her own place. She turned as the dog dragged toward the trees. "Thank you very much," she said politely. Mr. Spenlove waved to her.

He saw her stop and look at the swings on the big trees. He saw her stop as though she had thought of something.

"Come and have a swing," he called to her. "After I've put in new ropes. It isn't very safe now. Good-bye."

As she ran off he remembered what it was he had intended to do. He had intended to show her that book which had the tale about Tobermory. Next time, he said to himself. It can wait.

He saw her skirt the rear of his house, with Hector straining at the leash. Then only the bright, blood-colored beret was discernible among the young trees and bushes which lined the fringe of his property. Old Mudge had cut down a lot, but he had also planted—cedars, juniper and birch chiefly, and they were growing thickly down there. Then the beret moved rapidly across the next field, into a spinney, where it disappeared. In a moment he could see them both climbing the slope beyond which lay the plantations of large trees, patriarchal oaks and hemlocks, on the big estates, and the high open sky above the Sound.

Mr. Spenlove turned again to his workshop. He wanted to think, and he found thinking easier while working with his hands.

He moved the switch of the bandsaw motor and the place was instantly filled with the harsh, dry, rasping sound of teeth tearing through the wood of a pair of frames, a sound like a violent and prolonged mechanical snore. It stopped as the severed pieces fell apart and the hum of the machine died down, subdued yet sinister, like something dangerous shut up in a cage, like a creature with hundreds of sharp teeth, with tremendous muscles and coiled black viscera full of what Americans graphically called "juice."

Those same Americans were the principal subject of Mr. Spenlove's thoughts, now that he had nothing else to do but think, as he expressed it. It was all very well, on the ships, to study them as a scientist might examine strange animals in a cage. The very fact that they were in a cage, i.e., on a cruise ship, an expensive gilded social tank with almost transparent sides, so that they were on show continuously—that very fact made his study comparatively easy. He was like a naturalist working in a laboratory where all the specimens had been collected, classified in cabins of varying costliness, and unable to escape. Now he was studying the same creatures in their native haunts, and their habits were not quite the same as on board ship. They kept their feelings and opinions surprisingly under control. They were not nearly so gregarious nor so foolish as he had been led to believe. Indeed, they bore a striking resemblance, many of them, to analogous species in England.

Certainly, he continued, while the bandsaw took the last long inside curve of the ribs with a scream, he might almost be at home in the English countryside, so far as privacy went. Miss Penge might imagine she was being very American, bustling in to see if he had any antiques. But Mr. Spenlove was well enough acquainted with country life in England to know how soon there would have been a flurry of white cards on the table by his front door, if he had taken a small house near a village in Suffolk or Hampshire. The parson, for instance, would have called, to break the ice.

The others would have followed. The people were very much the same, he decided. The customs, the mores, were different.

The mores at that cocktail party at Church Yard had certainly been different; but the fact that Elliot Ducroy was a writer and possibly knew a lot of unconventional people, had seemed an adequate explanation. But those present were obviously neither artists nor writers. They were, Mr. Spenlove shrewdly suspected, the very same sort of people he had occasionally consorted with on board ship. They were people, nearly all middle-aged, of both sexes, who belonged to the financial elite of America. They were not, like Mrs. Colwell, his friend across the Sound, wealthy as Americans regarded wealth. They were part of the fringe both of plutocracy and of society, but they hardly rated either as plutocrats or as socially prominent. They wore, some of them, jodhpurs to the cocktail party, riding breeches and smart, loud checks, with preposterous hunting stocks. They moved easily in their own orbits and it was plain that they were reproducing, on their own level, a small-scale model of the equestrian régime in Long Island, New Jersey and the Carolinas.

Mr. Spenlove's desire to find out just where Elliot Ducroy fitted in with the pattern of his guests was not yet gratified. He had thought that when Mrs. Ducroy appeared he would discover something. But she had not appeared. She had not even been on the premises. Mr. Spenlove, holding his cup of punch in a corner and watching the scene with quick-darting dark eyes under tufted brows, had heard a snatch of dialogue behind him, in a window seat, that seemed to be authentic.

"What do you know?" said a man in a velvet coat of deep brown with a pronounced waist. "She isn't back yet!" He stressed the last word. "He said she'd be back . . ."

The woman who was listening wore trousers of carmine corduroy of amazing width, with a starched white shirt with red glass studs. Her lips were the same shade as the studs and her fingernails matched her toenails, as Mr. Spenlove could see because she was wearing golden sandals on bare feet.

She said, "Jesus Christ! How long will he stand it?"

The man said, "You can stand a lot when you're making his money, my lovely! It's only a question of time, though. Sydney Saxon . . ."

And she had tossed her head and complained. "Oh, you're so unsentimental, Roger! Now, aren't you?"

Mr. Spenlove, with bent head, moved quietly away as the conversation became much more intimate than he thought an elderly bachelor should overhear. It was a point he could never settle for himself, and he intended to ask Elliot Ducroy one of these days, how much of this sort of thing was genuine sensuality and how much mere showing off? Exhibitionism was the loathsome word they used. How much was exhibitionism?

His own theory, a mere crude outline so far, was that modern Americans were so fascinated with the novelty of a homogeneous social order, that the dividing line between affinity and fornication, between gaiety and hell-raising, became confused in their minds.

One thing they prided themselves upon, he noted, was their vicarious idealism. Not their own idealism. They themselves, in person, from their conversation, were desperately avaricious and promiscuous. They would, to hear them, do anything for money. They enjoyed having no inhibitions. But they all knew someone, generally quite rich, who was an idealist, who held aloft the banner under which they were all marching. Meanwhile they helped themselves without embarrassment to Ducroy's liquor and cigarettes, coming and going as if the place were a hotel foyer or railway station, making love in the gardens and in the parked cars among the trees, and having a foretaste, apparently, of heaven, which was, for them, "a good time."

That phase connoted a very important feature of American life. Mr. Spenlove was convinced that if he were to continue to live among them he would have to find out just how far one had to surrender to it. He had watched a group of those people at this party, all middle-aged, the women flushed with make-up and the men tanned by a month in Bermuda or Florida, doing an Indian dance in Ducroy's wide porch to the music of a radio. In a circle, with arms laced over each other's shoulders, their heads bowed toward the center, they had stomped interminably until they had become some sort of mystical, multipede organism. The stomping had become orgiastic, crepitating, verging upon a hysteria that might have had curious results if continued, when one of the matrons suddenly collapsed and brought the whole performance to an end.

The spell had been broken. Mr. Spenlove remembered vividly the grinning, painted mask of her face as she was helped to her feet, the sag of the flesh under the chin and the looseness of the sheer silk hose on her thin shanks. He remembered her simper as she confided to her escorts, "I'm tight!"

No doubt of that, Mr. Spenlove reflected; but, going on with his work, he reminded himself that he must be cautious in drawing conclusions from such a gathering. He could not help wondering why they behaved that way, however, and he was more than curious about Sonia's mother.

The remarks of the woman in the red corduroys might mean that Ducroy's wife was running around with another man, a depressing discovery. Mr. Spenlove had no desire to poke his nose into a smelly intrigue. It might mean she was a sociological freak and disliked her own kind. And it might mean, simply, that she was an impossible sort of person who made herself disliked by her husband's friends.

Mr. Spenlove was not prepared to accept any of these theories. As he marked out another pair of frames from the template, he decided that Sonia's mother was a person he would like to meet. The question was, how? The peculiar relations of the re-married might be simple enough to the residents of the shore estates, but to Mr. Spenlove they were as formidable as the society pages of a Sunday newspaper. He hoped to get some light on *them* one of these days, when he felt more courageous.

He fell back, in his revery, on the adventure of his first arrival, when Elliot Ducroy, driving his own station wagon like an erratic amateur, had been so distraught because someone he had been to meet several times had not come. That it was Mrs. Ducroy was an assumption, but it was probably correct. Crimson corduroys, as he called that woman with the blood-red claws and toenails, had not been any help. The thought that Mrs. Ducroy was in any way like that person haunted Mr. Spenlove for some reason. Probably not. Sonia was thirteen at most, and if she was the fruit of an ordinary first marriage her mother was in the thirties. Crimson corduroys was in the late forties.

Ducroy himself was another conundrum. He had worked at that party. Lugubrious Louis was continuously employed carrying around trays of food and drinks and carrying off the debris, but Ducroy himself, frowning or merely grave, made the drinks and set up fresh bottles of whiskey for those who disliked punch. He seemed to drink not at all, and when not buttling was meeting new groups, and introducing people, or going out to the door with some departing elderly couple who seemed to merit extra deference from the host. Mr. Spenlove noted the expression of serious concentration on the man's face, as though he were actually an employee, like the sad Louis in his white coat and thin wet black hair plastered flat. Elliot Ducroy's hair was neither thin, wet nor black, but as he went about the serious business of hospitality Mr. Spenlove observed that, apart from the prestige of his particular business of writing stories, he lacked anything to differentiate him from his servant. The impression Mr. Spenlove carried away was that Mr.

Ducroy was going through the whole business from a sense of duty. Which made it hone the less confusing, and Mr. Spenlove made up his mind to fathom it one of these days.

Mrs. Sankey, who had nearly finished her stint, came to the door of the barn and announced luncheon. She was a woman of hale middle age, reddish in complexion and decidedly robust figure. She often bore the marks of domestic battle on Monday mornings. Mr. Sankey was a jobbing carpenter by trade. His manly breast had given a fine sheen to the mahogany of the local tavern bar.

The relations of those two members of the American proletariat were difficult to define. The contractor who had done Mr. Spenlove's alterations, and who had recommended Mrs. Sankey as a reliable cleaning woman, had merely remarked that "Tom Sankey didn't work regular 'cause he was afraid that bar at Joe's place 'ud fall down if he left it for more'n a few hours." Pressed for details by Mr. Spenlove, who was unfamiliar with local inebriation, the contractor, a tall strong Scandinavian person, added, "He's a goddam souse, Tom is! He don't get stewed and he never gets sober. He's in between the hull time. And he takes all she makes, goin' out to clean, too. Now Old Jim, he works, an' then he goes off 'n gets drunk's a fiddler's bitch, and sleeps it off, and starts again. Meself, I'd ruther be him than Tom Sankey, any day."

Mrs. Sankey, who worked at some other house in Norbury most afternoons, was not communicative. The first day she came, when the time to leave drew near, she moved about with the restlessness of an animal in a strange house. Mr. Spenlove was reading the New York *Times* of the day before, which had just come by mail. She came to the door giving on to the porch and said she was through.

"All right," said Mr. Spenlove, smoking calmly.

"Thought maybe you was goin' in to Norbury in yore car?" she said.

"I haven't a car, Mrs. Sankey. When I go into Norbury, I walk."

Whether he ever recovered in her estimation, whether he had ever had a position to recover, Mr. Spenlove could not make out. Mrs. Sankey retired into herself. Mr. Spenlove might set out for a late dinner at the inn at Norbury with a stout walking stick. Mrs. Sankey, after a stand-up lunch in the kitchen, set off without a walking stick, but with a sharp eye over her shoulder for local cars, so that she usually got a lift as far as Sutton Corners, where the lady she worked for in the afternoon would call for her in a civilized fashion.

Today she called him as usual to the cold roast beef and pickles, with cheese and bottled beer, which he liked for lunch. Perhaps the most disturbing thing about him, for her, was his insistence on having the loaf of bread on the table, so that he could cut it himself. It set him apart as a strange alien phenomenon, not quite normal. It was like his peculiar trick of giving orders, and then looking to see if a room was clean. She described him to her other employer as a fussy old bachelor. With Mr. Spenlove himself, sensing without understanding his attitude toward her own class, she preserved a safe silence.

He saw her start off down the driveway today with a certain relief. It had been an adventurous morning. He wanted to reflect, to follow up a line of thought which had been occupying him for some days now. Since the weather had become warm, in fact, he noted.

It was nothing less than the problem of continence, now that he had left his accustomed way of life, his constant voyagings to the Mediterranean, to the isles of the tropic seas. He was retired now, on the shelf, and his mind was no longer preoccupied with professional cares.

Officially he was approaching sixty. It had never seemed to him a serious matter to pretend to be slightly older than he was. The fact that he was only just past fifty-five might seem of no significance. He looked, and had always looked, venerable because of his beard. Now that he was alone, he was confronted with another fact, that he either had to resign himself to continence or do something about it.

Mr. Spenlove had for many years prided himself upon his practical philosophy, and he had been moderately successful in regulating his life by its principles. He saw no reason why he should change now. The trouble was, he was aware of a subtle antagonism between himself and shore life, an antagonism that arose, not merely from his long years at sea, but from a deep-seated antipathy to continuous contact with human beings.

When he first went to sea he had been compelled to share a cabin with another engineer, a dark, dirty and shabby room, infested with bed bugs and smelling of rats, stale food and metal polish from the cupboards in the mess room next door. Nothing had compared in discomfort with the enforced propinquity with the third engineer. The fool had gotten himself a fine dose in Genoa, Mr. Spenlove remembered (even now) with annoyance. There had been a row over that. Mr. Spenlove had shown his mettle immediately. He had taken to washing in the engine room, had stowed all his clothes in the dry, clean storeroom there and had defended himself with disinfectants.

Perhaps that experience had warped his character a little. After that he had luckily always had a cabin to himself. Contact with men and women, save of the briefest and most sanitary nature, became with him what was now known as a phobia. The charm of his life at sea had been its privacy. He slyly described himself as an untouchable. Action—and speech—at a distance was his prerogative. Like Lorenzo de Medici, when he went in search of a woman he assumed what amounted to a disguise, for he never frequented the haunts popular with sailors, and he did not divulge his identity. Only in rare instances had he ever visited the same girl twice. On board ship he lived apart. In New York, once out of the dock gates he had been anonymous there too, and many were the legends about him in the nautical colonies of Brooklyn and Hoboken, when alien-born seamen huddle together in boarding houses and apartments. He had evolved out of this way of life a protective shell, a carapace for his sensitive and ironical temperament, within which he could exist philosophically, quizzing the follies of mankind and telling tall yarns, to amused passengers, of his bygone experiences.

Now the shell was in danger of being torn away. He was no longer married, as they say, to his job, no longer identified with the disciplined organization of a liner, no longer in possession of a unique place in the hierarchy of a ship. He was, to put it starkly, nobody at all any more. He had a feeling somewhat akin to nakedness since his retirement, a sense of solitude of spirit, a sense of having been amputated from the living organism to which he had been joined, of which he had been so long an important member. It was like being widowed.

The problem now, as he ate his cold beef and pickles and drank his beer, on a day in early June, was to establish some substitute for what he had left behind. When Mrs. Colwell, that extremely wealthy and intelligent person, who understood him better than anyone he had ever met, learned that he was actually retiring, she had immediately urged him to marry.

"I thought you were a friend of mine!" he had complained.

"I am. That's why I suggest it."

"Is that so? And you have someone in mind?"

"No! I wish I did. I'm not such a fool as to bring people together, though. I know I'm right, Spenlove. If I wasn't married I'd marry you myself!"

"I understand how you feel," he had told her. "The sentiment is mutual."

"Paying each other chaste compliments is getting us nowhere," she had warned him. "I suppose you've been so extremely cautious you've reached your present age without a stain on your character. Didn't you ever see anything you fancied? I can't say I blame you very much."

Mr. Spenlove, his hand on his heart, had bowed to the compliment.

"You had the sense to keep clear of that creature we both had the misfortune to know—what was her name again? You know the one I mean . . . Hm!"

Just to be subversive, as young Colwell was fond of saying, Mr. Spenlove had pretended he had forgotten the one Mrs. Colwell meant. She wagged an admonishing finger at him.

"There were so many," he said, smiling.

"Oh, go on with you! I said I knew her. I remember! Rhea Candleby! You said she lived in Florida now."

And Mrs. Colwell had then revealed what he already knew, that she was intelligent and liked him and paid no attention to his pretenses. She forgot Rhea Candleby (poor Rhea!), and said, shrewdly,

"Mr. Spenlove, you aren't an old maid, are you?"

Now that he was actually beached, an old discarded hulk, he realized the danger of becoming what she called "an old maid." The wine of his irony might easily sour into vinegar and originality of thought degenerate into the crotchety obstinacy of senile dementia.

He finished the beer and went over to get a fresh cigar. Was it any protection, he wondered, to see a danger too clearly? The longer he lived the less he believed in dogmas concerning the human mind. "Wisdom" was a weasel word, bearing no relation to intelligence. Having spent most of his life among men who confused both wisdom and intelligence with cunning, and who believed all of them were useless without luck, he indulged in introspection with extreme caution. He knew that he had always had too much imagination to be genuinely successful in his profession and had feared to abandon it for some career where imagination would pay. Advertising, for instance! He had had to go on a diet, as he called it, mentally. He had lived for long periods on roughage. He wondered, in passing, if the peculiar quality of the writings of monks and hermits was due to the restricted diet of those days.

Roughage was the word! He had restricted his reading, his thoughts, and even his speech, to the simple pattern of the average sea-going artisan before the days of wireless and predatory proletarianism. He had gone ashore and sat in wineshops and bordellos with his shipmates. He had learned the Sailor's Hornpipe dance from an old shellback during his apprenticeship and had won his way without fornication into the respect and admiration of many houses of fair reception. It had been a source of private amusement to him that the reaction of Mrs. Colwell and her guests, to this performance, had been precisely similar to that of the inmates of the Casa Miraflores in Havana or the customers of the Willing Hand Bar in Valletta.

He was proud, even now, of this achievement of subordinating his natural desires and aspirations to the common run of seafaring mores. It had evoked a rare blend of affection and contempt for the shipmates who applauded his skill. It had shown him how he could improvise a figure behind which he could conceal himself.

He had no intention of taking Mrs. Colwell's advice, however. That was no solution. Marriage was no longer a solution for any of his problems, he felt. He had seen almost every kind of marriage among his colleagues and subordinates in recent years, and the thought of following their example caused him to stop short as he held the match to his cigar. When the match had burned down to his fingers he threw it in the fireplace, frowning. No!

Outside, in the June sunshine, the fresh green foliage and the profound silence of afternoon in early summer enclosed the house like a trance. Mr. Spenlove got his cigar alight and walked into the porch to sit for a few minutes before going out to see Old Jim.

It was no illusion. The warm stillness, the h
near its equinox, blazed upon the invisib
Sound, so that the sky beyond the trees was
diant light, convinced him that the treacheries
England spring, the incredible reversions to b
and even snow, after days of heat, were now ove
sense the summer at last; its languors timidly ov
land.

The habit of years was still strong in Mr. Spen
liked to be obeyed, especially when his comman
confined to the simple rules which everybody know
and believes should be kept, by everybody else. O
the partly reformed inebriate whom he had found
wood stove in Mrs. Dooling's general store, was a cig
smoker. He was also uncertain in his movements and
in his reflexes. He had been instructed to keep out o
barn while smoking.

He was now in the barn, probably in the back seat of
Model T smoking a cigarette, and counting on his employ
being too busy, too forgetful, or too lazy to investigate. Th
place was so dry and so littered with inflammable, oil-soake
material that Mr. Spenlove was thinking of having it completely gutted. If it caught fire and the wind were right, the house would go too.

Old Jim was not the type to understand the reason why it was dangerous to smoke a cigarette in there. He was conditioned to smoking in garages where huge No Smoking signs hung on the walls and placid mechanics continued to smoke while investigating the entrails of trucks and conversing with Old Jim, who was also smoking. Stop signs, traffic signals, no-hunting and keep-off posters were part of Old Jim's cosmos, like the trash hoppers on the shore, and the no-parking warnings that were regularly obscured by parked cars in Norbury. All through the years of Prohibition he had got drunk regularly in a speakeasy once a week on near beer spiked with ether. Now, in the days of Repeal, he got

unk once a week on domestic gin. The only difference was at it cost more and the police took him in, instead of king him home, if he fell down in the street.

Mr. Spenlove was fond of Old Jim. He was a slow but teady worker. He was a tall scarecrow, the wreckage of a nan who, as a gangling youth of twenty, had served in the Spanish American war as petty-officers' messman in a transport carrying troops to Cuba. The pension, which seems to attach itself to every American who happens to have been even in the vicinity of military or naval operations, enabled Old Jim to keep soul and body within reach of each other. He was very infirm, and Mr. Spenlove believed the old chap really had gout in those enormous feet of his, due to prolonged but not excessive alcoholism. He was slow in his movements, extremely dignified in demeanor, and his deep sunken eyes, high cheekbones, bony forehead and gray walrus mustache, gave him a strong resemblance to the portraits of Nietzsche. The idea of having the author of *Thus Spake Zarathustra* working in his garden was irresistible to Mr. Spenlove.

He was about to go across the yard to make sure, when he heard a car coming in from the road. The sound of tires crackling on the strata of stove ashes laid down by old Mr. Mudge during many winters was very distinct. A heavy machine with large tires, was Mr. Spenlove's verdict as he stood by the porch door, listening. A long, low open car of foreign make came swiftly into view and stopped within a few inches of the shrubs in front of the porch. Mr. Spenlove, his hand on the porch door, well aware that behind the new bronze screen he was invisible, waited.

Sonia Pagett sat beside a woman of what Mr. Spenlove called the perfect age. She was more than thirty and not yet forty. Her brown untidy hair was squashed down under an expensively simple felt hat. Her nose, mouth and eyes were precisely the nose, mouth and eyes of Sonia on a slightly

more elaborate scale. She was the finished painting of which Sonia was the lovely sketch.

She sat, her heavily ringed hands grasping the huge steering wheel, looking about her, the sun drenching the equipage with light that flashed back from chromium and enamel like fire, and reflected the barn and trees in the glossy black panels of the tonneau. On the deep red leather cushions lay a short fur jacket, a bag of groceries, a large carton from a New York department store and a woman's pocketbook, very large, of yellow patent leather.

Sonia, who seemed to have been the organizer of this invasion, now sat in some confusion while her mother waited for the girl to do something.

"Well!" said a rich, plangent voice. "Get on with it, ducky! You said you'd made his acquaintance!" It was a voice softly resonant and full of rich tones. A lovely voice, Mr. Spenlove told himself, filled suddenly with a strange passion for England.

Sonia opened the door of the car and slowly descended. The car, Mr. Spenlove now saw, was a six-liter Virago, a car whose foreign sales manager had once been one of his passengers coming up from Rio. There were only about five hundred people in England who could afford a Virago, this gentleman had told Mr. Spenlove genially. The others had to go into debt to own one. So business was necessarily brisk among Brazilian coffee millionaires, Argentine cattle barons and North Americans who liked English cars for the same reasons that they liked English butlers.

Mr. Spenlove was again about to present himself when the lady struck the horn button with a quick blow of her fist. The Virago gave out a sudden, deep-toned hoot. Mr. Spenlove opened the screen door and went down the steps to dispel the girl's embarrassment.

Sonia was extremely glad to see him. She at once became self-possessed. Everything had suddenly become clear again. Everything fell into its place in her private cosmos—

the chase after Hector; the meeting with the man with the beard, who said he was English; the funny ginger beer; the cat in the story who could talk; the impulse to tell her mother and suggest coming back for the book about the cat who could talk.

She led the way, which was about three yards, to the door of the car, holding out one hand toward her mother.

"Mummy, this is the gentleman! Hector chased his cat. I'm awfully sorry, but I've forgotten . . ."

"My name's Spenlove." That gentleman put his left hand on Sonia's shoulder and held out the other to Sonia's mother. She reached over and shook hands with him. "Are you Mrs. Ducroy?"

She nodded, a smile playing around her mouth. Her eyes were long and almost nile green in the sunlight that was reflected from the new foliage into the polished windshield. She put her hand to her untidy hair and moved the little felt hat to and fro with lazy grace, examining her daughter's new friend.

"You must have made a hit with Sonia," she said slowly, drumming on the rim of the steering wheel, as if she were improvising an act. Her rich delicious voice moved Mr. Spenlove, so that he held the child closer to him. "She would have it we ought to come up and get some book you told her about. I hope it's suitable for girls, but I never interfere with Sonia. She reads the most awful things at school."

"It doesn't seem to have done her any harm."

Mr. Spenlove roused himself from the slight vertigo he suspected to be coming on, and opened the door for Mrs. Ducroy to get out. "We had a nice little visit, thanks to Hector's passion for cats," he said. "Come in, please. I want you to come in."

She uncoiled long limbs in flannel slacks and stepped out, her feet shod in white and scarlet espadrilles. He noted she wore conventional stockings. She looked at him over her shoulder with amused interest as he almost hurried her around the long machine with its enormous baggage trunk sticking far out over the bumper. He grasped her arm in its thin silk and wool sweater and guided her to the porch steps, where Sonia awaited them.

Mrs. Ducroy gave herself up to the mood of the moment, smiling and stepping with head slightly bent, conveying a subtle suggestion of having been captured.

Sonia went up and opened the door for her mother. Mr. Spenlove, who had not experienced his present emotion for a long time, wondered if there was anything symbolical about that impulse of Sonia's. He wondered, too, as he followed Mrs. Ducroy into the porch, if he were being a fool.

"I'll get Sonia her book," he said and led the way into the house. "Excuse the remains of the feast, please," he added. "My charwoman leaves early."

"Charwoman? I haven't heard that word for ages! Sonia says you're English too."

Mr. Spenlove, his face to the bookshelves, was heard to say he wasn't the only one who came to America to try and live it down.

"I'm not trying to live it down!" Mrs. Ducroy said with sudden indignation. Then she sank into the most comfortable chair, which was of dark green leather, and smiled.

"I know what you mean," she added.

Sonia was oblivious of the two grown-ups. In front of the bookshelves was an Armenian rug which Mr. Spenlove had brought back from Smyrna long ago and had kept in storage for sentimental reasons. Sonia had sunk to her knees on this, her hair falling over her face as she became absorbed in *The Chronicles of Clovis.* Mrs. Ducroy contemplated her daughter with the abstract impersonal stare of the woman who has survived maternity and who has no intention of regarding her own life as over.

She looked around at the simple arrangements of the living room, smiling at the loaf of bread and the triangular hunk of sharp yellow cheese, the empty beer bottle and the jar of mustard pickles. She smiled as if to herself. Lying back in the chair her felt hat was thrust forward over her eyes, giving her an expression Mr. Spenlove decided was raffish and provocative. On the instep of her red-heeled espadrilles he could read the word "France."

"It's easy to see they haven't Americanized you," she said. She put a strong beautiful hand, with its galaxy of costly rings, on the crown of her head and slowly moved the hat to and fro, and then took it off and dropped it on the window seat at her elbow. "What do you do?" she demanded. "Or what *did* you do? My husband"—the word was brought out with slow emphasis, but Mr. Spenlove was not sure what it emphasized—"My husband told me you were a naval officer."

In her rich voice, resonant, neither loud nor husky, she laid a stress on words like husband and naval that conveyed interest and intimacy, as though the matter were something almost conspiratorial between them.

"He was right in a way," said Mr. Spenlove, "but it don't signify, as Mr. Toots used to remark. You can get nearer the mark if you accept me as a merchant marine officer, now on the shelf. Naval officers are specialists. They spend their lives in the fighting ships. People like me are only reservists."

"You on the shelf?" Mrs. Ducroy, he saw, was interested. She lay back in his most comfortable chair, her hands behind her head, her body full of mature beauty, her hazel-green eyes watching him. "You on the shelf? Any one would think you were in the sere and yellow. I suppose you'll fool any number of people with that beard."

"Really!"

"Yes, really! Sonia came back so fascinated, I was amused. You know what kids are."

He looked down at the kid. Sonia was reading. She seemed to have the faculty of ignoring her mother completely.

"I'm not to be drawn into any such admission," he said. "I do not know what kids are. I know Sonia is charming. I'm very fond of her already. I was surprised when she told me Elliot Ducroy was her stepfather. He and I got acquainted when I came down here for good."

"He told me. Did you know the Mudges?"

"Slightly. I came up once when I bought the mortgage."

"Were they . . . ?" She made an expressive movement of her body to describe swinging. He nodded.

"They were much more part of this place than I'll ever be," he said. She said quickly, "I should think so!" She looked around critically. "What do you want to go into business as a hermit for?"

The question made him laugh. Then he laughed again much louder. The barb sank in, for all his laughing. The question was so perfectly in line with what he had been thinking as she swirled through his driveway in her six-liter Virago that he stopped on his way to the corner cupboard and looked at her.

She was glancing out of the window at the bright June afternoon, the weaving tracery of new green leaves, listening to the faint sound of Old Jim slowly driving in a stake.

"What will you have?" he inquired as the cupboard door swung open. "Glass of sherry?" It seemed suitable.

Sonia looked up quickly from her book.

"Mother doesn't drink," she said.

"Not sherry?"

"Mother doesn't drink anything."

Mr. Spenlove glanced from one to the other, his hand resting on the bottle in its shelf. Sonia returned to Tobermory. Mrs. Ducroy was still looking out at the summer afternoon with tender glances. Her face, in profile, was intoxicatingly beautiful. It was beautiful and very desirable. She seemed lost in her thoughts. The shadows of the leaves played delicately over her features.

At length she said, in that lovely voice that evoked in Mr. Spenlove's brain the sound of far-off chimes of bells within a sacred wood, "All right, ducky!" She smiled enigmatically at Mr. Spenlove. "Make mine ginger ale." She added, "Sonia takes care of her old mother."

She began to walk about the room, and while he was on the back porch getting ice, she looked into the kitchen. He saw her walking upstairs. For some reason, which he could not at the moment define, this pleased him. She pleases me no matter what she does or says! he thought, with sudden vehemence. He entered the living room again and stood waiting. He saw Sonia stretched on the Armenian rug, her bob hanging over her face, which was supported on her hands. She was absorbed in her book.

Footsteps moved around upstairs. Now she was looking out of a window. Now she was examining the books, or perhaps the picture over the bookshelf which he could see as he lay in bed in the morning. How did she react to such things? Rembrandt's "Man in a Golden Helmet" didn't appeal to everybody.

Why should he care so very much whether it appealed to her or not? Why was he so extraordinarily excited, all at once? The recollection of his coolness and amusement, while Miss Penge invaded his privacy and gave him a preliminary glimpse of the world of local gossip, astonished him. Miss Penge was a woman not unattractive in a practical, domestic fashion, a capable, sociable, reliable creature, sound in wind and limb. Yet she might have been one of those inanimate female models one sees in store windows, so far as he was concerned.

Now, as he waited for Sonia's mother to rejoin them he was aware of an exaltation of spirit, a profound happiness, for which he could not find an adequate word, unless he was in love.

He stared down at Sonia, extended on the rug, her chin on her hands, reading. He listened to the sounds upstairs. He had all the touchiness of men who have been long in authority and who resent the intrusion of strangers into their privacy. Why did he not resent this entirely unknown person walking about his house? Sonia seemed as much at home as if she belonged.

He walked heavily into the front porch and stood looking out at the afternoon sunshine. Instead of Miss Penge's ponderous old car there was now the long, lithe, glittering Virago. Mr. Spenlove was inclined to be impressed by a machine of such august prestige in his own country. He knew you had to be in considerable funds to afford a thing like that. And her rings! He had not been able to resist the feeling that there was "a lot of capital locked up there" as he phrased it in his mind.

But these things no longer had any significance. They had no significance at all. What was of significance, he decided, was that instead of being retired, on the shelf, and of no importance to women, he was down in the arena, being challenged. And it was a challenge he could not ignore, even if he had wanted to.

He heard her step on the stair and then she was beside him.

"Show me your place," she said in a low tone. She took his arm and he opened the screen door.

"I'm just clearing it at present," he said. There was a touch of irritation in his voice. He had seen the long fine stone walls, the blue-stone driveway, the costly landscaping, the deep solid banks of rhododendrons and the exotic lilac trees, at Church Yard. He had appraised the cost of the lawn and the laying on of water to the blue oval swimming pool. And he had nothing of that to show at all.

"It doesn't matter," she said in her musical soft English tones. "Oh, there are the swings! Do you ever . . . ?"

"No, the rope's rotten and I haven't had occasion to renew it," he told her. "I'll get it fixed for Sonia if you like. Would you come this way? There's nothing at the back except a bit of grass and the part my man's clearing and fencing to make a garden."

"What are you going to show me?"

He led her around the barn to the door of his workshop, which was open. He saw her peer in at the skeleton of the boat, at the bench and the machine tools, the white walls and the clean concrete floor.

She made no remark at all, leaning forward, glancing around continually, holding his arm, as though she thought he might run off and leave her.

"A boat!" she said at length, smiling. "We have a boat. So that's what you do! That's what you like?"

"When I haven't any interruptions," he said gravely.

"Don't be nasty," she urged him, still smiling. "I'm enjoying this visit."

"Don't you want your ginger ale?"

"I'm not mad for it," she said. "Of course, I suppose people come out of curiosity and take up your time."

"What did you come for?" he asked. "I particularly wish to know."

"Sonia said you were nice," she told him. "Why did you particularly wish to know?"

"Well, I was wondering about you, you see."

"Why?"

"I had a visitor this morning, a Miss Penge."

"Oh, did you? That explains it. I bet Miss Penge said something to excite your curiosity! I call her place Ye Olde Curiosity Shoppe."

"That's the lady. Route Eleven, she told me. Invited me to pay her a visit. She wanted to know if I had any old things to sell. She collects glass."

"She collects scandal, too! What did she say about me, if it isn't too disgusting?"

"She didn't say anything about you. She started to, several times, but sheered off."

"She's a great one for that. I bet she's on the telephone now, talking to her friend Mrs. Cagliari, telling her about her visit to you."

"Who's Mrs. Cagliari? She sounds interesting."

"She's our gardener's wife. He's a Sardinian, but she's American. Early American! Used to be a schoolteacher, she said. She's a big fat woman and a wonderful cook, and the original idea was for us to employ them both, as a couple. Our houseman made a fuss. He said he wouldn't stay if she came, so we didn't press it. He's an old employee of my husband's. Mrs. Cagliari's the other end of the local grapevine. What those two don't know, they invent."

"You know more about this place than I do," Mr. Spenlove admitted. They were standing in his workshop and she drew her fingers along the stem of the boat, which was being built on high trestles. "I suppose it will be only a matter of time before they know you've been here to see me."

"I hope not," she said. "But they probably will. I'm not very fond of gossipy females. In fact I'm not fond of females at all. Is that a bad sign?"

"I lack jurisdiction," he muttered. "Let us go back to Sonia. I'm fond of *her*. She's a female."

"Oh, so am I, though I am her mother. Sonia's a brick. You heard how she stopped you giving me a drink?"

"Yes, why?"

"Because she knows what's what. Do I make myself plain?"

"That would hardly be possible," he pointed out, and she gave him a delighted grimace, pouting her lips toward him provocatively.

"I'll tell you something," she said, and they began to walk back to the house. She contemplated the short, springy old turf which grew thick and strong under the great trees. "It's a long story, so I'll make it short. I'm leaving my husband."

"What about Sonia?"

"That's just it. He's awfully fond of her. He's—never mind now. There she is."

She pointed to Sonia on the front porch. The girl came out and stood on the top step, silhouetted against the bright new bronze screen, which seemed to enclose her in a lustrous frame.

"I'm not surprised he's fond of her," Mr. Spenlove said in an undertone. "Who wouldn't be? And what you intend . . ."

"Sonia!" her mother called, "Mr. Spenlove's building a boat. In there," she pointed. "Go and see it. Are you"—she turned to him—"going to join the yacht club?"

Sonia ran, fleet limbed and lovely, past them to the barn.

"I don't know," he said. "I thought of it. Yes, I thought of it. Why are you leaving him?" he said suddenly.

"I said it was a long story," she pointed out. "Could I call again? Would you mind if I came . . . ?" she made a gesture toward the invisible Sonia.

For a moment she met his glance, which was very bright and burning. Then she looked down at her feet and walked toward the car.

"Funny how things happen," she said, as if to herself, under her breath. She remembered her hat and started toward the house. Inside she said, earnestly, standing close to him, "I had to tell someone! Sonia said you were . . ." Her rings flashed as she set the hat on her bronze-colored hair . . . "English. All the same, it was an impulse. Was it a mistake? You don't think me a trollop because I . . ."

"That'll do," he said. "Sonia's in the car. I'll be here."

"Will you?" she said. Her face became extraordinarily seductive and her voice low and musical. She closed her eyes for an instant as though in rapture.

Then without further words they walked down to the car together.

"What do you drive?" she said, as she got in and he closed the door.

"I haven't driven a car since I was a young man in England. I worked in a garage in London for a while. Panhards, Mors and De Dion Boutons. And the old Benz with a belt drive."

"You'll soon pick it up again," she said lightly. "De Dion Bouton! It sounds like a French perfume."

"It was. *Parfum de Petrole!* But I like it here. I can always send for a taxi when I get a phone."

"Oh, of course. But excuse me. One gets the habit of rushing about." She started the engine.

"Good-bye, Sonia. When you've finished that book come and get another."

He stood and watched the car start down the narrow drive, Sonia holding up her hand to him and smiling.

iii

NOW THAT he was actually on shore, living among these Americans whom he had been studying for so many years, Mr. Spenlove was far from certain that the relations of husbands and wives would ever be clear to him. Mrs. Sankey toiled all the week and took her wages home to her husband, who apparently used her for a punching bag before going out to join his pals at Joe's place. Mr. Ducroy had been apparently in some sort of trouble with his wife—Mr. Spenlove was quite positive it was the wife—who had failed to come back from New York on schedule. Mr. Spenlove presumed it was New York. Mr. and Mrs. Mudge had evidently outlived their marital troubles. They had swung gently together from the branch of the big white oak in the yard, in companionable silence. Now they were in Abraham's bosom.

What disturbed him so much, as the days passed, was the effect of this encounter upon his complacency. He had become so accustomed to having women to talk to on the voyage, so practised in provoking their interest in his own past and the adventures of his soul among the amorists, so dependent upon the end of the voyage to restore them to their families, that he had not foreseen how it would be when he was finally drawn up on the beach.

He decided one evening to go for a walk to the shore before dinner. The lighthouse was about a mile and a half by the road. Across the fields it was about half that.

Old Jim was washing his withered bony arms in the

kitchen as a preliminary to trudging the half mile to Sutton Corners. Nietzsche at the kitchen sink! Like Nietzsche, Jim had a small pension, and Mr. Spenlove had more than once reflected upon the queer quirks of destiny whereby an entirely illiterate ex-messman and orderly in a naval hospital had evolved into an unconscious philosopher. Old Jim, whose hirsute auricles hearkened to no Townsendites or utopia-mongers, had achieved in his own life the perfect balance sought by sages and mahatmas. His needs were few; he lived in a furnished back room above a store in Sutton Corners, a room whose equipment was no more than that permitted a Carmelite prior. He might have assumed a vow of silence, he spoke so little. Only when the day came for him to get drunk did he fail to hold the even tenor of his way. It was a perfect existence, Mr. Spenlove concluded, for anyone without intellectual resources. And as ninety-nine percent of the population were entirely destitute of intellectual resources, even Bentham's greatest good of the greatest number could find no defect in Old Jim's way of life.

"Finished?" said Mr. Spenlove loudly, smiling in spite of himself. Old Jim was a bit deaf.

"For today," he mumbled behind the fierce Nietzschean mustache.

"Coming tomorrow?"

Old Jim dried his sharp elbows, lean as dead cedar branches. He had been working nearly a week now. Human nature would not be able to bear much more, Mr. Spenlove surmised. Old Jim began to roll down his sleeves. He uttered a sound midway between a murmur and a grunt, partaking of both. It was accepted around Sutton Corners as an assent.

"Well, don't keep me in suspense, Jim. I'm going for a walk now. Leave some kennel food on the back porch for the cat. And change his water, will you?"

He went out by the front way and struck across the fields, which were drained marshland, toward the estuary. The sun was setting beyond the flats that at low tide were sheets of glistening, bronze-colored mud. A speedboat was tearing a long slit in the water, which resembled zinc-colored satin. Two clam diggers with baskets on their backs, like industrious hunchbacks, were clearly outlined in the foreshore, to southward, tiny black figures silhouetted against the brightness. The clumps of bright green sea grass against dark rocks were vivid in the slanting rays.

The road along the shore wound among hummocks of coarse grass and clumps of wild cherry that were bounded by a sandy slope above the beach. The lighthouse stood on the point beyond the yacht club basin. A dredger was at work scooping out the mud brought down the river by the spring freshets. Some of the yachts were still boarded up. Others were huddled together on the dock, or being painted. The yacht club house seemed deserted, though a flag flew from the signal halyards in the lookout tower.

Mr. Spenlove followed the road behind the sacred precincts of the club. No one would have challenged him if he had gone through and walked by the basin. The season was not yet started. But he disliked trespassing upon the privacy of the local magnificoes. The road behind the property was good enough. It was a right of way to the lighthouse and could not be closed.

As he came out upon the point and the sharp black and white angularities of the lighthouse enclosure confronted him, he had a feeling of nostalgia for his old life within the bonds of discipline. There might be, as Mrs. Colwell shrewdly suspected, something old-maidish about him, something that was more in tune with the lighthouse, perhaps, than the yacht club. Was it old-maidish to wish to live a life of quietude, to avoid the hot lather of modern social intimacies? Was it not the utmost wisdom to evade any contacts that made a man look as spiritually defeated as Elliot Ducroy had looked during that cocktail party? It was a look, Mr. Spenlove told himself, much more desperate than any man at sea ever had, unless, unless he was bedeviled with shore worries!

The clean bright sharpness of the lighthouse lines, the lovely perspective of the lime-washed walls of the yard, the huddle of green and red buildings behind it, the blue window-boxes and the black dog outside a white kennel at the gate, all this was a great solace to him as he contemplated the day's events. A man had to have safeguards, he thought, dikes against the great seas of humanity surging in to overwhelm his spirit. At sea, so it seemed now, it had been easy! He was beginning to believe that much of the crazy behavior he had witnessed among passengers had been due to the lack, in America, of these safeguards. They had to pretend that they must never be alone. Or they honestly dreaded solitude, and would turn on the radio in their cabins until it was a roar, rather than be alone. They professed a religion of being good fellows, of mixing interminably with other damned souls, of suspecting a solitary person of being un-American, possibly a radical. They chanted "Safety First!" and worshipped their pioneer ancestors, who put safety last.

It was no wonder, then, that they seemed deranged while on holiday, rocking in the cradle of civilization or storming along the Spanish Main in air-conditioned galleons. The wonder began when one studied them in their ordinary daily lives, when they were not going through the mystical incantations of "a good time." No tribal witch doctor could compete with their magicians when it came to erecting barriers between them and their angry deities, especially the fierce god with his two rows of grinning teeth, his wide-open laughing mouth, his maniac eyes and waving arm, the god who immolated his victims on the altar of good fellowship. Mr. Spenlove called him "the Get-together God." There seemed to be no escape from him save into some institution, where the patient was camouflaged as "a nervous breakdown," and the cure was called "a complete rest."

Rest from what? he asked himself. Because these people were well off. They were handsome, cultured, gifted beyond anything he could achieve himself. They controlled industries, wrote novels, confected cinematographs, cackled over the ether and painted pictures. One never heard of a subway motorman having a nervous breakdown and needing a complete rest. Or a twenty-ton-truck driver, who kept up a steady fifty miles an hour through a snow storm on the Federal Highway; or a coal miner; or steel worker! It was only when people of this class became suddenly rich through a lottery or something that one heard of them running amok and needing a rest.

The lighthouse lantern was turned on as he watched. The golden heart of the light suddenly burned full on him in the dusk and turned away for a few seconds. Far out on the Sound a white steamer moved steadily toward New York, a pale phantom on the gray water. Lights began to wink on the Long Island shore. A smear of smoke showed where a coaster was hull down toward New Haven. The speedboat was now rushing across the estuary toward the yacht basin. The thunder of its engine exhausts was diminished to a soft patter by distance and the moist evening air. Mr. Spenlove watched it as it suddenly swerved from the shore and fled away to sea, its absurd red port light almost buried in foam. Then the stern light came into view, followed by the starboard lantern as the boat went over the bar and tore along the westerly side of the river mouth.

Mr. Spenlove started back. He would have an appetite by the time he reached the inn at Norbury, which was all of four miles by the road. He started back, but he found himself watching the speedboat, which had swung in a wide arc to the eastward and was now coming around behind him, the crepitation of its engines growing louder because of the southerly breeze. Someone, he thought, was having "a good time," going nowhere fast!

Instead of skirting the yacht club this time he climbed

through a fence and walked around to the jetty. The speedboat's racket grew portentous and overwhelming. As he reached the wooden dock it became a thuttering roar, and then suddenly stopped. The silence was delicious. He felt an involuntary gratitude blending with his rage against the unknown defiler of the evening peace.

The boat floated in quietly; the twin engines, throttled down, were turning over with barely a sound. There was a solitary figure in the cockpit. With one more burst of explosions the uproar died for good. The boat drifted alongside.

He saw a lithe, leather-coated, goggled figure reach out with a boat hook and then pass a line through a ring bolt on the dock. A youth wearing a blue jersey with a white monogram came out hastily from under the club house and ran toward the boat, ignoring Mr. Spenlove completely. As he ran he smoothed his hair and pulled down his sleeves, which had been rolled to his elbows.

He ran, sprucing himself meanwhile in a manner calculated to arouse curiosity in a seafaring mind. Mr. Spenlove turned again to watch the disembarcation. The manner of the young man was explained. The operator of the speedboat was a woman.

She came toward the solitary stranger with what was now the familiar easy stride, carrying a white rubber raincoat, leather gloves, and goggles. It was as if she were breasting a slope. She wore oil-stained jodhpurs that revealed the full vigorous curves of her limbs.

Mr. Spenlove held back a quick breath of astonishment, finding himself looking into those curiously-colored eyes that changed as he looked.

He halted, resting on his ash plant. All his precautions had been entirely useless. She was here, smiling with surprise and also with anticipation. He had not even the consolation of telling himself that she had schemed this. She couldn't have! It was fate! He said so.

"Kismet!" she echoed and made a downward movement

with the hand holding the gauntleted gloves. "You've been following me!" She laughed in his face. "Won't you come in? The place is not really open yet. The season . . . We can have some—you know—ginger ale! I have to change. Won't you?"

A steward in a pale blue page-boy suit saw them ascend and cross the wide verandah, and opened the glass door leading to a large lofty hall with a vast stone fireplace. She hurried away, looking over her shoulder at him, as though trying to ascertain his thoughts.

He sat down and waited. After all, he told himself, he had had nothing to do with all this. He was not responsible for it in any way whatever. Sonia was the agent of destiny. He had used the word "Kismet" in joke, but it looked very much as if there were something in that superstition. She had accused him of following her! Why now, he wondered, did the tone, the lovely timbre of her voice when she uttered that amazing impertinence, thrill him like an aphrodisiac?

He sat by the long center table, which was littered with the magazines known as slicks, especially the slicks connected with yachting, motor boating and off-shore fishing. On the walls were stuffed sailfish, tarpon, marlin and swordfish. There were silver cups and shields, photographs of boats and yachts. In the corner was a ticker machine covered by a blue hood. Mr. Spenlove wondered whether that wasn't stuffed, too.

A waitress, also in pale blue, click-clocked across the hardwood floor and said Mrs. Ducroy would be right out, and would he please order?

"I'll wait," he said. She turned on her heel and click-clocked away through a swing door in a far corner.

What made him ponder was her assumption that he was worthy of her confidence. Was he? That was the really important point. Was he? Did he put so high a price on the meditative life (which could wait a while, perhaps) that he would put an end to this performance of hers? It was all

very well to talk about Kismet and assume that sh
merely making a convenience of him. He knew the
She was not. He knew the signs, and he was filled w
pleasurable anxiety.

At any rate he understood now what lay behind
phrases Miss Penge had used.

But what of that? He was not under an obligation to
Penge. He was under an obligation to nobody. He co
walk out of the club and go home in the twilight and resu
his solitary existence. In theory he could do that.

But he could not conceal from himself the fact that
solitary dinner at Norbury, followed by a long walk in t
darkness back to an empty house, seemed particularly una
tractive tonight. For once, he thought, he would enjoy hav
ing company. He had been alone, practically, for nearly si
weeks. There was scriptural authority, if he needed it, fo
occasional indulgence in society, if he so desired.

He knew, of course, that it was not quite so simple as that.
Miss Penge, for instance, would not arouse all these perplexing thoughts if he happened to meet her in Norbury and invited her to dinner at the inn. He knew he was only dodging the issue. He was in full possession of all his faculties, and they were all informing him at this moment that there was no fool like an old fool, and he was therefore heading for a life the reverse of meditative if he did not put an end to the present situation. It was perfectly simple, the faculties chanted in chorus.

Possibly so, he commented to himself, when the chorus had retired. Possibly so; but there was a catch in the argument, which was, that a man is merely the sum of his faculties. He was much more than that, Mr. Spenlove believed. He was the product of his emotional experiences, for one thing; experiences during which many of his faculties were absent without leave, as they said in wartime.

Another thing, he continued. He had been led astray by the rules and regulations of the economic system in which he

had been enmeshed for forty years, for he had begun his apprenticeship when he was fifteen, just before the Boer War. He had assumed that when a man retired he was on the shelf, destined to gather dust until he became dust. Most of them did, he admitted. But most of them were men whose emotional resources had never been remarkable and had been dissipated, anyway, on wives and children. They had become ossified in their personalities. Most men who survive a life at sea long enough to retire cling to the rim of the economic machine in silence, as it revolves according to laws they have never remained on shore long enough to understand. They continue to obey orders until Death gives them the final order of all.

Mr. Spenlove had often used the metaphor of the mouse in a revolving cage to describe the futility of a seaman's life, but he always made a mental reservation in favor of himself. And now that he was refreshed and restored by his retirement to the country and had made a few tentative, experimental contacts with American life, he had lost any feeling he might have had at first, of being a septuagenarian. Quite the contrary. And besides, his friend Mrs. Colwell (who had promised one of these days to come over and see him) had perceived this before he had. And she was a woman of intelligence and integrity. He liked her, and he flattered himself that she liked him, enjoying his pungent comments on what he called the predatory culture of Long Island. It was lucky, of course, she pointed out, that everybody didn't have his views, which to her were fundamentally immoral.

Having disposed of the arguments of his guardian angels, Mr. Spenlove felt better. He felt infinitely better than if he had caught himself slipping into the sort of pismires some of his most respected colleagues were occasionally discovered patronizing. Like himself they had a Puritan background, a tradition of middle-class integrity behind a façade of lower middle-class hypocrisy, and this was a combination that sometimes disintegrated in the American air, as do

ancient monuments when brought over to American museums. He had had numerous examples of men like himself caught in the toils of transatlantic Circes. There was that staff captain, who shot himself in his cabin one morning in New York. . . .

Still, I'm not a staff captain, Mr. Spenlove told himself; nor was Mrs. Ducroy a nightclub hostess, which had been the reason the staff captain put a bullet through his not very steady brain. Mr. Spenlove turned suddenly away from the glazed stare of a sharp-nosed varnished sailfish as though he had again seen that figure, through the half-opened cabin door, crumpled against the bunk board, the intolerably bright scarlet pool of wetness spreading on the white bed cover. He could again hear, for an infinite fraction of time, the hoarse bellow of the commander: "Ah-h! God dammit!" Disgust, contempt, shame and pity were all there. What distress of spirit, when one of one's own people did such a thing! And how quickly one experienced, after the distress, a complacent thankfulness that it was he and not one's self! Mr. Spenlove, his hands folded over his walking stick, remembered it was called a tragedy in the Liverpool papers. Liverpool was the staff captain's home port and nobody there knew anything about the New York nightclub hostess. A tragedy accomplished the purification of the soul through horror; but there was nothing of that, nothing of that! Mr. Spenlove knew his own kind too well to believe in purification.

What they did achieve was a feeling of superiority over the shipmate who had let a woman get hold of him and play him like a fish on a hook. Mr. Spenlove, however, had always suffered from a secret but furious pride in his own intelligence. He had looked down from the heights of that intelligence so long, contemplating the follies of seamen, that he now automatically flinched away from even the beginnings of such a situation as he had observed in the lives of other men of his condition. Their pathetic ignorance of shore life landed them literally in the most dismal shipwrecks. They went ashore as a ship did, often becoming a total loss, eventually breaking up on the beach.

Faulty navigation was the cause, of course. Mr. Spenlove had an idea he was a better navigator than most of them. He knew a hawk from a handsaw, anyhow!

He had withdrawn into himself for many years. It was a curious thing, he often thought, that the woman who had enslaved his heart when he was a young man in the Aegean trade, was now only a bright shadow at the back of his mind. An empty shape, like an almost completely faded photograph. She had died in his arms, during that silly street battle in Salonika, from a random bullet glancing off a house, a bullet fired off vaguely by a soldier reluctant to hit any neighbors in a suburb where he was well known. She had been the innocent victim of a million-to-one or a hundred million-to-one chance. And now, twenty-five years afterward, though the events were still clear, he could not remember what she looked like! She would be between fifty and sixty now, he reflected, smiling sourly.

That, however, did not alter the fact that he had been enslaved by Artemisia Macedoine. No other woman had ever had a chance with him. All the beauty and poetry of his life had crystallized around that lovely, unfortunate creature in the Grecian isle of Ipsilon. It had so captured his young romantic imagination that nothing that could ever happen afterward could take its place. It had been perfect. Perfect for him, that was to say. A jewel of memory enshrined in his heart. But the jewel had lost some of its luster, the image on his mental retina was now only a shadow. It had served its purpose, possibly. It had enabled him to keep all the other women at a distance, both the affectionate and the comfortable homebodies who thought he "ought to settle down." He had navigated himself into a quiet harbor. He ought to be safe now. He had paid his respects to romantic passion and he was now in Arcady!

That was the future he had figured out for himself when he got out at Norbury that spring day and established himself at the Mudge Place. No pretentiousness for him! Frugal, thrifty, and a healthy life in retirement. This he had enjoyed for going on two months; but so far from feeling a fondness for the chimney corner growing within him and gentle resignation to a slowing pulse, he was aware of the sap rising again. . . .

He had been deceived by the conventional attitude toward his age. Only the other day he had read about that French war poet, who had said that he did not fear death (Mr. Spenlove privately disbelieved the fellow), but he did fear reaching the age of fifty, and the impotence that would fall upon him then. Fifty! A stripling!

All his life Mr. Spenlove had heard the slogan, "Too old at forty, finished at fifty." Like all slogans it would not bear scrutiny; but anything constantly heard without contradiction leaves a faint but indelible stain on the mind. You think it probably is true for the other fellow, and therefore for yourself also. The French war poet had been misinformed, however.

Mr. Spenlove experienced a glow of pleasure that was both mental and physical. But he had a sudden remembrance of an episode in his life, when he was a young man not long at sea. He remembered it perfectly, though he had not recalled it for many years. It was something of a shock to realize that he had, on that occasion, seen into the future!

He frowned and concentrated on that scene. The lofty club house, almost deserted because the season was not yet officially open, was barren of all disturbing elements. The employees, in their blue uniforms, were in their own secret chambers. "In the glory-hole," Mr. Spenlove thought of them. In some subtle fashion the place seemed to hold a promise of them, although they were invisible. There were no sounds at all. The western sky, red and dark amber beyond the estuary, could be seen framed in the glass doors through which he had entered. An electric clock at the end of the room moved its minute hand with a nervous jerk every sixty seconds. He frowned in the effort to reconstruct that scene which had been, although he did not know it then, a glimpse of the future.

It was now a long while ago, he mused. He had been at the time what is known as a relief. The regular chief engineer had gone home, "to meet his children," as he put it sardonically, and Mr. Spenlove, the second, was appointed for the voyage. He remembered having a drink with the captain on his twenty-eighth birthday, which fixed the year. So it was twenty-seven years ago.

The skipper had been an unusual type for those days. He was about fifty—the age the French war poet was so afraid of—and he not only took his pleasure ashore but liked to have his chief with him. Mr. Spenlove was invited "to give the natives a treat" in Alexandria, in Egypt.

Mr. Spenlove remembered that night after all those years. The ship had been lying far out at the buoys and they took a splendid sailboat, with a huge yellow and brown sail, which flew across the harbor like a bird, keeling over in a way that made the skipper laugh like a boy. They had had a good dinner and a bottle of Greek wine and then had seen a show at the Ramleh Casino.

It was all vivid, after twenty-seven years, to the man who sat in the yacht club, for a special reason. Later the captain had called a gharry and they had driven to a distinguished-looking house in a fashionable street. No Jack-ashore business for this skipper. He did things in style. It had been like calling on a consul-general or the minister to a minor republic. A handsome madame received them in a noble drawing room. Servants in white gowns and red sashes took their hats and canes and other servants brought drinks on brass trays. The furniture, the pictures, the soft-shaded lamps, were astonishing and made Mr. Spenlove, only twenty-eight, suspect the captain of fooling him—this place was surely the home of some wealthy friend.

The lady of the house had bowed and thanked him when he made this remark. The captain said, of course, this was the most respectable house in Alex. Then the girls came, Rumanian, Austrian, Greek, Syrian and Circassian, in beautiful robes and with modest manners, almost blushing when accepting a grenadine or a water-ice. The folding door at one end of the room had opened and through the portiere hangings he had seen other girls and men, sitting on cushions at little Egyptian coffee tables and listening to a young man with blond marcelled hair playing and singing "Viens, Pupule!" at a black upright piano.

Mr. Spenlove reminded himself that he was only twenty-eight then. The Greek wine had made him fall in love with a violet-eyed, bronze-haired Austrian girl who came and sat beside him on a divan in a corner. In the dim rose-tinted light of the alcove she was, he remembered, so extravagantly lovely, so seductive, though he could no longer recall her features, that he suffered from a slight vertigo. He had fantastic notions of being at last in the Mohammedan paradise. What did he not say, in hurried whispers, while she looked at him with her lovely violet eyes over the glass of syrup she had ordered? He remembered how she smiled and nodded and confirmed the invitation with intoxicating glances. And every moment she glanced over her shoulder toward the entry.

Mr. Spenlove concentrated his gaze on the floor as he thought of that girl. He was young, not bad-looking, and fairly conceited. He began to preen himself like a male peacock, he remembered. He was filled with manly pride to have dazzled so splendid a creature, the prettiest girl in the room. He saw the lady of the house making gestures, as though even she were annoyed at his success. He saw both the girl and the madame look sharply toward the dim-lighted hall, and then the girl sprang up and hurried out. He saw a tall, broad-shouldered elderly man, with a fine beard, a gold-rimmed monocle and a cigar in an amber holder, enfold the girl in his arms, lift her off her feet and carry her into another room.

And the memorable thing about that adventure had been his own revulsion from the thought that a man so old—he must have been fifty at least—a man with a beard, too, should be in such a place at all. Yes, he had been revolted because in his youthful imagination a man of that age, with a beard, would have no charm, no romantic appeal for a beautiful girl.

Good God! What a callow ass he had been in those days! Now he was a man of fifty-odd himself, with a beard into the bargain, and he was waiting for a beautiful woman. . . .

There were hurried footsteps behind him. He closed his eyes for an instant and opened them to find Mrs. Ducroy's face close to his shoulder.

"Did you think I was dead or gone away?" she said, smiling. "I had to have a bath. That boat is as dirty as an old oil stove. I expected you'd have got sick of waiting."

"I said I'd wait," he said.

"And you haven't had anything to drink? I told them to . . ."

"I waited for that too. You look as if you were worth waiting for."

She held out her hand and moved toward the door. "I'm glad. Come on then," she said.

He rose and followed her. She wore a light wool dress of turquoise blue, with a hat, small and chic, of the same shade. She had a short fur coat, dark and rich, and from the hat hung a bluish veil that reached just below her eyes, a veil designed for coquetry, for suggesting, ever so faintly, the seductions of a seraglio in a perfumed garden.

The blue-clad steward appeared silently and opened the glass doors, with a glance at Mr. Spenlove's baggy corduroy trousers and well-worn brogans.

"Do you own this place?" Mr. Spenlove inquired lightly. "I thought it was a yacht club."

"It is a yacht club." She hurried ahead of him around the main building to where several cars stood in an open-fronted garage. "The season doesn't start for a week or two. I was tuning up our boat."

"I heard you."

She looked over her shoulder at him, her eyes mysterious through the blue gauze of the veil.

The six-liter Virago stood in one of the stalls of the garage, its enormous trunk distinguishing it from the glossy bulging posteriors of the American sedans. It was, Mr. Spenlove thought, like a bustle.

What does she think she is going to do? he asked himself, but he refrained from putting the question into words. She seemed perfectly clear as to what she was going to do. She got in and started the engine, waving to him to go around and join her. He did so. The Virago slid out, in reverse, in a wide arc. The haughty hood, with its radiator cap in the shape of a female figure with streaming hair and draperies, rose like the forecastle of a destroyer in front of them, a symbol of arrogant power. Mrs. Ducroy drove forward again, going over a small boulder at the edge of the driveway as though to demonstrate springs of incredible resiliency. She sped swiftly through the gateway, where a watchman touched his cap to her, and then let the car out on the shore road.

At first she did not speak and Mr. Spenlove had no idea of playing her game by exhibiting curiosity. So far it might be a kidnaping affair! Using the arts of a siren, she had carried him away in her glittering chariot. The music of her voice would ensnare any man, he thought, even a blind man who could not see the beauty of her person.

The sea was calm under an evening sky of soft fleecy clouds faintly illumined by the afterglow of a sunset beyond the Connecticut hills. Only a few cars were parked at intervals among the wild cherry copses that lined the shore, cars facing the sea and with lights out. A winking orange light at the intersection warned Mr. Spenlove that here was his way home. He was about to point this out when Mrs. Ducroy swung to the left and the car fled toward Sutton Corners. He sat silently in the deep red leather cushions. The headlights flashed on, twin beams of broad soft radiance. Soon they would illumine his entry. They did. The car slowed slightly, swung in among the trees, swept into his yard, and stopped as softly as a feather coming to rest.

"This is very nice of you," he said as he sought for the door handle, "but it wasn't necessary. I was out for a walk. Exercise! Exorcise too, as a matter of fact."

"What?" she said, and laid her hand on his. "Say that again!" She leaned toward him, smiling.

"Presently," he said. "It'll wait. Where were you going, when you came ashore, if I hadn't happened along just then? If it isn't an impertinence?"

"Here," she said. "I was coming to see you."

He got out slowly and closed the door.

"All right," he said, "but I usually go to Norbury for my dinner."

"We can have dinner all right," she said. "The car will take us to dinner."

"Aren't you dining at home?"

"Not tonight."

"You would not have found me at home."

She was already out of the car and coming around to the steps of the house.

"I'd have followed you," she said smiling. "I wanted to see you and you hadn't any telephone, you said, so that was the only way. You went out for a walk and walked to the lighthouse. I saw you when I was out in the boat."

"I walked straight into the trap," he said, going up and opening the screen door.

"That's right," she said, affably.

It was now dark in the house. The large trees shut out the sky. For a moment he stood beside her in that darkness, his hand grasping her arm strongly.

"What?" she said. She turned her face directly to his so that he was aware of the veil touching his eyes.

"I think we are being indiscreet. I'm not experienced in the customs of the country, but I couldn't help overhearing two of your husband's guests talking when I was there once. . . . Yes!"

"Didn't leave a stitch on me, I suppose," she said quietly.

"They were busy skinning you alive when I moved out of earshot," he said, still holding her arm. It was a strong, round, warmly resilient arm and she made no protest.

"What did they say?" she asked, naturally.

"Later, later!" he suggested. "I didn't believe them. I'd never seen you and didn't pay much attention. I was only perplexed because you weren't there, at the party."

"I was in New York," she said sharply. "I don't have to consult those horrible creatures if I want to go to New York. I told you what I'm doing."

"Horrible creatures! That's strange. I thought them not only horrible but obscene."

"They're *his* friends. They're not even his *friends!* It's his idea he has to entertain them, because of his position."

"His position?"

"Don't you know he's one of the highest-paid serial writers in America?"

"I don't read serials."

"Neither do I. But he is. He can do that magazine stuff so fast the others accuse him of having ghosts to work for him."

"I would have thought he would be independent of everybody in that case, except the ghosts."

"You don't know anything about it. Why do we stand here in the dark?"

"I find it easier to ask you these questions in the dark." He shook her gently. "I was thinking about you. A woman can be indiscreet and marvelous. The more marvelous the more indiscreet, sometimes. I was just wondering. Those people at the party, now . . . Hm."

"I suppose you think badly of me, coming here, then? Coming here and telling you I'm leaving my husband."

"No."

"Think I'm a *femme fatale,* anyway?"

"Not in that sense. I daresay you're fatal enough, but not in that sense."

"You're nice! Let us go in, please."

"And have an *apéritif?*"

There was no answer. He kept hold of her arm and moved toward the switch. It was a warm night, but not too warm. He felt extremely excited. When the light in the room came on, an amber-shaded floor lamp which he used for reading, he was surprised to see that she was agitated.

"What's the matter?" he said. "Better sit down, perhaps?"

He steered her to the deep leather chair and she subsided gently into it. He watched her hunt in her bag for cigarettes, waiting for an explanation. He struck a match and held it out and she thrust her face forward. She drew on it and then looked up, smiling.

"All right. I'll have an *apéritif,* as you call it. What have you got?"

"You seemed to be making a fuss about it," he pointed out. "Are you a *femme mystérieuse* as well as *fatale?* Are you sorry you came here, after all?"

"It was nothing much. I'll tell you later."

He went away to get the drink. The memory of Sonia suddenly assailed him, and he stopped in his tracks. Sonia knew something, it seemed. He went back to the door of the room where Sonia's mother sat smoking, drawing nervously at her cigarette and knocking the ash into a tray, although there was no ash to knock. She looked up and smiled.

"How about sherry? Sherry and bitters?" he said. He added, "Now Sonia's not here to forbid it?"

She shook her head. Then shook it again, violently.

"Can I have a whiskey and soda?" she said.

He went to the corner cupboard and took down a bottle of whiskey and a siphon of soda.

"Sonia said you didn't drink," he remarked without emphasis.

"This is a celebration," she said.

"Gin for me," he said, and went out once more to find glasses and some ice.

A celebration! He repeated the word as he broke off a lump of ice and dropped it into a wooden bowl for cracking. He got two glasses and put everything on a tray.

"What celebration?" he asked when he got back.

"Meeting an intelligent person, for one thing," she said, smiling.

"Intelligent?" Mr. Spenlove looked vague and unconscious of any compliment. He stood at the table preparing the drinks. "Is that a cause for celebration?"

"I said intelligent, not intelligentsia!" she explained, and this time she did not smile.

"Oh! Ah! Quite so. But your husband, he isn't one of the intelligentsia, is he? He didn't give me that impression."

"No. They make him think he is."

"I wouldn't imagine him to need to worry about those people. I would have thought he was too successful to be dependent on . . ."

"He's successful, of course. Very successful. But did you ever try to analyze what makes a magazine writer successful?"

Mr. Spenlove shook his head. He didn't want to talk to her about her husband. "Magazine writers" was a phrase that conveyed very little to his mind. Mr. Spenlove's mind was highly specialized on the technical side, and for refreshment he depended principally upon reflection. He did not actively dislike magazines. It was simply that to him they seemed to be designed by maniacs for the entertainment of the feeble-minded. They were substitutes not only for thought but for reality, for the actual experience of the world, its color and romance, with which his own life had been filled, and which were inaccessible to the readers of magazines. He knew also that most of those readers were quite incapable of adventure and romance themselves, that they did not recognize it even when it came to them. He had seen that happen many times in his own life. He had known men to confront romance and fail to recognize it. The magazines were brightly packaged goods, proprietary drugs, distillations, sedatives, pick-me-ups, stimulants and aphrodisiacs.

He knew the consumers of these things. They were bought in drugstores, he noted with a smile, but the men and women who manufactured them were not so clear to him. A consul, a harbor master, a stevedore or a shipowner, was to Mr. Spenlove a sharply conceived image. He knew them as he knew mates, engineers, stewards and passengers. He even had a few fugitive memories of passengers who were professional authors, whose names were to be found on books. He had imagined magazine writers were the same people.

When he said this, Mrs. Ducroy shook her head slowly.

"Do you know any professional authors?" she asked. It was his turn to shake his head.

"An occasional stray on a cruise," he said. "They come to get away from it all, of course. Their wives take care they are put at the captain's table. And the photographers mysteriously discover them on the boat deck contemplating the New York skyline. I know a writer of detective novels slightly. Norah Kavanagh."

"What's she like?"

"Amusing. Not a bit like her books. She gave me an autographed copy. *The Gilded Skull* it was. It's here somewhere. Like to read it?"

Mrs. Ducroy took a long sip of her drink and put it down again.

"Oh!" she said, and then stopped for a moment. She looked around the room, at the almost stark simplicity of the furnishing, the half-burned log in the fireplace, the shelves of shabby books, the scrubbed boards of the floor, the delicate colors of the worn Armenian rug. And then she looked at the owner of it and studied the solidly masculine figure leaning forward from the waist, one black-haired hand on the powerful thigh, the knees heavily muscled and spread wide. Finally she raised her eyes to his keen dark gaze, with the heavy black brows, to the mobile, satirical, sensual lips above the sharply trimmed beard.

"We're just making conversation," she said at last. "We're not saying what we think, what we mean, at all."

"Hm." He smacked his lips over the last of his drink and set it down. Instead of returning to his seat beside her, he stood over her, his hand on the back of the leather chair, looking down into her upturned face.

"Hah!" he said. "I can see what it is. You've always had everything you wanted, and . . ."

"No, I haven't!" she said. She stamped her foot. "How do you know what I wanted? I'll tell you one thing I've always wanted, and never had. I've always wanted to own myself, be myself, be on my own, be independent, be somebody!"

"Is that what you're celebrating?" he asked. Her glass was empty. "Your final emancipation?"

"You don't understand. You don't *want* to understand!"

She sprang up and faced him, her face glowing in the light of the amber-shaded lamp. "I thought you would, when I saw you with Sonia. You were sweet with Sonia."

She turned to the window and looked out.

"I suppose a man with the necessary intelligence for a woman like me is inevitably cynical. You don't have to be cynical, do you? I dare say you think terrible things of me now, because I've been honest with you. I am honest with you. I don't want to talk about magazine writers or any kind of writers. I would like to forget all about writers! What do you think of that?"

"All right," he said quietly. "But I had no reason to assume all that. Now you've told me, all right. Possibly I'm as honest as you are. I was in a state today, I can tell you. Yes!"

She turned quickly to look at him.

"A fair state!" he continued, without looking at her. "That honest enough for you? I went for a walk this evening to get my bearings. I hadn't realized, when I came down here to live—in retirement, mind you—I hadn't realized I was so easily—hm—well, so easily upset."

"Afraid?"

"At first. Plain fright! I'm a stranger on shore, you know. I haven't got my bearings."

"And have you got them now?"

"I thought you were one of those women we have sometimes on the ships," he went on without answering. "We call them body-snatchers, man-eaters, rattlesnakes. All sorts of names like that. Wait now!" He put up his hand to silence her. "I say, that's what I thought at first. The people at your husband's cocktail party talked rather loud, some of them, and they gave me a wrong impression. They seemed to have it in for you, yes, but only because you were beating them at their own game. That was my impression. It was all strange to me."

"I see. And my coming here, and telling you that—confirmed the impression. I must seem an awful bitchy person to you! I . . ." She looked quickly around the room again, as though endeavoring to confirm a mental picture she had been cherishing. "Oh! I *am* so sorry!" She turned to him with hands outstretched. "I've spoiled it all, I suppose. You think I'm one of those . . ." She pressed her fingers to her mouth.

"No, it's not spoiled. And you aren't one of those. Oh, no!" He laughed and stepped to the table to replenish his glass. "And I'm not one of the others, if you know what I mean. We can dispense with making conversation, as you call it, until later. And I'll say what I think."

"What are you thinking now?"

"It's hard to put into words. Your voice. Do you know you

have a voice that is like a benediction? That's not the right word. In fact it's the wrong word. Benison? No; benison's too archaic. You see, I was thinking of the voice, but not in words. When you speak to me, I can hear the song the sirens sang!"

He smiled and came over to her, and took her by the arms. She stood close to him.

"Yes?" she said softly. "You're awfully nice! Tell me some more. Say something to me, please!"

"All right," he said.

iv

SEE THAT?" she said, pointing. "Do you see it?"

He saw it, very plainly, through the binoculars.

"Now do you understand my side of it?" she inquired. "Or do I have to go over it all again?"

Mr. Spenlove did not reply immediately. He was standing not far from where he had been that afternoon when he struck across the dried marsh to the path that took him to the lighthouse. He was a little farther up the river. It was about ten o'clock, a clear, soft, cloudless, moonless night. The estuary below them was invisible except when the lighthouse beam swung across the entrance, half a mile away. To the right the headlights of an occasional automobile heading for Sutton Corners showed through the trees.

The only other light, save a red lamp by the yacht-club fuel dock, was directly across the river, below a dark wooded slope. Mrs. Ducroy had said, pointing to the house, whose one immense window was a square of soft diffused light with a background of bright flames from a stone fireplace,

"See that?"

He had taken the binoculars she had suggested bringing down with them, a pair of high-power German glasses, and adjusted them while she stood close to his shoulder, her hand resting lightly on it. Even while he focussed the glasses on the square of radiance, across the dark river, he had a sensation of glory all around him just because she was there, invisible in the darkness.

The great raftered room of the house across the river was

suddenly revealed to him. The window faced the river, and the occupants of the room were oblivious of any possible observation. A man and a woman were outlined against the firelight of large logs. The woman had her arms around the man, who stood looking down at the fire. The heads of two other persons were visible above an immense divan that cut across the foreground. The heads were close together, Mr. Spenlove noted, and the firelight struck through glasses and bottles on a table between the couples.

They were small but very distinct, and he had a peculiar sensation of possessing, just temporarily of course, supernatural powers. Those people were so completely unaware, or so careless (this was a bare possibility) of any one being able to see them, that they fascinated him. He kept them in view much longer than he had imagined necessary. He could not identify any one or anything. Less than an hour ago, in a roadhouse ten miles away, he had first learned of the existence of the house into whose interior he was now gazing. But those tiny figures could not be identified by him. It was his companion who had brought him down here after their return from dinner the other side of Norbury. On Route Eleven, he reminded himself, and a very good dinner, in an alcove that was almost a private room, overlooking an orchard. He had asked where her husband was. Was he in New York?

"He hardly ever goes there," she had said. "He doesn't need to."

She began to tell him a tale so fantastic that to him, a man of the sea, it sounded slightly cracked. He told her this and she said, simply, "All right. I'll prove it to you. I dare say it sounds slightly improbable and I'm not a bit flattered! No woman would tell a story like this about her husband unless it was true. She wouldn't tell it even then except to someone she trusted absolutely."

"And you trust me absolutely? Why?"

She had said, touching his hand lightly and smiling, in the shaded candlelight, into his eyes, "Just because."

It was when he asserted his right to details that he heard, for the first time, about a person named Sydney Saxon.

"You mean to say you've never heard of Sydney Saxon?"

What is it in her voice? He asked himself as he shook his head. Admiration and hate? Or perhaps just contempt? She possessed that musical gift of evoking a character in tones that had the qualities of a caricature in bright color. "Sydney Saxon!" He had never heard of the creature, yet he was aware of a resplendent orb in that world Elliot Ducroy inhabited, the world of shiningly successful Americans. Whereas he and the woman who stood beside him were invisible microcosms, fragments of the darkness which formed the background of their brilliance. Nobodies!

Mrs. Ducroy chuckled musically and indulgently.

"It's evident you don't read magazines!"

"And I ought to, you mean? All of them?"

"She's in all of them, almost! If not one week, the next. Sometimes two, or three at a time. Like Gentleman Church. Only she writes *treacle,* not mystery stories. Sydney Saxon, America's Public Friend Number One! The Dark Red Lady of the Slicks! Do you know what I mean by treacle?"

"You seem to admire her!"

"You notice she does more than admire my husband. They're the Douglas Fairbanks and Mary Pickford of the magazine world. They ought to get married!"

> *"Make her take him and keep him,*
> *That's hell for them both,*
> *And you're shut of the curse of*
> *a——"*

Her hold on his shoulder tightened and she laid her head on it.

"That house," she said slowly, "is only rented, of course, by the person we're discussing. It was built, they told us, by a big Hollywood man. He came back here to retire with a fortune and a star. But he rolled to his rifle and blew out his brains one night, as Kipling puts it, and the star vanished of course. It's a huge place. We looked at it when we first came down to look at places. I would just as soon live in a public building. Tudor, with a hall suitable for public meetings instead of private ones. That's it there. The fireplace, oh, my word!"

"Yes, it seems quite baronial," he said.

"Seen enough? I took liberties with Kipling's ballad, adjusting it to the situation: *When you're wounded and left on Afghanistan plains, and the woman*—that's Sydney Saxon—*comes out to cut up what remains!* But I'm not going to blow out *my* brains!"

"Certainly not," Mr. Spenlove said. He was still staring at the scene by the roaring fire. Sparks streamed out of the chimney straight up into the night as one of the party moved the logs in the grate. He was not seeing any more than the first glimpse had afforded him, but he continued to gaze in order to make some sort of comprehensible picture in his mind of these people and the, to him, strange world in which they lived.

"No, you mustn't do anything like that," he said and, closing the binoculars, he slipped them into their case, which hung by a strap over his left shoulder. He was aware of her now only by the pressure of her body against his other shoulder and the faint breath of her perfume.

"With a high-powered rifle I could pick them off from here. How would that do?"

He heard her chuckle again and felt the vibrant motion of it too.

"Let's go back," he said in a low tone. "And don't talk about high-powered rifles."

"All right. It does sound like a Gentleman Church story. Just suppose! From these cherry bushes there wouldn't be any flash, the sound wouldn't carry as far as a truck backfiring on the road up there. They backfire a lot coming down that hill, you know. The bullet would flatten itself against that stone chimney. The window would prevent them hearing the sound of the gun."

They moved carefully toward the road in the darkness, avoiding the tussocks of rush grass and the occasional rain gullies.

"Would you, if you could bring it off as smoothly as that?"

"No! I don't think I'd commit murder because of Sydney Saxon. She's a talented trollop!" she added quietly, recovering her poise. She was holding his arm and keeping in step. "Lives on other women's leavings. Are you going to give me a drink when we get back to your house?"

"You're driving a six-liter car, and from what I remember that's about two hundred horsepower in the case of a Virago with supercharging and dual carburetion." Mr. Spenlove steered her past the broken hedge that bordered the beach road. "You might bear it in mind."

"You're an engineer, so you can remember things like that. I couldn't. I drive the same as I breathe, without thinking. Do I have to take orders?"

"In matters like drinking, possibly. Keep out of trouble until you've taught me how to drive."

"I believe you do know how to drive! You're only pretending. It's part of your pose as an old man. 'On the shelf' you said! You know all about Viragos, and pretend you don't drive! Sonia can drive the station wagon; only of course she can't, legally."

"Well, neither can I, legally. You have to get accustomed to local conditions. My motorcar experience dates. You wouldn't remember those days. Women took the veil when they went motoring! You got into the tonneau at the back and you had traveling rugs and electro-plated sandwich boxes and foot warmers full of boiling water unless it was high summer. Only adventurers used a car except on fine warm days, however. I had a little experience of those cars just before I went to sea. Did you ever see a White steam car? We had one to repair in a garage where I worked in London. If we needed a spare nut or screw we had to send to New York, and they had to send to the factory. Americans were really independent in those days. They even used a different shaped thread and nut for their screws."

He guided her carefully up the dark narrow track that led to the Mudge Place.

"You could write a book about motor cars!" she said, with her comforting chuckle. He loved the sound of it and the feeling it conveyed to him that she was at peace while in his company. "Tell me some more."

"Nothing easier," he said. The porch was dark. Only the amber-shaded floor lamp behind the door was burning. He was feeling extraordinarily elated, even though that restless analytical intelligence of his, which had controlled his emotions for years, was busy with the reasons for that elation. "*You are an old fool,*" it was saying feverishly. But he did not feel either old or a fool. "*That is part of the illusion,*" the analytical intelligence cackled. "*It is like the beauty of a sunset, the prelude to the death of the day. Or the red sky at morning, if you prefer it. Prelude to a hurricane. Old fool!*"

Mr. Spenlove listened. He always listened to this inward monitor. He had an idea that his analytical intelligence did not know all the answers in this case. He felt justified in assuming that his faculties were unimpaired, that he was able to take care of himself even if there were a hurricane. *This,* he thought, as he opened the screen door and reached out in the gloom to bring his companion up the steps, *is far better than what I feared!* What he had feared was infatuation for some young creature in whom he would inspire only derision. The analytical intelligence had often taken that possibility as a probability when warning him.

But this was something entirely different, he thought with exultation. It was as it should be, he told himself, with a faint touch of complacency, the complacency that is integral in the completely male animal.

He had once told a lady passenger, who had been arguing about it, that her lack of logic was a clear proof she did not grasp the implications she had raised. She was complaining that love was "woman's whole existence," which placed her at a disadvantage with men. Mr. Spenlove had pointed out that she could, and did, balance that disadvantage by her superior skill in pursuit. "You can't have everything, but you can have a jolly good try," he had told her, adding, "and the glory of the sport!" That phrase had been her own, uttered in a thrilling contralto, but used in connection with deep-sea fishing, of which she was a passionate devotee. She had turned on him triumphantly.

"What if he's a heel?" she had inquired. Mr. Spenlove had an answer for that too. He said heels kept away from women with intelligence. He added that a woman could not expect to receive credit for intelligence if she did not use it on elementary problems at least. To which the lady had retorted that only a heel would say a thing like that!

All that was in the realm of theory and had no bearing on this woman. She was something new, and unexpectedly stimulating. She was intelligent without being intellectual. She was free from the quaint provincial arrogance of the college woman. She was sensuous, but without that fantastic sensuality which women who have ideals sometimes cultivate like an orchid, to create glamor for themselves among men. She was delicious by virtue of the perfect blend of her bodily and spiritual qualities.

He enumerated them to himself at this moment. There was the beauty of her voice, never loud, or flat, or brassy; the infectious gaiety of her chuckle, which seemed a most inadequate word for that little laugh of hers; the marvelous cosiness and companionship implicit in her. "Tell me some more!" Most of all, the impression she gave of being without anger.

"Can any one see us here?" she inquired. She took off her hat and laid it on the window seat.

"I don't think so. I have sat here, night after night, and someone may have been watching me. But I don't think so."

"What were you doing, night after night?" she asked. She lay back in the green leather chair and watched him as he opened his corner cupboard.

"Reading, thinking, smoking a cigar, and somewhere around eleven o'clock I would have a noggin of rum to sleep on."

She made a lithe forward movement and took the book that lay open on the side table. It had been there since the afternoon, forgotten. She held it so that the light fell on the page and she began to read. For a moment a faint frown crossed her forehead. Then she smiled.

"I can't make it out," she said. "This book, is it supposed to be good? You aren't religious, are you?"

"That? Supposed to be good? It's good to me. Good if you like it. You think, because a man reads a serious book, he's religious."

"It sounds gloomy. *Urn Burial!* That's cremation, I suppose. Are you morbid?"

Mr. Spenlove, without turning round, laughed.

"Am I making an exhibition of myself? You know, I'm not a reader. I've no education."

"Oh, of course!" he murmured.

"What do you mean, of course? Have you any idea what it is to be brought up in a literary household? Where everybody was writing except yourself? You'd know what being morbid was, if you had."

"I meant that nobody who has had no education ever admits he has no education. Not in the tones you used when you said the words. They may brag about it, as great industrialists do, or they may tell it mournfully to young people. In either case it's obvious without any confession. You can be educated without being a reader. And there's no compulsion to read Sir Thomas Browne."

"Who was he? I really don't know. I read *Tom Brown's School Days.*"

"This Tom Browne lived earlier. He went to Winchester, not Rugby. He was a medical man. The first medical man, so far as I know, to write a best seller. One of his books is still going along, and it came out nearly three hundred years ago. I prefer it to some of the books doctors write nowadays."

"You like old books?"

"I like them sometimes. I like Sir Thomas. He was a civilized man of his day, even though he believed in witches and helped to get a couple of girls burned for witchcraft."

She closed the book with a snap and put it down. Her eyes were bright as she looked at him without speaking, her thoughts concentrated upon this extraordinary good luck of hers. She was not going to ruin it by talking about old books. She said suddenly:

"I hate books!"

He went on with his preparations, sure-footed, neat-handed, silent, almost stealthy in his movements to and from the kitchen. In the silence she could hear tiny noises, the sounds of an old house adjusting itself, settling to a night's rest after a warmish day.

When he was ready he came in again with an old black lacquer tray, on which were a highball and a glass of rum and water.

"You said something like that at dinner," he remarked. "You said something about your being warped by books. I thought you were trying to be clever. Did you mean it?"

"I was talking about my childhood. . . . Something made me forget what I was talking about, and we went off at a tangent. When you enjoy talking to a person you digress, I think. Well, I meant it. I was brought up in a literary home. We were up to the eyes in it. There was no getting away from it. They were all writing."

"Who's 'they'? Your family?"

"Father, mother, brother, cousins, uncles, aunts. My little sister inherited the family genius. My father used to be rather famous in an obscure way."

Mr. Spenlove restrained himself. She meant something special, no doubt. But he wanted to laugh. She was so absorbed, now, in getting the memory of that time clear in her mind, she had not noticed anything unusual in her words.

"You see," she went on, "it was a family business. Grandfather started it in the sixties. It was called the Chimney Corner Miscellany, a sort of Family Herald thing."

Mr. Spenlove nodded vigorously over his glass of rum.

"I remember it," he said. "We used to have it down at Threxford when I was a boy. It had an ornamental cover. The title was printed in rustic style over the mantel of an old-fashioned chimney corner. There was a little girl on one side and a little boy on the other. Am I right?"

"You are!" she said, smiling. "Grandfather founded it and Father edited it and wrote serials for it. Mother wrote stories for it too, and my brother wrote some of the advertisements. My Aunt Phoebe—she wore tight red curls on her head—wrote on cookery, though she was a terrible cook herself. Uncle Jack, Aunt Phoebe's husband, wrote on temperance. His knowledge was purely theoretical, I'm afraid."

"Didn't it die out during the war?" Mr. Spenlove mused. She nodded.

"But that didn't stop the family," she said. "Grandfather was dead, and Father never liked being in Fleet Street. He didn't like living in the Fulham Road, either. Grandfather wouldn't move from the house he'd bought when he got married. They were very Victorian."

"We have that in common," Mr. Spenlove said in a low tone. "Your people were metropolitan Victorian. Mine were provincial Victorian. Lower middle-class Victorian!"

"I don't know about lower middle class," she said, regarding him steadily. "You can't pull the wool over my eyes that way, my boy! You've got us wrong too, as the Americans say. We *were* middle-class Victorians, but that isn't the whole of it. We had contacts with Bohemia. One of my uncles . . ."

She stopped, smiling.

"I've never told you my name," she said. "My given name. Or my other name either, for that matter. Well, my Uncle Claud was on the stage. Nothing much. Just an ordinary character actor. He was once with Wilson Barrett, but on the road. Not in London."

"*The Sign of the Cross!*" Mr. Spenlove said in a tone of hushed awe. "I saw it when I was an apprentice. It made a very deep . . ."

"No. It was *The Silver King* Uncle Claud was in. But he was doing Autolycus in *Winter's Tale* when I was born, so he said I ought to be called Perdita."

"And you don't like it? I am absolutely certain you don't like it!"

"I'm used to it now. I hated it at first, all right, when I was a kid," she said. " 'Perdita Price, stand up!' " She imitated the shrill, spinsterish soprano of a schoolteacher. " 'Perdita Price, do a hundred lines! Oh, what price Perdita Price!' That was the way it went at school. Hardly any of the girls had ever heard of Perdita. It was so easy to dance up and down and chant 'Perdita Price is made of ice!' or 'Perdita Price is far from nice!' "

"Was there any foundation for those innuendoes?" Mr. Spenlove inquired. Mrs. Ducroy stretched out luxuriously in the green leather chair and put her hands behind her head. *You are magnificent!* he said to himself. His eyes were extremely bright and made the unuttered thought clear to her. She responded with a glance of grave ecstasy.

"Yes," she said, nodding. "As a matter of fact, I was a rather bitchy child. Disagreeable was the word most people found applicable to my case. Leggy, skinny, freckled and bad-tempered! I didn't get on with my family and wanted to run away. I simply hated the Fulham Road! All this of course was while I was a kid. After the war we moved into the country. Down in Suffolk. A place called Brandeston Knights. We were buried alive down there."

"Out of the frying pan . . ." Mr. Spenlove mused. Unlike most garrulous men he could let others talk. And he was experiencing a sudden attack of homesickness. Brandeston Knights! The name was like the sound of church bells across a misty valley at dusk. It evoked a memory of an old, gray, gabled church, where woolly sheep made a soft stealthy sound as they cropped the rich grass among the sunken gravestones.

"Just about that," she said. "Though there wasn't anything very hot about Brandeston Knights. You know, the parish was almost empty; all the people had gone to London or Ipswich, for the taxes were so heavy nobody could afford to live there so far from everywhere. There was no employment, either. So the church people, Ecclesiastical Commissioners, made the vicar of Brandeston Hundred take over Brandeston Knights, and they let the rectory to Father. Father by that time had dropped his Fleet Street work. He'd been toiling away like a beaver in an upstairs back room in the Fulham Road, writing stories. He worked very fast, and once he had struck his line, he had more work than he could do. And very soon Mother was helping him and starting to do girls' stories on her own."

"Where did these stories appear? Magazines?"

"Weekly newspapers and penny numbers," she said. "Boys' papers. Not the *Boys' Own Paper* or *Chums*, or swanky magazines like the *Strand* and *Windsor*. Father never sold anything in his life to those magazines. The people who used to read Father only earned about thirty bob or two pounds a week. They'd have the *Weekly Echo* on Sunday, with all the divorce cases reported in full, and one of Father's serials on a back page. Their children would have *Pluck* or *Idle Moments*, a penny a week each with a serial by Father, and their wives would buy one of the Marchioness magazines, a penny a week. Nothing but love stories in which virtue got all the breaks in the last instalment. Mother was always good at those."

"Then it was a sort of family monopoly. You owned the paper and produced the stories."

"Oh, no. The paper—the *Chimney Corner Miscellany*—was gone. It couldn't have fought the big trusts, even if the war hadn't killed it. We couldn't get any paper! No, Father and Mother worked for the Fireside Syndicate, one of the companies controlled by the *Daily Echo*. Aunt Phoebe was in that. She didn't write, exactly—she dictated. She thought up themes for Father and Mother to write on. She was editor of a paper called *Girls of England*, a penny weekly."

Mr. Spenlove nodded and began to clean his pipe. "All the same," he said, "it was a sort of home factory like those families I used to know in Clerkenwell, who made clock parts at home. Every member of the family helped. Some families made nothing but escapements, others coiled springs, or cut the teeth of the brass gears, or perhaps made faces. For clocks, I mean."

"We did that! We made faces," she said, smiling. "No, I wouldn't make the comparison quite so close. Father got twenty-five shillings a thousand words. Mother only got a pound for her stuff. But they had to keep grinding it out. You can't take a week or two off. The whole house was run on the principle that Mother and Father mustn't be disturbed under any circumstances while they were at work."

"But who took care of you children and the house, and so on?" Mr. Spenlove tried to picture this extraordinary household, entombed in an old rectory in the depths of the country, pouring out thousands of words, for the delight of the proletariat, behind closed doors.

"Servants. The gardener and housekeeper had lived in that house all their lives. I mean at the rectory. The gardener had a cottage in the garden with the greenhouse built against its south wall. And the girls of the village all expected to spend some time in service there. We had a horse and trap. It was seven miles to Marks Tey Junction, where we got a train to London. And on week ends the house was full. That was how I happened to get married."

"Sonia's father?"

She nodded.

"You aren't bored, are you? I really do want to explain myself to you. I think the one character in life I loathe and detest is the 'woman of mystery.' There's nothing mysterious about me."

"I am not bored," he said quietly.

She watched him moving about, very deliberate and quiet. He opened the door concealing the old bread oven built into the fireplace and drew out some kindling, which he arranged in an intricate pattern on the dogs. Then, without her having seen him withdraw it from his pocket, he had a jackknife in his hand, with which he was whittling long thin splinters and a few shavings from a clean yellow stick. He knelt on one knee with a match, and then began reaching into the oven for larger faggots.

He stood back and took up his glass again. The fabric he had constructed was a cage of yellow flame. She leaned forward. Her eyes shone in the firelight. Then she laughed, not harsh and flat, but with her low musical chuckle.

"That's what Boy Scouts always pretend to do, but they never seem to bring it off. You didn't start the fire with two sticks, though. You used a match!"

"Next time you come to see me I'll have a flint and tinder, if it will please you," he said. The fire was drawing strongly and a brisk crackle of dry pine filled the arched fireplace.

Her face, with the flames playing on it, became serious again. She rose and drew the chair nearer the fire. Mr. Spenlove watched her with a certain anxiety. He had some peculiar antipathies. One of them was women who always had to get down on the floor in front of a fireplace, even if the fire were artificial or non-existent. To his relief this woman resumed the chair.

"I must tell you about the house at Brandeston Knights," she went on, "because that place was my beginning, and because it was so different from this place here, and I'm so different too, from what I was then. . . . It was dark!"

"Dark?"

"Very dark. An old, old house, with heavy stone walls and overhanging eaves, in a sort of hollow full of great dark trees. The roof was dark red tile and the outhouses stood at right-angles to the front of the house, so the driveway was in a court where the sun could never shine. The windows were small, and Mother had that very Victorian mania for lace curtains and side curtains of dark blue velvet with brocaded loops. The front door was set in a porch in the house front, a porch as dark as a coal cellar. At the back there was a French window from the drawing room on to a lawn. On one side of the lawn was an enormous box hedge. On the other a very high wall belonging to the farm buildings. You see, it had been a glebe farm, and there was room for all the farm animals in that barn. Our pony and trap looked lost in it."

"How far from anywhere?" asked Mr. Spenlove.

"Miles! There was one row of cottages down the lane, where a bridge crossed a small stream, and beyond that fields, fields, fields! The church was close to our house, of course; a small church with a huge tower that shut off more light. That's why I say that house was dark. It was damp, too, and in winter awfully cold."

"No heat, of course."

"Heat!" She shrugged her shoulders and looked at him. "No heat since the Norman Conquest! I believe it was burned down at that time. Fire and rapine business. But it wasn't the cold so much as the damp, owing to being in a valley, and the darkness from those wet evergreen trees. It made me feel as if I would go mad. In holiday time, I mean. I went away to school soon after we moved to Brandeston Knights."

"What was the real trouble at home?" Mr. Spenlove asked. "Incompatibility of temperament? Or shall we say, no heat?"

"Partly," she smiled, staring into the fire. "Father was very conventional, in spite of our Bohemian connections. For instance, when I wanted to ride astride on my pony, he put his foot down. No riding astride! Unladylike! And when Uncle Claud bought a motorcar—a second-hand Daimler—and I wanted to learn how to drive it, Father nearly had a fit. No woman should have anything to do with those beastly, smelly things! Father was an Oxford man, and he never lost the feeling that even if he did make twenty-five pounds a week at writing stories for errand boys and slavies to read, he was somehow disgracing himself. You know, he sat at his desk from ten in the morning until ten at night, very often, writing, writing, writing; but he always wore a starched shirt with big cuffs, and a wing collar, and an old frock coat. In the winter he wore spats."

"In the country?" wondered Mr. Spenlove.

"Yes, buried away in that dark old house at Brandeston Knights! In summer he would have a gray frock coat for evenings or afternoon tea. He used to say none of his family had ever seen him in his shirt sleeves or in deshabille. I think it was true, too. I know I hadn't! He used a small room off his bedroom for a dressing room, so I dare say even mother hadn't either."

"Go on," Mr. Spenlove urged. "He interests me, your father. He was very English."

"Oh! Weren't we all? My mother was the same in her own way. She looked like a stage duchess when she was ready to go to London to order things from the Army and Navy Stores. And Harrod's. She wouldn't go anywhere else. If Aunt Phoebe praised another place Mother would sniff and say, 'It's a second-class shop!' Nothing second-class for Mother. She and Aunt Phoebe were wonderful when they went out together in London. They always hired a victoria by the hour. No cars for them. Mother was a very good driver in the country. She could handle a horse, I mean. We'd drive into Ipswich and put up the trap at the White Horse, if it was a fine afternoon and she had finished her number. That was what they called their instalments, numbers. A number was about six thousand words. Father did three a week, year in year out, when he was in full production."

Mr. Spenlove sat up in his chair by the fire—it was one of his idiosyncrasies that he could not lounge; he always sat up straight—staring at the woman in his green leather chair, but without making any comment. He was trying to take it into his mind, this picture of a man in a frock coat in one room of a dark house in the country and a woman dressed like a stage duchess in another room, writing penny novelettes all day long against time, against a dead line, while their daughter grew up, neglected.

"When the old gardener died—he'd worked, man and boy, all his life in that rectory garden—Mother got a young man who lived in the village, and then made the cottage over into a week-end guest house. Father liked to have Aunt Phoebe and her husband, and Uncle Claud's wife and kids, and a few Fleet Street men, for a Saturday-to-Monday. He liked to feel himself a lord of the manor, I think, dispensing hospitality! My brother and I sometimes had to have our meals in the kitchen passage, at a little table set for us, because the dining room was so full of guests.

"You see, Mother and Father had peculiar Victorian ideas about us kids. We were important because we belonged to *them,* but we were unimportant because we were only kids. Why, even when Father made thirty pounds a week, the year after we went to Knights, I didn't have a pair of stockings without holes. And I'd grown so fast my clothes were half up my thighs and half way to my elbows. Mother made us go to church Sunday mornings, and I was so ashamed! I felt absolutely naked. It was only my being sent away to school that brought the matter to a head, and then she took me to London. I think Mother suddenly *saw* me when she looked at me one day; saw me as a female animal, and not merely one of 'the children.' For people who spent their lives writing romances, Father and Mother were very unromantic. They didn't seem to me to have any imagination either, though that sounds rather daft, I admit."

"Did they write under their own names?" Mr. Spenlove inquired, frowning. He was trying to think himself back a quarter of a century.

"Oh, no. Father thought it ungentlemanly to use one's own name. He wanted to be completely dissociated from commerce. He called himself Norman Tower."

"No! Why, I . . ."

"Mother was Vivienne Vavasour."

"Again, no! You bring it all back!"

Mrs. Ducroy raised one foot and gazed meditatively along the shining curves of her stocking to the small sharp shoe that pointed toward the fire.

"It does sound fantastic. What's even more fantastic is the fact that I ran away from that noun-and-adjective factory, because I couldn't stand it. And here I am, in another noun-and-adjective factory, and a rival factory across the river is bitching things up for me!"

"Norman Tower? Hm. I remember the name. Boys' stories, I fancy. 'Rattling New Serial by Norman Tower.' "

"Father was very successful with boys' stories," she said. "I mean stories for working-class boys. I don't believe he set eyes on one, in the flesh, for years, except George, our house boy, and he never spoke to him except to say, 'I want my boots; quickly please!' or 'Bring me some hot water; quickly please!' Very brisk and polite, but firm. It was the same with Mother. She wrote dozens of love stories for servant girls—skivvies we called them at school. I've seen the maids at school devouring novelettes by Vivienne Vavasour. I don't know how Mother got to know they existed, or what they did out in the kitchen. It was as much as the maids' jobs were worth to let me go in there. I had to stand at the door and tell them what I wanted. Or better still, in Father's opinion, ring the bell. The Rectory had old style bell-pulls in every room; and in the kitchen, which had a lumpy red brick floor and a huge open range with a turnspit and a crane, there was a row of bells on springs along the top of the wall."

"You describe it exactly," Mr. Spenlove said. "It must have made a strong impression on you, that house."

"I suppose you know hate can make you remember as well as affection," she suggested lightly. "Better, I fancy! They talk about the eyes of faith. What about the eyes of hate? It's love that's blind, and deaf and—dumb!"

"We'll go into that later," he said, shaking his finger at her. "The house! Tell me about it. You had a room looking out over the dark lawn?"

"I had a dormer window in my bedroom in the darkest corner of the house, in the shadow of that great end wall of the glebe barn. It was half-timbered, that barn, and its roof overhung the walled passage where the kitchen pump was. I could hear that pump, *clank clackety clank*, in the morning when George was filling the pitchers and the big iron pot for Teeny the cook. George wore a green baize apron and had to black all our shoes, scrub the kitchen floor, and fill all the kettles and pots by seven o'clock. He had to build up the fire and get it hot with the bellows. And run when one of the bells jangle-jangled over his head. Then he had to fill all the lamps, table lamps, floor lamps, piano lamps, hall lamps and the bedroom lamps . . . ! Clara, the housemaid, brought them down and George carried them up. Father wouldn't let us children do anything menial. When it got dusk, which was about three in winter and four in summer, we rang and Clara brought in the candles. We all had candlesticks to take up to bed."

"You grew up a perfect lady."

"That was the idea. The funny thing was, it didn't take! My brother—he went to Father's old school—was always the perfect gent. He is now. He's head of his own advertising business. He was younger than George, but all the same George was afraid of him. George would cringe before him! My brother would never raise his voice either. I hated it. I was a rebel. I thought George a grubby little beast, but I didn't want him to grovel!

"Well, when Clara went into the dark hall and whanged on the big gong it sounded like the end of the world! We all came marching in, except Mother. Clara set everything ready, soup tureen, ladle and all that, and stood by Mother's chair. Sometimes we had to stand like idiots for several minutes. Then there was a *whoosh!* on the stairs and in she'd come, like a battleship going into action at thirty knots. She'd sit down, take the ladle and be serving the soup almost before Clara could move the plates.

"Father would hold up his hand above his shoulder and Clara would hurry round and pass him the claret bottle from the sideboard. Father always wanted a glass of wine at table. I never saw him drink at any other time. When some week-ender told him about cocktails coming into fashion in London, he would pish and pshaw and say it was 'a beastly American bad habit.' "

"So it is," said Mr. Spenlove. "I like it."

"Victorians didn't. They really had convictions, and they were always ready to make other people suffer for them. We were not supposed to answer back. My father wasn't really unkind. He just didn't think. He had a set of standards. It was his belief that if you had standards, and stuck to them, then you didn't need to think or consider individuals. My brother Gerald is exactly the same. Unless somebody has murdered him."

"You didn't get on with your family," Mr. Spenlove decided. "I can't feel much sorrow for them."

"When the long summer holiday began," she went on, "I came home. I was sixteen. I'd failed in the exams at school."

"What year? After the war, of course."

"Well, it was 1921, I think. Yes, I was married in 1921. Are you awfully disgusted?"

"No. I was thinking about your brother. What makes you suggest he might have been murdered? I know it's merely figurative, but why bring it up?"

"Because he began by being an unimaginative snob and he went on until he's now one of the Mosley crowd. One of the Élite! Black jerseys and sweaters with silver fasces!"

"That's an awful thing to say of any one, let alone a relative." Mr. Spenlove shook his head. He was really delighted. He had not had such an intimate conversation with a woman since that time when he was stranded in a tropical hospital. The women he had met as passengers hardly counted, if he excepted Mrs. Colwell. And *she* didn't count in one sense because she did not live in his world. She was a fine, wholesome person, but she did not live in his world. No, passengers did not count. If they told him anything it was because he was so far away from their real lives it didn't matter much and it was a relief to tell someone.

This was different. She was telling him all this because they were coming together. They had their roots in that extraordinary country of England, which no American had ever understood, and they had left it to live in America, a country even more extraordinary in many ways. They had had marvelous adventures before they had met, and she was explaining the beginning of hers. She was filling in the background with figures familiar yet astonishing. They corresponded to the figures he had glimpsed afar off when he was a young radical apprentice; the prosperous upper middle classes who lived in Maida Vale, Hampstead and St. Johns Wood, and who became petty gentry in the country if their prosperity continued.

"Awful or not, Gerald's a humorless bloke!" she said. "He really believes he could run the British Empire singlehanded if he had unlimited power, a trained secretary and an office boy. He worships Mussolini. When he was only a schoolboy he would stamp his foot and say, 'If people would only do what they're *told!*' He was the one to tell them, of course!"

"He has standards," said Mr. Spenlove, drily. "He ought to find them useful in the advertising business."

"I suppose he does. I haven't seen him since I married the first time. I wrote him when I was at the end of my rope, and needed help, and he didn't reply. But the point is, he only developed out of Father and Mother. They were both frightfully class conscious. It was in the air, the difference between us and the servants. The way Mother would say 'the maids,' or Father 'the servants,' was marvelous."

"And yet you say they wrote stories for them. How do you account for that?"

"I don't account for it. All I wanted was to get away from it!"

"What seems so strange to me," Mr. Spenlove mused, "is people like your parents burying themselves away in the country like that."

"Well, they had to have seclusion, you know, and they wanted to avoid any contamination by the suburbs. My mother would say 'the subbubs!' as if there was something disgraceful about living at Swiss Cottage or Tufnell Park. But they couldn't afford to live like the county people, to hunt and ride point-to-point. They were county, but not quite —quite . . . I can't quite explain it. Alternate week ends we were Bohemian. Father had his friends down; Mother invited Aunt Phoebe and her husband; and Uncle Claud's family turned up with one or two friends. Father was always saying, 'Come, and bring a friend.' He was doing very well in those years. They were all doing pretty well, and I and my kid sister were almost forgotten. We were packed off to school."

"Tell me about—you know—the man you married. What was he like? One of the chosen?"

"Chosen? Oh! Yes, he was. A cousin by marriage. One of Mother's cousin's children."

"Name of Pagett?"

"How did you know? Oh, of course Sonia explained that. She told me. Yes, Archie Pagett. Does the name give you an idea?"

"It gives me an idea, but how do we know it is the right one? I can see him, though!"

He pointed his finger at her and made a sort of good-humored scowl at the fire, which was now bright and lively.

"Good-looking?"

"Rather! Mother always said, 'Archie's a pretty little boy.' She was fond of his mother—her cousin. Go on."

"Nobody's enemy but his own?"

"That's a darned good shot," she said. She drew up her legs and sat ensconced in the big green leather chair. "As a matter of fact, he wasn't even his own enemy very much. Archie was known in the family as the Imperialist. He had a rather bad case of Old School Tie. He was fifteen when the war began and nearly twenty-one when it was over, and, having been at Father's old school and Oxford during that time, he didn't seem able to settle down. People were giving all the jobs to those who had fought, or who said they'd fought, you see. So Archie's people sent him to the colonies."

"A remittance man? The Lost Generation?"

"He didn't stop anywhere long enough to be called that. Archie was more of a visitor. He decided Australia, or New Zealand, or Canada wasn't the right place for him, and he would move on. It was a sort of grand tour. And he wasn't lost, as you call it. There was nothing cynical about Archie, nothing bitter. He thought the world owed him a living, but he wasn't nasty about it. Then he came to visit at Brandeston Knights in the summer. He fell in love with me."

"Not you with him?"

"Yes, I did. He had glamor. He was a Prince Charming to me, a kid turned sixteen who felt jolly superfluous. He was a way of escape from all those damned writing people who came down and used Brandeston Knights for a hotel without any bills. Father might be a fine old Tory to the servants, but he was very loyal to his old Fleet Street pals. And of course he enjoyed having them see him doing so jolly well. Most of them couldn't make more than three or four hundred a year. They had to live at Ealing or Tooting, with an occasional week end at Brighton. Better still, a week end at Brandeston Knights, with free board and lodging, tennis and billiards, and plenty of drinks. They were absolutely the most selfish and inconsiderate lot of bounders I ever knew in my life!"

"Strong words, those! Very strong words!"

"I mean them to be! I've heard so much of the culture and intellectual superiority of artistic people! All they talked about was what So-and-so was making or how somebody else did an editor out of a few bob on space rates. All sordid shop talk! They never took the slightest notice of me. I wasn't seen and I wasn't heard."

"Then one day Mother said, at breakfast, 'Your cousin Archie is coming to stay with us.' She took me with her to Marks Tey to meet the train. I wasn't very keen about it. Mother wouldn't let me drive. She said I wasn't capable. She didn't think anybody could do things the right way. She was always telling Father how he ought to improve his output, as she called it.

"When the train came in, Mother let me hold the reins while she got down and waited near the barrier. There was a small crowd of people. Archie came out last, because he'd had to get a dog out of the guard's van."

"Yes, I can see a man named Archie Pagett getting a dog out of the guard's van!" Mr. Spenlove said with relish. "How you take me back! Do you know you are making me homesick? Ever since you said that afternoon, that you hadn't heard the word charwoman for years! Yes!"

"Well . . ." She gazed into the fire for a moment and then raised her eyes to his, smiling. "That's how it was. Archie and his bull terrier came through the barrier and Mother went forward like a duchess and put her arms round him and offered her cheek to kiss, and the bull terrier was introduced, and then I was brought into the business. 'This is Perdita,' Mother said. 'My little girl Perdita. Darling, this is your cousin Archibald. He's just returned from a tour round the world.'

"That was Mother's way. I didn't know it then, but all his family had been contributing to get Archie off the hooks, as we used to say, and start him in a colony. And here was Archie back again, 'like a bad penny' he would put it, very cheerfully. He had an uncle by marriage in the Home Office, and through this uncle they had been trying to get him into the Consular Service. You know, vice-consul in some small place the other side of the world! It wasn't easy, because Archie has the family weakness. He can't pass exams. In fact it was impossible, because Archie didn't think exams should be essential. I heard him tell Mother, 'I don't think it's essential, do you?' Mother didn't, of course. It was lucky we didn't have to pass exams. But in the Consular Service it was essential.

"It may sound silly to you, but to me Archie was marvelous then. Mother told him to take care of me and went off to her writing room. Father was in his room all day. Gerald was with school friends at Cromer, and my little sister was down in Devonshire somewhere. My sister was delicate, and couldn't stand the relaxing air of Brandeston Knights. I could stand anything, it was supposed. Did I tell you my sister writes too? Poetry and stories for children! So Archie and I were thrown together all the week. Archie and I and the bull terrier.

"I think it was the way he used to keep his end up with the Fleet Street men who came down for the week end, which made me admire Archie. He wasn't a fool by any means, which you might think he was because he never settled down, and just lived off his relations. He used to talk to those men as if he knew more about the world than they did. He'd say, 'But you see, Old Chap, I've *been* there.' He really interested one editor with his impudence. The editor said, if he knew so jolly much about South Africa, to write an article about it. That started something. Archie began to write!"

"You seemed destined to be among writers," Mr. Spenlove said. He put another billet of oak on the fire and busied himself with the glasses.

"I wouldn't call Archie one of them. Writing with Archie was like everything else, including marriage. It was a sudden impulse. He couldn't keep his mind on it. What he really wants to do is to wander."

"And—if it isn't an impossible question—what's he doing now? Wandering? He sounds most engaging."

"He's been married twice since he divorced me. He's in Hollywood. That Old School Tie is worth ten thousand a year out there. He's married now to a Nicaraguan dancer. He has a job in the studios."

"Go on. What happened?"

"Well, I told you. We fell in love. Mother was having a very busy time just then because Aunt Phoebe had got her a new job on one of the Fireside Magazines, giving advice to lovers, so she never noticed anything. When I asked her one day, 'Mother, can I be engaged to Archie?' she nearly fell out of her chair.

"It was really very complicated for Mother. It wasn't simply getting used to having a daughter old enough to be engaged. It was Archie. All he seemed to have in his own right was his big portmanteaus, full of sporty clothes and covered with steamer labels, and the bull terrier. He had no money and no job. That didn't worry him at all. When Father told him, if he wanted to marry me he would have to get a job of some sort, he said, 'Righto, I'll get a job.' Father said, 'Righto. I'll give you a hundred pounds for a wedding present in that case.' Mother promised me a trousseau, which was pretty decent of her. I hadn't had any clothes for years, really!

"Archie went to London and started to look for a job. He

hadn't been able to sell the things he wrote about the Empire. Archie isn't really a writer. In fact he's a lousy writer! He just fell into the pardonable mistake of thinking it must be easy because everybody except me seemed to be making a jolly good living at it. He called at all the offices in Fleet Street. Father gave him cards of introduction to lots of people. No soap! Fleet Street was full of Old School Ties trying to wangle jobs from editors.

"The second time he called on the editor who had printed that thing about South Africa, Archie actually got into the chap's office. He told him he was engaged to me and needed a job. He showed Father's card. There wasn't any job, really, but the editor happened to pick up a letter that had come in that morning. It was from a Hollywood studio, and it invited him to send out a special correspondent at their expense to see the studios and write them up in his paper. There was a movement just then in England to exclude Hollywood pictures, or slap a duty on them, and they wanted to do something about it, and change English opinion.

"This chap was in favor of the duty, wanted British pictures for British patrons, and so on, so he wasn't very keen on this scheme. But he saw a chance to get rid of Archie. He said, 'Want to go to Hollywood?'

"Archie said, 'What ho!' when he read the letter. 'Will this complimentary ticket take two?' The editor said, 'I'll see it does.' Archie said, 'What about expenses?' But the editor wasn't having any. He said, 'You pay your own expenses, unless the picture people want to pay them. Take it or leave it.' Archie said, 'I'll take it.'

"It sounds the maddest thing now, but we were very young and the idea of going to Hollywood was simply intoxicating! It didn't seem important what might happen afterward. We had a ticket, and Archie's people gave him a hundred pounds. So we were rich! We had a ticket and two hundred pounds!"

"You went? You got married and went? Of course. I can see now what it was puzzled me about you. You confused me when you came in here with Sonia. I couldn't place you. Now I am beginning to see you in a setting. You've had experiences."

"I should think I have had experiences! Some of them very unpleasant. I won't talk about them."

"Did he leave you?"

"I left him!"

"So what?"

"I said I didn't want to talk about unpleasant experiences. I had a difficult time when Sonia was born."

"But didn't your people take care of you?"

"They did after things were straightened out a bit. You see, Archie had given them the wrong idea. He'd cabled Father several times without my knowledge and Father had sent him fifty pounds several times. When I'd left him and wrote Mother to help me get home they couldn't understand. It was then I had the experiences, as you call them. Did you ever starve?"

Mr. Spenlove was aroused from his reverie. He rose and carried her empty glass to the table with the idea of refilling it. Something made him turn around. He saw the tears running straight down her face and raining on her hands in her lap. He went over to her and put his hands on her shoulders, and shook her gently.

"Don't!" he said. But he felt very helpless as the tears rained down. Suddenly she dashed the moisture away with her fists and found her handkerchief, and put an end to the scene.

"I won't," she said. "I'm sorry. I'm a fool. But it's your fault, really. You have a way of listening, and you make me feel you understand and have sympathy. And I got to thinking of when Sonia was little, and I couldn't get a job. . . . Sorry!"

"Have another drink?" he said. He did not feel competent to handle the situation if she gave way again. He was alarmed. That view through the binoculars had been too much for her.

"Oh, no!" She uncoiled her legs and rose suddenly out of the chair. She put her arm around him and laid her head on his shoulder for a moment, regaining control.

"I must go," she said hurriedly. "Sonia has gone to the movies with Louis. She'll wonder where I am. I feel I've been a bad guest. I'll tell you everything, but not now. Excuse me."

She was cool and collected and smiling as he guided her down the porch steps to the car. She pointed to a star setting over the sea.

"I'll look at that when I'm in bed," she said. "Will you see it too?"

He nodded. She smiled again as she settled herself in the car and started the engine.

"I know what you're thinking," she said, and then leaned out with a swift, caressing gesture. "You're afraid!" she added, as she let in the gears and turned on the lights.

"Please don't be! Good night!"

V

WAS HE afraid? As the days passed, the marvelously benign days of early summer in New England, and his boat approached completion in the barn, if he had at first cherished a craven fear that he was being imposed on by an unscrupulous woman, that fear faded.

He was, on the contrary, filled with pleasurable anticipations. He was aware of a subtle change in himself since he had settled down in the Mudge Place. He was getting the hang, as he called it, of this unusual way of living.

At first it had seemed to him that there was no such thing as solitude compared with the countryside in England. It had struck him as curious, in his walks into the hills, that in so vast a country as America it seemed almost impossible to get out of sight of houses. He remembered with affection a tramp he had taken in the west country at home, while on leave. Taking the train to Dorchester, he had walked south through Portisham to Abbottsbury, and up along the hills above Chesil Beach to Swyre. He had found long miles of loneliness, without even a cart. The old land breathed softly, holding in its ancient bosom the long barrows and cumuli of prehistoric men, the bones and shards of aboriginal Britons.

Like most seamen from Europe he knew nothing of continental America. He was unaware of the Western deserts and prairies. He could have no conception of the immense and magnificent silences of Wyoming. He knew they were there, having read of them, but he cherished a subconscious reluctance to have his British prejudices dissipated.

Here, he reflected, the earth was possessed by the living, who seemed always to have something to sell. Now that he had a telephone, it rang and rang. The Norbury *Times-Echo* wanted to know if he had any social items to impart; and could they take care of his stationery problems?

Someone, during the first few weeks, was always calling, or appearing in person, with something to sell—a car, a vacuum-cleaner, a washing machine, a broom, a book, a magazine subscription, a newspaper, a ticket for a dance, a fire extinguisher, puppies from pedigree kennels and eggs from certified hens. He was disappointed, after what he had read about America, that no one tried to sell him a lightning conductor.

The irritation these intrusions caused him became less noticeable. He even enjoyed some of them. The boy who came on a bicycle with a basket of crumpets on his handlebars, for instance, and the telephone chats with Miss Penge.

He liked Miss Penge. She was apparently the real thing in local primitives, he believed. The people on the shore were hardly less recent than himself. Old Jim was a piece of floating wreckage which had got caught in a local eddy and had remained. Mrs. Sankey declared, without bitterness, that her family had come from Ireland.

Miss Penge, however, had roots in the soil. He derived a certain secret amusement from Miss Penge because she always spoke over the phone in a loud, dominant voice to drown out her radio, which was apparently near the telephone. She told him that for her antiques were a sort of company; but she did not exclude some of the more modern broadcasters. She seemed to have the radio on most of the time.

He liked her, and intended to go out there, on Route Eleven, and see her antiques, and her great-grandfather's beaver hat, which he wore when he fought the British in 1812. She had, she shouted, the very thing for him—a captain's desk from one of the famous clipper ships out of Norhaven. One of her uncles had been a clipper ship captain. Did he know that where the yacht club was now they built clipper ships in the old days? They did so! He told her that was interesting, because he was going to join the yacht club when his boat was ready to take the water.

She began about the yacht club, and he hoped no one could overhear her. Any amount of gambling on those cabin cruisers week ends, she said. And liquor! And other things as were nobody's business.

He protested about that. He said his neighbors, the Ducroys, were members. They had a speedboat. Miss Penge said, not being deaf, she knew that. Jimmy Munzinger at the yacht service dock had told her that boat burned up twenty gallons an hour. Well, he said, that was fine for Jimmy Munzinger. He was to have another customer soon, Mr. Spenlove told her. And he heard Miss Penge, after a pause, say, "Is that so?" He said it was so, according to the Ducroys. Did Miss Penge know the woman writer who lived across the river?

Miss Penge said, did he mean the house on the bluff, with steps down to a boat house? That was Sydney Saxon, who wrote stories for the magazines. Miss Penge had heard things about her too. Did Mr. Spenlove know her?

No, he said, he only knew of her. Miss Penge said she only knew of her too, as a customer who tried to beat you down a few dollars. If she, Miss Penge, got a thing cheap, she sold cheap. If otherwise, well, otherwise. That was all there was to antiques, except, of course, rare pieces with a famous name on them. Mr. Spenlove ought to come over. Some time when he wasn't busy with those grand friends on the shore.

He inquired whom she referred to specifically. She said she wouldn't mention any names, but there was a big foreign car seemed to know the way blindfold into his yard. Ask her no questions and she wouldn't tell him any lies, she added, and laughed like a trumpet.

He said he was afraid she was hearing a lot of old wives' tales in Norbury. They weren't old wives' tales, neither, she assured him with animation. What about the story she heard, that he himself was in government pay? That he was watching the shore every evening on orders from Washington? They said he was an ex-naval man keeping tab on smugglers from boats in the Sound, coming in from Canada. Things like that they were saying.

Mr. Spenlove had said, "Oh, indeed!" His solitary strolls along the shore, to the lighthouse, and into the hills, beyond Norbury, with his binoculars in their case, had not been unobserved, it seemed. Possibly Mrs. Sankey's remarks had touched on her employer's habit of receiving calls from New York and consulting mysterious blueprints while talking over the telephone.

So he said, "Oh, indeed!" and Miss Penge laughed again and said she didn't believe it, of course. Leastways, it was only one speedboat he was interested in, maybe. Naturally there'd been considerable talk all over town when a single man bought the Mudge Place, payin' cash, and yet had no car. Now, if he was to get a car he could come out on Route Eleven and see her place. He knew his way to the Norbury Inn, she heard.

"Well," he had told her, "that's what I intend to do. They'll be taking *you* apart, then! There seems a lot of gossip going on."

"Sure!" said Miss Penge cordially. "Most of 'em have nothing else to do. Why, they're sayin' you were lookin' for to settle down. Get married, maybe."

He had made a sound indicating shocked surprise at this. He said he was surprised to hear her say a thing like that. Was she really interested in such irresponsible talk? Was it . . .

Yes, indeed she was, she assured him. He heard her hearty and disarming laughter. It was perfectly natural, she said, and she didn't want to be forgotten. To this he said "Well!" but as she was still laughing he made some allusion to what Americans called, he understood, making passes. Wasn't he justified in thinking that her pretense of looking for antiques was a pose, for instance?

This brought the conversation to an end. Miss Penge had been severe and occasionally not too certain of herself in a personal interview, but she was as bold as a brass bugle over the telephone. The instrument gave her voice a booming and harsh quality that was neither masculine nor feminine, but metallic. She became a disembodied voice urging him for his own good to see the good "horse sense" of her remarks. The meaningless phrase "horse sense" seemed to assume significance when applied to the loud, impersonal neighing jocularity of her voice over the wire. The word "wire" made him think of barbed wire and a fence, with himself as a nearby horse swishing his tail. . . .

He refrained from going too deeply into that. Miss Penge, he was sure, could wait. She might make flirtatious passes over the telephone, but she would not die of unrequited love. She was, psychologically, ruggedly constructed, a sound New England mare.

He tried to imagine what she was telling her friend Mrs. Cagliari over the wire, which took the place of the old Victorian garden wall, he supposed. The discovery that all these people observed and discussed each other made him thoughtful. It was the same passion for gossip he had so often experienced among his juniors on the ship; tales about So-and-so's wife having roomers while So-and-so was at sea; of the mate of a ship keeping a girl out of a cat-house in Havana, and the chief of another ship being secretly married to a schoolteacher who would be fired if the authorities knew of it. He had been staggered by the almost mystical fascination such tales exerted upon his shipmates and had imagined, in his simplicity, that it was because they were largely naive, illiterate sailor men.

How naive, and (in a social sense) how illiterate he had been himself all this time! He thought his walks, his visitors, his custom of dining at the Norbury Inn, were all too insignificant to any member of the public to be worthy of observation, to say nothing of comment. Perdita Ducroy, turning in to his place, or driving out, had been noted. Walking on the lonely foreshore beyond the lighthouse, where the dunes ended in a low bluff about the sea, strangers had kept an eye on him and exchanged comments in the town taverns concerning his habits.

He might have enjoyed a sort of prankish flirtation with Miss Penge had she been a passenger. He was beginning to understand that his relations with passengers had been conditioned by the fact that he had no responsibility beyond carrying them safely. They had not been actual fellow creatures with whose fate he felt vitally concerned after they stepped down the gangway. They were highly fragile and perishable freight, or they were beautiful, costly phantoms moving athwart his vision, living in exotic luxury, regarding him with smiling benevolence as a decorative, uniformed feature of an unusual existence, whom they forgot as soon as they resumed their own life on shore.

But a flirtation carried on by going up Route Eleven and involving himself in the local village life was, he discovered now, inconceivable. He wasn't equal to it. He shrank from it. As he thought of it, while working a ten-hour day on the boat, he gave an actual physical shudder. Then what, he asked himself, about Perdita?

He put that question to himself very often until the day her husband suddenly came to see him. He had reached the point where Elliot Ducroy was no longer a fantastic legendary being, who was known for his underworld stories from coast to coast, whose film creations were stared at by Mongolian, Tonkinese and Malay children in hot little oriental cinemas. Instead he was a man with whose wife he, Frederick Aspinwall Spenlove Esq., late of His Majesty's Royal Naval Reserve (E division), based on H.M.S. Victory II, Portsmouth, England, was in love.

Another fantastic and legendary being had come to life,

the sea-rover, hard-living Fred Spenlove, ship's engineer, who had loved and lost Artemisia Macedoine, who had been the confidant and counselor in the spectacular love affairs of others (but who had kept his own to himself).

If Miss Penge knew of those days in the past in the eastern seas! If she could even faintly imagine the sort of life he and his shipmates had lived when they were young and furious, trained down to the last ounce by toil, tropic heat, plain harsh food, and the enforced continence of the voyages! She might have something to tell her friend Mrs. Cagliari then, he thought, smiling.

Neither Miss Penge nor anyone else knew anything about that time now. It had been followed by the years of executive responsibility, keeping a liner on schedule, so that in time he had come to believe his real inner self was not dormant but dead, that he was an old bachelor, that he could retire into a hermit's cell and live a life of contemplation.

He had been a confirmed Victorian sentimentalist under his mask of irony all these years! He had believed that the memory of Artemisia would preserve him, like an amulet, from further passion. He had believed that amulets retained their potency unspent, indefinitely.

He had been wrong. So wrong that this woman, for whose young daughter he had conceived a chaste affection, had almost instantly swept that long-cherished fancy out of his mind. It was as though, laying her hand on what seemed a solid, indestructible part of his personality, it had crumbled silently into dust.

So he had no excuse now, for backing out. If the woman one was in a moment falling in love with, chooses that moment to say that she is leaving her husband, what was the answer? What was the correct attitude toward the husband?

So far it had been an academic question. Elliot Ducroy had not appeared. He was to be seen, driving his station wagon in a hurried, preoccupied manner, through Sutton Corners, turning left at the intersection instead of continuing along the valley road to Norbury. That left turn took him over the plank bridge and up the hill on the west side of the river. Mr. Spenlove had been passed by him while walking to Norbury, and noted the quick turn left. One evening he had gone down to the shore with his binoculars and taken a look at the house on the bluff. He had seen nothing, and had returned, slightly out of humor with himself, resolving not to do that again.

Ducroy was over there frequently, Mr. Spenlove knew, because Perdita had told him so. Then again, what was the answer? What was his own position in this business? Mr. Spenlove was aware that men who had mistresses sometimes revealed extravagantly lofty standards where their wives were concerned. It did not alter his conviction that he would go through with the affair, but he felt a certain grim curiosity about Elliot Ducroy's attitude. How did authors regard the "unwritten law" about which so many stories were written?

Mr. Spenlove did not brood upon these problems. Day after day he worked on his boat. Soon he intended to visit the plant where the engine was being built. As the craft grew under his hands he discovered fresh enthusiasm for living. Independence at first had been like a new suit of clothes. It took a little time to mould itself to his personality. Now he was becoming used to it, so that he forgot he was wearing it. His old uniform, which had been the symbol of his service to the Company, and that older naval uniform, its gold lace and insignia now gone dull and dusty, hung in the cedar wardrobe he had built against the chimney on the landing upstairs. At first he had not cared to face the fact that he would never wear them again on duty, and he was therefore being a bit of a sentimental fool for keeping them. Now he was able to put them on for a few minutes and walk to and fro in meditation. *This and this I have been and without dishonor*, he thought. The strip of colored service ribbons high on the left breast, green-white-red, blue-gold-green-orange, blue-black-white-gold gave him more satisfaction now than when he received them. After that submarine business in the Aegean, when they had run it down and sunk it, he had received another medal, a real one, the Reserve Decoration. It had been a long time coming, however, and he had never taken the ribbon out of the original envelope. It lay in a cigar box (those good Dutch *Reclames* he used to smoke!), and there it might stay. There had been nothing particularly valorous in standing by the engines while the ship cut a submarine in two at full speed.

The question of valor was much in his mind now because he knew—always had known—that the quality seemed to be lacking in himself.

If so, how was he going to behave when Elliot Ducroy suddenly discovered the situation?

There was time enough, he decided. He was not "breaking up a home" in the newspaper sense, nor was Elliot Ducroy a "wronged husband." The whole business had unfolded, as though it were a living organism, in the minds of the woman and himself. After a couple of hours on his porch after dinner she would say, "I have *such* a good time with you!" She would stop her car far out in the Connecticut hills and they would alight and walk down some narrow road into a valley, where a stream ran over gray stones and the cattle stood knee deep in mist. Once, as they paused to let a herd of cows cross the road and the lights came on in the farm house, she said,

"It's like Brandeston Knights, something. The smell of manure reminds me. We had cows all round us there. Wouldn't you like to see it?"

"With you," he said.

Then, when he had been thinking less and less about the matter, Elliot Ducroy came to see him.

He was taking a shower after a warm day, working on the boat. He heard someone on the porch. He was planning to go to town next morning, and had knocked off early. He put on a bathrobe to walk down the steep little stairway, and he found

Elliot Ducroy on the porch. The room door being open, the visitor was in full view. He was taking short steps to and fro, smoking a cigarette very fast, as was his custom, and pausing to glance at the book on the table.

He's come to have it out about Perdita! Mr. Spenlove said to himself. *She's told him; or he has suspected something; or been told something. Well . . .*

Well, had he? He started fluffing over the leaves of *The Notebooks of Samuel Butler*. He turned his head quickly and in welcome when he heard Mr. Spenlove's bath slippers slapping on the stairs. He spoke with obvious sincerity.

"Hello. I saw your gardener out there. He said you were in the house. He said you were upstairs, so I came in. Busy?"

"No. I'm going to New York tomorrow so I knocked off. Have a drink?"

"No hurry. You going to New York? Coming with me? I'm driving up tomorrow morning. Got some engagements."

"Hm! It's a suggestion. If you're sure it won't put you out."

"It'll be company. We'll take the Packard."

"Not the Virago?"

"I don't like a right-hand drive. And besides, the Virago's my wife's car."

"Well, you make it difficult to refuse. If you'll wait a bit, I'll get dressed and we'll have one."

"This book . . ." Elliot Ducroy had held it up. "I don't know it. I been looking at it. It seems good stuff."

"Out of print," Mr. Spenlove told him, going up the stairs. Ducroy nodded, studying the pages.

They had a cool drink with a stick in it and Elliot Ducroy borrowed Samuel Butler. He said he understood Mrs. Ducroy had made Mr. Spenlove's acquaintance and had called on him once or twice.

"We had dinner," Mr. Spenlove informed him. "Didn't she tell you?"

"That's right. She told me you're building a boat. That a fact? Sonia's been full of it too. What I was going to say, yes, she told me. I'm glad about this. My wife's been a bit dissatisfied with things lately. Before we came here she was in a pretty fast set in New York. She gets restless. Now you can find time—uh-huh—to see her sometimes. I'm pretty busy these days, you understand. A writer has to work all the time. My work keeps me jumping. Yes, it keeps me jumping, all right. I have a schedule for a series." He made a characteristic gesture, closing his eyes as he pressed his hand slowly upward on his brow.

He kept hold of Samuel Butler while saying this, as though that ironical, nonjumping person might have some words of salvation for a man driven to turn out thousands of words a day to make a living. A man whose work, as he phrased it, kept him jumping; a phrase which, when applied to a writer, fascinated Mr. Spenlove. *His work keeps him jumping,* he had repeated to himself all that evening. He tried to imagine such a man at work, producing stories in a series—of convulsions.

Mr. Spenlove had already made a few cautious moves in the direction of his "scrap log," as he called it, that projected record of his adventures in his new surroundings. Samuel Butler's *Notebooks* had been in evidence because to Mr. Spenlove it was the only model he dared attempt. Butler put down his thoughts as they occurred to him. One of the chapters was even called "Higgledy-Piggledy." It was one of Mr. Spenlove's incessantly read volumes. It lay, as a rule, on the pine table beside his bed, with *The Anatomy of Melancholy, Urn Burial, Amiel's Journal* and Stendahl's *Le Rouge et le Noir.*

Cautious, timid moves only, so far. The emotions aroused by the blank pages of a large, marbled notebook had astonished him. He had felt suddenly "stark naked in his mind," as he put it; or at any rate, as if he were suddenly to find himself in his shift among strangers. That had been followed by an extraordinary sensation of insignificance. He became reduced to microscopic size in the world of thought. Time after time, after a long wait for inspiration, as he supposed, he had closed the book without putting anything in it. The difference between merely thinking or talking, and writing it down so that it did not appear to be nonsense, staggered him, but he supposed this was because he felt self-conscious. If he had been required to express a professional opinion in a report, or to issue an order, he would have had no difficulty. But would it be possible to write down, as in a report, how he felt about Perdita Ducroy's voice, her hands, her walk, or the way she looked at him? Could he make a simple, businesslike statement concerning Sonia's eyes, which were as perplexingly changeable and distractingly beautiful as her mother's? Would it be possible to describe, in that projected scrap log, the divine loveliness of children's tanned limbs on the beach, divine because they were innocent of desire? Or the grace and precision of Tobermory, his belly flat to the earth as he moved swiftly and stealthily through the grass upon a rabbit?

Not even Samuel Butler had helped him to overcome this ridiculous bashfulness when confronted with a blank page. *There is some secret in this business!* he told himself, smiling, and put the book away, untouched, time after time.

When he did make a start, after Elliot Ducroy paid him that sudden visit, he surprised himself.

Temperature 75° he wrote hastily, half ashamed. *Barometer 29.7 ins. Prevailing wind southerly; smooth sea. Elliot Ducroy, one of the native chiefs, told me his work "kept him jumping." He lives in a very expensive way, large house, three cars, possibly four, some horses, servants and a speedboat. About 95% of his expenses are not essential to his business or his pleasure, if his conversation is a guide. In fact he deplores the necessity of doing it. A sort of slave of the pen. He came to see me, he said, about his wife. Said he hoped I would be friends with her. When I said I was going to town next day, said he was too, and invited me to go with him in his car. I accepted both offers, as a matter of course, just to be agreeable, not as anything important to me, etc. I don't understand why he has come here or why he should be friendly. At least not yet. The motives of the people here are obscure. Only P. (Perdita) does anything because she wants to, not because it is a fashion or what they think is "correct." But Ducroy's desire to have me friendly with P., who is leaving him, can hardly be based on any code. Or can it? So far I am as puzzled, apart from Perdita, concerning the way these people act and react, as if I were in Tibet, or on another planet. Or in another century.*

Of course there may be a perfectly simple solution of this mystery. We shall see!

Pouring himself a second cup of coffee, next morning on the porch, Mr. Spenlove saw a bright yellow car with a sharp nose roll into view. Inside was Elliot Ducroy wearing a double-breasted business suit and a fedora. Mr. Spenlove had once again, as at the party, the feeling that aside from his unusual gift of spinning stories of mystery and crime around the sinister figure of the master gangster, Gentleman Church, Elliot Ducroy was a man of almost perfect mediocrity. Dressed in the uniform of the average commuter on the nine thirty-seven from Norbury to Grand Central, the creator of Gentleman Church, whose adventures were the perfect answer to a circulation manager's prayer, was indistinguishable from the "Wall Street men," the industrial-insurance statistical research clerks, or the gentlemen who bought hides and coffee on the Produce Exchange. Indistinguishable, Mr. Spenlove perceived, from the public who devoured his Gentleman Church stories. The man might be the smart mate of a fast freighter, apart from his car.

This, no doubt was democracy; but to one who had obstinately fed his mind on another kind of democracy, who had acted on the presumption that he had a right to enjoy the finest works of man, who was preoccupied with the questions, *Who am I? Whence do I come, and whither do I go?*, Mr. Ducroy was a curiosity. He seemed, quite agreeably of course, to have the mental stature of the newspapermen who boarded incoming liners, or a semi-professional baseball player. There was, moreover, a curious humility about the man, all the more bizarre when seen against the background of his expensive house, his enormous garage, his blue-tiled swimming pool, the landscaped grounds, the fine, crushed-stone driveway, and (above all) his wife. The explanation, of course, was simple, if one could only find it.

He wears a mask! Mr. Spenlove said to himself as he opened the screen door and welcomed his visitor. Not the mask of the rich, not the mask of Mr. Colwell and his banker friends in the Westphalia Trust, the grand seigneurs of business. No, it was the mask of a man who, in spite of his obvious success in a peculiar calling, was not sure of himself spiritually. The mask he wore was that of the well-to-do merchandisers and dealers who swarmed in New York, the camp-followers of the capitalist armies. Mr. Spenlove wondered whether Elliot Ducroy wasn't just one of those camp-followers himself, a vivandier of red-blood fiction. Perhaps a closer acquaintance would provide a glimpse.

Elliot Ducroy shook his head and held up a hand when offered coffee.

"Can't take it," he said. An offered Havana cigar caused him to pretend horror. "If I smoked those things—" he said, closing his eyes. "Gee!"

"You have to lead a Spartan existence, then," Mr. Spenlove surmised, getting into his coat. He gathered up a bundle of blueprints and thrust them into a large manila envelope. "Sonia told me you had some trouble." He touched his breast.

"If you said I lead a hell of a life, you'd be nearer the mark!" said Mr. Ducroy. "Where do you want to go in New York? Yeah, I have to watch that."

"Don't bother about me. I'm going over to Brooklyn on the subway. I'll get out anywhere. I suppose you're for uptown."

"Okay. Let's go."

The car slid down the curving driveway into the road. Elliot Ducroy was not a good driver. His performance with the station wagon had impressed upon Mr. Spenlove the remarkable difference between a preoccupied amateur and, for example, Mrs. Colwell's English chauffeur. Elliot Ducroy had a habit of absent-mindedly using the exact center of the road until an oncoming vehicle was almost upon him, its indignant driver suddenly pulling far over to avoid him and letting out blares from his horn. Another trick was to proceed at fifty miles an hour up to a red traffic signal and stop with a shriek of brakes. Mr. Spenlove felt a certain lack of ease until they swung into the Merritt Parkway at Greenwich.

"You save time this way," Mr. Ducroy explained, and the car accelerated to sixty-five miles an hour.

"Take all the time you want," his passenger remarked. "Heaven can wait."

Elliot Ducroy laughed. It could not be said he was unaware of his idiosyncrasies as a driver, but he did nothing to improve them. He laughed again.

Mr. Spenlove said at last, "I'd rather go slower, if you don't mind."

Elliot Ducroy nodded and reduced to forty-five.

"Thanks. And now, there's something else I'd like to ask you."

"Shoot."

"You said Mrs. Ducroy had been in a pretty fast set. Fast in what way?"

Elliot Ducroy kept his gaze on the ribbon of white concrete.

"Well," he said, "I'll tell you. You've never been married? You're a bachelor?"

Mr. Spenlove made no reply.

"Silence means consent," said Mr. Ducroy. "And besides,

sailors don't care, so I've heard. My wife takes fancies to people. Some of the people she takes fancies to aren't so hot, if you ask me. They're a bad influence."

"What do you call a bad influence, Mr. Ducroy?"

"Well . . ." Elliot Ducroy took his right hand from the wheel, turned toward Mr. Spenlove and made a gesture of raising a glass to his lips.

"You mean she drinks too much? I haven't noticed it. On the contrary . . ."

"No," said Ducroy, a curious expression on his face. "Maybe you're a good influence, or you've just seen her in between the cycles."

"Between the cycles? You mean . . . ? Hm!"

"That's it," said Ducroy. The car's speed went up for a moment as his foot unconsciously pressed the accelerator. "Well, this crowd in New York . . . Ever hear of a place called Greenwich Village? Eighth Street and so forth?"

"I've heard it described as a state of mind rather than a geographical area," Mr. Spenlove remarked. "Yes, I've been in it, never of it."

"Yeah, a state of mind! Well, my wife lived there, in that state of mind, off and on, before we came here. She had an apartment. I had to stay out on the Coast, you see, to finish my contract. So she had an apartment, close to MacDougall Street. Down a blind alley about ten feet wide. St. Giles' Alley. Very artistic. Ever hear of a poet named Caxton Derrick?"

Mr. Spenlove nodded vaguely.

"Yes," he said. "I saw where he committed a very spectacular suicide not long ago while crossing the Atlantic. Went over the side from a promenade deck full of people taking afternoon tea. Naturally we liner men discussed it. He was a bit too complicated for me, from the samples of his poetry I saw."

"Complicated! You said it! He didn't know himself what

he was driving at. *Crimson Cantilevers* was one of his books. I didn't get a line of it! Sort of talking to himself."

"He may have written for posterity," said Mr. Spenlove, smiling.

"So? I wouldn't wish posterity that luck," said Ducroy. "You don't suppose posterity can't supply its own writers? Posterity isn't that dumb, eh?"

"Go on," Mr. Spenlove suggested. He did not wish to argue about that, even if it was a good idea.

"Well, he had an apartment in this alley, just below my wife's. From what I found out later Caxton Derrick had been told so often he was a genius he believed it. He'd convinced some big banker too, and this banker had staked him to trips to Europe, because, being artistic, he couldn't write in America. Had to go to Paris and write there! America was too crass! So he went to Paris. Get that? Then he couldn't write in Paris, although he got outside of plenty of Scotch in Paris, and came back to Greenwich Village. All the time he was being told by other snide poets he was the world's new Homer or Elbert Hubbard, or something, and he went on believing it. He comes into this because of my wife."

"Where was Sonia?" asked Mr. Spenlove.

"Oh, she was in the country. You can always find a place to park a kid. Well, there were hot doings down St. Giles' Alley. Motor trips to Cape Cod, for instance, and a good deal of drinking in penthouses, especially Mrs. Ducroy's penthouse. What they call a penthouse in those parts. Pest house would be more like it, if you ask me. Caxton Derrick was one of the serious drinkers of Greenwich Villege, and there's quite a few serious drinkers down there."

"I've seen them," said Mr. Spenlove.

"They're conspicuous, yes. Derrick's special line was Scotch. Wouldn't look at rye or bourbon. It seems he had to be full of twelve-year-old Scotch to get inspiration for these jigsaw poems of his, *Crimson Cantilevers*, and *Purple Pontoons*. Jesus, I guess he saw 'em that way! He had friends to stand treat, too. And this banker, who staked him to his fare to Paris, and one of these scholarships serious drinkers get hold of so's they can write their poems without worryin' about the circulation manager. And in time he gets to know Mrs. Ducroy, whose husband is workin' without benefit of bankers or scholarships, but bloody hard for all that, in almost solitary confinement, in a motion-picture outfit, three thousand miles away! That's the scenario, you see. Married woman in a penthouse; non-rhyming poet in the apartment below; husband on the Coast."

Mr. Spenlove touched Elliot Ducroy's arm with his forefinger.

"Yes, yes!" he said. "Before you go on, why pick on me? Where do I come in? Are you suggesting . . ."

"Who's telling this story?" Elliot Ducroy swung the car into the Cross County Parkway. "You asked me what I meant when I said my wife had been in a pretty fast set. I'm tellin' you."

"That's right. I did. I didn't expect you to go into details."

"Well, all right. But you asked me! And you could be just the right sort of influence. . . . See what I mean . . . ? Advise her. She'd take advice from you. . . ."

"Advice about what?"

"I'll tell you. She wants to leave me. Wants a separation. After I spend pretty near fifty grand on that place, so's she'd have a background, she wants a separation! I'm not the man to keep a woman on a chain. No, sir! I'm not that sort of guy. She can do what she likes. But it 'ud bugger things up for me if she left me legally now. That's all. If she cleared out—again."

Mr. Spenlove, contemplating the mountainous regions of upper New York, shook his head.

"I couldn't possibly interfere. What do you take me for?"

"A square shooter. I got that the first time. Sonia thinks so too. So does she."

"Did you say—again?"

"Yeah, I said, again. So you advise her. You could make her see the folly of goin' off and leavin' me."

"You mean you don't want the publicity?"

"That's what I do mean. Instead of going to a law firm in New York or New Haven, for advice, she'll do what *you* advise. Now you know the background."

"I doubt if I do. This Caxton Derrick business . . ."

"It was a bloody mess," said Ducroy. "I told you he went to Paris. A bunch of them went to Paris. She was one of the bunch. She went to Paris."

"Are you suggesting an affair with him?" inquired Mr. Spenlove.

"It wasn't so simple as that. This Derrick, he had a peculiar reputation. Some people said he never slept with a woman in his life; had a mother fixation, whatever that is. I was told he had a sailor fixation at one time. German bellhops and Swedish quartermasters. The man who told me said they still talked about him around the Hamburg docks."

"I see," said Mr. Spenlove.

"Of course he had women friends too. In fact women made a fuss of him. When he went to Paris several of them went along to take care of him, so's he could finish this *Crimson Cantilevers* masterpiece. To keep him out of trouble, and to give themselves a special thrill."

"Quite a mess."

"I'd say so. He ran away from 'em to Cherbourg. They found him livin' in a sailor's flophouse."

"They? The women . . . ?"

"No. The police. Aliens have to report to the cops. He had to go back to Paris to get the old passport stamped at the Sûreté."

"I'm not interested in your poet apart from Mrs. Ducroy." Mr. Spenlove spoke in a low tone. They had pulled up suddenly at the toll barrier to pay a dime. He handed it out.

"That's right. He was a heel; but he wrote these things, and he was supposed to be a genius, don't forget. The poor son of a bitch couldn't write a line anybody could understand, couldn't sell it when he'd written it. He was just a joke to everybody in the business. Never mind. Never mind! He must have had something. That banker who was stakin' him to finish his book, and the board of estimate that give him his scholarship—you can't make 'em *all* out crazy! I don't know the answer. If I did I wouldn't have to work for a living.

"Well, he got back to Montparnasse and the twelve-year-old Scotch and then he had a breakdown. Cracked up. They had to put him away. My wife was the only one to go near him. She went to the institution when he got better, and read to him. He got better and they let him out, and she took him to her apartment to take care of him."

"Wouldn't that be to her credit?" Mr. Spenlove said. "She never mentioned all this to me."

"I don't suppose she did. Credit? I guess so. I guess so."

"What makes you say that? You don't think she was his mistress?"

"I didn't suggest it. They tell me Caxton Derrick never slept with a woman. Against his principles, I guess. You can never tell with these geniuses. Look at Villon. He was a Dead End Kid, they say. Baudelaire was a dope. Caxton Derrick had what you might call precedent for what he did."

"What did he do? I mean, what else did he do?"

"I'm tellin' you. She took care of him, and I dare say there was more drinkin' than you'd approve of. There was always a bunch of free-loaders in the place. Too much drinkin'. And at the Dôme. It's easier to get plastered at one of those Frog joints than to sell a short story to a magazine with a seven figure circulation."

"She told me she hated books . . . Her people were writers," Mr. Spenlove said, trying to get the story straight.

"I know! Writers who can sell what they write! Anyhow, it wasn't his writing she was interested in. He didn't do enough of it to worry the printers. It was the social life, I guess. Bein' with those Left Bankers, so long's the old bank at home was on the right, you may say, was stimulating. They'd sit around a table at a cafe and exercise their chins. That was all right. Perdita wasn't the only married woman runnin' around in Paris, France, at the time."

"Well, let's hear the end of it," said Mr. Spenlove. "What happened?"

"He skipped," said Elliot Ducroy. "He ran away again, which would have been an ideal solution if he hadn't taken her mink coat, a wallet, a couple of rings and a wrist watch. He was ready to start on his rounds again, you see, thoroughly rested, but he hadn't the cash. The banker hadn't sent him any more money and his scholarship was all shot too. So he tried to hock my wife's things, and they caught him right away and jailed him."

Elliot Ducroy turned south on Riverside Drive. Mr. Spenlove admired the splendor of the Hudson River, the bold line of the Jersey shore and the beauty of the suspension bridge. He didn't want to hear any more about Caxton Derrick. His curiosity about Perdita's adventure made him feel ashamed. He said nothing at all.

"Yeah, they jailed him, and when they wanted her to charge him she wouldn't. She went to the court and asked the judge to let him off. Said he was sick and didn't know what he was doing. It might have worked if the judge hadn't had Caxton Derrick's dossier. The French don't care a hoot if you do sleep with sailors, but they make a note of it just the same. The judge bawled her out. He told her to go back where she came from and learn a little sense, 'stead of runnin' around with a drunken gigolo in Paris. And then he gave Caxton Derrick six months."

"How did you come to hear about it?" Mr. Spenlove inquired.

"It was in the news. I had a pal in Paris in a wire office. He tipped me off and I phoned all the city editors in New York I could get hold of and got 'em to kill it. It wasn't very important to anybody else but me, I guess. Besides, God-damn it, I did that poor bastard a good turn! If his banker friend had seen it he'd have dropped him.

"So she came back, and I bought that place and we went to live in the country. Derrick came back too, when he got out, and set up in Greenwich Village as a hero. Can you beat that? He couldn't write in Paris, it seems, so he came back to Greenwich Village. He must have had a wonderful line! He got a renewal of his scholarship. Maybe it was a smaller one; but there he was, on top of the world again."

"What do you mean by on top of the world?" Mr. Spenlove demanded.

"Well, I'll tell you. I told you before, he must have had something. I don't pretend to know what it is. But he had something. What he hadn't got was the guts to earn a living with what he had. So nobody except his own pals had ever heard of him. Those guys look down their noses at money, but they want to be famous. They want like hell to be talked about. But nobody in the street's ever heard of 'em! So they compromise on a bunch of faithful followers. They get together and drink, and tell each other what wonderful guys they are, and he's the super guy. Caxton Derrick was one of the elite. He'd lived on the Left Bank. He'd been jailed—very unjustly the others said—and he could drink more Scotch than any of them. He was bigger'n Homer and Eddie Guest combined, to hear them tell it. So I say, he was on top of the world.

"He believed it, too! He used to open his window and bawl that he was the greatest, most marvelous author since William Shakespeare Shelley. To prove it, he once heaved his typewriter through the glass and nearly beaned another great poet who was rollin' home from Christopher Street, full to the guards!"

"So he jumped off a ship," said Mr. Spenlove. The incident had come back clearly to him now, also the peculiar arid quality of the man's writing. To read him was like listening to the rattling of something dry and hard in a closed casket of no particular beauty. The sound might have been caused by jewels or pebbles. In any case Mr. Spenlove, who was conservative in his taste in poetry, found little of interest. He recalled one grotesque simile, in which the New York skyline was described as "the carious dentures of a decaying god."

"So he jumped off a ship," said Elliot Ducroy, nodding. "He found he couldn't work in Greenwich Village and started for Majorca. That was the latest fashionable dump. He jumped. The only mistake he made was in not doin' it ten years earlier. He jumped; and now they say he never had a chance. They say he was crucified by the philistine editors who wouldn't buy his stuff."

"Well," Mr. Spenlove said, "at any rate you don't have him to worry about any more. Very unpleasant business for you."

"Yeah. So I got a place in the country, and sent the kid to school, and joined the yacht club, and the net result is, she wants to go back to it."

"To what? Greenwich Village?"

"Yeah. Says she wants to have her own apartment and get a job."

Mr. Spenlove said nothing. The car had turned south and now turned into Fifty-second Street. He decided that in a society so completely dedicated to enlightened self-interest he might as well practise that virtue.

"Where do you want to get out?" Elliot Ducroy asked. The traffic was heavy and he was crawling along, watching the line of cars at the curb.

"Here," Mr. Spenlove said. "I'm going to Brooklyn by subway."

"Okay," Ducroy saw a car leaving the line and nipped into the vacant space. "Bit o' luck, that!" He stopped the car and locked the ignition. "See what I mean now? Perdita's taken a fancy to you. She's interested. Do her good to talk to a man like you. You've been around. Done things and seen things. She'll see what tramps that bunch are. She'd quit all that business.

"You exaggerate," Mr. Spenlove said, as he followed his companion out of the car. Elliot Ducroy locked the doors.

"This is a good place," he said.

West Fifty-second Street was cluttered with sidewalk cafes, screened at the sides by gay awnings and in front by evergreens in tubs. Elliot Ducroy led the way toward an awning with the name El Tobalito in pink glass letters across the top. Three steps down into a sub-basement gave the outdoor customers a view limited to the legs of pedestrians. At the back, what had once been the garden of a private house was now a narrow dance floor with a fantastic ceiling of revolving colored glass. A small "private saloon bar" was furnished as replica of a London West End pub.

They sat on stools in a sort of nook screened by glass panels from the other customers. Elliot Ducroy ordered gin and bitters. "I generally come here. This is an off day, for me," he explained. He made some expressive gestures to indicate what he had insisted on from the first, that his work made abstinence compulsory. "Besides which . . ." He touched his left breast. "Got to be careful," he said quietly.

"When you retire you'll be able to do as you like," Mr. Spenlove suggested. He was still suffering a vague discomfort. He wanted to say, without giving himself away: *"Look here, old chap, I don't want to discuss your wife! I know about you and Sydney Saxon. I don't want to be involved."*

He wanted to say this, and he did not want a gin and bitters quite so early in the day.

"Retire? Me retire? Writers are like donkeys. They die in harness. It takes me all my time to earn enough to pay the bills!"

Mr. Spenlove thought of a political phrase used as a slogan in his boyhood—Peace, Retrenchment and Reform. This man apparently needed all three but was unaware of it, he mused. He merely nodded sympathetically. He had a suspicion that he was applying the wrong standards to a man like Elliot Ducroy.

Elliot Ducroy leaned his head on his arms as they rested on the bar. When he looked up again he smiled.

"Retire? All right for you. But listen: Know what I've come to New York for? To get an advance."

"You mean a loan?"

"Yeah! Call it by its right name, it's a loan. An advance on a contract. I need some money."

Mr. Spenlove, thinking of the fuel consumption of the speedboat, the probable dues of the yacht club, and the cost of the Virago, was technically not surprised. Yet he was surprised. He was English, and the apparent solidity of the success embodied in the handsome house, the lovely grounds, the solemn solvency expressed in the presence of the lugubrious Louis and Mr. Cagliari, made it difficult for him to imagine such an establishment operated on a margin.

"You're exaggerating again," he said, looking around the bar appreciatively. *It's too clean!* he said to himself, sniffing. The American passion for refrigeration made it impossible to reproduce the odor of sawdust, wood sodden with the lees of ale and wine downstairs, and the perfume of corks. *No barmaid!* he suddenly noticed. Elliot Ducroy nodded.

"Maybe so, chief!" he said smiling a little, "I'll need a lot of money pretty soon, and I'll have to roll some together. So I'm having lunch with my agent. How long you going to be over in Brooklyn?"

"Oh, I'll be finished in time to get back on the five o'clock train," Mr. Spenlove said.

"Hell, don't do that, man! This is my off day. Come here at five, and we'll go some place and eat. I'll drive you back."

"All right," Mr. Spenlove said. "I hope you get the money, but there's no need to squander it on me."

"Money?" Mr. Ducroy looked puzzled. Then his face cleared and he laughed. "Oh, sure! You mean you thought I hadn't money for a drink? I wasn't talkin' about that kind of money. Don't you worry!" He took his second gin and bitters, diluted it largely and drank a little. Mr. Spenlove shook his head at the bartender.

"Well, what kind of money were you talking about?" he inquired. Elliot Ducroy had become suddenly benign. He smiled again at Mr. Spenlove's naive notion that the trouble might be a lack of petty cash.

"Don't you worry," he said again. "This is my day off. Squander it?" The word had caught his fancy and he savored it again. He thrust some bills toward the bartender and turned away without waiting for change.

Mr. Spenlove withdrew into himself, smiling hypocritically. He could never enter into the successful American's grandiose conception of money, and was forced into hypocrisy to hide his prejudices.

Elliot Ducroy was amused. He took Mr. Spenlove's arm and led him out into Fifty-second Street.

"Got to go now," he said, in a low confidential tone. He was looking down at the sidewalk. He seemed to have something on his mind. Suddenly he said, hurriedly:

"Keep it under your hat, but I'm seein' a lawyer."

"A lawyer? You mean to . . . I thought you said you didn't want . . . Well, it's your affair, not mine. But you did say you didn't want your wife to leave you. You going to leave *her*? Is that the idea?"

"Take it easy! It's about Sonia. I'm goin' to fix up a bit of a trust fund for Sonia, so she can go through college, no matter what happens. Keep it under your hat, now! I don't want Perdita to know about it. She'd think I was . . . Well, she'd think it was gallery play."

"All right. But I can't advise her. And I can't tell her to go away."

"Sure you can't. I wouldn't wish that. I think it's a fine thing for her, to have a friend like you. A square shooter. You'll be a fine influence."

He nodded gravely and stood, his hand raised in a genial gesture, and then walked off toward Fifth Avenue.

VI

Mr. Spenlove, entering once again the dusky foyer of El Tobalito, where the air was heavy with perfume and tobacco, saw Elliot Ducroy talking to a small, neatly tailored person who wore no hat. Mr. Ducroy was sitting crablike on a stool, his knees outspread, his arms occupying a considerable area of the bar.

He turned as he caught sight of his neighbor and spun his companion around by his shoulder.

"Meet Mr. Spenlove, Irving," he said. He introduced the other man, punctuating his words with thumps on his back. "Meet Irving," he said. "My script agent."

"How'd you do, Mr. Irving? What's a script agent?"

"Irving's his given name. His other name's on half the police blotters in New York. A script agent gets you a contract for ten thousand dollars and sends you a check for about six hundred. The rest is his commission."

Mr. Spenlove glanced at Irving's round black head. His round black eyes, with round shell-rim glasses, and his round blue chin were all extremely amusing and attractive. Mr. Spenlove liked him. He was not entirely in love with Irving's clothes. The flashy check coat with a narrow waist, the loud silk shirt, the sharp-toed moleskin shoes, the stentorian cravat and the dazzling socks, were a shade on the noisy side. They suited Irving, however, and he was evidently suited to them. He ran a shrewd appraising glance up and down Mr. Spenlove's clothes, and noted his trim beard and keen eyes. He was merely trying to decide whether Mr. Spenlove's practise as a doctor was legal or illegal.

"Now you know," he said, as he smiled. "Mr. Ducroy can take the hide off a rhinoceros with his tongue when he's in the mood."

"He seems to be in the mood," Mr. Spenlove surmised, looking around.

The bar of El Tobalito was comfortably full of prosperous middle-aged men and youngish women enjoying the cocktail hour. There was a deceptive air of *bonhomie* about the place, Mr. Spenlove felt. The smoothly manicured and barbered persons, in morning coats and striped trousers, had watchful, preoccupied expressions as they patrolled the rooms. It was like being under the supervision of well-dressed detectives. Mr. Spenlove saw one of these men give him a sharp glance, which changed to a courteous, masklike grin when he found the glance returned. Mr. Spenlove had an uncomfortable sensation of being, as he said to himself, in the wrong pew. He had spent several hours that afternoon in the invigorating atmosphere of a machine shop and drafting room, in direct contact with the realities of production. There were realities behind the silken dalliance of El Tobalito, of course, but they were not the realities he cared about. He saw the bartender watching certain customers in the small mirrors placed correctly among the bottles for that purpose. He noted glances, which were obviously signals, passing between the swift, silent waiters. And he experienced a strong desire to get out of El Tobalito.

Elliot Ducroy was telling his friend Irving that the hide of a rhinoceros was wet tissue paper compared with the epidermis of a script agent in normal health.

"You might think Mr. Ducroy was drunk," Mr. Irving remarked in his smiling, tightly controlled fashion. "He's just being complimentary. If he ever got drunk he'd seem sober. Pleased to meet you, Doctor."

"Drunk? I'd take care not to be drunk doing business with

Irving," Mr. Ducroy said impressively. "One of Irving's ancestors made a fortune skinning fleas, marketing the hides, tallow, entrails and exporting the mandibles. That sort of thing is hereditary. Over my typewriter there's a framed text. 'Keep one eye on Irving.' That's how drunk I am. My friend Spenlove is a sailor, not a doctor. He doesn't approve of intemperance."

"Mr. Spenlove is without prejudice," said that gentleman. "But that does not mean he is not human. He is, for instance, hungry. You can't expect him to live exclusively on highballs and wisecracks."

"There's plenty make the experiment," Elliot Ducroy muttered. "That Caxton Derrick I was telling you about, for one." He seemed to be talking to himself. "The Great Caxton Derrick!" he snarled. His friend Irving gave him a quizzical smile and then turned it on Mr. Spenlove.

"That's his pet subject when he's signed a good contract," he said. "It's a sort of reaction. You know who Caxton Derrick was? Well, he's a symbol, sort of, in Mr. Ducroy's mind. He uses the idea to . . ."

"Has he signed a good contract?" Mr. Spenlove said. "I would have gathered, from his looks, he had lost every cent he owned."

"You don't know Elliot Ducroy. His work takes it out of him, and when he comes to see us in New York he lets his hair down, sort of."

"It's been a big day," Elliot Ducroy admitted. "Come on, fellows, let's go and eat."

"Not here!" said Mr. Spenlove firmly.

"No, not here. Hey, Irving, let's go to your place. Think Terry 'ud mind?"

"I'll have to telephone," said Irving, smiling.

"Well, telephone. We'll buy a steak and take it along."

Mr. Spenlove said he had no desire to be the fifth wheel of the coach. Elliot Ducroy shook his head. He seemed full of suppressed excitement under a mask of unsmiling good humor. His features had become keener and a shade more haggard. He watched his friend Irving go to a telephone booth without changing his expression.

"Irving's a good scout," he said, examining the check for the drinks. "Fifth wheel to the coach? Oh, no! Irving's girl friend has no exclusiveness. I mean, Terry's broad-minded. You'll like Terry."

"So?" said Mr. Spenlove. He smiled. "I'm broad-minded too."

Elliot Ducroy leaned forward, studied his guest for a moment, and laughed. In that sudden eruption a number of deeply native emotions were releasing themselves. He had taken an instinctive liking to his new neighbor on sight. He could not explain it, but it was there. And the strain of his last few weeks, working like a demon against time to finish a series of sensational stories, struggling with his domestic difficulties, and his affair with Sydney Saxon, had been almost too much for him.

Now he laughed and beat Mr. Spenlove on the shoulder with his fist. Irving came back from the telephone.

"Okay?" said Elliot Ducroy.

"Okay," said Irving.

"Then let's get out of this ye olde tappe room. I'll bet a dollar you think it's phony," he said suddenly to Mr. Spenlove.

"I didn't say so," Mr. Spenlove insisted, smiling. "Where are we going now?"

"In my car, to Bannister Street. That's in the Village."

"Always the Village," Mr. Spenlove mused. The hat-check girl, as slender as a wasp, striped in black and gold, and with supple, wasplike movements of her body, as though she had a sting in her behind, gave him his hat and a professional smile, all teeth and mascara.

"Well, the Village has certain advantages for shady characters like Irving," Elliot Ducroy said. He unlocked his car and got in.

He drove with care in the turmoil of Fifth Avenue early evening traffic. Mr. Spenlove found Irving's arm affectionately over his shoulder as they sat, three abreast. The smiling round eyes and round blue jowls were close to his own.

It occurred to him, as he looked at Irving, that what he himself habitually avoided, this clever, cheerful little Jew revelled in. To huddle close to others, to clutch and to embrace, was to Irving a sensuous pleasure.

"You don't like New York," said Irving smiling. There was a faint fuzz on his upper lip, shaved to a narrow thing like a shadow, or a smudge. Irving called it a mustache.

"Don't I?" Mr. Spenlove inquired. "I wonder why."

"Well, sailors. Mr. Ducroy said you were a sailor. You married? They say sailors have wives in every port."

"It's not confined to sailors," Mr. Spenlove informed him. He looked into the kind, wise, smiling, Semitic dark eyes. "What about you? Are you married, and how often?"

"Married, but separated," said Irving. "My wife's bringing suit for alienation."

"Irving's like a lot of us. He's had a raw deal," said Elliot Ducroy. He gave a cruising taxi-man, who was swerving out upon him, a sarcastic glare. He then swerved in front of a massive limousine and in turn received a contemptuous glare from the ascetic, elderly chauffeur.

Mr. Spenlove resigned himself to living in what he called, privately, hell. The peculiar psychology of motorists in action, the close contact with the bodies of the two men between whom he sat, and the bedlam of New York traffic made him wish he was back on the hill beyond Norbury. Yet behind this distaste he was aware of a vast and nebulous curiosity about his companions. It was plain, humiliatingly plain, to him that he had lived his own life on an extremely simple pattern, compared with theirs.

"No, not a raw deal. I got the breaks," said Irving. He chuckled, all his big white front teeth, one of them with a gold crown, gleaming at Mr. Spenlove. "Mr. Ducroy has very high ideals," he added.

"Has he? He never mentioned it to me." Mr. Spenlove was not quite sure what the phrase meant to Irving.

"Well, of course he wouldn't. A feller don't speak freely on pers'nal matters."

Mr. Spenlove kept his face straight by firm resolution.

"Of course not," he said. Elliot Ducroy, who had halted for a red light, kept his face averted from his passengers. "Otherwise I'd be asking you your girl friend's name. I often miss names in introductions. Not that it matters."

The car spun around into Washington Square, along Waverly Place and into the maze of narrow lanes, mews and crooked passages which are the heart of Greenwich Village.

Irving laughed and patted Mr. Spenlove's shoulder.

"Oh, sure! Her name's Terry Florence."

"You mean Florence is the surname? Or is it Florence Terry?"

"Nope. Both names are Christian names. Her surname's so terrible nobody can pernounce it or spell it. She can't either, she says. So she's Miss Florence, if you want to be formal. Call her Terry."

"Oh, she hasn't your name yet?"

Irving said no, not yet.

"Bigamy is frowned on in Irving's set," Elliot Ducroy said. He turned toward them and his face suddenly relaxed.

"I'm only kiddin'," he said. "I kid Irving all the time. From coast to coast I've kidded him. He lived on me in Hollywood. Now I live on him, you may say. Let's get a steak, Irving."

"She's got a steak," Irving said. "It's on the broiler now, I guess. Hey! You can't park this side, Elliot."

"Well, get out and I'll run the bus to where I can park."

As they climbed the dark stairs, to which numerous sour smells clung, Irving drew Mr. Spenlove to a landing window. He looked down on a solid cement area from which sprang, miraculously, a tree with foliage.

"How the hell can it grow from concrete?" Mr. Spenlove said suddenly. "Its roots must be among the cables and water mains." He was surprised Mr. Irving should notice it.

"Never mind that," said Irving. "What I want to say, keep this place under your hat. This is confidential. Mr. Ducroy, he likes to get off the chain now and again. He likes to come here and forget his pers'nal troubles. Any friend of Mr. Ducroy's is welcome; only, you understand, this is off the record, see? Don't mention it, please."

He spoke in a low tone, jerkily and with his hand fondling Mr. Spenlove's shoulder.

"Oh, yes, that's quite understood. Don't worry."

Mr. Spenlove, following Irving to the top floor and watching him as he gave certain knocks on a green door, really did understand. He understood that while Elliot Ducroy and his script agent were involved in a highly complicated pattern of living, their emotions were extraordinarily simple. Irving could have easily avoided prying eyes on his hideaway by not inviting strangers. But Irving was the victim of pride and vanity. He wanted to show someone what he had got.

Mr. Spenlove was familiar with this peculiarity of men whose lives were beset by women. The urge to show off waged an endless war against the instinct to hide their passion. It was like a struggle between two demons for the man's soul.

He heard the latch of the green door click and saw it open upon a flight of steep stairs. He saw Irving turn and make a gesture and then run up the stairs. *Yes!* he reflected, *I am hot on the trail! Elliot Ducroy wants me to think he is off the chain, as Irving says. It's a justification, all this business.*

He peered up the stairway and saw the smartly trousered legs of Irving close to a pair of silk-stockinged legs that were visible as far as the knees. The legs ended in feet encased in bright scarlet, high-heeled shoes. Above the knees were red garters and a school dress. Mr. Spenlove waited.

Irving clattered down a few steps and beckoned. He was

still holding the hand of a plumpish fair girl whose features were not very clear because of the window behind her. She waved her other hand benignly.

"Terry says come on in," said Irving.

Mr. Spenlove detected the tremor of pride in Irving's voice as he introduced the girl whose surname was so unpronounceable and unspellable she had discontinued using it. Terry Florence smiled and led the way into her apartment, which was an immense attic with a terrace encumbered with skylights. The odor, rich and delightful, of a broiling steak, filled the chamber.

Terry Florence pointed to a low table where there was a tray with bottles and glasses, and went behind a partition of yellow wall board, where she had her kitchen.

"Make yose'f at home." Irving grinned, and he took off his coat. He had the air of a conspirator introducing an old and tried accomplice to the secret rendezvous of the organization. "When that door's shut I'm home, see. This is . . ."

The bell buzzed three times and then, after a pause, once again.

"That's Mr. Ducroy."

Irving and the girl collided as they both hurried to release the latch. He took her in his arms and carried her. It was as much as he could manage. She pressed the button, smiling, and holding off her lover's caresses.

"Now, Irving!" she said, smiling again.

Mr. Spenlove set his hat out of the way and sat down to admire the general scene. The large room was painted yellow. French windows, which were open, gave him a view of the terrace, which was the roof of an office downstairs. A canary bustled about in a cage suspended between the windows. It was obvious that Terry was energetic. Crates, boxes, butter tubs, and an old iron drinking trough had been filled with earth and were growing pansies, geraniums, tulips and ferns. Mr. Spenlove's experienced eye noted that the floor of the room was immaculate and the muslin curtains fresh.

The yellow walls were decorated with startling modern pictures, in black frames, of naked Negresses in tropical settings, cats with arched backs, and landscapes drenched in blinding sunshine. There was a poster of some bal-masque, with a nude kicking a silk hat. He saw a typewriter, neatly covered, on a side table. There were some photos of Terry in shorts and several photos of stars, signed by the stars or the stars' secretaries, and inscribed to Terry.

The low table was an antique cobbler's work bench, and on the mantelpiece Mr. Spenlove observed a Cape Cod ship in a bottle. There was a shelf of books, too, clean copies of first-rate recent works and about a score of reprints. There was a carton with some sewing in it and an evening paper not yet unfolded.

"How you like it?" Irving said. His face was suffused with pride, as if he were responsible for it all. He saw Elliot Ducroy coming up the stairs.

"I like it all right," Mr. Spenlove said quietly. He caught Ducroy's eye as the girl came out to greet him.

"A love nest!" Ducroy said. "Irving's love nest. Hello, Terry! How you keeping?"

Mr. Spenlove saw them embrace and kiss. The casualness of it extracted all significance from it, as it were. It was like shaking hands, he supposed. He felt suddenly inexperienced and old-fashioned and ashamed.

Elliot Ducroy took off his coat. The girl made a smiling gesture for Mr. Spenlove to do likewise. Ducroy laughed as he examined the bottles.

"Englishmen don't take off their coats. Not in the presence of ladies, Terry," he warned her. "They're civilized. They'd as soon take off their pants. I mean trousers. Say, do you know I got a suit in London, once, from a tailor who spelt trousers with a 'w'? It's a fact. Fourteen guineas." He laughed again.

"I only want you should be comfortable," Terry said, and she went back into the kitchen.

Irving came to the table with a tray of ice cubes.

"You ain't a woman hater, Mr. Spenlove, are you?" he said.

Mr. Spenlove did not reply to this. He was looking at his neighbor Elliot Ducroy, who was mixing two whiskies and sodas.

"No, he's not a woman hater," Ducroy said. "What he hates, I should say, is everybody."

"No!" Mr. Spenlove held up his hand. "Oh, no!"

"Well, landsmen," amended Elliot Ducroy. "That's pretty near everybody. Lives alone and likes it. He's got an old New England cottage that simply ought to have a girl like Terry in it, with chickens in the barn. And do you know what he's got in the barn instead of chickens? A lot of electrical machinery for boat building. It's a waste of good acreage!" He handed Mr. Spenlove a drink.

"Mr. Spenlove, will you rent it to me this summer?"

The round smiling face of Terry Florence looked out from behind the wall board partition. Mr. Spenlove found it hard to believe she was not a young girl but an experienced woman in the middle thirties. She wore a school dress and her hair was done exactly the same as the high-school girls' in the drugstore at Norbury.

"She'd make it a love nest for Irving," said Elliot Ducroy, amused, pouring a soft drink for himself.

Irving said to Ducroy, "You could use that idea."

"I can use any ideas," said Elliot Ducroy. He took a good swig of his drink. "But I prefer ideas to situations. And that isn't even a situation. It's just a setting."

Terry came into view bearing a platter on which a thick steak was still spitting in a mass of fried onions. The two men cleared a card table hastily and spread a cloth. Irving produced knives and forks. Ducroy set chairs.

Mr. Spenlove watched the proceedings calmly. It was obvious that Elliot Ducroy enjoyed this sort of thing. He knew, as though from experience, how life in these establishments went on. He accepted Irving's intimacy with Terry

Florence and seemed almost to share it. There was nothing incongruous in imagining Elliot Ducroy having a duplicate of Terry in the next apartment, or even in sharing Terry herself. The lines of their behavior were sometimes shadowy and wavering. What was incongruous was the immense place on the shore, the useless extravagance of his life there, his strenuous existence as a producer of fiction.

They sat down and Irving cut the steak into strips. The girl brought an Italian loaf and a glass of milk for herself.

"Don't you drink?" asked Mr. Spenlove.

She held up the milk in answer.

"Abstinence makes the heart grow fonder," said Ducroy sententiously.

"I just don't like it," Terry explained.

"She gets her stimulation from men," Ducroy remarked.

"Sure," said Terry. "I like men. I mean, I like them to associate with."

"Not to live with?" said Ducroy.

"Be yourself, Elliot," she said. "You know what I mean. I don't care very much for *any*body to *live with, all the time.* I wouldn't like to have anybody under foot all day."

"It sounds like an ideal arrangement," Ducroy said. "Irving's a lucky man. The wicked always prosper." He said to Mr. Spenlove, pointing with his knife at Terry, who was spooning up gravy for her bread crust, "She's one in a thousand. She's in love with a man and she doesn't want to make a meal of him! She doesn't even want to make him divorce his wife."

"I'll get a divorce all right. I don't need making," said Irving hastily.

"And then?" said Ducroy, still holding his knife upraised.

"I never cross bridges until I come to them," Irving said.

"Don't spoil everything, darling," said Terry in a casual tone.

"Didn't I say she was one in a thousand?" said Elliot

Ducroy. "When she was made the mold was broken. The Great Artificer couldn't bear to repeat himself."

"How much of this am I supposed to take seriously?" Mr. Spenlove inquired.

"None of it!" said Terry smiling.

"All of it!" Irving contradicted. "Mr. Ducroy likes kidding, but they's a lot of genuine cerebration in what he says."

"There's a testimonial for you!" said Ducroy, giving Mr. Spenlove a solemn wink. "Irving knows his stuff. He wouldn't know a preposition from a superstition, and he wouldn't recognize a split infinitive if he fell over one. As for double quotes, don't make me laugh. But he knows fiction the way an oriental carpet merchant knows rugs, by the seamy side. Half the time he couldn't say why one story's good and another one stinks. But he knows all right."

"Most of 'em stink," said Irving, cutting more steak.

"He can tell by the feel, like the carpet merchant," went on Ducroy, gesturing. "He knows what the customers want all right. By instinct."

"Intelligence," corrected Terry. "Irving's very intelligent."

"What about us? Aren't we all intelligent?" said Ducroy.

"Not in the same way," Terry said, pleasantly, and Mr. Spenlove gazed upon her with mild approval. Her kind eyes flickered toward him as though there were things she, too, knew by instinct, and others that she wished to know and which she suspected he could be persuaded to tell her.

"Let's quit talkin' shop," said Ducroy agreeably. "Mr. Spenlove, you know, he won't think much of our intelligence if we harp on it. He's a retired ship's officer; been at sea for years on liners. He thinks passengers the lowest form of life."

"Did I say that?" Mr. Spenlove inquired, amid laughter. He refused any more steak, but took a piece of bread to mop up his gravy. "Mr. Ducroy has exaggerated. Haven't you noticed how he exaggerates?"

Terry Florence nodded vigorously.

"I'll say we have!" she said.

"Well, it must have been a chance remark," Mr. Spenlove suggested.

"There's an idea!" said Irving, nodding to Ducroy, "for a script. You start with a chance remark, and . . ."

Elliot Ducroy waved him aside.

"A chance remark!" he said, explosively. "I said, I expected you'd seen some life all right on these cruise liners. I said I bet, if you told all, you'd be able to give a fiction writer some good leads. And you said it would be unprofessional to tell on the passengers. You said it was like havin' a job in an institution for the feeble-minded! They weren't responsible for the crazy things they did on a ship. And now you say *I* exaggerate! Well, it was a lead. I got a story of sorts out of it."

"He gets a story of sorts out of everybody, though you can never recognize yourself in them," said Terry. "It's just the idea he's after—just a hint."

"I have no objection," Mr. Spenlove told her. "I know so many stories. They don't strike me as suitable for publication, though."

"They wouldn't to you," Ducroy agreed. "I'd not worry about that, if I were you. Leave that to me. Just go ahead."

"You want to write me up? You want to get copy? Is that what you call it?"

"No, that isn't quite the way things are," Elliot Ducroy said quietly. "I was only givin' you an illustration. I suppose you have the usual ideas of the gaping public. You think we can put you on the stand, like a witness. Or on an operating table, like a patient, and cut a story out of your innards. I used to have letters accusing me of stealing another fellow's stuff, or using another person's experiences. It isn't that way at all. You tell what you call a story. You relate an incident. Why, man, there's only nine plots in the world, so they say! All you can do is to be yourself. All I can do is rearrange the same old counters."

"I thought we weren't going to have any more shop," Terry

complained. She rose to start the coffee and bring some cheese.

"Well, it was you, Terry, who started us off on intelligence. And Irving had to bring up what he calls cerebration. Mr. Spenlove here is the man for cerebration, if you ask me. He's takin' it all in—yes."

"But I'm not a writer, or anything like that," Mr. Spenlove pointed out. "I keep a sort of journal, what I call a scrap log; but so do thousands of other people. All I do is watch the performance. I wouldn't presume to . . ."

"To write? That's where you show your cerebration! You know, they say monkeys are too smart to talk, 'cause they know men 'ud put 'em to work. If some of you fellows who have been around and used your eyes began to get on to the writing game, us poor authors 'ud be right out o' luck."

Mr. Spenlove had lit a cigar, and he looked through the smoke at Terry and Irving, smiling.

"There's more exaggeration than cerebration in this discussion," he said briskly. "How do you know we are so innocent? I notice a certain condescension in that attitude! It's a mock humility to say, 'us poor authors,' when you make as much in a day as most of us make in a month! Come, come! What are we here for? To pull each other's legs?"

"You mean, what are we on earth for? I would say just that, to pull each other's legs. First we succeed and then someone else does the same to us. It's great sport, if you're moderately successful. But most people, what I call the gaping public, aren't successful at all. They've lost the knack of pullin' each other's legs. They get their salvation in instalments, out of the magazines, and movies, and radio and sports. That's where we come in, Irving and me, and the rest of the amusement industry."

The girl seemed to be pondering, her eyes on a cracker she was crumbling with capable fingers that ended in nails resembling chips of polished red amber.

"Don't be cynical, Elliot," she said. Mr. Spenlove helped

himself to a slice of sharp Provolone cheese and ate it with enjoyment.

"He isn't being cynical," he told her. "It's a realistic conception of our life. We're just the same on the ship. Keep them amused, and interested. Keep them guessing. Keep them smiling. Keep them from thinking, in short."

Elliot Ducroy struck his hand on the arm of his chair and nodded, his lips protruding, his eyes stern.

"That's it! That's what it is!" he said.

"Well, it's only since you've become so successful that you've talked that way," Terry said, looking at her own hands. "Out on the Coast you had ideals, don't forget."

"I've got ideals now, but—well, maybe they've changed." He frowned.

They heard the telephone ringing behind the partition which half concealed Terry's bed. She rose to answer it.

Irving looked at Mr. Spenlove, smiling.

"We're expectin' a phone call around now."

Again Mr. Spenlove had the impression of having lived an almost absurdly simple existence both ashore and afloat.

"I'll excuse you," he said, smoking imperturbably. He saw Terry turn toward them, leaning forward from behind the partition, holding her hand tightly over the mouthpiece.

"It's for you, Elliot," she said. "You know . . . She asked for Irving . . . She doesn't know . . ."

"Say you can reach me," Elliot said hurriedly. "Say Irving'll get in touch."

They heard Terry speaking with the exaggerated lucidity one woman uses in speaking through the phone to another woman she dislikes. They heard her say,

"Yes, Irving's here, Mrs. Saxon. He was out on the terrace. Yes, he has an engagement with . . . Yes, sure he will. I'm telling him. No, no trouble. I said, he has an engagement with Mr. Ducroy. That's quite all right, Mrs. Saxon. G' bye, Mrs. Saxon."

She set the receiver down with enormous deliberation

and came back to get the coffee. She brought it to the table with an inscrutable expression in her fair, irregular features. Mr. Spenlove allowed his glance to rest alternately on the two men. It was a whimsical glance, committing him to nothing, but indicating that he felt more sure of himself now than at any time during the day. He had noted Elliot Ducroy's idiosyncrasy, to assume control of anyone with whom he associated. Possibly Perdita had not been sufficiently malleable material. Possibly she had incurred criticism. Mr. Spenlove knew how quickly a man could change into a god in his own estimation. And now, here was Sydney Saxon, whom he had seen that night through his binoculars, while the splendid Perdita pressed close to him in the darkness, her hand on his shoulder.

"I don't know if she believed me, but there it is. Irving, you've got to call her at the apartment. And not from here, please!"

Mr. Spenlove began to wonder if Americans, with their extraordinary talent for complicating the simplest emotions, had achieved a combination of love, hate, shame and pride. All four were traceable on Elliot Ducroy's keen features, as he sat, his chin on his hand.

"I wasn't sure she was in town," he mumbled. And to Mr. Spenlove it was obvious that he expected no one to believe him. "No, I wasn't sure she . . ."

"Suppose I decamp," Mr. Spenlove said, looking at his watch. It was past eight, but he knew there was a train on the hour. "I can catch the nine o'clock all right."

"No! You wait!" Elliot Ducroy said. "You're drivin' back with me! We won't be more'n an hour. Eh?" he said to Irving.

"Less'n an hour," said Irving. "It's important money though, if we can swing it."

"You wait here 'n talk to Terry," said Ducroy, in his midwestern, twangy voice.

Mr. Spenlove made a hasty mental note to the effect that

his reputation for reliability was evidently well founded, and spreading. He continued to smoke as the other men drank coffee, resumed their coats and hats and prepared to leave.

"We'll take a taxi," said Ducroy. "It's quicker . . ."

They descended, and Mr. Spenlove contemplated the light of the western sky through a slot in the dingy brick battlements around Terry's zinc-floored roof garden.

"I hope you won't be bored," the girl said. She brought the coffee pot over to refill his cup.

"On the contrary," he said. She brought her own coffee and cigarette to the chair nearest the window.

"What do you think of this joint?" she said, smiling. "All right?"

"Yes, it's all right. What do you do? Are you in a business in New York?"

"Oh, yes. I have a job, but it's very irregular hours. Today, you see, I was free from noon on. I work for a newspaper syndicate, Regal Distributors. I do the beauty shops, mostly. I'm a writer. I keep working until Irving gets organized."

"How does one do a beauty shop? You mean call on them? Write them up?"

"Yes, get the dope—all the new hair-dos, face creams, foundation lotions and packs. Perfumes too, but only conservative ones for my public. I'm Alix Fayre. That's my nom de plume."

"It sounds like something in a dream to me," Mr. Spenlove admitted. "You advise your public? You advise them to buy this or that?"

"Only so long as we get the advertising," Terry Florence smiled over her cup. "But we won't go into either this or that. I interview stars too. I used to be in pictures, and knew the stars some. But my voice didn't record too good. So I interview the stars, and they endorse the preparations."

"I suppose they do. Well, you live an interesting life. You all live interesting lives. Were you talking to a Mrs. Saxon?"

"You heard me? Yes, she called. She is . . ." She looked

doubtfully at Mr. Spenlove, wondering how far she could assume a knowledge he might, quite conceivably not possess at all. "Do you know her?"

"Who? I? Oh, no. I know of her. I mean I know where she lives, for instance. Across the river from my place. But it's a much more elaborate residence than mine, I imagine. She's a writer too, I understand. I can't recall anything of hers . . ."

"She made a hundred and forty thousand last year," Terry said. "Counting motion picture and radio rights."

"Hm! She must be talented. Is she a friend of yours? I rather thought, from your voice, you weren't enamored . . ."

"She's talented, all right!" Terry said grimly. She crossed her legs and drew down her short skirt. "Too talented in some ways. She's a man-eater."

"You mean she's a *femme fatale*?"

"So it seems. You wouldn't think so to look at her! Dark red hair. She has a good strong chin, and another one under it coming. Black eyes, like an Indian's. They say she has Navajo blood, but I wouldn't know about that. I guess she must be attractive to certain types of men."

"Irving said it was important money they've gone for. Just what is 'important money'?"

"Well, several thousand dollars. Irving is trying to arrange a contract with a magazine for a collaboration serial. *Gentleman Church Falls in Love* is Irving's idea, you see, and there would be a domestic angle with a Sydney Saxon treatment."

"Do you think it's a good idea?"

"No, I don't! I don't believe Mrs. Saxon would even consider it if she hadn't something else on her mind. Her public's so different from Elliot's. Absolutely."

"What do you mean—something else on her mind?"

"I don't know if I ought to talk about it."

"Why not?"

"Well, you're a friend of Mr. Ducroy's and maybe you'd feel—well . . ."

"I'm a friend of Mrs. Ducroy even more," Mr. Spenlove said quietly. "I came to New York on business and he asked me to ride in. But Mrs. Ducroy and Sonia, that's her daughter, are my friends, yes. Do you know her?"

Terry Florence nodded.

"Sure, I know her. I don't mean as a close friend. I know her, yes. She's very glamorous."

"She told me about Sydney Saxon," Mr. Spenlove said. "I had never heard of the woman. Perhaps you haven't anything to reveal that would shock me," he added. "Or Mrs. Ducroy."

"I guess that's so," said Terry slowly. "Well, it only shows how queer men are."

"Some men."

"Yes, some men. Irving's different. Irving's very reliable. But I never try to influence him. He's absolutely free, s'far as I'm concerned. The mistake many women make is to try to boss a man around. But that isn't the only trouble. With Elliot it's money. He was pretty well all right while he was only making around a couple of hundred a week. His first wife married again, and that let Elliot out, s'far as alimony went. Now he's in the big money, he's changed. Do you know, I really believe there's some sort of magnetism in money. It's partly Sydney Saxon's success that is causing this split-up. I don't mean he wants her money. Nothing of that sort. It's just the fact he feels she must understand him better than anyone else because she makes so much money the same way he does. I don't seem to explain it very well," she ended lamely.

"You explain it admirably," Mr. Spenlove said. "It's a sort of cosmic gravity. The psychology of what you call important money used to be one of my hobbies when I was at sea. You're probably on the right track. Mrs. Ducroy seems to know what's going on."

"I thought it was pretty raw of Mrs. Saxon to take a house so close to his. But she's that sort of woman. And after all . . ."

"How old a woman?"

"Oh, she's forty, I guess. I first met her when she was out on the Coast doing a continuity for Rex Pictures. I'd say she's forty now. She's got a boy in college. She's had an awful lot of affairs since she got her divorce. I don't know why, but men fall for her, hard. She's entirely unscrupulous. I don't suppose you ever heard the Sydney Saxon version of the traveling salesman story. They say he called at her shack at Santa Monica, selling typewriters. She kept him there demonstrating all day. When he wanted to quit she wouldn't let him go. They went down to Tia Juana together in her car. It was quite a while before he saw his family again. That's the story."

"And now she's got our friend, apparently."

"Well, she never was a one-man woman, but she's really mad about him. I'm sure of that."

"Is he a one-woman man?"

"It depends. He's like most successful writers. He's an idealist."

"It must be quite expensive, being an idealist."

"You can afford it if you're successful. In a way, it's a sort of symbol of success. If you're poor you just have to make out the best you can."

"I don't see the idealism unless he marries this Mrs. Saxon."

"Oh, I wouldn't say that! *He* might, but she can keep her head. She's mad about him, but she can keep her head. She's a first-class business woman. There was a man she'd met on a cruise once, one of these big huskies who grow bananas down in South America some place. He stuck around too long. She had a serial to do on contract and she told him he'd have to clear out so she could work. When he wouldn't, because he was so madly gone on her, she simply cleared out herself and took a room in a hotel in

Atlantic City for a month while she got her serial written. When she returned he'd gone back to South America or wherever it was. Sydney's too clever to marry a writer. Irving and I have had a lot of argument about this idea of his. They're up at her apartment now with the editor. I say to Irving, you'll lose a good friend if it blows up later. An agent has to watch his step. It's like handling a couple of prima donnas, sometimes."

"Well, all this is very surprising to me. What do you suppose will happen? You see, I live next door to them, as it were. I mean, my small place is tucked away in the hills behind the Ducroy place. Sonia, that's the kid, comes over to see me. She's thirteen or so. I'm fond of Sonia. Mrs. Ducroy drops in too. So does he, for that matter. Without having any designs on them, I've become a friend of the family. But I've never seen them together. I've even been to a cocktail party, a big one, at their house, and she was away. I thought that peculiar until I heard some of the guests discussing her rather freely."

Terry Florence nodded.

"I know. She was in New York. Irving told me. Irving knows everything that's going on. She expected Sydney Saxon to come to that party and she knew Elliot wanted them to be friends. He didn't want any quarreling. She came to New York."

"Wanted them to be friends? That's a very extraordinary thing to say. Do you mean to tell me a man likes his wife to associate with the woman he is in love with?"

"I told you he's an idealist."

"Suppose you explain what you mean by an idealist. Mr. Ducroy and I got into a discussion about the word intellectual. He means something special. Just the opposite to what Mrs. Ducroy seems to have in mind. And now you say he's an idealist . . . !"

"Well, that's what he is. He feels he has an obligation to

take care of her and the kid. Knowing what he does, he's afraid what might happen to her if . . ."

"Is that idealism? I'm not sure you've made it absolutely clear, but there's a sort of insane integrity in such a course. Now, you and your Irving . . . ?"

"Why, I'm his common-law wife!" she said, with rising inflection. She seemed shocked. "He wants to get a final divorce so he doesn't have to be hypocritical. I tell him, take your time. I tell him, let your wife bring suit for alienation and not defend it. It's much simpler if you don't hurry. Irving wanted to get a Florida divorce when he was down at Miami Beach last winter, but I told him he'd much better wait, and let her do it. For alienation."

Mr. Spenlove finished his coffee and lay back to enjoy his cigar. He laughed. Terry Florence, rising, looked down at him kindly and gravely before going over to enshroud the canary in a blue cloth for the night.

"What's so funny?" she said, her back to him.

"You seem to have thought of everything," he said, "except what Mrs. Ducroy might do. This idealism seems to inflict a certain amount of hardship on third parties, hm? Do you know how the wind sets in that quarter? Remember she's not a writer earning a hundred and forty thousand a year."

"Oh, if Elliot hadn't lots of money, Sydney Saxon would take care of that."

"Buy him up, eh? Pay compensation? Heart balm's the word, I believe. But I wasn't thinking of that so much. I happen to know Mrs. Ducroy has resources. She'd be all right! But—what if she was in love with her husband? Or is that unethical?"

Terry Florence dimpled happily.

"Now you're being cynical! I hope you won't repeat anything I say to Mr. Ducroy. Of course Irving and I are on his side, but don't tell him anything I say, please. Her first husband's married twice since. To La Conchita now. I forget who it was the first time. Mrs. Ducroy didn't get a cent from him. He's English. Elliot paid for her divorce as well as his own. His first wife wanted to marry again. No, it isn't unethical, but it isn't the truth. You know, there was a man committed suicide at sea. A man she was in Paris with."

"That's rather an improbable story," Mr. Spenlove said gravely. "Knowing her as I do it sounds a shade improbable."

"It's true, though," she insisted, frowning a little. "It was while Elliot was still on the Coast. She was living just around the corner from here, and she was playing around with a lot of writing people. She was very restless socially. Irving used to fly east about four times a year and he would see her. That's how I know."

Mr. Spenlove smiled.

"It strikes me you dislike her," he said.

"I was never in love with her," the girl said. "You can't like a person who doesn't know you're in the room."

"Well, about the man in Paris. You mean she had a lover?"

Terry sat with her hands folded, not saying anything for a moment. Mr. Spenlove continued, vehemently, "Incredible!"

Terry dimpled again.

"I can see she's been on her very best behavior at your house," she said. "When she's with you. But aren't we all?"

"You mean to suggest everybody's under restraint in my stately presence?" Mr. Spenlove grumbled. He stood up and began to walk about the room while Terry, after examining her highly organized fingernails, put her hands behind her blonde head and leaned back, watching him. "One of the first things I ever heard about Mrs. Ducroy," he said, "was a vague innuendo. One of my neighbors, a good sort of woman, in the antique business."

"A woman in the antique business wouldn't get much change out of Mrs. Ducroy," Terry agreed. "As a matter of fact, Elliot's wife gives another woman the impression she's thinking of something else all the time. That accounts for the innuendo, as you call it. It's hard to explain, though. It's as if she belonged to a different social world. I remember, before Elliot married her, he gave her a cream-colored Duesenberg roadster, the sort the stars have. She used to leave it outside the Brown Derby and walk away after lunch and forget about it! I can't *imagine* a woman like that! She had no sense of property at all. That was part of her charm for Elliot. The girls on the coast are not so subtle. They're fast, or they're thrifty, or greedy, or they get one of these freak Californian religions, but you can always figure them out. Elliot's wife was never one of the crowd. And she came east soon after they were married. Just got on the train and came east. Said the climate out there was so horrible she couldn't stand it. Said her kid needed a more bracing climate. Irving did everything for her. Elliot began to make more money than ever before. Gentleman Church was everywhere. There's even a Gentleman Church comic strip now. As for the movies and radio sketches they make out of his adventures, you can imagine! The money poured in. He got offers from advertisers. He made himself into a corporation. Gentleman Church Features, Inc. That was stopped after a while, by the Government. Gentleman Church dolls earned him thirty thousand dollars."

"So he had to have a country estate?"

"Well, what else was he to do with it? He bought a lot of stocks one year. You know what a good idea *that* was. So he got that place on the Sound and put a good many thousands of dollars into it. His idea, you see, was to make a setting for her, to give her a background. He thought, maybe she'd been unhappy in Hollywood. He still owns a big property out at Encinitas, but they never lived on it. He thought, maybe it's all too new and crude for her, coming from England. So he bought that old place on the Sound and remodeled it, like all the other men were doing, and persuaded her to live in it. That was after she'd been to Paris."

"Well, she does live in it. What does he want? Why the Sydney Saxon business?"

Terry clasped her hands around one knee and rocked herself gently. She said, slowly, "You wouldn't say a thing like that if you'd been married."

"How do you know I haven't? What gave you the idea . . ."

Again Terry dimpled.

"Oh, that's obvious, Mr. Spenlove! Excuse me. What does he want? With a man like Elliot his demands are terrific! Most of all, he wants a woman to be absolutely absorbed in their partnership. Not in him personally. Of course, I don't explain it very well. It's like a soldier, you know, and—his armor-bearer. I was an extra in a Roman picture once. A spectacle. The centurions had armor-bearers who followed them. When a man's in the thick of it, making lots and lots of money, and he has dozens of problems and contacts, he needs a woman who's with him, thinking of him, pulling for him, for both of them. You understand?"

"Not entirely. Perhaps she doesn't want a lot of money."

"Every woman wants a lot of money," Terry said casually. "If she says she doesn't she's a liar."

"You really believe that?"

"I don't simply believe it, I know it."

"Mrs. Ducroy is the exception, then?"

"She doesn't take any *interest* in what he's doing! See what I mean? He hasn't ever had her pulling for him in her mind, thinking for the two of them while he makes the money. . . . If a woman isn't *absorbed* in her husband's life, she isn't married at all, really. Why, Elliot was marvelous to her when they met. She was practically starving! She was trying to get taken on as an extra, and not having any luck. Her first husband was a heel if there ever was one. Well, Elliot saw her one day, with the kid, in the casting office, and fell for her. He was awfully chivalrous about it too. She'd been having the same hell of a time as most of the girls, but she isn't the sort to live in an apartment with half a dozen others, on call on the telephone. On call, that is, any hour of the day or night. She couldn't do what I did for a while, wash dishes in an eatery on Figueroa Street. So she was having a thin time. Money from home had almost stopped."

"I know. She told me about that once," Mr. Spenlove said. "Not about the apartments on call and so on, but about her thin time. And about her people in England."

"Irving says she's always been very mysterious about her background. I suppose she's good people."

Mr. Spenlove made an abrupt movement.

"She doesn't confide in Irving, does she?"

"She doesn't *confide* in anybody! One night last winter Elliot was here. He was very restless and at a loose end. He'd had an awful disappointment. . . . He told us his wife had never asked him a single question about himself or his folks, or his youth, or anything, since they were married. She hadn't taken any interest in that place he calls Church Yard. Just lived there as if it was a hotel."

"I didn't know men, American men, expected their wives to be wrapped in their careers and personalities. It seems to be monogamy gone mad, the way you explain it."

Terry looked at Mr. Spenlove doubtfully.

"Monogamy? That means only one wife, doesn't it?"

"And one husband, of course," Mr. Spenlove said drily. He noticed that whenever Terry lost control, which was rarely, her voice became strident and flat, like the other New Yorkers he knew.

"Yeah, well? Who's talking about that? You've missed the whole point, Mr. Spenlove! When a man is a big money maker, like Elliot, he wants his wife pulling for him; but it's not to say they can't have their fun on the side. Not if they're a *team!*"

"You practise that?" he inquired.

"Oh, that's a different thing altogether. I'm in love with Irving and he is with me. We wouldn't *want* to sleep around. It's a matter of temperament. Now Elliot . . . Well, we don't think it's so important."

"You think sexual integrity isn't important?"

The girl looked at him gravely.

"A man I used to be fond of—before I met Irving—before I married my first husband—told me, if I couldn't keep my own secrets I needn't expect anyone else to keep them. But this isn't a secret, except to you, maybe! A man, or a girl, may wander off the reservation now and then, and nobody pins a medal on them for it; but if they keep together as a team, believing in the man's work and all, it's not important."

Mr. Spenlove sat in the shadows which had gathered around him, shadows tinged with the haze of cigar smoke. For some time he sat silent, resolving the words he had heard into some co-ordinated pattern. It was a strange sensation, this sudden impact of the girl's soft-spoken philosophy. It was not a new philosophy even to him. He had read countless books of the modern age and its modern menages, but he had never before heard anyone enunciate it, calmly and dispassionately, and believe in it as a matter of course. He had, compared with Terry and Irving, lived an unsophisticated, secluded, almost bucolic existence on the ocean. His colleagues, in their Brooklyn apartments, in their close-packed suburban villas in Bayside and Flushing, would have been stunned into scandalized silence by Terry's simple statement. They had been conditioned to accept certain astonishing features of modern life, but they retained their faith in hypocrisy. According to them, a fellow might go to a brothel in a foreign port, but he would never allow his wife the same privilege at home, nor would he dream of suggesting that she should approve of his behavior, supposing she heard of it. Such a wife, Mr. Spenlove knew, would be given a harsh name. He himself, while less naive, had not previously met this new, streamlined morality face to face.

"Well," he said, "this explains a lot of things that puzzled me."

"As how?" Terry said. She rose to take the coffee things into the kitchen.

"A lot of things about him. And about his wife."

Terry's head, leaning backward, appeared from behind the partition.

"He's a fine, generous man!" she said warmly. "Imagine! She left him and came to New York, and when he was ready to come to New York, she'd gone to Paris!"

Her brown head vanished again. Mr. Spenlove heard the gentle clatter of dishes being piled. Terry was quiet and gentle in all her movements, as though she were perfectly at ease and at home in her world. Or perhaps because she had discovered that unless she watched herself carefully she became less charming. She came in again and sat down.

"I don't suppose you ever heard about her and Caxton Derrick," she said.

"Yes, I have," he told her. "He was a poet and he committed suicide. I read about it in the papers. I read one of his books."

"That was the man she was in Paris with," Terry said, looking at her hands in a way she had. When Mr. Spenlove made no reply her glance flickered toward him obliquely for an instant, under her lashes.

"That's all over and done with," he said at length. "The man's dead. If what I heard about him is any way true the women with him might have been foolish. They weren't vicious."

"Sure. They were crazy, those people. But Caxton Derrick attracted a lot of women, and it had nothing to do with his being a homosexual. He could talk about poetry and art and all that. They say he was wonderful when he recited his own things. I have been told. I was never in that crowd. Too high for me! I wasn't talking about that at all, as a matter of fact. It was the drinking. I don't know quite how to explain it to you because you've seen her in such a different light in the country. Mother and child business. Misunderstood wife business. I can see"—she folded her hands and looked angelic for a moment—"I can see you're on her side. So maybe you wouldn't believe me if I told you."

She got up suddenly, went into the kitchen, and brought out a diminutive red watering can.

"I must give my flowers a drink," she said, dimpling. "I call this their cocktail hour."

Mr. Spenlove sat and watched her. Her attitude indicated that she suspected him of nothing except friendly interest. *I suppose it's my venerable appearance* he said to himself. *She has no suspicion!*

"How do you know I wouldn't believe you?" he called to her. She was a vague figure out on the terrace, bending over her boxes and tubs, in the shadow of the tall buildings.

"You'll find it pretty hard," she said in a gentle voice.

He waited. He knew that much anyhow, that if he waited she would tell him, and having to make the move herself, would tell it more truly. If he pretended it didn't matter to him, it would be more dependable.

As he told himself this, he felt he knew something about it already.

The watering can was empty at last, and her figure suddenly filled the opening of the window. She went into the kitchen and re-filled her can slowly at the sink. Slowly she passed out into the dusk. Bright rectangles in upper stories showed in the darker masses of brick, with occasional figures moving about the lighted rooms.

"Yes," she said, coming in and putting the can down somewhere. He heard her lighting a cigarette in the gloom and smelt the first fragrant puff before the paper began to burn. She came over and sat near him, facing the night, her left hand in her lap, her feet in the scarlet shoes, crossed. Her glance flickered several times in Mr. Spenlove's direction as she drew on the cigarette. "Of course, this is in confidence. You ought to be able to see Elliot's side of it too. And I'm sure *I* never had any desire to see her the way she was. I wouldn't wish my worst enemy . . ."

"You are telling me she was the worse for drink?" he said.

"The worse for . . ." She looked at him. "You think we—

Irving and I—make a fuss over anybody just getting tight? Worse for drink doesn't describe it. She was insensible! Irving brought her here."

"When was this?"

"The time you went to a party at Church Yard and heard them talking about her and you worrying because the hostess wasn't present. Irving found her, at Jock's Place."

"Who's Jock?"

"He has a bar. It used to be a speakeasy. It was the speakeasy where Caxton Derrick would drink a whole bottle of Cutty Sark at a sitting. Irving had been phoned, and went around on the chance. Jock took him in back and showed him. It was just as if she was dead! Irving had seen her that way before, but even he was scared. Jock thought she *was* dead. The funny thing was, the waiter who'd been serving her swore she'd only had a few drinks. He found her with her head on the table, glass upset."

"You sure she wasn't doped?" Mr. Spenlove said, sharply. "I've heard funny stories about those places in the United States."

"No. She'd been drinking all the evening in other joints. Well, Irving knew what to do. The job was, to put her into a taxi without people getting suspicious. It took four of them to lift her and hold her as if she was just sick. And he brought her here. I can tell you, getting her up these stairs was worse than a grand piano.

"We managed it at last. It was an awful thing to see a beautiful woman with her face in . . ."

"Oh, shut up!" Mr. Spenlove said, and rose abruptly. "This is very painful. I beg your pardon!"

"Shut up?" said Terry gently. "If you'd had the work I had to do you'd have found it painful. We did it for Elliot. Elliot's our friend, see. We're on his side."

"Oh, all right. So you played the Good Samaritan."

"The Good Samaritan was a real white man if he did what we did," Terry said in her quiet tones. And said no more.

"It's so incredible. I can't possibly believe you made it up," Mr. Spenlove muttered. "I've had vague premonitions. Well, now I know! Now I know!"

"Most people know," said Terry in a low tone.

She heard the man beside her say something to himself.

"What?" she said.

Before he could answer the door bell buzzed and she rose at once.

"There they are," she said. "Of course–" she stooped to bring her face close to his, her finger on her lips–"Irving wouldn't like it if he knew I'd said anything."

He did not reply save by a nod. The two men found him lighting a fresh cigar.

vii

Mr. Spenlove, in his shirt sleeves, his large hairy fore-arms on the pine table, read the latest entry in his scrap log.

In his hands, their backs tanned with sun and dark with hair even on the powerful fingers, the wooden penholder and the bowl of his pipe seemed out of scale.

What he had written seemed out of scale too, he reflected. It was a report of what he had heard in New York. He had added these words:

The personal equation cannot be solved by reference to third parties. Listening to that girl, Terry, in New York, was a mistake. No one is ever what words make them out to be. Never as vile, or as good. Everybody bears false witness.

He was waiting for Perdita in a mood that was neither complacent nor gloomy. The sound of her voice—on the telephone —*Can you endure me alone?*—was still echoing in his ears. *I've something to tell you!*—like a benediction.

He dipped the pen in the ink bottle and wrote:

Why does that girl give me a feeling of uneasiness and even alarm? Is it because she is so completely in harmony with Irving and Ducroy? They all belong to the same clot in the social bloodstream. They are fundamentally pluto-cratic, though that word is usually reserved for the wealthy.

It is not that they have no principles, but their principles are not operative in the realm of the spirit. They only function during banking hours.

They give me the impression of wearing masks over their minds, Terry and her Irving. These masks are extremely well made. They look exactly like real minds. But the real minds never appear. Perdita's is the only real mind I can see here. What are their real minds like, I wonder? Miss Penge's, for instance? Or Old Jim? He looks like Nietzsche, and his mind does not need much masking. Sonia's mask is delightful, but it is a mask; very much so. She condemns her mother because Perdita does not wear one at all.

He set the pen in the ink bottle and transferred the bottle to the corner cupboard. He was getting hungry. The problem of an assistant to set up the engine and gearing of his boat had been decided that morning. The builders were sending a young machinist who had a Ford of his own and who would live on the premises while working. The young machinist had inquired if he could bring his wife, and the office in Brooklyn had made the arrangements. It would be a few days yet before the engine would arrive, and those few days would be busy ones on the hull.

Besides the letter from Brooklyn there had been one from St. James. Mrs. Colwell had written announcing her desire to come over and see him in his sylvan retreat. She had even mentioned an early date.

He was aware of a certain pleasure that she had not forgotten him, but he had always maintained a guarded attitude toward such intimacies. He knew how easily wealthy people forgot their casual enthusiasm for those outside their own circle. He was wondering what she might think of his adventure with a woman. *At your age!* she would probably remark. She had urged him to marry. But the idea of marrying Perdita was simply inconceivable. It was grotesque, after the glimpses he had had of the complexities of matrimony among these people. He was more likely, indeed, to rescue her from marriage than to involve himself in it.

Mrs. Colwell, of course, would want to know, *Well, what are you doing?* She would get it all out of him in no time. And he felt that he would enjoy the inquisition. He would relish hearing what she would say when she had met Perdita. And how would Perdita regard Mrs. Colwell?

He got up suddenly and walked out into the porch. Behind the pleasure he felt—yes, really felt—at the thought of meeting Mrs. Colwell again, he detected a shyness at having her in his own place, so much less grand than her chauffeur's quarters at St. James; and behind that again, a grim reluctance to be drawn into the turmoil of human contacts. *Because of the masks!* he told himself, smiling. Those people at Elliot Ducroy's cocktail party, for instance. They were not sinister to each other, whatever he might think of them. No more sinister to each other than are reptiles and certain horrific insects. The effort necessary to appease them, to put them off their guard, to inspire them with confidence, so that he would be accepted as a tolerable minor acquisition on occasion, was too uncongenial.

No! He was no more eager for that than to be added to the antique collection of Miss Penge. . . .

He walked up and down. *What I want,* he told himself, *is still solitude, with her coming here for an hour! There's only that shadow, the shadow of what that girl told me. It might be pathological. And it might be exaggerated by that girl. Evidently she doesn't expect me ever to check what she said. She was gratifying some obscure feminine urge.*

He went in and got ready to go to dinner. Perdita had not come at once after all. He stopped in front of the corner cupboard and pulled his beard. To be consistent and the austere disciplinarian he enjoyed imagining himself, he should have it out with her when she came and announce his decision as a commander of their friendship. He must be allowed to issue orders. She must obey orders. And so on.

But he found this idea preposterous the moment it appeared. It conflicted with the shadowy but splendid conception he had formed of the woman and their possible relationship. He had no desire to have her chained up in the yard, as it were, or to assume responsibility for her eternal welfare. A woman passenger had once explained a furious battle she had been waging with her husband in their suite during a voyage, by saying, with a wan smile over her fourth side-car:

"He wants to dominate me and I won't let him."

Domination, Mr. Spenlove reflected, could be as intoxicating, apparently, as side-cars to certain temperaments, and probably far more degrading. Men who could not impose themselves upon their associates took it out on their wives. He had sailed with shipmasters like that, soft spoken, quiet men with cowed families.

He did not want to dominate anybody. There was something obscene to him about the idea, and the suggestion that marriage involved a man in it, either as a bully or a menial, was almost a nightmare to him.

He had written in his scrap log:

There is nothing in marriage that could possibly appeal to a man of my temperament, training and age. I asked Mrs. Sankey how she liked being married. (She had just remarked that it seemed "funny" to her, my living here all alone.) She did not take the question quite as I expected, considering the wretchedness of her domestic existence. She looked suddenly very pleased. "Why, Mister Spenlove! You aren't thinkin' of it, are you?" I said, "Would you say it was a good idea?" She said, "Sure! If at first you don't succeed, try, try again."

It was the longest speech she had made since she came here to work. She seems to believe it too. Even if she divorces that drunken husband she would at once marry again. But when I said she might be better off if she had her liberty, she shook her head violently without turning to look at me!

These people all talk and act as though in a trance. Only Perdita seems without delusions, and she does not discuss other people at all. Even the Saxon person has not been mentioned by her since that night we saw them.

She is pure delight. What a fool I would be to . . .

Mr. Spenlove had discovered that the words came more easily so long as he thought of Perdita. But he often let several days pass without putting down any comments. Often, again, he would write something that antedated most of his entries, or he would copy out a paragraph from a book he was reading which seemed to express his own thoughts better than any words of his own. But he was alert enough to admit, early in this journal of his, that if he copied out a thought it was not his own. Unless, he reflected, he had hammered it out himself, it was not his thought.

And even then, he added, *it may be that I have heard it, or read it, and forgotten it. All men are fishing in the same waters. I have only a short rod, a small hook and no fishing license.*

He would be a fool, he was convinced, to spoil everything by giving way to what he called sentiment. That was an intelligent resolution. If these modern people were evolving their peculiar ethic of the relations of the sexes, he had a right to steer his own course too. But he was aware of another and less noble motive. At any rate it was more selfish. It was due to his cautious reluctance to be legally responsible for another person's fortunes.

He was no zealot. He desired no "cure of souls," as the old phrase had it. His conception of freedom was realistic to the point of austerity. He had never belonged to any particular stratum of society by right of birth. Mrs. Colwell, calling him an Ishmael, was promptly contradicted. "I'm not an Ishmael.

Ishmael was a gypsy. His hand was against every man and every man's hand against him. Another thing: Ishmael had no idea of birth control. He had an immense concourse of descendants, flocks and herds of black sheep. You've forgotten your Old Testament history, Mrs. Colwell! The Lord made him very fruitful. Too fruitful, the anti-Semites would say. Now, I'm not in the least like that. I'm certainly no black sheep, dear lady."

So he was no outcast, but a dues-paying member of the bourgeois working class. He belonged to it by his upbringing as apprentice, improver, and artisan in London, and he preferred it to any other class on earth. It left his mind free to philosophize, and it had preserved him from the pallid servitude of the white-collar races to middle-class conventions.

There was another thing. He had had to tell Mrs. Colwell about that too. She had enjoyed charging him with a suppressed desire for that Rhea Candleby. "The Candleby creature," she called her. Mrs. Colwell having actually seen Rhea in the flesh, thought of her in that connection. Rhea was getting on in years now, down in Florida, embedded in the very sort of life Mr. Spenlove regarded with amused dislike—the life he saw in full flower along the shore below him. Mrs. Colwell probably envisaged someone like Rhea for a wife for him, a mature female embedded in an adequate cocoon of profitable real-estate mortgages and sound gilt-edged stocks. She only used Rhea as a symbol to tease him; but she was so saturated with the capitalism in which she lived that to her such a woman was the only eligible wife for a man like him.

He had told her, with a sudden rush of frankness, about Captain Macedoine's daughter. Not all of it. Not that Artemisia Macedoine's mother had been an octaroon of marvelous loveliness, or that Captain Macedoine himself had never been a captain, but was only called that in derision. Or that Artemisia had been a nursemaid and then the mistress of a rich Greek merchant. None of that. Only the essential fact that he, Mr. Spenlove, twenty years earlier, had been in love with her. It had been one of those passions which drain a man of all desire ever to love again. It had been the peak of his emotional existence, he told her, and believed it.

"Where was this?" Mrs. Colwell had inquired.

"In Salonika," he said, "and in one of the Greek islands of the Cyclades. I too have lived in Arcady."

It had been no Arcady, really. He nursed the popular illusion of those days, that there was no domestic happiness out of England. But he had never taken her home to England. She had died out there in Salonika. A crazy wounded soldier in the street fighting had fired at random in his agony, and the bullet had ricochetted from a stone wall into her heart. So she had died there, in the house on the hillside above Salonika, and he had carried her memory over the world.

"Devotion to an ideal," Mrs. Colwell had admitted. "But you don't mean to sacrifice . . ."

"No," he said. "I'm not suggesting I've been a celibate at any time. I'm only telling you of the greatest thing in my life. In one sense the only thing. It was complete—a marvelous experience. It was entirely selfless. I hadn't a thought of myself. The average man would say I was crazy to love such a girl. The average man is just that—average."

"And that affair . . ."

"It wasn't an 'affair,'" he reminded her. "It was never consummated. It was a young man's—a moderately young man's—splendid gesture. I was going to take her away from all the dirt and shame and sorrow she had suffered, and make her happy. A beautiful dream, such as only the young can have."

"Well," Mrs. Colwell had remarked, "it's to your credit; but you ought to marry, all the same, if you're going to stay on shore."

Now this had happened, capsizing his smug plans for "a serene, careful old age," as he put it satirically to himself. She hadn't taken the place of Artemisia because he was no longer the sentimentalist of those days. He did not believe Perdita, after her experience of marriage with Pagett and

Ducroy, wanted any more of it with anybody else. He didn't know what she wanted. That was one of the things he intended, since talking to that girl Terry, the common-law wife, to discover. What an expression! he thought. "I'm his common-law wife." Mr. Spenlove for some obscure reason, detested a phrase, a relationship, of which he knew nothing save on vague hearsay. It was a euphemism, in his opinion, for something not esteemed.

The great blaze in the sky beyond the river was declining. Tobermory crouched, somnolent, by the barn door. Mr. Spenlove wondered why she did not come. He would not admit it to himself, but he wanted her to say she was not going back to the house for dinner, that she would go out and dine with him. She came often enough, yet he could never convince himself that she would come on this occasion. He wanted to discuss his plans for putting his boat into the yacht-club basin when the time came; for erecting an awning framework outside the barn for the final work of installing the engine, finishing the cabin and painting the hull. It was incessantly in his thoughts, that boat. He had written, in his scrap log:

> *Of no importance apart from myself, it symbolizes my freedom. I have never, since I was an apprentice, done anything that was not to the order of the owners. This boat is my idea. I can destroy it, or alter it, or sell it, or use it, exactly as I please. I could go out and sink myself in it, and nobody can tell me I must not do it.*

It was in his thoughts now. The thought of his boat and the thought of Perdita coming into his life drugged him somewhat. He sat in his porch in the deepening twilight, reflecting upon his good luck. Never having made the extravagant demands upon life so fashionable among the younger generations, he thought some credit was due to his philosophy of intelligent individualism. He was unable to discern any part of his life pattern which had injured a single human soul.

He believed in what the older economists called "the rewards of abstinence." He believed in the theory of entropy applied to human happiness. It was like heat, and could be dissipated. There was only so much of it in the universe, he suspected, and in the course of aeons it would diminish. He believed that a life of strict regard for duty and integrity, for loyalty to his principles of conduct, entitled him to create his own private world.

But he was finding it was none too easy, now that he was away from the familiar landmarks. If he had, for instance, imagined himself being entangled with a woman, he would never have foreseen a girl like Perdita. He wasn't even entangled, in the vulgar sense. She made no demands on him at all. She was pure delight. He had been saying so ever since she came with Sonia, to see him. When she had shown him that extraordinary scene through his binoculars, her husband in the arms of Sydney Saxon, she had said she trusted him absolutely but she had not demanded his help. She wasn't that sort at all!

What sort was she, in the light of this story the girl in New York had told him? He had to find out her side of it. She could not retain any respect for him if he was afraid to ask. He was going to mention it this evening.

It was almost dark. She had not come. It was past his dinner time. He got up and went to the telephone. Perhaps she had gone home, not wishing to be late. He could then walk into Norbury to dinner. He called Elliot Ducroy's house.

The telephone at Church Yard was in a sort of cloak room by the front door, with an extension line to the pantry. Mr. Spenlove heard a slow, vague voice, which he suspected belonged to Louis, Sonia's friend, the sad houseman. No, said Louis, Meesiz Ducroy wasn't home yet. Was she expected? Mr. Spenlove inquired. There was no answer. Louis probably hadn't got that.

"Well, she said she would call, and she hasn't, so . . ."

As he set down the receiver the room was suddenly flooded

with the high-power glare of headlights coming up the drive. The shadows of everything in the room, silhouetted against the black wall, grew furiously and agitatedly smaller and sharper. There was a slight crash as a fender struck the stone well-curb, and the car stopped with the lights still on.

He stepped down into the yard, shading his eyes with one hand. He said gently, "Put out the lights!"

There was no answer. He recognized the high radiator, the flaring fenders, and the huge headlamps of the Virago. He stepped around and looked in behind the wind shield.

She was sitting with her shoulders pressed against the upholstery, her arms rigid and her hands clenched on either side of the big steering wheel. Her legs were rigid too, in the position she had held since striking the well-curb. Her feet held the pedals hard down. The engine was running, like a watch ticking, and the great car at intervals gave a slight shudder.

As he leaned over the leather-cushioned coaming of the door she smiled, and leaning forward, cut the ignition and the lights.

"What are you trying to do?" he said. He laid his hand on hers and opened the door. "What's the matter with you?"

Her head fell back against his shoulder and her eyes closed. He could see, by the faint radiance from the burnished instrument board, a tiny bubble at the corner of her mouth.

He put his arm around her shoulders and drew her to him. Then he became aware.

"So?" he muttered, and looked at her closely. Her head fell against his breast. *Well, here it is!* he thought. He bent down.

"Can't you come in and lie down a bit?" he said in a low tone.

There was no answer. She seemed quietly asleep, or unconscious, as though she had been drugged; or even dead.

"That's probably the size of it," he said aloud, following up his unuttered thoughts of drugs. He took her left hand from the wheel and lifted her, with a backward movement, out of the car.

"I'm quite the gallant hero," he said aloud, "rescuing the woman in the magic forest. *Sono il Cavaliere Errante!*" he said in her ear. He wondered if he could remember enough Italian to add another line, to rhyme. What about *pesante?* She was heavy like this!

He remembered, long ago, seeing in the Tate Gallery in London, Sir John Millais' painting of the Knight Errant releasing a nude woman with long golden hair, who was bound to a large birch tree. The contrast between the silver sheen of the Knight's armor and the voluptuous, pale, rose-tinted nakedness of the blonde captive had impressed the young mechanic as he studied it. Mr. Spenlove in those days had had an almost pathological dislike of unfinished stories. The Millais story was unfinished. What did that dark handsome Knight, with the long sharp nose and pointed chin, do when he had rescued the handsome, full-breasted wench whose tresses fell in a golden shower to her thighs? Where did he take her, and what were their precise relations when they were safe from the evil spirits of the wood? What was he thinking as he severed the cords? And who had bound her?

Mr. Spenlove remembered that period of his life, when ladies in captivity did not cross his path. Now he wondered if Millais would have been able to make anything of this business. He got the screen door open with his knee, carried her into the porch, and laid her down on the long swing seat. He fetched a cushion from a stool in the front room and put it under her head.

He had seen a lot of intoxication in his time, but this was much more literally toxic than anything in his seagoing experience. Women! He sat in a chair at the other end of the porch, reflecting. They were never at rest because they *were* women! Their viscera betrayed them when they tried to be men.

A few minutes more or less would not change the situation.

He had to think, not only of himself, but of her and of the world in which she lived. Apparently Louis, the sad major-domo, expected her home to dinner. Mr. Spenlove rose with a glance at the motionless shape on the swing seat, went in to the telephone.

"Mr. Spenlove speaking. Mrs. Ducroy is here now. She's just arrived."

There was no answer.

"You understand? Is Mr. Ducroy at home? Mrs. Ducroy is not very . . ."

"Meesta Ducroy, 'e's eatin' out."

"All right. Mrs. Ducroy's eating out too. Get that?"

He heard the telephone cluck, and he set down the receiver once more. He made a face over the cool way these menials took it on themselves to run things. But what else could you expect when their employers behaved like enchanted lunatics?

He stood at the door leading to the porch, trying to decide what to do. This stupor would pass eventually, he supposed. He went over and looked closely at the face he now knew so well and which he thought so marvelous when alive. It was dead now, he said to himself, frowning.

He stood up and gazed through the screen at the deepening dusk. It was now night. The sky was full of stars, and their light, together with the glare, like a luminous mist, from Norbury, made the darkness under his trees impenetrable.

Sir John Millais, he thought, with his Knight Errant, knew very little about modern women. *They* were not bound to trees in a dark wood! What a modern knight errant needed was not a sword to sever bonds but a coil of rope and a whip! Or perhaps a graduate degree in psycho-pathology!

They gratified his vanity, and there was a faintly sensuous tinge about such ideas; but they gave him no assistance in dealing with Perdita lying there. It was more to the purpose to see her, after all, as the prisoner of a very real Gorgon who was turning her, not to stone, but putting her into a dreadful, corpselike trance.

It was now night, and he had not eaten. There was food in the house, of course, but he wanted his dinner. He could not go away and leave her. Well, he could, if he were the ironic, completely emancipated intellectual man he often imagined himself. Faced with the problem, he found he could not. She had a hold on him. She made demands. Without premeditation and without forfeiting his strict loyalty, she had woven a net about his imagination and his desires. This was a challenge, as if she had known, in some sacredly secret fashion, what that girl in New York had told him about her, and was resolved to put him to the test, once and for all. Even if she had not known, that was what it amounted to. He had to make up his mind, not merely for this adventure but for the future, whether she could depend on him to take care of her, no matter what she did.

He sat down for a moment and thought, and he found he could not run away. He got up and went into the kitchen. He put on the kettle to make some strong coffee. While he was exploring in the icebox he felt a soft pressure against his legs. Tobermory, being black, was only a presence in the darkness. Here was another creature who had thrown a subtle noose over him, claiming comradeship and support!

There was cold beef and cheese and a bottle of beer. Tobermory, following deftly into the kitchen as the screen door swung, purred decorously and ran to the scraps of meat flung on the stone hearth. Mr. Spenlove cut himself a couple of sandwiches and broke out the beer. He carried them on a tin tray to the front of the house, and sat down in the darkness.

No, he told himself again, probably for the third time, he was no longer capable of leaving her to sleep it off and drive herself home. It was plain now that he had to take care of her. He had underestimated the immense void made in his life by leaving the sea. He had been fooled by the ease with which he had sloughed off the casual, negligible acquaintances he had made during voyages, the friendships with passengers which often ripened so rapidly and went rotten with even greater speed! What he had been depending on, all the time, had been the *ship,* the strong ligament of his life. Now that was severed he had to have something to take its place. He had to have something to be responsible for. That was the penalty of a well-spent life.

He got up to grope for a cigar. He did not want to put on the lights while she was lying out there. It was symbolic of his uncertainty of mind at this moment. He didn't like the look of things at all. But when he tried to define what it was he wanted, he could not say.

Ducroy, of course, was the man in theory who ought to be in command. In theory! Mr. Ducroy, according to the laconic major-domo Louis, was "eatin' out." That meant he was probably either across the water at Sydney Saxon's place or with Sydney Saxon in some roadhouse. She had a telephone. How would it affect the *mores* of this region if he called Ducroy there, and told him to come and carry his wife home?

It seemed to be almost as natural as breathing for people to burst into each other's privacies at all hours. *Would you like to send us a subscription? Would you like to have two tickets? Would you be interested in the exciting new menus now serving at the Whiffletree Tavern? The Wharfinger's Summah Theatah wants you to know their production of She Stoops to Conquah—can you heah me?* Often he had come from the barn, called by Mrs. Sankey, or had hurried, towel in hand, from a shower, to answer these blandly imbecile questions uttered by the thrilling, extravagantly articulated voices of local sirens. They were all beating a path to his door, to sell him a mouse trap he didn't want.

On the other hand he could call the taxi-man, drowsing in his little glass office at Norbury station. That would end the matter, probably.

He could not bear to think of the matter ending. Outwardly and to the careless beholder, Sonia and Sonia's mother had been merely two amusing casual callers. In fact they were becoming the substitute for the life-long preoccupation he had lost when he came on shore for good. That sense of loss, which had been almost a sense of fear, in his heart those first few weeks he now knew for what it was. Since he had known Perdita, had gone places with her to dinner, had walked with her down on the shore that night, had had her warm vital presence in his house, the sense of loss was gone.

He sat smoking, an aromatic haze around him, waiting for her to rouse. He had set a coffee pot to boil. Coffee would help, possibly, he thought vaguely. He was unfamiliar with the exact methods of recovery now in vogue, but coffee might help, he thought.

He had never foreseen this sort of thing when he came to live in what he sometimes called Arcady. No doubt, in the original Arcady, men discovered nymphs and goddesses under the vines, with purple-stainéd mouths. Perhaps he had a number of foolish misconceptions to get rid of before he could make the most of American life.

Misconceptions of himself too, he suspected. It was impossible, he was aware, for him to feel as he thought he ought to feel, about women. Instead of being realistic and dispassionately ironical, he was actually romantic about them. He could be as satirical as he liked over the *Cavaliere Errante*, but the reason why he did not telephone the taxi-man at once to take Perdita home was simply that he did not believe Elliot Ducroy's house was her home any more. He did not want anyone in the world to see her like this, moreover. The idea of taking the taxi-man—or anyone—into his confidence, was revolting. So was the idea of her being exposed to her own menials.

Now, as the event took on perspective, he could not endure sharing a knowledge of it with others, which was why he resented Terry Florence, of all people, knowing so much. As regards himself he had an extraordinary exaltation of spirit. It had a sensual pagan significance for him, as though he were in the midst of Dionysian mysteries.

He went out to make the coffee. The old cat, waiting at the kitchen door, vanished on his night hunting. While the coffee dripped Mr. Spenlove went out into the yard, where the fence Old Jim had been building showed white against the foliage. Over the rise of land toward Church Yard he could see the blaze of a yet invisible moon rising. The fireflies were intensely brilliant in the shadows under the trees. The darkness sparkled with them, as though it was full of minute electrical charges.

Animals have sense! he thought. *They never explain.* The reflection struck him at once as spurious and he smiled, because spurious philosophical reflections had long been a native product. He remembered Ralph Waldo Trine and Elbert Hubbard when he had first visited the seaports of America, and their subsequent tremendous vogue. It was contagious, he had discovered. Every newspaper had a midget Trine or Hubbard cackling in a syndicated corner. He felt ashamed because the origin of such sententious wisecrackings was fear and intellectual anaemia. One had to guard against it all the time while on shore!

Well, he did. The story of St. Anthony and his temptation took on a new significance. St. Anthony had an easy time of it, compared with an intelligent recluse in America. A man never knew who would call him up, using all her arts to sell him something, infecting his mind with a blend of synthetically sexual excitement and social cowardice.

Perdita did not do that. That simple fact obliterated everything Terry Florence and her kind might say about Perdita. They—the Terrys—did not dream how profound was his suspicion of their genuineness, his contempt for their picayune ideals and their smug acceptance of spurious evasions.

Perdita was not like that. She had no evasions and nothing spurious either. He exulted in the splendor of her personality. The very fact that those lacquered and brittle people at the cocktail party could speak of her with venomous dislike was to her advantage, in his eyes. As for Terry and her Irving, they would have let her die in the street, if she hadn't been Elliot Ducroy's wife. That was their ethic, and it was the measure of their intelligence too. They were on his side.

He carried the tray with the coffee pot carefully into the front porch. As his eyes grew accustomed to the darkness he saw that the swing seat was empty. She was not there.

He looked to see if the car had moved. It was untouched. He hurried out to it, thinking she had made a sudden decision. He saw then a light upstairs, in the bathroom. He returned to the porch and resumed his cigar, waiting for her to come down. He switched on the lamp at the foot of the stairs. That she should use his house as her own filled him with delight. He went downstairs to the cellar and shook up the small furnace that heated the water supply. The reservoir was only warm. So she was having a bath. Mrs. Sankey always left it boiling hot. He was very pleased as he went up, and was about to pour himself some coffee when the telephone rang.

"Hello! Spenlove? Mr. Ducroy speaking. Louis says my wife didn't come home to dinner. Says you called him."

"I told him she was here."

"Is she all right? Louis don't talk very plain on the phone."

"She's all right," Mr. Spenlove said, in a low tone.

"Okay. I guess I'll be late back."

"Don't worry," Mr. Spenlove said.

"Thanks a lot. I appreciate it."

Mr. Spenlove said distinctly, "Do you want to speak to her?"

"Wall!" the midwest ejaculation was like an explosion in the receiver. "Maybe you can take care of it . . ."

"You want to leave your number, so she can call you?"

"No. Say, I'll drop in tomorrow. Got an engagement . . . Remember Irving? My agent? Got an engagement with him."

He set the telephone down on its pine shelf and stood at

the foot of the stair. What did that conversation mean, unless it was a quittance, an abdication? What had Elliot Ducroy got to explain, except that he was running off and leaving his job to a stranger? He seemed excited. Mr. Spenlove tried to imagine him, exalted by his continued success, which was snowballing in a way that had nothing to do with his present exertions; and by the affair with Sydney Saxon. With Irving, who no doubt had Terry with him, Elliot Ducroy would be in an exalted condition.

There was nothing unique about his behavior, to an outsider. Men of ability, Mr. Spenlove was aware, were the surest victims of such illusions. They were the most easily deceived by success, and they gave themselves the credit due to their good fortune. They were always able to explain their defects in terms of generosity.

In the few moments of absolute silence that followed his conversation with Perdita's husband, Mr. Spenlove recalled, with the speed of light, other successful men he had known, shipmasters and naval officers, who had behaved in exactly the same way in essentials. Vanity and pride were their companions by day and by night. This man was financially in another class. He was extraordinarily successful, and thereby all the more vulnerable. But he was in their category.

As he thought it out, Mr. Spenlove recovered his own poise. He had been upset in spite of himself. He stood at the foot of the stair, waiting. Then he decided to go up and call her.

There was a crack of light under the door. He saw there were cracks in the door itself where the tongued and grooved boards had warped, which he had not noticed. He would have to attend to that. He stood in a neutral position and knocked.

"All right?"

He heard a splash as she said, "I'm perfectly all right now. I'll be down in a minute."

"I've made some coffee."

"Splendid! I'll come."

"Want a bathrobe? I'll leave one outside the door. And an extra towel."

"You think of everything, my dear! What time is it?"

"Half-past nine. Had any dinner?"

"No."

As he went down he decided to say nothing at all. The one thing a woman in such a situation would never forgive was stupidity. To know, yet never allude to it; to support and strive with her; to make her feel he would never let her down, no matter what she did—that would be his policy.

He tried to explain it—her clarity of soul. Why was she so immensely superior, apart from the beauty of her physical being, her *élan,* to respectable females like Miss Penge and clever hetairai like that Sydney Saxon? That was all Sydney was, of course, he decided, not knowing her. You had to grant her cleverness if she made the money Terry Florence said, which was probably exaggerated forty percent. And to enslave Elliot Ducroy—was that cleverness? It would pass for ability in the ranks of high-class hetairai, those who embraced their profession as brilliant and wealthy amateurs take up the arts. The point was, Perdita had none of that cleverness. She was so completely alien to them she might be—and probably was—a different species. He almost said, a different sex.

She came down carrying her shoes in her hand, his bathrobe over her slip and stockings, and stood before him, dark shadows under her eyes, her lips pale yet smiling, her glance without fear or challenge.

"All right now?" he said. He moved the table with the coffee tray to stand near her chair.

"All right now." She sat with her hands folded, her body inclined a little toward him, as he poured two cups.

"It's still hot. I didn't know how long you'd be. Bath all right?"

"Yes. I had a soak. Best thing for a soak is another soak." She did not laugh; merely shrugged her shoulders and with a faint shudder accepted the coffee. Then, as she stirred it, she looked up at him.

"The telephone. I heard you . . . Was it . . ."

He nodded.

"Hm."

She went stirring abstractedly.

"Everything's all right," he said, "except that you must be hungry."

She shook her head.

"I wish you were right," she said. "But that's the least of my troubles."

"Well?"

"I can't go back there. I can't go to that house again."

Her voice was steady, dry and full of pluck. She drank half the coffee and set down the cup. Holding her knee she contemplated the night.

"What'll you do?"

She shrugged and then seemed to remember something. She leaned forward and looked out at the car. She got up and gazed steadily until she made out the sheen of the metal in the darkness. She turned to him with an expression of perplexity.

"Did I drive in here? I thought . . ." She looked out again, frowning. "Hm! . . . Damn!" She sat down again.

"You bumped the well," he said.

"I don't mean that. I can't *remember!* I thought you came into Norbury and brought me back. It seems you didn't. I must have come in here–subconsciously."

"Never mind."

"No damage?"

"Only the fender."

She whistled softly and made no further comment. She finished the coffee and held out the cup for more. She seemed to have forgotten the car for more important problems.

"Not going back!" she said again suddenly. She sat with

her chin on her hand. He nodded. She turned to him slightly and went on:

"We had a row," she said in a low tone. "He took a new line and I couldn't stick it. I said I was leaving definitely and told him why. He said I couldn't keep myself. He made comparisons. I didn't mind him sleeping with that fat little bitch over there. I suppose she's his type. I didn't mind that. It was comparing me with her. He's got a new word—economic. She's my economic superior. You can have economic comradeship with a woman who earns a fortune. Economic! Who's got the economic? He says, 'What can you do if you quit?' I said, 'I can give you and the Saxon comrade a punch on the nose.' "

She pressed her hands between her knees and looked down at them.

"Do advise me! I lost my temper. I was furious. He's so simple in some ways! He honestly is mad about that woman. She's hypnotized him, I think. So I can't go back. I thought it was a temporary affinity. Writers have them like measles. This is serious. She's *absorbing* him! What must you think of me? After a frightful row I drove into Norbury and had a lot of drinks at the Inn. I was so excited I don't know what I was doing. Did I faint? I don't remember driving back! No . . !"

"I'd advise you to have some dinner. I've only cold stuff here. You hit the fender. Go and look at it."

"All right. Tell me what to do and I'll do it," she said in a low tone. She rose obediently to go out to the car and he caught her strongly in his arms.

"Yes!" she said, desperately holding to him. They stood for some seconds, silent, molded together in half darkness of the porch. "Yes! I want to, so much! There! There!" He held her a moment longer, the formidable barricades he had built up through the years between himself and the world crumbling away. He held her long enough to hear her say, in a resonant whisper, "You are sweet. . . . I'll be good. You didn't reproach . . . There!"

She drew the bathrobe about her with unconscious grace

and went out to the car. He saw her get in, and then the lights came on. The engine gave a faint sighing sound; the beam of the lights swung sharply as she backed toward the barn. She switched them off and got out of the car. He saw her examining the well, which had its flat wooden cover askew.

"Marvelous luck," she said, as she came in holding her bag. "Fender bent a bit; that's all." She poured some more coffee and drank it down without milk or sugar. "I'll put on my clothes."

She stood for a moment one foot on the stair, looking around the severe little room, and then ascended, holding up the bathrobe like a skirt, to avoid stepping on it.

He heard her moving about upstairs. The sound filled him with vague pride and satisfaction. All the same, what was she to do now? Tomorrow was another day. What was she to do?

He heard her coming down, heard the clip-clop of her high-heeled pumps on the stairs. He put on his coat and took a couple of cigars from the box. His first impulse, to ask her again what she was going to do, he saw at once to be clumsy and crude.

They went out to the car. She took his arm with a gesture he already knew and loved. As he opened the door she said, in a low tone, as though someone might overhear her:

"I say, I do wish you would drive! You can take the wheel when we are out on the turnpike. It's wide and straight for two miles, so you can get in the way of it. You could, couldn't you?"

"All right," he said. "Where do we go for dinner?"

"Do you remember the first time we had dinner together? That's where I'd like to go tonight. They keep open for late customers, late suppers and dancing and that sort of thing. It's awfully late now."

She clutched his hand tightly as they sat together in the darkness. There was a touch of excitement in her voice that made it hoarse and mysterious to him. She leaned close to him urging him.

"I do so want you to drive!" she said huskily and with passion. "It means a lot to me, really it does. You will, won't you? Not much traffic now."

"You mean, on the way back?" he said.

"Yes, I want to come back with you," she said. "That means a lot too." She held to his arm as though for safety. "I'll know, my dear, where I am then. I made up my mind just now, in the house. Your house."

"You will come back and stay in my house?" he said. She sat looking straight ahead in the darkness for a moment.

"Yes," she said. "That's what I want."

PART TWO

What Led Up to It

i

ELLIOT DUCROY was being interviewed for a motion-picture magazine soon after his arrival in Hollywood, when he had what he called a flash.

Louis had just served the interviewer an old-fashioned cocktail. She was a bit old-fashioned herself, Elliot observed, a queer, tiny, nervous, black-eyed creature who lay back, almost invisible in a big chair and smoked furiously through a long white cigarette holder.

"Mr. Ducroy, you must have *some* faith!" she protested. He had waved away Numerology, Christian Science, Yoga, Astrology and Rosicrucianism. When she learned the day and hour of his birth and had consulted a battered little book in her bag she said his success was obviously due to the stars.

"Your Jupiter is in Taurus, now, so it's in conjunction," she told him gravely. She was obviously sincere. He said nothing to spoil it.

"I'm a writer too," she went on rapidly. "I wish you'd run through a manuscript of mine. Would you help poor little me?"

"A script?" he said.

"No, a novel," she said. His heart sank. He had heard of men who were brutal to this sort of interviewer and envied them. "It's about a star who's lost her mascot and can't act until she has found it. It had been stolen, you see. She has all these adventures searching for the thief."

"Is the thief another star?"

"How did you know?" she wailed.

"Well, it might have been a jealous dresser, or a crazy doorman."

"But how did you *know?*" she insisted. She looked imploring.

"I'm a seventh son of a seventh son," he told her.

It was then she said he must have *some* faith, and he had the flash.

"I've got a mascot," he said. "Only the mascot doesn't know he's a mascot. If he did it would break the spell."

"Who?" she said breathlessly, leaning forward. Her black, damson-like eyes were very bright. Elliot Ducroy thought she was probably a mild T.B.

"My houseman," he said. "The one who brought the drink. It was when I found him that I began to sell good. Yes, I guess Louis is my mascot, all right."

It wasn't a bad article.

It wasn't such a crazy idea after all, either, when he came to think of it. A year earlier, after eighteen months of free-lance work on short stories for the slicks (with a featured serial in a pulp) he had felt so stale and washed up he decided on a trip abroad. He had not had a vacation since the Great War. His wife, Myra, had gone back to Ohio, where the hundred and fifty a month he gave her went three times as far as in New York and where she was thirteen times happier. He himself had been living frugally in a two-room apartment on West Fiftieth Street. He had several thousand dollars in the bank and editors were beginning to ask for more underworld stuff.

When the interviewer inquired where he had obtained his knowledge of the underworld he had told her:

"The same way H. G. Wells got to know about Mars, and Rudyard Kipling learned about the jungle."

It was a fact his specializing in gang wars and crime had been largely accident. The stories had caught on. It was because he had done a series of six stories about a character named Gentleman Church and had sold the first serial rights for three thousand, that he decided to travel. No *Normandie* stuff for him, of course. He took a round-trip ticket on a Red Star cabin liner to Paris and London. Coming home on the old *Gothland* he had met Louis, his dining-room waiter.

Something in the saturnine sallow features, seen foreshortened above his own shoulder, as well as the stealthy precision and silent speed of the man's work, attracted him. Louis was without conventional charm as an attendant. He was taciturn because of his limited English. He preferred freighters to liners and had been a sailor as well as a messman, for he liked the sea. He had gone to sea in the first place because wages as a cook in a restaurant had not been very large. There were, moreover, no tips.

He had tips on the liner. His services were so dexterous that many of his patrons did not notice them, but they tipped him. When he received a bill he could make it vanish as if he were a conjurer. In fact he had a number of conjuring tricks, and a dry, unpretentious humor.

Elliot Ducroy, slipping him a ten-dollar bill, asked him if he would be open to take a job as a butler. Would he buttle for twenty-five dollars a week and all found? He gave Louis a card with a telephone number penciled on the corner.

Louis was a Belgian, a Walloon. He went back to Antwerp and got a passport, and then the American consul in Arlon, where he was reared, visaed it. Then Louis returned to Antwerp and worked until there was a vacancy in the Belgian quota.

When Elliot Ducroy returned from this voyage the Gentleman Church boom had begun. He had a number of stories, already written or drafted, which he remodeled to fit the series. The saturnine features of Louis he used for the leading character, who was a sort of supreme gangster of all gangs, an intellectual recluse with a secret passion for regenerating the world by means of his power over evil doers.

There was something hieratic in the demeanor of Louis, as though he were a skeptical priest offering sacrifices to gods in whom he did not quite believe. "Like a parson who had committed a crime," Elliot Ducroy had noted. It was a face into which one could read the remorse for tragic follies, the ravages wrought by deep sorrow and the melancholy of lost illusions. An ideal face, in fact, for the character Gentleman Church.

Louis was unaware of this conception of him. He did not know—and it was irrelevant to a man like Louis—that he was the "original" of Gentleman Church, the money-making master criminal character whose sardonic and deeply lined features were becoming as famous as Sherlock Holmes or Mutt and Jeff.

The comparison had been made by a reviewer in the Middle West when Elliot Ducroy's first volume of short stories appeared. The book contained twenty stories which had earned in first, second, and foreign serial rights about two thousand dollars each. Four of them had been bought for the screen, netting another ten thousand.

Elliot Ducroy had been mildly surprised at the calmness of the book reviewers when *Put 'em Up!* had burst upon them. The size of his checks from magazines, the flamboyant display of his name on covers and outside the newsdealers' stands, the honeyed letters from script editors in Hollywood and the requests from the compilers of anthologies to include one of his stories (without remuneration) had warped his perspective. With the surface of his mind he had been half humorously expecting to be accepted as a new Conan Doyle or O. Henry. When *Put 'em Up!* sold exactly 2742 copies in six months, which netted him in royalties less than a third of his latest price for one magazine story, he was surprised. He thought there had been an error in the publisher's office. There had been no error. It was, from the publisher's viewpoint, not at all bad for a first book.

Elliot Ducroy had accepted the verdict, though he wondered privately how the authors of books made a living. He wrote three stories during the following month at prices which salved any wounds in his pride. In fact those wounds were not deep, or vital. Story writing for the big magazines was his business, and he enjoyed his business. He had merely mistaken it for something else out of inexperience. He was a craftsman, not a thinker, and there were many things about his own trade which puzzled him at times. It was easier to ignore the deep problems and get ahead in his own line of work. He cultivated a faintly ironic pose toward what he called high-brow stuff in those days, a pose that was like a protective shell under which his real ego hardened. After all, he concluded, there was something pathetic about those complicated books which secured lavish, classy reviews, yet which netted their authors a mere chicken-feed of a living. There was something wrong with this argument, he knew, yet he could never make up his mind what. It was this permanent perplexity which had caused the vertical crease to form in his forehead, as though he were embittered.

He was not embittered. He was not even jealous. The rewards and the excitements of his business kept him from brooding upon the possible losses he had incurred by not "boning up on the art of the novel," as he expressed it. Sometimes it seemed to him, when he had done an especially good job, finishing a story with a bang like an explosion in the reader's brain, he suspected he knew something about "real art." He did not give way to this sort of dreaming very often. He enjoyed picturing himself as a sort of Hebrew slave in Egypt toiling to build a pyramid, making bricks without straw while the circulation manager, a swart Egyptian with a whip, made it coil around his limbs and drove him to incredible exertions to make a sensational finish.

There had been a time, after the rate for one of his stories had been raised to a thousand dollars, during which Elliot Ducroy had played with the country-gentleman fantasy. He had the idea of importing an English butler. He realized he was much more comfortable with Louis. An English butler would have kept him in his place as a vulgar rich American.

Louis was apparently unaware of either social or financial distinctions. He was silently, mysteriously, efficient, and continuously sad and taciturn. He neither saw nor heard anything, so far as a stranger could discern. He was like some harassed poor relation moving around in his black alpaca or white linen coat.

Out on the Coast Louis refused to leave his benefactor. Attempts were made to lure him away to the Beverly Hills seraglios and the palaces of the minor movie moguls, who were always having trouble with their help. Louis remained with Elliot Ducroy. He preferred the known to the unknown, and he had no woman interfering with his arrangements.

He hoped there would never be another Mrs. Ducroy. His professional feelings were exacerbated by the amateurish clumsiness which women revealed in domestic matters. They were all right, tolerable in an imperfect world, as subordinates. In command of an establishment, compared with the chief stewards who had taught him his business, the chefs who had shown him how to cook, they were incompetent nuisances.

He was perfectly happy looking after the bachelor quarters Elliot Ducroy had rented, a bungalow half way up a precipitous canyon road. It was built, in the lavish, theatrical, Californian style, on stilts on the slope. The verandah faced the sea and gave the observer the feeling that he was looking down from an airship. There was a garden at the back and Louis, who suffered from vertigo, kept his eyes on his work if he had to go into the verandah. His own quarters were cut out of the rock, like the garage.

Elliot Ducroy lived in this place, rattling away on three typewriters alternately, sometimes speaking into a dictograph, sometimes pacing up and down the long verandah and scowling at the incredible beauty of the valley's vista. Sometimes he would drive away and be gone all day and all night. Sometimes he had a party, during which many trays of drinks were ordered and some of the guests became intoxicated. But this was a rare event.

Elliot Ducroy was not enamored of the work he was doing. He would have preferred to write what he called "straight fiction." Editors were eager for more Gentleman Church stories, but the vogue had reached Hollywood, and Elliot Ducroy was a businessman. He regarded himself as a manufacturer of a certain product. He was fond of emphasizing the not surprising fact that he had been a newspaperman. He believed, he once told an interviewer, who happened by chance to be a newspaperman, that fiction was a branch of journalism, that the training a man received on a newspaper was the foundation of success in literature. Elliot Ducroy convinced himself this was true and, as no one ever contradicted him, the conviction became part of his philosophy. There is nothing more soothing for the successful than the assumption that their success is part of the broad intellectual movement of the ages, something integral with Walter Pater and Honoré de Balzac. Not that Elliot Ducroy wished to suggest that his fiction was highbrow. On the contrary, he pointed out to the interviewer, Shakespeare and Homer wrote thrillers, didn't they? The object of writing—his object anyway—was not to make people gloomy. It was to make them brave, make them forget their own drab lives for a while, inspire them to go on. The great thing in writing, he opined, was to be sincere.

For a man without experience of being interviewed, it was a success. Editorials in California and Florida quoted Elliot Ducroy's simple creed (To thine own self be true) with approval. It harmonized with their own belief, that the dividing line between newspaper work and the classics was largely imaginary.

He was entirely businesslike in his attitude toward his employers in the motion-picture industry. "Why sure!" he said to another newspaperman who was collaborating in a story. "I suppose when I've made a bit I'll blast Hollywood like all the rest of 'em. Just now, I'm singin' for my supper."

He continued to sing and Louis kept his bungalow, stuck like an eagle's nest on the steep mountainside, in good shape. And then the whole quiet tenor of their monastic lives was shattered by Elliot Ducroy meeting Perdita Pagett, who had been sitting in the waiting room of the casting director as Ducroy came rushing in, his hands full of papers and photographs, for a conference.

Perhaps the deciding factor had not been Perdita so much as Sonia. Sonia had been what she called "little" then. She had been sitting on the rug at her mother's feet, her page-boy bob resting against Perdita's knee. She had been gazing thoughtfully into space, unaware of the people swishing and rustling around her. Elliot Ducroy had stopped in his tracks to look at her. And then for a moment, before he turned the door knob and passed in, he loooked at Perdita.

The costume director, a thin, intelligent woman in rimless pince-nez, was showing some designs. To Elliot Ducroy there was nothing incongruous in the casting director selecting an actress to go with a certain décor. He accepted the crazy structure of picture making as he accepted the California climate, carrying an overcoat through a landscape of tropical verdure to guard against chill. He looked at the designs which were to be draped around the lithe slinky form of the adventuress in a Gentleman Church story with an Anglo-Indian setting and thought of the fair girl with the short nose and angry eyes in the waiting room.

"Who is she?" he asked the costume director, who looked at the names on a pad on the desk of the casting director.

"Nothing," she said. "An extra. She comes here . . ." She shrugged.

"What is she?"

"English. Starch. You'd be surprised. You'd think she was Ellen Terry or something. Just a not-so-good extra."

Elliot Ducroy, like many American businessmen, was able to combine a suspicious contempt for the British with an almost romantic weakness for certain features of English life. It was almost as if he had a subconscious conviction that those features were in the wrong hands. He liked English clothes, and although, with many of his countrymen, he believed all Englishwomen had big feet, red faces and ugly teeth, he had cherished a boyish admiration for "The English type." Like the English butler, the Englishwoman at her patrician best was something he wanted as he might want an Isotta Fraschini, an Hispano Suiza, and a Sulka house suit. They were symbols of success.

Perdita Pagett and the little Sonia, sitting in a Pacific-Electric trolley, roaring along the Boulevard to Santa Monica, where they lived in a tiny bungalow made of what Perdita called "pink mud," were unaware of being followed. At that time Elliot Ducroy owned a Stutz convertible which could out distance any Pacific-Electric street train, and he was skimming along just behind them, on a romantic quest.

It was romantic because the time he had spent in Hollywood had conditioned Elliot Ducroy to the standardized loveliness of the women. Glancing around him in the Brown Derby at lunch time they all seemed turned out of the same factory, as if there were in America huge plants with transmission belts, off which beautiful human models, lacquered and enameled and chrome plated, came under their own power and were shipped to Hollywood. There seemed no difference between a made-up star and a made-up orangeade girl at the road side. They all had beautiful bodies and superb eyes, and they were all a manufactured product. He had come to accept them, like the architecture and the palm trees, as integral with the landscape.

Perdita, with Sonia at her feet, had flashed on his brain as something entirely and brilliantly different. It was because she was so different, so completely unsuitable to the screen, that he was attracted, he was enthralled. His imagination had been captured by the posing of the mother and child, which had been unstudied, unintentional. Sonia was then a very thoughtful little morsel, gravely contemplating the California scene while her mother seemed oblivious of it. Perdita's indignant gaze was fixed on something in the distance as she sat in the roaring, rocking trolley car.

When the Stutz drew up in front of the shabby pink bungalow and Elliot Ducroy pressed the bell, which did not ring, Sonia opened the door. Her smile gave him the lead he required.

She said "Mummy, it's a man from the studio," and Perdita said, from the tiny kitchen:

"Tell him to go to hell, ducky."

She was able to explain after he had refused to go. She liked him because he told her flatly she was not screen material at all. He had not come to give her a role.

"I know I can't act," she said as she sat studying him. He was exactly the lean-jawed American type she had heard of so often and imagined to be the original "vanishing American."

"You don't photograph," he said. Then he told her he came, not to make passes or get her on a payroll, "which would be helping you to get money by false pretenses," but to have the pleasure of her acquaintance.

"But what's the matter with me?" she inquired.

"You're a lady, not a screen actress," he said. "I suppose you're broke."

"I suppose you've done this so often you are an expert," she suggested.

He let her fight him, and counted on Sonia to pull him through. He was in a fury of emotion. He was inflated with an enormous vanity, for it was an accepted canon of the Hollywood creed of those days that Englishwomen were cold and proud and generally inaccessible. His erratic movements plunged Louis into a profound perplexity until the stage was reached when Perdita and Sonia came to dinner.

Perdita sat in the verandah that seemed to be hanging in mid-air, and looked out over the canyon without speaking.

At first Elliot Ducroy, who had been in the pantry with Louis, giving orders about drinks, imagined that she was stunned by the view. She was struggling with her own confused emotions. Her recent experience had been a severe strain on her. It had been a magnificent gesture, leaving her husband and taking Sonia with her, but it was a gesture which impressed Mr. Pagett as merely unwise for her and a wonderful bit of luck for himself. And it had depended, far more than Perdita had quite imagined, on money from home. And money from home no longer came.

It had arrived; but her husband had found it extremely handy. Well, there was no use in going over all that again. What occupied her mind now, as she sat in that high place looking down the canyon at the queer black derricks beyond the house roofs in the valley, was the nature of the fortune that had befallen her. Elliot Ducroy had left her in no doubt, even at the end of their first meeting, that he wanted her. Wanted her to get a divorce and marry him. And Sonia, who was at that moment in the kitchen with Louis, liked him.

That, as she sat there, was uppermost in her mind, not the scenery. Oh, no, not the scenery! She had never told anyone yet, and perhaps it was colored by the discovery, out there, that Archie Pagett was an outsider in spite of his swank and polish; but to her California was not beautiful at all. It was nightmarish and touched by madness even in the daytime. Now that she was so far away from the English countryside, it seemed marvelous. She kept her mind sealed from the sights and sounds of Hollywood, her senses immobilized, waiting for deliverance.

So she meditated, oblivious of the view, oblivious even of the silent Louis at her elbow offering perfectly cooked food, and eventually she capitulated. Yes, and for Sonia's sake, again, yes!

Louis, as a rule not hospitable toward strangers in his kitchen, enjoyed having Sonia around. He moved about his work with an added alertness and good humor at such times.

She was English, which for men of his race bore a special connotation. He was, in a mildly religious sense, in love with her. She told him many things she withheld from the rest of the world. She would sit on a stool in the pantry, or on the back porch, and converse. Louis did most of his work on his feet, a habit he had contracted while at sea.

Sometimes his austere, sallow features would undergo a peculiar convulsion, when she made one of her naive remarks. As when she said, munching a cookie, "I'm glad Elliot's going to marry Mummy 'cause you're my best friend."

She grew out of those confessions, but their friendship continued. Later, when the inevitable readjustments between Elliot and Perdita took place, the two became closer friends. When her mother took a small apartment downtown, coming to the bungalow once or twice a week, Sonia explained to Louis that "Elliot needs absolute quiet for his work." She developed a quaint habit of using long words. She said a kitten at the apartment became "seriously indisposed" and "had to be destroyed." It was not long before she learned how to get off the Sunset Boulevard trolley at Gardner Junction by herself and trot up the canyon road to visit the bungalow.

It was true that Elliot Ducroy worked better alone. "I suppose," Sonia said gravely to Louis in the pantry, "I suppose that's why *you* haven't ever married, isn't it, Louis?"

Louis was not clear about it. He felt it was unimportant. He now had Sonia and her mother to think about. And Mr. Ducroy was saying that if his contract was not renewed he would go back to New York.

This was the situation a year after the marriage. Perdita had a tendency to ignore the social life of the picture community. It was difficult for her to appreciate the importance and prestige of people whom Ducroy called, in private, the moguls. She did not read the studio gossip and formed no friendships with the artists. She made no concessions to their terrific vanity, which had been fed and even gorged by publicity and studio sycophants. She was even unimpressed when other script writers and famous novelists and playwrights came to the bungalow on Sundays.

"I don't care for myself so much," he pointed out to her. "It's for you. I'm thinking about you. You miss a lot. These people are the top of the heap. They're cultured people. They've got a very cultured community out here. Why don't you like them?"

"I just don't," she said. "However, I'll do what you suggest. Yes, I'll be nice to them. But I won't kiss! These men kiss every woman they can catch hold of. They pat them and feel their hindquarters. They don't actually have sexual intercourse in the open, but they do everything else at their parties. I'm afraid to pass a bedroom door."

"Some, yes. It's only a pose."

"It's a pose I can't hold. I dare say you think I'm squeamish and provincial, Elliot, but I get nausea when these people make a *maison de tolérance* of your house."

"*Maison* . . ."

Elliot Ducroy was one of the hardest workers in the script-writing colony at that time. He lived in a highly charged atmosphere of sanguine hope, sudden flashes of inspiration, and periods of black despair. Half the time he hardly knew what he was eating, drinking, or wearing. There were conferences late at night or in the small hours, hurried trips to location and more hurried trips back to the studio. Sometimes they chafed and chaffered while a director fled East in a night plane, and then they sat around the telephone in a conference room, equipped with manifold receivers, quarreling with the man three thousand miles away.

Elliot Ducroy was under no illusions about these people. He really considered them cultured because they employed the highest possible talent to get a picture authentic, and entertained these birds of oriental, archeological, historical and pictorial wisdom in their homes. He wished to exhaust this mine of wealth before going back to his main source of inspiration, magazine fiction. He felt himself associated with them in business, and a businessman had to make allowances for business associates. Their occasional naive sensuality under the influence of exhausting nervous strain and strong cocktails he regarded as no more than a silly lack of good taste. The great thing, he felt, was to make as much money as possible.

It was here that Irving began to hover on the edge of the scene in which Elliot Ducroy and his wife were playing the leads. Sonia, in Irving's opinion, was an ideal juvenile, while Louis was comic relief. Irving saw everything in real life as a scene, a situation, or a setting. He took a simple pleasure in directing the pictures he saw thus. He had an ambition to be more than an agent.

There was a childlike simplicity of intellect in Irving which aroused in Perdita a subtle antagonism. Irving had a "perfessor," as he called him, to coach him in English, to give him lessons in history and geography. Did Mrs. Ducroy know that New York used to be called New Amsterdam? Irving no longer said Joisey for Jersey or hunnerd for hundred. He was sure Mrs. Ducroy would enjoy getting posted.

The odd thing about their acquaintance, for it was impossible to call it a friendship, was that it never degenerated into dislike. It was rather a gentle clashing of traditions. It was impossible to convince Perdita that her ignorance of a fact had any significance at all. Subconsciously she was aware that facts were irrelevant to the soul.

"I don't care what it used to be called," she said. "All I know is, I'd rather be in New York than here."

Elliot Ducroy turned from the view down the canyon. He had been struggling with a sequence.

"You can go to New York if you want," he said patiently. "It's all right. I mean it," he added. "You go."

"This climate is bad for the brat," she said, meaning Sonia. "I sometimes think, if the sun doesn't stop shining I'll shoot myself."

Irving said, soothingly, "It's an asset, the sunshine. The state's biggest money-maker. I'm for it."

"Well, I've had enough of it. Sonia catches cold if she's out after eight o'clock. It's the most—the most brainless sort of existence!"

That was the solid obstacle between them. Elliot Ducroy would ask her, "Anybody'd think you were a whiz, intellectually, yourself, to hear you pan these people. I can't see what you mean by 'brainless.' "

And she would say, quietly, "I don't suppose you can. I don't suppose I'm good at explanations and discussion."

"Well, how are we going to find out if we don't explain and discuss?"

What was it she wanted? he would ask himself, in a pause in the frenzied life of the studios. All his values were completely ignored by a woman who, in his view, owed everything to him. He himself was aware of the rootless and ephemeral nature of the California scene. He knew that the morality, the religion, the culture and the intellectual achievements of the people around him were somehow different from the East. But why should that prevent a man and his wife getting along together when he was making five hundred dollars a week?

Such moments were rare. He was too absorbed in his work to be hypercritical. When Perdita suddenly went East by train, taking Sonia with her, he made all arrangements and resumed the hard-working bachelor life she had interrupted.

There were fewer drinking parties, however. Ducroy drank very little, owing to occasional warnings from his physician. Louis had very little beyond the regular routine to occupy him. He was more than ordinarily silent and solemn, now that he had lost Sonia.

One new caller interested Louis. She was a middle-aged woman of aristocratic appearance, apparently out of place in a script-writer's establishment. Elliot Ducroy, one morning, starting his breakfast of orange juice, bran, and coffee without milk or sugar, told Louis she was "the Ph.D." Her job was to coach her employer in French, classical art and advanced literature. If his engagements permitted, Elliot Ducroy proposed to go to Paris later, then Berlin, Munich, Florence, Venice and Rome, taking ship at Naples. Miss Linkweiler had a degree from a Western university, and she had conducted study groups to Europe by arrangement with steamship agencies.

She interested Louis because the phrase "Ph.D." was incomprehensible to him. He imagined at first that she was a new California kind of wife. She slept on the premises in order to be on duty before breakfast. She demanded a number of unusual vitamins, and instead of the perfect coffee Louis enjoyed making she drank Paraguayan maté, which Louis thought unfit for human consumption.

Elliot Ducroy had a definite motive in employing Miss Linkweiler. As a former script editor for one of the smaller studios (she had once done the continuity for a silent screen version of *The Beggar's Opera*), she understood that subtle element, the female public. She reacted unerringly to the various stimuli incorporated in a series of scenarios Elliot Ducroy was drafting for use in short stories.

And besides, he wished for culture unashamedly. He gave Miss Linkweiler the job of dredging the highbrow magazines for suitable material and commissioned her to buy books for him to read "when he got time." It was a regular thing, long before the stars took lessons in elocution and pronunciation, for the best people in the colony to engage coaches for their minds.

Elliot Ducroy, within a month of Perdita's departure with Sonia to New York, had signed a new contract for a year at seven hundred dollars a week. It was the only way to keep him there, he told them. Miss Linkweiler had less and less to do, and she spent more time buying whole shelves of books, sets, encyclopedias, and limited editions, using them herself while Ducroy was absent on location or working in his office in the studio. Like dozens of such schemes, Elliot Ducroy's cultural plans disintegrated. Miss Linkweiler herself faded out, as she expressed it to Louis. More concretely, she was experienced in Hollywood customs and was aware how tenuous was the hold of an employee on a private job. She told Mr. Ducroy she had accepted a position as a period costume consultant with the American-Hispanic Corporation.

Ducroy and Louis survived this desertion, but neither of them was happy. Louis received picture post cards from Sonia and once a week Ducroy used the transcontinental trunk line telephone to talk to Perdita for five minutes. He told her what he was doing, what people he was going around with, now she was no longer there to disapprove, and asked after Sonia. "Louis wants to know how Sonia's making out." And then he asked her if she was happier in New York.

She always said yes, she was happier, and he invariably replied, "That's swell!" But the words, as so often happens with those whose coinage and capital consist of words, were inadequate. He himself, as he would replace the receiver and made a note in his record book, knew that there was something missing from their relationship. He could detect, in his feelings, under the pride of ownership and his own success in the world, under the surface pleasure of hearing her lovely voice across the continent, a canker of unhappiness.

He had married twice, and so far happiness had eluded him. The first time had been impossible. Myra and he had married exactly as thousands of other young couples had married in 1918. They had had a week together before he sailed for France. When he came back they were two strangers who loyally slept together for a while and finally gave it up as a bad job, an impossible job. Elliot Ducroy never wanted to think about that time. He had been so crude, so inept emotionally, so inexperienced. He had helped her get a divorce and sent her a nest egg when she married

Holker, the truck salesman from her home town in Ohio. She was probably so changed he wouldn't recognize her.

Well, would he recognize happiness if it came to him, he wondered. What was the matter with him and Perdita? Why could she not settle down with him?

Irving, who had been in New York, supplied him with a hint of what line Perdita was taking, and it had surprised him. Perdita with poets and painters! She had always been excessively astringent in her attitude toward literature and art. He could not call her indifference to American life complacency. It was more unawareness. Famous names had meant nothing to her, not because she despised their modern achievements, but because she had never heard of them. Literally never heard of them! That time, for instance, when a director had made a wisecrack about *Ulysses,* and she had said, blankly, "Homer's?" As for the newer fashionable cults, they never registered with her at all.

Elliot Ducroy noticed that Perdita inspired a diversity of men with individual sentiments quite distinct from sexual love. Louis had a feeling of inarticulate, gloomy reverence for her. Irving was full of admiration of something he called her décor. And it was Irving who gave her husband a hint of the reason behind the new development.

"She's on her own now," Irving said, smiling. "She's got the stage to herself, see. You're Mr. Big here, if you know what I mean. Now she's got something, as you might say, exclusive. Décor."

"She isn't running around with anybody, is she?" Ducroy inquired. Irving was definite. He made a downward gesture.

"What you think? She's an aristocrat." Irving emphasized the second syllable. He used the word in a special, personal sense. There were several classifications for human beings in Irving's private world, and the word "aristocrat" did not necessarily include some of the stars' titled husbands he had met. They were merely tramps.

"Is she?" said Elliot Ducroy. "Well, so long as she's happy . . ."

Whether he was happy himself in his furious industry, his monastic existence with the taciturn Louis running his bungalow, he became increasingly doubtful. His doubts rose out of an unexplored swamp and jungle of thoughts, which the world he was living in was being taught to call the unconscious. He was amazingly inventive in constructing new combinations of the age-old materials of fiction and he was sensitive to influences he could never completely comprehend. When people at the Writers' Club talked profoundly of "the Russians," Elliot Ducroy ordered all the Russian translations available in Miss Linkweiler's catalogues, and read a few pages. Most of the books stood on his shelves in virgin solitude. He hadn't time. And in his opinion Chekov could neither construct nor complete a story. But he got the idea. There was something in the Russians different from the writers in Hollywood, but not very different from what a Russian would write if he had been raised in Ohio or Iowa instead of Podolia or Kharkov, and had no editors to show him where he was off the track with regard to circulation. If you want to write you want to be read, was Elliot Ducroy's philosophy, and the only concrete success was circulation. He was able to feel a certain thrill when he thought of the ten to fifteen million patrons who paid to see the pictures he was doing. It made even the several million readers of magazines appear small potatoes. Whereas Chekov never got to first base. . . .

He had a curiously double intelligence because he was aware—down in that uncharted area of his mind, they told him, somewhat confusingly, was his unconscious—that his lack of positive happiness and his acceptance of the editors' standard of achievement were two faces of the same coin. Like a cloud at the back of his mind was this awareness of the spurious nature of that standard.

He strove with this problem at times. It was not an easy

one because he experienced the satisfaction of an artist when he succeeded in what he was doing, which was the expert manipulation of conventional situations. That was an art in itself, wasn't it?

Then why was it that he could never impress Perdita with his importance, with his success in a specialized branch of this art? Why was everything he did apparently of no *importance* to her? Why was he mortified because she ignored, or neglected, the material luxuries his success enabled him to give her?

Even more perplexing was the failure of the other women he met in Hollywood to perceive the qualities he saw in her. Men were aware of her, but not in the sense that they were aware of their own kind of women. They were, to put it in simple phrase, scared of her. Or they appreciated her glamor while not liking her. Only Irving was articulate enough to define the emotions she inspired, and Elliot Ducroy suspected most of Irving's definitions came from Terry, a young woman with a good level head on an extra-girl's body. Irving and Terry were devoted to each other, living in an idyllic, if slightly irregular, fashion in a miniature villa out on the road to San Fernando.

Terry was the sort of girl, in Ducroy's opinion, a man ought to have, if he could clear his head of illusions and delusions. She was the ultimate useful mate for a worker. She was entirely adaptable, unspectacularly efficient as an extra, an orange-juice waitress, a typist, or a home-maker. She was serenely capable and independent, in a small way. Above all, she wore well. She kept her head and her figure, and life ran along pretty smoothly for Irving, whose legal wife was back with her mother in the Bronx, sulking and making life miserable for her family.

But Elliot Ducroy knew that he himself would never be able to jog along the way Irving did. Some devil inside him made him hanker after the unattainable. He wanted someone of his own stature, he supposed, someone who could grasp his ambitions, enter into his only half-formulated plans for the future, and share his confidences. The nervous strain of the work he was doing, which was, he admitted, making everything in life that was true seem false and all that was false in life seem true, made it all the more imperative for him to share that strain with a partner. That, in real life, was art. You had to fake all the time if you were a real artist. And it took it out of you. If you didn't drink, or smoke marijuana, or fornicate, or go in for the milder forms of sexual inversion, or become converted to a phony religion, you had to have a partner, a wife who could act as a confessional box, a safety valve, or you went crazy.

ii

It was perplexing to him, with his Midwest traditions, that she should ignore material and artistic triumphs. What did she want? What the hell did she want? Obviously, from Irving's report, it wasn't a lover. He knew it wasn't a lover, in his mind. She was not that sort of woman, of course. But what did she want?

He was perplexed by the depths to which this inquiry led him. He saw suddenly the spuriousness of his calling in a new light. Part of his work was called psychology. If it meant anything, it meant that he was supposed to know what went on inside people. But if he had absolutely no knowledge of what was going on inside his wife, or inside that efficient and gloomy Louis, what was the use? The Hollywood answer, of course, was that Love Opened the Door. Love revealed the mystery. Well, it was all balls. Love did nothing of the kind. Love could not be All-seeing and All-understanding, and Blind as well! People in pictures and fiction acted on motives that would only inspire real people with ribald laughter. People were always doing things in real life that would bitch up the motivation of the finest script in the world. Real people, he observed, were incurably corny. You had to fake. . . .

There were some radicals who said, "No, you only faked if you were a faker. The great men did not fake." That was getting off the reservation. The great men were dead, mostly, and did not have to make a living in competition with the radio and the automobile.

Now and again you found a poet like Elliot Ducroy's friend, Piers Mallinson, who lived like an anchorite on a lonely promontory where the cypresses streamed inland with the everlasting wind from the Pacific. Mallinson was as poor as Dives and looked very much as Dives must have looked. His features were emaciated with frugal living and inward ecstasy. It was as though the wind had scoured the flesh from his bones. His poetry was well-nigh incomprehensible; but occasionally Ducroy was uplifted by a phrase like a wild beast's howl in the night. Mallinson didn't earn ten dollars a week by his verse. Ducroy had read the book when Miss Linkweiler bought it for him. "He is important," she had said, impressively. "Who?" "Piers Mallinson," she repeated in a resonant contralto. "Important modern poet."

Elliot Ducroy had not had much luck with *The Waste Land,* when it was forced on him, and he took some time to get around to reading Piers Mallinson's *Shining Vampyres.* He persuaded Miss Linkweiler to get in touch with the poet. One day, instead of driving straight home from location a hundred miles north of Los Angeles, he went to San Luis Obispo and on to the sea.

He had been impressed by Mallinson's integrity. He might be crazy, but he practised his philosophy. Ducroy liked him because he was practical in spite of his craziness. Ducroy asked him if he would accept assistance to buy necessities. Mallinson was trying to live on what he could grow himself and he had no farming ability. He said at once that he would accept assistance. Fifty dollars a month would be enough, he said, his lean sharp face shining like a sword.

It was in Mallinson's hut on the headland, drinking the local wine out of an enameled mug, that Elliot Ducroy first heard of "a great poet, a really great modern poet," named Caxton Derrick. He wrote, Mallinson said "like a man inspired! Such passion! We have waited fifty years for an authentic Voice, and now we have it. *Crimson Cantilevers!* A masterpiece of American literature!"

These casual contacts with the real thing did not interfere with Elliot Ducroy's own work. Nothing interfered with his work. He worked harder than ever to produce the sort of thing he now knew very well how to do quickly. He was making more money than ever. It gave him a feeling of pleasure to be able to render assistance to Piers Mallinson, who was doing important, if slightly difficult, literature. Miss Linkweiler agreed with Mallinson about Caxton Derrick. He too was "definitely important," she said.

Sometimes Elliot Ducroy wondered to himself why important writers never seemed to have any idea at all of constructing a readable story. But he discovered that he could combine remorse with money making. He could recognize with manly candor that working in Hollywood, doing what were called "treatments" of masterpieces of literature, supplying supporting sequences for stories by writers of international fame who were plainly incompetent in the studios—all this was routine stuff, no doubt, and not to be regarded as inspired. But the final result was art, just as the stage play was a supreme example of the combined efforts of a lot of people producing a great work of art.

Some of the masterpieces of literature needed a great deal of treatment, he found, and he preferred to do his own stories whenever possible. He often forgot not only his ignoble position as one who was, according to Piers Mallinson, prostituting himself for money, but even his personal problem of what he was going to do about Perdita. He was absorbed in the great game, and the money he was making (it was now nine hundred a week) took care of everything. Irving, who deposited the balances in Eastern banks, reported a total that made Ducroy thoughtful and suddenly loving toward Perdita.

How would it be, he reflected, how would it be if he cut Hollywood and came East, hook, line and sinker? How about a place in the country? A country estate? Not Long Island;

Connecticut? And live together again? He would take Louis with him, of course. Old Louis, his mascot.

The idea attracted him. Life on the Coast in the shadow of the enormous fortunes of stars and moguls, even if you had a pretty big salary for a writer, was extraordinarily uninspiring. He remembered the English author who had come out to "supervise" the screening of his best seller (that supervising was a joke!) who had remarked "What I like about America is your absolutely classless society! Truly democratic! Now we . . . !" He had shrugged his shoulders and given that peculiar Oxford snigger, that rougish grimace which had enslaved the New York women interviewers.

Classless, my eye! As Terry had commented at the time, "Ixnay! He's a dumb bunny if you ask me." They were both only obscure members of an immense mob of loquacious egotists. The leaders of that mob were walling themselves up in their villas and chateaux, while their press agents worked tirelessly to create synthetic substitutes for public consumption. More and more exclusive became the society of these wealthy *émigrés*. They had an order of precedence, and Elliot Ducroy, whose name on the screen was often, like those of the immortals, omitted altogether, was never given a by-line in type more than one-twentieth the size of a producer's or a star's; was never held for more than a few feet of film. Even photographers and sound-track specialists had larger type and longer exposure.

It was far from classless, he reflected grimly, and the idea began to attract him, to go East while he was still good, to settle where he would be somebody, maybe, have a nag and a boat. He had, he now realized, the money to do it. You could spend half a million dollars out in Beverly Hills and it would hardly rate a quarter column in *Script*. You could have ten million fans gaping and gawking at your dialogue and situations, and they would never hear your name. They would never know you existed. Somehow even famous writers, writers who rated A1 with the highbrows, became invisible and without significance in the blare and blaze of the stars and moguls.

These were his thoughts when Irving returned on the airliner from New York a few weeks before the end of his second contract. What Irving had to say was in his own special jargon, but it was obvious that he had something unusual on his mind.

Irving had a number of clients whose money he collected and cared for, whose domestic relations were well known to him, and whose desire to spend more than they earned demanded tact and patience. Elliot Ducroy was no trouble at all, practically, and Irving's interest in Mrs. Ducroy had been always platonic and chastely sentimental. Now that Terry had gone to live in New York, Irving was on the plane about once a month. And through Terry he kept in touch with Perdita.

"Chief, I think you ought to go back to your wife," he said to Elliot in his office.

"Go back to my wife! I like that. That's an understatement, Irving."

"I mean, she's runnin' around with a bunch as crazy as bedbugs," said Irving.

"I'd have to learn the exterminator business from the ground up. All right! All right! I'll go. Is it serious?"

"There's a lot of liquor in New York," Irving said glumly.

"She didn't use to drink. Not much."

Irving made no immediate reply. He could be diplomatic. Terry's wise aphorisms were not lost on Irving. He said, after a long pause to light a fresh cigarette. "It's a sort of nervous relief. They're a very nervous bunch, those writers."

"What do you mean, those writers? What writers you talkin' about? My wife wouldn't be found dead with writers when she was here. She . . ."

"One of 'em's supposed to be America's greatest poet," said Irving. "Guy who took Terry to one of those book teas, where they have poets givin' recitations, he said this Caxton Derrick's a sort of American White Hope. There's smokes writin' po'try nowadays, see. Caxton Derrick's white."

"Colored?" Elliot Ducroy frowned. He could not get the picture focused. Perdita drinking. Perdita running around with a lot of Greenwich Village poets, some of them colored! It made very little sense as Irving told it. But Irving was a friend as well as an agent. He knew the world without being either boastful or malicious. He was reporting this because, in his opinion, Mrs. Ducroy was in some danger.

"What do you suppose is the attraction?" Ducroy said, half to himself. He found that he was automatically making a script problem of it for a Gentleman Church film. What, in that case, would be the attraction? His mind ran over the possibilities. Very few of them fitted Perdita, as he knew her. But how much did he know her? The idea, of knowing nothing about the woman one had legally married and slept with, was technically taboo, unavailable. You'd never get Hays to admit it.

"Attraction!" said Irving. "Listen, chief. You go East and everything'll be hunky dory. Married women always run around when they're left alone too long. It's always the man's fault."

"I've noticed that," said Ducroy. "It's one of our standard motivations. Well, I said I'd go, didn't I? Does Caxton Derrick make real money?"

"Don't make me laugh," said Irving. "No, I would say he has independent means. His old man used to give him an allowance. Then he got a Finkelberger Endowment. He has a lot of rich patrons, I understand, some of 'em women."

"Sounds like a louse," said Ducroy, but without animus. He was vague about Finkelberger Endowments. Rich patrons meant Caxton Derrick must have a line. Miss Linkweiler had spoken of him with awe.

Irving waved his ringed hand, squared his shoulders and nodded.

"Terry wanted me to tell you," he said. "She thinks it's

inexperience. You know. Nothin' to do; parties with poets doin' their stuff; high-class conversation; artists askin' everybody over to see their etchin's. See what I mean?"

He made a gesture of raising a glass and downing a drink. His round, black, east-European eyes were wide open as he looked at the man with one leg over the arm of the office chair.

"I'll go. I intended to quit and I will, too. So long's she's not leaving me. She wouldn't do that, now." He mused. "Would she?" he said to himself.

"Oh, sure not!" Irving knew Elliot Ducroy never meddled with women at that time, and he had Terry's word that Perdita wasn't anybody's pick-up. He'd take Terry's word for that.

"I'd like to see the kid again," Ducroy said. He saw, in his mind's eye, the file of paid bills for board at Shadowcrest Farm, where Miss Sonia Pagett was living; and the other file of very short, very strenuously written letters to "Dear Dadda" which they made Sonia write him. Dadda! When she had always called him Elliot!

He went away from Irving's office, which was cunningly situated downtown in Los Angeles, and drove meditatively toward home. In the back of his mind lay a resolve to leave the screen stuff to Irving, to live in the country, and buy a new car. The one he had now he would turn in and have the new one delivered in New York.

Elliot Ducroy had a desire—not a violent passion, but a reasonable desire—to own a foreign car. He was as sick as anyone else of seeing advertising in magazines of glamorous stars stepping into their new Jalopede Sixes, six hundred and ninety-five dollars F.O.B. Detroit, while they actually used Renaults and Isotta Fraschinis with two chauffeurs. What he really desired was a life comparable with the money he was earning. He did not even want to drive the foreign car. All he wanted was to own it.

The new Virago catalogue had caught his eye one morning. The Virago was a six-liter English machine with a top speed, guaranteed silent, of ninety miles. He was not a speed hog. He was a somewhat absent-minded motorist who spent quite a few dollars monthly on minor repairs. The Virago was a symbol of his rise into the middle-income brackets.

He was glad there were no other prospects to be seen as he entered the show room. He walked around the erubescent monster enthroned on a raised dais of red velvet roped off with silken cords. It was long and low. It had upholstery of cream leather, several windshields, a gigantic pair of headlights, and a transparent steering wheel resembling crystal. It carried a silver statuette of a woman in armor on the radiator.

It seemed to him more suitable for the favorite dancing girl of a very rich maharaja in India than a married woman. He decided that the model he bought would have to be less ritzy.

"It's for my wife," he told the salesman, who was English, extremely urbane and perfectly dressed. "She's English." He got in and tried the driver's seat. Most of the arrangements made his old Stutz seem like a ten-year-old Ford.

They took him out to the demonstration model and started for a drive. The salesman, as he threaded the traffic, explained the silent valve action, the duplex lubrication, the dual ignition and the differential braking. The model he recommended had an aluminum and leather body which reduced the weight about twenty percent. The speed might seem modest, he went on, letting the car out, but while other makes offered a hundred and more miles per hour, this was silent. And so on.

"She's in New York." Elliott Ducroy said, when they got back. "You quote me in New York? Black, with red cushions. This has too much flash." The salesman opened catalogues and folders. "Just so," he said. "You care to place an order? We can cable at once, you see. A month ought to have it in

New York. This one's nine thousand, including duty and taxes."

"I'll give you a check."

The salesman steered him toward an inner office. He was as calm as though he sold a Virago every day. The slightly older man in the office, who wore a monocle, might have been selling them over the counter. Elliot Ducroy studied them with interest. He signed his name to the order after reading it, wrote a check for twenty-five hundred dollars and handed it over. They both gazed at the signature. The name, his name, which was printed on the end of the check, evoked no emotion. Evidently it meant nothing to them, which was about what he expected.

It's the truth, he told himself as he drove along the Boulevard toward Hollywood. *A writer out here is incognito and incommunicado. Well, what the hell! I'm through. I'm the original man without a contract. The only specimen west of the Rockies, of a man who quit while he was good!*

"What would a Virago do to Perdita? And a speedboat? He had a vision of a house with a covered dock, where a speedboat could be housed. He saw himself going down through his grounds to the dock, starting all twelve cylinders with a roar, and hurtling out across Long Island Sound. Speedboating had for him, in prospect, all the thrill of motoring without any traffic trouble. It would do him good to take a spin in a speedboat. Perdita would like it, he thought.

He wanted her. He was in that mood (unusual for him) in which he was conscious of monetary success, in which that success, reacting on his glands, made him desirous of authentic sexual happiness. He was too much of an American to follow the example of rich Europeans and South Americans, and set a girl up in an apartment and lead a double life. What he wanted was to express his achievement in a sexual formula. In its way, only half emerging, what he felt was the same desire of the successful British soldier, statesman or merchant to buy an estate in the country, an old manor house, and set up an establishment with a modish, aristocratic wife from a good family. He had seen such places in England, with a row of cottages down beyond the paddock, which went with the place. It must make a man feel damned feudal to own a place like that. In California it was different. The moguls made anything under a thousand acres and twenty bedrooms seem suburban. The atmosphere was not right for it.

In the East it would be different. He saw that the change from England to Los Angeles county must have been difficult for Perdita. What could he have been thinking about to expect her to settle down in California? He would go back and be a devoted parent and husband. Sonia was a swell kid. He wanted to see her again.

He had to drill himself into thinking that now, with his name in the mags, with his accumulated savings from his years of slavery in the movies as a sort of abnormally well-paid hired hand, doing the rough work around the place for the moguls, he could be somebody and live, not a life of ease, but of comfort and security in the country, doing the work he preferred.

He wanted Perdita. He wanted her as a mirror, a magic mirror, in which to see his own success, his own emergence from the reporter, the special correspondent with a by-line, the pulp fictioneer and the free-lance serialist in the slicks, to the moneyed screen writer with a name, a man with a glittering future as good as Kipling's or Jack London's, come to that! Yes, sir!

Back in his lofty perch on the canyon edge, he smiled. Louis, who practically never smiled, brought him a long drink of lime juice and soda with a slight lacing of Jamaica rum for taste. Miss Linkweiler had told him of writers who did their work on alcohol. She mentioned Richard Brinsley Sheridan, who wrote an immortal comedy with a bottle of port or Madeira at his elbow. Elliot Ducroy shook his head at that. The physician to whom he went at irregular intervals had told him he was in no danger at all with his heart so long as he avoided hard undiluted liquor and violent physical exertion.

"It wouldn't do for me," he told Miss Linkweiler. "Port wine? It sounds batty. I'd either fall asleep or get sick. Maybe I'm not a genius."

"Oh, Mr. Ducroy!" Miss Linkweiler wailed. "You demean yourself!"

"Well," he said, with a faint grin, "my scripts aren't immortal. Maybe, if I drank wine, they'd be immortal; but I doubt it."

Sometimes he hated the work, in fact. It was the endless going over and over that was the real drudgery; the conferences, the imbecile suggestions of underlings trying to get their names up with the director, the sudden scrapping of weeks of work because someone decided it stank, the starting again from scratch, and then the abandonment of the whole thing, followed by weeks of rushing about to find a star, or weeks of waiting while the moguls decided on a new story. Yes, he would like to be his own property again.

"Louis," he said to that silent person as he was withdrawing to his pantry, "Louis, how would you like to go East again? We'd see Sonia. How'd you like that?"

Louis studied the Navajo rug under his feet. He seemed to meditate. For twenty-five dollars a week this man was Elliot Ducroy's slave. He ran the house, cooked without any apparent effort, made drinks (which he did not touch himself), purchased his stores without graft and spent his spare time, like an Indian philosopher, in meditation.

Having considered the matter, he drooped the corners of his mouth and nodded.

Elliot Ducroy wondered sometimes whether his art, as he called it, encompassed all the emotions and secret thoughts of even the dumbest of the toiling masses. After all this time he knew nothing of what went on inside the head of his houseman. Yet wait a minute! Louis had been obviously fond of Sonia, and Sonia had been as obviously fond of Louis. What could be done, photogenically, with a situation like that? A real situation. Not an Uncle Tom and Little Eva fake, but a human story! Drama, not slop!

He drained the drink and set the glass down on a side table with a firm hand. Not a thing, he decided. Breen would think you were trying to slip some continental stuff past him and would throw the whole script in the ash can. Well, you had to work to a pattern and within the limitations of the medium. Miss Linkweiler had said that Shakespeare and Molière had taboos to wrestle with too. And that other man she recommended. What was his name? Some Russian, who had to camouflage his stories to keep the police from sending him to Siberia. Miss Linkweiler had ordered the books.

Elliot Ducroy went to the shelves packed close with new books he had not yet had time to read. He would make time now, when he got a place in the country where there was plenty of peace and quiet. He could take a month off before going to work in earnest on that new series of Gentleman Church stories. Yes, he would have a regular banquet of reading. Somehow the atmosphere of Hollywood was not conducive to quiet study of great masters. It was like a vibration in the air. You were constantly in high gear. An English author had said it made him feel as if his entrails were being drawn out of him. Funny how well the Russians stood it. Miss Linkweiler had said that if they could stand what went on in Russia, Hollywood would seem peaceful and quiet by comparison. It was an idea—that the hectic nervous strain of the studios was similar to a revolution. It *was* a revolution—a new art being born. . . . Weren't there dictators, purges, exiles and spies?

He ran his tongue along his lips as he thought this out. It was a sure sign that he was aware of the spuriousness of his life while continuing to believe in it. It paid well; and he knew that all integrity west of the Rockies was necessarily based on the ability to make money. Even the religions took in hundreds of thousands of dollars a week. This library in which he sat, the money in the banks, even Louis, who was going East with him to be his butler and general factotum, all were part of the edifice of integrity which he proposed to erect. The indispensable façade was Perdita and Sonia. Behind them was Irving, the indispensable man of business. Even Piers Mallinson, as a recipient of his bounty, would be part of the structure he had in mind. He must ask Piers to come East and have a long visit.

This, he supposed, was ambition; or was it merely the natural result of living such an unnatural life in the studios? A life devoted to working always to a rigid pattern? A life devising new arrangements of Trouble–Conflict–Complication–Predicament–Supporting Sequences–Crisis–Black Moment–Climax–Fade out! How horrible and unreal it was at times! Never any Frustration, yet ninety percent of our own lives was frustration. In other words, what he had to do, to earn his thirty thousand a year (and it would be fifty thousand witih this new Gentleman Church series for Unity) was the Bunk. There seemed no way of bridging the gulf between this Bunk, which was Art, and Life. Not in Hollywood, anyhow. Hey, and likewise Ho!

The thing to do was, get back to the magazine game. Let Irving market the stories to the pix. Playwrights were coming more and more into their own in the films, as was only right. They knew the stage, and you had to have actors and actresses as the raw material for stars, which made it easier for playwrights to get the hang of it. But it did not follow, oh, most emphatically it did not follow, that if you knew the screen you could write plays!

Elliot Ducroy recalled a recent example of that. A man he knew slightly, a man with a real flair for the screen, a man who never used the word "montage" yet did it better than anybody, had this bug in his brain for writing plays. He wanted, more than anything else, to get away from pictures and into the theater. He had gone off to Monterey, lived in one of those rented cabins, and written his play. Boy, was it the berries! It was a blend of O'Neill's *Hairy Ape, Outward Bound* and *Tobacco Road.* As one ink-stained continuity writer said, over his vermouth cassis, it had everything, swimming pools, cesspools and sex-pools.

And it had lasted just two nights on Broadway. The author sank seven grand in it and was still in Hollywood, living what he called a life of prostitution and hoping some day to become an honest playwright.

No, thought Elliot Ducroy, that was no way out. There might be a play in Gentleman Church, but he was not going to mix with Broadway. Irving could find a buyer for it. Or an adaptor, like those boys who did *Rain.*

He relaxed. Apart from a few odds and ends waiting to be cleared up at the office and some retakes, he was through with what he called "inter-office rumble-bumble." Then he had to see about that property he had bought at Encinitas. Better put it on the market. He had been told it would go up. It hadn't. If he put it on the market he could put a reserve price on it. Lovely place, but you'd think there was a jinx on it as well as a nice five-room bungalow. Nobody wanted it. The trend was away from Encinitas, apparently. Now for New York.

He wouldn't, he was quite determined, live in New York. Definitely not in Greenwich Village. That place Perdita had, a penthouse in St. Giles Alley, was not what he wanted at all. He knew it all too well, that part of town. After the war, when he got back and out of uniform, he had kicked around the Village for a while, working on a newspaper, trying to write a novel and wondering what was going to happen to him. Those crazy dives and speakeasies! Good for a young fellow without much money, maybe, but a hell of a dump once you got going.

He went to his desk and saw a telephone message in the

vague, sprawling hand of Louis: *Mr. Ducroy call Mr. Cavoura Plaza 7409 before six.*

"Okay, old son," he said to himself, and went over to the telephone.

Josef Cavoura was a frustrated genius, in Elliot Ducroy's opinion. He was frustrated, because he directed commercial co-features, instead of designing huge symphonic treatments of mighty classics which would probably cost three times as much as *The Miracle*. Plaza 7409 was Cavoura's villa, an immense stucco edifice which resembled a Gothic dragon's castle from the outside and within seemed as vast as the Grand Central waiting room. Cavoura's bedroom was entirely furnished with original Napoleonic pieces, including a huge tester bed with the imperial "N" on the coverlet. The main hall was done in imitation of a monastery refectory with a great oak table. Tattered medieval banners hung from the roof beams and stained glass adorned the casements.

It was probably a party. Cavoura was an abstainer, but he had good liquor and gave enjoyable parties.

Elliot Ducroy listened. "To meet—to meet—a new wrater. She want—she want—to meet—wrater—of Shentleman Shurch."

"Whassa name?" Ducroy inquired.

Here was an impasse. He could not make out what Cavoura was saying. He sometimes fancied high-salaried foreigners talked like illiterate immigrants out of vanity.

"Well, all right. I'll come. Deelighted, old son."

New writers were always arriving in Hollywood. Always departing too, he thought, gravely. Very few had much aptitude for working; that is actually writing, on the set, or on location. They were useless in a conference when ideas were wanted on the jump. You had to improvise as you went along. Made you work fast!

He had a shower and changed into fresh clothes. Cavoura preferred informality—or said he did. Oh, Jesus! Why was everybody in the place pretending to be somebody else? Was that the reason Perdita ran out on him? Had he been acclimated to it, so that he accepted the flapdoodle, the pretence, the weakly wicked hypocrisy of the life, without question or derision? What Cavoura really preferred was expensive pornography. He had a library of it, including an illustrated copy of *Lady Chatterly's Lover* and another of *Fanny Hill.* It was his hobby.

Elliot Ducroy was not censorious. It was no longer of any real importance to him. He was going back East, to civilization. He was going to be sincere, where he would never see a palm tree, an orange grove, or an extra girl gazing hungrily at him as he passed her to hurry into the office. The beige-colored hills and the flat blue sea off Santa Monica would be behind him.

Some Englishman had once made a remark that stuck in Ducroy's memory. They were out on location doing a Riviera sequence. It was precisely what was wanted—a background of blue sea, creaming surf, a craggy island, yellow sand below a cliff, with a corniche road coming down from mountains covered with semi-tropical verdure. It was a scene from a story in which a fight took place in a char-à-banc traveling from Nice to Monte Carlo. Gentleman Church, escorting an escaped man to his yacht, was set upon by masked men who leapt into the vehicle as it skirted a precipice. The whole machine lurched and rocked and hung over the abyss, held by invisible wire ropes, of course.

And what was it the Englishman said as he took little sips of his Scotch and soda? He had said that the defect of California scenery was, nothing had ever happened there. It had no historical tradition, no memories of human joy and sorrow. So it was, he said, psychologically inert. Whereas the Mediterranean . . . And he began to quote Ruskin, between sips.

One of the staff had muttered that if those two steel hawsers broke, something would happen plenty quick right there.

But on recalling that remark and the subsequent conversation, Elliot Ducroy knew now what the guy was driving at. Was it a fact, that there were moods and emotions you couldn't express except in a sort of prose-poetry?

His life, in spite of his success, was not a success. You couldn't keep on forever wanting and wanting something splendid if it never materialized. Like a presence just behind him, but which he could never quite glimpse fairly, and which he did not really want to face, the vague fear haunted him that Perdita had perhaps married him without passion and on an impulse to escape an intolerable penury.

What was going to happen to him, then, when he arrived and carried out his plan to live with her in the country? He did not know which he dreaded most, her refusal or her indifference. He frowned as he thought of this, biting his lower lip, becoming uncertain as to the real reason for this anxiety.

She would like that Virago, at any rate! He had given her a big car at the beginning. She had had a number of minor accidents with it and sometimes left it around in the streets, as though she wanted to lose it. That had been a complicated psychological situation. It had enlightened him as to the futility of trying to discover what was in a woman's mind. She could have given it away if she had wished. It had been hers. But suddenly she exclaimed that she simply must go to New York; and after a while he had disposed of the Duesenberg.

Now she should have a Virago and he a speedboat. He had to keep on reminding himself that these things were really within his range. He had become so absorbed in the game he had not realized, until Irving insisted on an audit, how the money had accumulated. He had given up investing. After his one disastrous excursion into stocks he was cured. Irving was not to blame. He, Elliot Ducroy, had imagined stocks to be safe. They had not been safe. They had declined in value. Even bonds had ceased to be much use. The banks had finally refused to cash the coupons. Writers, he supposed, were part of the great army of suckers. So he left his money on deposit in New York banks.

He thought of this financial success with pleasure but without pride. By professional standards it was nothing at all. His vanity demanded that Perdita share what he did and what he had. He hungered for her solicitude, her preoccupation with his work, his problems, his ambitions. He imagined her telling other women about him, speaking not so much with pride as with a grave consciousness of his importance to her. You could hear that note in Terry's voice when she spoke of Irving. You could see the expression in her face.

It was not that he did not want, and hope for, passion. Passion was part of the stock-in-trade of his business. Cavoura would take and take and take, until he had, or thought he had, the real thing in a love sequence. Passion as it were, was chilled and preserved, like food, for use on location. You were everlastingly aware of it in the studios. Cavoura was of the opinion they'd never get real passion again until they went back to silent pictures. Those were the days, he said, when you could get the stars so worked up, with an orchestra playing sensuous music just off the set, that they'd be carried away completely. Cavoura had an almost tumescent humor at times in conversation. In his position, as one of the old guard, he could say what he liked, and generally did. That little, sharply waxed mustache of his, the points thrust up toward his ears, would twitch and become almost alive as he told some unprintable anecdote of those days.

He hoped for passion, not realizing that he did not really experience it. He was merely accustomed to hearing it talked about. Perdita, for all her brilliant loveliness, and the way in which she had (he imagined) embodied his ideal, did not inspire him with passion. As he drove down the hill to the Boulevard he wondered, was she his ideal? In some ways she fulfilled his early dreams, which had been mainly of wealth and magnificence. The artist in him had matured in a somewhat warped and twisted form. His originality was not remarkable. His intellectual and emotional resources were those of a good newspaperman. He could not rid himself of the conviction that time spent in reflection and reading abstract books was wasted. He had a swift and supple dexterity in assembling his ideas into the salable patterns of magazine fiction. His very narrowness of outlook helped him to maintain the humility that directors loved in their writers. He was adaptable, so that he was aware, now, of a picture in projection, as though he sat in the long narrow darkness of a movie house in some jerkwater town, himself a jerkwater patron, desiring diversion and the fulfillment of his dreams. He understood how simple motivation must be for such a patron, and he could combine that understanding with a humorous perception of the highbrow's dismay at such tripe.

When Miss Linkweiler had given him Joyce's *Ulysses* to read, telling him it was "important," he read it, in spite of what he called its "complications" and "lack of continuity." When she told him that Joyce had gone blind he had told her, tranquilly, "It reads like he'd been blind from birth, that bird. It's all sound-track, without any photography or direction."

Wealth and magnificence he had dreamed of, in that Midwestern village where his father had been a "judge." Like any other lusty young hick with ambition, he had had dreams of fair women. They, and the sudden romantic emotion of assuming the role of protector of the lovely child that Sonia was, had made him fall in love with Perdita. She had been honestly grateful to him for his interest in Sonia, but the bonds between the mother and child had always been mysterious to him.

Sonia seemed to have fallen politely in love with Louis! He received affectionately-inscribed colored postal cards from Connecticut, where Sonia was living. They were stuck in the mirror in his bedroom off the kitchen along with small snapshots of Sonia on a pony, Sonia holding a puppy, Sonia riding a bicycle at Shadowcrest Farm. Louis had taken Sonia from him, he thought, smiling. Kids were the only real democrats.

He longed for Perdita as he wanted her to be, and hoped she would be, in the Eastern countryside. He knew just what he wanted in the way of an estate. He saw it, richly secluded, with a boathouse on the dock and a place to work among trees. He saw Perdita among flowers, and Sonia, with her kittens and puppies. It would be all his, bought with the money he had earned. . . .

• • •

iii

APPROACHING the medieval chateau occupied by Mr. and Mrs. Cavoura and a dozen servants, he put away his dreams—for they were nothing more and came from that part of his mind which was useless to him in his business —and drove his car to the end of a line of vehicles. A white-coated Japanese revealed a complete set of large and perfect teeth and ushered him into an oak-paneled great hall with a fine stone fireplace. Here the company was assembled and Mrs. Cavoura, a quiet mousy lady who had never had any connection with motion pictures, had never been on the stage, and who was supposed to go to church for fun, gave him her hand and immediately left him to amuse himself.

Elliot Ducroy had developed a system adapted to these gatherings where the great, the almost-great and the would-be-great were mixed with nobodies and nonentities. He cultivated the affable manner of a shopwalker and remained quietly outside the various groups until he found someone he knew. This time he went toward the broad figure of Cavoura himself, who sat on a lounge in an alcove with a dark girl. Cavoura had his hand on her arm as he leaned toward her, telling her something that made her laugh diplomatically.

When he saw Elliot Ducroy he held up his left hand, still holding the girl's arm with the other. He struggled to his feet.

"I introduce," he said, "Shentleman Shurch, Sydney Sahxsohn."

He smiled at the girl, who sprang up and stood close to Elliot Ducroy.

"Oh!" she said, taking both his hands and thrusting her face toward his, "are you really the creator of Gentleman Church? I must kiss you!"

Mr. Cavoura smiled even more broadly.

"And Mees Sahxson—she write stories . . ."

Cavoura was not acquainted with the full extent of the girl's fame in the magazines.

"When Mr. Cavoura said he knew you, actually knew you, I made him ask you to come."

"You Sydney Saxon?" Elliot Ducroy saw Cavoura, smiling broadly and without malice, lumber away to the bar. He sat down.

Her hair was a solid dark red bob which seemed to have been cut away in front so that she could look out. Her skin was white, almost translucent, against a costly and simple black dress. A necklace of small red coral beads had an extraordinarily seductive effect. Her bosom was deep and full and her eyes were dark and bright and searching. She looked at him with frank admiration and critical approval. There was a curious blend of business acumen and sexual acquisitiveness in Sydney Saxon.

Elliot Ducroy knew her by reputation. He knew she was one of the spectacular successes of the last two years, not only in serials but in short fiction. Now at last she was in Hollywood, and the first thing she wanted was to meet the famous author of the famous Gentleman Church stories.

"Just as I'm leaving," he said. "Don't pass it around, but I'm through. I mean I'm through here."

"Oh, don't go away just as I'm needing someone to tell me what it's all about!" she said. He had got her a drink and was now getting a cola for himself.

"You'll find it all out for yourself," he said. "The great thing is, don't worry. Let them do that. Take it easy."

She thought this over. As he looked at her he had confused thoughts. She had kissed him the moment she heard who he was. She was confident and admiring. She gazed at him with the familiarity arising from their exactly similar backgrounds and professional achievements. Yet it was something more. She was not only a conspicuously successful woman writer, with such a phenomenal output that her serials seemed to follow one another without a break, but she was a desiring and desirable woman.

He tried, as he gave himself up to the intimacy of their conversation, to recall what he had heard of her private life. He knew she had been married and divorced several times and that was all. It did not matter. He saw she was completely interested, and he was aware of an upsurge of emotions that had been dormant for a long time.

When he asked her if she wanted another drink she shook her head.

"No," she said. "I have had two. Two more than I usually have. I don't drink."

"Me too. I'm celebrating."

"Celebrating what?"

"Meeting you. Will you have dinner with me tonight?"

"I can't tonight. I've got an engagement."

"All right. What do you suggest?"

"Call for me." She took a card out of her pocketbook and showed him the address. "I'll say I'm expecting you. We can have dinner tomorrow."

He copied down the address.

"I'll be there at ten," he said.

"Do you really want to? It's a long way out of town, Mrs. Cavoura says."

"Yes, I want to."

"What shall we do?"

"That's telling."

"All right. Show me your etchings if you want. . . ." She made a mouth at him and her smile was provocative. It was the smile, not of an odalisque but of an independent woman in full vigor of mind and body.

"It's an amusement," he told himself, as he drove to the Writers' Club for dinner with Irving. "She's marvelous, too."

Irving nodded when he heard Ducroy had met the new arrival. He knew all about Sydney Saxon coming to Hollywood. She had no agent, he said.

"No agent? She'll have to have an agent," said Ducroy with vehemence.

"Sure," said Irving, "but who'll tell her? She thinks she knows it all. Thinks she's going to save agent's commission. Thinks agents are the bunk. Says she's her own agent."

"I'll mention it," Ducroy said.

"Don't just mention it. Mention me," said Irving. He grinned.

"That's what I mean," Ducroy said, without grinning. He was thinking of Sydney Saxon.

He mentioned it. He was convincing. Sydney Saxon's resistance to the agents in New York had arisen from her lack of experience and from the stories she had heard from other writers. It had taken a personal letter from the president of the corporation to get her to sign a contract to supervise the "picturization" of her best seller, *All on a Summer's Day*. When Elliot Ducroy told her of Irving's many virtues she said she'd give Irving her contracts in future. If Elliot Ducroy thought he was all right. . . .

"All right? He knows more about my financial position than I do!" said Ducroy.

They were in the verandah of his bungalow looking out at the constellation of lights that was Los Angeles and Santa Monica and Venice and Hermosa, with a luminous presence behind which was the Pacific. They had dined at the Ambassador, where she was staying in a cabana in the grounds until she found a house, and then he had driven her up the canyon road.

"All alone," he had told her, as he unlocked the garage

door. "My man's out this evening. Probably sitting in one of those Mex joints and drinking a gingerale. He's another faithful soul, Louis is. Like Irving."

The view, when he led her up the steps cut in the rock, to the house itself, and with his arm around her, to the verandah, made her exclaim. He remembered how Perdita, sitting in precisely the same chair had seemed not to notice the view at all.

"You get used to it," he said. "It's like the girls. At first they attract attention. They knock your eye out. Then they become part of the show. All the same, this is one of the things I'd like to keep. But it's only a rented shack." He waved toward the view.

"I'll rent it if you're really going East," she said.

"I'm really going East," he told her. "I've got plans, yes, and it's too bad you have to come out just as I'm headed back there."

"I'll be coming East," she said. "I've no intention of giving up my real work. I want some local color, for one thing, and, well, it's real money, isn't it?"

"Some of it is. This is a hell of a place for polite panhandling. A woman can dodge it better'n a man. And there's a lot of politics in the office, and humbug. Don't forget that you, as a writer, are less than the dust beneath the second deputy assistant supervisor's chariot wheels."

"Oh, is that so?" said Sydney Saxon.

"Yes, that's so! You'll suffer less than most. You'll suffer, though. It's like seasickness. You get used to the motion of the pictures, and then you don't notice the insults."

Elliot Ducroy laughed. He was enjoying himself. In this girl's company he unfolded, whereas with Perdita, who preserved an air of resignation while he was talking of his work, he felt strangled. It was not that Perdita disapproved of what he said, or that she was bored, but that she hadn't paid attention. She was somewhere else, he believed.

Sydney Saxon laughed, but she was not convinced.

"The first second deputy assistant supervisor who . . ." she began calmly and broke off. "Oh, the hell with them! I'm mad at you because you're going East just as I . . . You'll think I'm one brazen hussy." She looked out across the night.

"No," he said. "No. I think you're swell. I've wanted someone like you!"

"Those words you take right out of my mouth," she said hoarsely. She put her arms around him, and he lifted her, holding her to him. She delighted him.

She was his exact complement. He comprehended her rhythm, the complex blend of feminine yielding, ruthless business ability, and the artistic sensitivity that made her a facile and popular writer. She had a delicate boldness toward him that suited him without alarming him. He discovered, also, that his preoccupation with Perdita's physical type had been an illusion. What he really wanted was something utterly contrasted, something Sydney Saxon possessed in its full maturity and vigor.

"You're sweet!" she said in a low, measured tone. Her voice was thrilling to him, yet it was without the disturbing intensity of inexperience. He did not feel a cad for not being fantastically romantic about her. He understood that for her, having been through the rigors of earning her living, the struggles to make her way as a writer, and the business of marriage and maternity and divorce, sex was now something to be enjoyed richly and soberly. Love was no doubt the crown of life, but you did not wear a crown all the time, was Sydney Saxon's private credo.

What she advocated in her stories was more romantic. Her first serial in a woman's magazine, she who hated women, had been called *Love Will Find a Way* and it had caused a number of editors of women's magazines to make immediate inquiries about her next story. It was, they felt, the real thing.

High on the side of the canyon, on Elliot Ducroy's verandah, she who had never before crossed the ranges, having gone from Ohio to New York, had a momentary suspicion. It was so romantic! She had a job to maintain command over her intelligence. It was so like fiction, up here, with a man she admired as only a woman writer can admire one of her own trade. The suspicion, that there might be people who did not write romance, but lived it, who actually achieved in their lives passion and heroic folly, was so confusing that she blushed. It was illumination, she thought, as she lay in his arms. And that, she was able to note, would be a swell title for a long short, a novelette, in which her favorite woman character, a smart young married woman who had been to college and who had ideals as well as experiences, would be illuminated by visiting a dude ranch near a canyon in California, run by a swell man.

The following Saturday evening he was connected to Perdita's apartment in New York. He heard a faint far-away voice saying "Hollywood on the wire." He sat waiting for her "Hullo!" He was not feeling very well at the moment. He wondered if she would express any solicitude if he told her about it. Nothing much, just a sort of oppressive feeling after running up those stairs. Sydney Saxon was coming in her own car later and they were going to Cavoura's for a buffet supper. Cavoura had a distinguished European playwright staying with him. A highbrow.

He listened. He was trying to make up his mind whether he ought to resume his life with Perdita without telling her about Sydney Saxon. He had a good measure of provincial conscience in his system. It seemed a cheap, scabby trick. A man whose wife was in the East might make a casual date with an extra girl in one of those apartment hotels in Los and then forget all about it. This was different. It was an affair. Sydney Saxon was in love. She made absolutely no claims on him. He knew without that what she wanted.

It was the sort of problem a man instinctively stalled in

solving. But he was honest. He wanted to tell Perdita. He decided to ask her what they ought to do in such a case.

He listened. A voice, a thin, hesitant, and suddenly African whine, came over the wire.

He thought to himself "Hell, it's the smoke."

"Mr. Ducroy speaking. Come alive there! Get Mrs. Ducroy, please. Hollywood talking."

"Miz Ducroy gwine awaye! Note heah naow," the voice wailed.

"Gone away? Where's she gone?"

"She gwine to Pairiss. She sent you night lettah dis mawnin'. She sailed dis mawnin' fo' Pairiss."

He sat with the thing to his ear so long he heard the line cut. He walked to and fro for a while, his fingernail against his teeth. It was one of his habits when thinking.

"What do you know about that?" he said to himself out loud. Louis came to the door and looked in, thinking he had been called.

Elliot Ducroy's first reaction was to get Irving. Irving was in New York. He was close at hand, really, with Terry in an apartment. The only thing was, he might not have a telephone, and if he had it wouldn't be in his name. Moreover, it was supposed to be a strictly clandestine abode until Irving got his matrimonial affairs unsnarled.

The night letter might not arrive until Monday morning. He could find out. Yes, he could do that.

He had been going to surprise her. She had surprised him all right. Paris? He tried to imagine what had happened to make her do that. Her monthly allowance had been paid a few days before, he reflected. Of course, if she wanted to go to Paris, she had the price. There was no reason why Elliot Ducroy's wife shouldn't go to Paris. But she had never mentioned the place!

It made him angry, all at once, to think of this happening. He felt imposed upon. He had always been on the level with her! He had made up his mind to keep it up, too. Now, well, God damn and blast!

He had it all planned, to do the thing well. He wanted a nice place in the country, in Connecticut, on the water. He had it all etched on his imagination, and the woman in the picture was Perdita with a Virago, Sonia riding a pony and himself keeping a speedboat at the yacht club. He saw Louis installed as his faithful seneschal.

He kept saying to himself, "God damn and blast!" faster and faster, his heart pumping. He had a sensation of walking wildly alone on an immense quagmire, of collapsing suddenly with a frightful pain in his breast, a pain burning and unbearable.

When he came to, he was in bed. The light was shaded, a nurse was at a side table with her back to him, and a doctor sat at ease in the living room, smoking a cigarette and talking to someone out of sight.

The nurse glanced at him and spoke to the doctor, who rose and came forward. Elliot Ducroy did not know him. Then he saw Sydney Saxon at the door. She came in and stood a little away from the bed.

"You scared me stiff," she said sternly. She looked at the doctor, who was calm.

"I don't remember," Elliot Ducroy said, looking at the doctor.

"Don't try," said the doctor. "Take it easy. Bed for you. Who's your physician?"

Elliot Ducroy told him. The doctor nodded.

"You'll be all right now," he said. "The nurse knows what to do."

"What happened? I don't feel so bad."

"Just a mild attack of angina pectoris," said the doctor. "Haven't you had it before?"

"Not like this. I thought I was run through with a red-hot iron."

The doctor nodded.

"Absolute quiet," he said, and prepared to remove his white coat. The nurse went out with him. Sydney Saxon, her eyes very bright, came to the side of the bed.

"I remember," he said, "you were coming up. We were going to Cavoura's."

"Don't talk. Yes. And I came, and found you lying on the floor as if you'd been shot in the chest. All doubled up. Louis was phoning for a doctor. The police came! He called them, said you'd had an attack. They thought he meant you'd been attacked. I found a couple of cars at the door."

"When was this?"

"Hours ago. Don't talk. You heard what he said."

"Don't go away."

"Of course not. You need someone to look after you."

"Sure do." He put out his hand. He looked at her with a fixed, tight smile. "Stood you up for that date."

"Louis fixed us a drink. The doctor . . ."

The nurse came back and took the hand he had given Sydney Saxon, for his pulse, watching her wrist watch. She had long lashes, he noticed, and humorous lips. When she released his hand she gave him a discreet smile.

"That's what I call nerve," he said to her. "Don't you want a hand of your own?"

"Just as you like," she said, smiling at both of them. She made them think she had a lover and was in love herself. She went into the living room and sat down to smoke a cigarette.

Elliot Ducroy made Sydney Saxon sit on the bed, so that he could talk without effort.

"I had a shock," he said. "I thought I'd ruptured a blood vessel. I was very upset. I was calling New York . . ."

He paused, holding her hand.

"Go on," she said. "What did she say?"

"She didn't say anything. She wasn't there. Colored girl

answered the call. She'd sailed for Europe this morning. It's still Saturday, isn't it? Well, she'd sailed for Paris."

They sat for a moment, hand in hand. This neither of them had bargained for. Sydney Saxon had bought her last divorce from a mail-order Mexican agent on Park Avenue and she was not at all sure it was actually valid in any state in the Union.

Neither of them had bargained for this, because marriage would suit neither of them. At any rate marriage to each other would suit neither of them. They both knew this and knew the other knew it and accepted it as a feature of their adventure.

"Do you suppose, maybe, she'd heard about us? From some kind friend who wishes her well?"

"No," he said. "It's not that. In fact I was goin' to tell her about us. Yes, I was. I didn't want to have any undercover business."

"You were? Oh, well, yes, I see."

"Not to embarrass you. I was going to tell her I had a friend, you see, and if she wished to split up, I'd see she was all right."

"I see."

"So she's gone to Paris. And I don't know why. She isn't the sort to run off with a man. It's inconceivable."

"How do you know?"

"Well, because I'm married to her and do know, darling, that's all. The smoke said she'd sent me a night letter. I might get that tomorrow, maybe Monday. You know, she does things like that without meaning anything. It's because . . . I dunno . . . She's another sort of person. Different from us."

"I understand, darling. Don't talk. You don't mind if I stick around, do you?"

He put out his arms and she sank into them softly, comfortably, humbly, thankfully. She thought: *He's mine when I want him, anyhow.*

He woke so gradually that the two worlds, of sleeping and waking, were imperceptibly blended. Was this, he wondered with a mental wink, the subconscious? It was very enjoyable. Wouldn't be a bad idea to live here, he thought. He could reflect with ease, as upon an immense, resilient cloud of nebulous memory.

He saw everything he actually looked at with extreme clarity. For instance, he saw that Perdita was not deceiving him over this Paris business. With Sydney Saxon holding his hand it was not so clear; but he knew that she herself did not believe it. She only wanted to believe it in order to justify herself conventionally.

This sudden physical collapse, which was credible only because of the memory he had of that intense ferocity of pain before it became unbearable and he fainted, had done one thing. It had brought his life into focus. It was sweet to have Sydney close at hand, as understanding and loving and efficient in many ways; but that was in focus too. It was in the foreground, while Perdita and Sonia were in the background. In fact they were the background.

Another figure in the background was Irving, who had been wired and who had phoned back that he was arriving on the transcontinental on Tuesday. By that time everything would be straightened out.

He lay luxuriating in the novel sense of languor and complete freedom from responsibility. He saw how he had been distorting things. He saw his own personal vanity in buying the Virago. He saw also, that some of his ideas would have to be modified. His original conception of a great house with servants and a boat dock . . . Oh, much too grandiose!

It had been inspired by the almost fabulous structures around him in Hollywood, reproduction of Carcassonne and the terraced palaces of Persepolis. He had grown accustomed to driveways, a mile long, through eucalyptus, orange and ilex groves leading to forty-room air-conditioned bungalows of white marble with cedar paneling.

His eyes closed, his body relaxed and motionless he saw all this as nonsense. He was on the verge of doing what thousands of crazy Americans did every year, living beyond his resources, loading himself down with possessions. He had a flash of inspiration. Possessions possess a man. He becomes their prisoner.

He would take care of that now. And he was not going to be stampeded into breaking up his life with Perdita. He refused to imagine her running off to Paris with another man. When he was ready he would call the telegraph office and try to get her night letter sent over. He did not regret telling Sydney Saxon about Perdita; he hoped she'd understand, that it was a private matter between him and Perdita. That the two things were separate in his mind.

He saw his mind as a multi-cellular organism, in which a number of smaller organisms were existing in various stages of maturity. It was a hive . . . !

It was delightful to lie still and think nonsense. Yes, the mind was a hive in which there were precious few drones, so there was plenty of honey. He didn't think of Perdita as a drone, but as the queen bee. . . . He had read that queen bees always hunted down and killed all their rivals. . . .

Yeah, he thought indulgently, the great trouble is always the truck a fellow has read. He himself had always been afraid of metaphors and abstract, metaphysical musings. He tried to keep his professional mind objective, telling only what happened, giving the story a beginning, a middle and an end. A sensational, startling beginning, a swift-moving middle, and an end as much like a crack on the jaw as he could invent.

They weren't always good. Everybody wrote seconds and mavericks, with a few stinkers. So did the mighty dead whose stories he had sometimes to adapt. The mighty dead had been mighty lucky in having small competition, he thought. This attitude of patronage toward the great was always accompanied by a realistic conception of his own work. But he knew he had something, and the real reason for everything being the way it was, was just this—Perdita had never understood or appreciated that something. It was hard to pin it down and give it a name. It was himself. It was what made an Elliot Ducroy story different from the stories of a dozen other writers of his class.

Sydney Saxon saw it and had seen it before she ever set eyes on him. It thrilled her and made him dizzy to hear her tell him about it. When she read one of his stories the other day she said, "I'm proud!" and kissed him.

This was a rich experience. A man had a right to savor and enjoy it when it came his way.

On the other hand there ought to be some way in which he could become adjusted to Perdita as a plaything, who would live in the seraglio he was going to have in the East, who would know nothing about his business and who would be merely ornamental, a recreation for his leisure hours.

What was wrong with that picture, he thought quickly, was that a writer hasn't any leisure hours. Not in the usual sense. When he had he was more likely to spend them in some other fellow's seraglio!

He was curiously ignorant of how Perdita would function in a home of the conventional sort. So far as he knew she had never had one with that heel Pagett. Since their marriage, because of his work, there had been no real opportunity to live that way. A woman ought to have domestic tastes or artistic tastes; Perdita had neither. She might have been a socialite at home in England, but in California she was a total loss. No doubt the change from old England to Hollywood was too upsetting. He clung stubbornly to the conviction that when he did get her set in the East, things would be all right. Because of Sonia, he added, "We'll live happily ever after." It was only in fiction nowadays that stories ended unhappily. In real life it was different. . . .

He saw Louis with a tray and the nurse following him into the room. He decided to ask her to get the night letter.

"It's here," she said. "Are you sure you ought to do any business? The doctor . . ."

"It isn't business," he told her. "It's pleasure. Where is it? Hello, Louis."

She brought it in.

He opened it and read it quickly, the nurse and Louis on each side of him.

Terribly sorry could not get you on telephone last night have invitation to join party going to Paris sailing NORMANDIE *hope no objection Sonia all right returning early March weather beastly in New York please cable thousand dollars care Cooks Paris*

regards P.

He laid it down and smiled at the nurse as she took the dishes from Louis and arranged them on the table. There were also flowers.

"Thanks a lot," he said. "I had to know what this wire was. It's from a friend of mine in New York." He smiled again.

"Mrs. Saxon called," the nurse said. "She's coming to see you. She sent some flowers."

"Suits me," he said. "What about Doctor Seligman? Has he been? Or has he sent flowers too?"

"You were asleep and he wouldn't have you disturbed," she said. "He said Dr. Vasey gave the right treatment."

"That makes it unanimous. They always back each other up. Are you going home today? Or are you waiting for a relief?"

"Mrs. Saxon said she'd be here in an hour." She looked at her own wrist watch as a matter of habit. The curve of her arm and the elbow itself were charming. It was, she added, half of eleven.

"She'll make a good substitute," he said. "There's nothing the matter with me, really. It's a racket you and the doctors organize when business is slack. I don't need professional care."

"Is that so?" she observed with pleasure. "I'll mention it to Doctor Seligman."

"And Dr. Vasey," he urged. "He ought not to be kept in the dark."

Louis looked lugubriously around the room. It was hard to determine whether the experience of finding his employer lying on the floor, apparently dead, or the later experience of finding so many strangers in the place, was the more disturbing to him. With a faint Latin gesture of his hands he went away. The nonsense his master was talking only made him vaguely uneasy. To Louis frivolous conversation could only indicate a flirtation.

When he was alone again Elliot Ducroy re-read the night letter and found that his first reaction to it remained. He had been right about Perdita. She had called him on the phone. She probably picked an hour in the evening in New York when it was afternoon in Hollywood and Louis had been out. He still didn't see why she should suddenly bolt like that; but some people did things that way. Picture people, for instance! Everybody liked to make a sudden impulsive gesture at times. He did not resist a secret grin at her mention of the New York weather in March. She had fled from the everlasting sunshine of California. That was human nature, of course. Nobody was consistent.

Irving's theory was that she was an aristocrat, with the accent on the second syllable. Irving would be in soon with something that might or might not substantiate his theory. Elliot Ducroy called Louis and gave him the telegram in its envelope to put in a desk drawer. When Sydney Saxon's coupé appeared at the foot of the canyon road, he was reading the newspaper. And so she found him.

She made no reference to what he had told her. She looked unusually young and attractive this evening, full of new enthusiasm and tenderness that was not to be resisted. He had known, when he first met her, that she was the acquisitive, possessing type. It was a type that suited him secretly on account of a faint indolence or nonaggressiveness in his character. He pinched her chin.

"What happened?" he said. "You look like a million dollars. Got an assignment?"

"They've given me a collaborator," she said, smiling. "A boy."

"What's his name?"

"An admirer of yours," she said. "Dryden Turneur."

"More likely of yours. Yeah, I've met him. We've given him work now and then. Did he tell you he was a descendant of the poet?" She nodded.

"He took me out to lunch."

"Did he? Must have sold a script. The studios are full of 'em. They stick around for years, but they don't make much. He'll give you a lot of hints. He can kick a story around."

"What kind of hints?"

"I mean . . ." He laughed and then nodded. "If he takes you out to lunch the first day . . ."

"I got an idea at once," she said with energy. "He was a new one to me and I wanted to hear him talk. He had the strangest youth."

"I've heard it. He made a script of it and mailed it and it was read and they sent for him and gave him a contract. He married a girl and they wrote a script together on the bridal-night theme. I know Dryden Turneur."

He could see she was slightly disconcerted because what she had imagined was a newly discovered personality turned out to be common property. The neat, twenty-five-year-old Dryden Turneur's pointed mustache and quick glancing eyes, his excessively Hollywood haberdashery and footwear, had attracted her. There was something of the boulevardier, who had been a gentleman-adventurer, about him. He was romantic if slightly tarnished.

"Well, anyway . . ." she said. "He knows more about pictures than I do. I guess I'll make use of him. Hasn't he talent?"

"Maybe. He knows there's gold in them thar Beverly Hills. He may strike pay dirt yet. He isn't a yes-man and he isn't a faker. As I said, the studios are full of 'em. Have I made myself clear?"

"It's all very well for you," she said. "All your talk doesn't alter the fact that scripts aren't easy to write if you're used to straight fiction."

"They're not easy to write no matter what you've been used to. Remember what I said? Take it easy. Let *them* worry. As a matter of fact, I expect they've let young Turneur sew them up with some crazy scheme connected with your stories, and to get rid of both of you for the present they've given him this collaboration job. I give them a month to start wondering what the heck you're doin' here anyway. The man who made the original suggestion has been fired, maybe; the president, who wired you to come, is in Florida or Arizona, and nobody else cares."

"What am I to do?" she said.

"Take care o' me. Let Turneur have the typewriter. He's probably writing a novel on the office time. Or a play. Yeah, it 'ud be a play."

"You make the whole thing senseless," she told him.

"It is senseless. After a while, 'less you go East, you go batty. I'm goin' East."

He expected her to allude to the night letter, but she did not. She had had an amusing time, the previous day, with Dryden Turneur, clarifying his attitude toward her and, making him understand there was no chance, at present, of having an affair with her. It was all part of the extraordinary tempo of the place. Young Turneur took it in his stride, and was charming in a she-loves-me-she-loves-me-not fashion. And she was thinking how far would it be prudent to tell Elliot Ducroy about him. The mention of his going East steadied her nerves.

"Not for a few weeks, you aren't," she said. "The doctor said you could get up in ten days, maybe. Did you ever go to La Jolla?"

He shook his head. "Too busy," he said.

"Young Turneur says it's a dream place."

"All right. We can go down there. Near San Diego. I got a bit of property at Encinitas. Tryin' to sell it. We'll go, and we can take in San Juan Capistrano for dinner on the way back."

She said, suddenly, "I love these Spanish names. They're the only romantic thing about this country. I mean," she added, "I like to see them with you."

iv

"You were right," Elliot Ducroy said to his friend and agent, Irving. Irving was sitting on the bed practically where Sydney Saxon sat. He was nursing his leg. "I ought to have gone East when you suggested it. But how was anybody to know she'd go off to Paris with a crowd of poets and artists?"

"Only one or two are that," said Irving. "There's Caxton Derrick. It was him gettin' this stake from a rich banker to go to Paris and finish his new book, see, that started the caravan. There's an artist and his wife—she's a sculptress. The others are goin' along for the ride, to hear Caxton Derrick do his stuff. In the cafes."

"I still don't get it," Ducroy said. "She never mentioned Paris before and she always seemed to think writers were the lowest form of life."

"What I told Terry," said Irving. "*She* says it was just what you might expect."

"What does she know about it? She didn't run around with Caxton Derrick, did she?"

"No, but she's got this job for Regal Distributors. She's in a taxi half her time chasin' stars 'n' socialites, interviewin' 'em for Regal Distributors Cosmetic Club. She thought up the club idea herself. She's smart, Terry is. Calls herself Alix Fayre. She hears a lot o' gossip. And she's just around the corner from St. Giles' Alley, where your wife lives. It's a sort of Bohemian social bunch. They have talkfests and they's plenty to drink. I told you the sort of the mob they were."

"I know you did; but I didn't figure on this Paris business. It looks as if I might as well not go back East at all."

"Now listen, chief! She's sailin' on the *Ile de France* end o' the month. You can take it easy and be there to meet her. You see what she says in her cable."

"I can read. It also says 'please send five hundred care of American Express.' Does this bird Caxton Derrick charge admission to his poetry reading? And what was Terry gettin' at when she said it was only what we might expect? What did she mean by that?"

Irving caused his foot, with the startling shoe and Scotch-plaid pattern sock, to waggle to and fro across his knee.

"I guess she was referrin' to the liquor side of it," he said, irritably.

"Liquor side of it?" Elliot Ducroy put his hands under his head and stared at the ceiling. He reflected. Perdita had once or twice, long ago, given evidence that she was better off without it. As a rule she didn't touch it. Once or twice, though . . . Yes. Terry had no inducement to color the facts. There had been quite a few cases in Hollywood of women who drank to excess. Some made a secret hobby of it and seemed almost religiously proper when sober in public. Others behaved beautifully for months and then, suddenly, up went their tails and they flew over the fences to open country. Others sat tucking in side-cars and old-fashioneds and smiling, getting quieter and quieter, and smelling awful. And others suddenly keeled over into your lap and were sick, dead to the world.

"Yeah," Irving said, harshly. "Better get back and see for yourself, chief."

"I will, when I'm through with this lyin' around. The doc says I have to keep in bed a bit. Say in a fortnight. That'll give me time to travel by train and meet the boat. I'll have to look for a place."

"I heard of a place," said Irving, feeling in his pocket for papers. "It's near Norbury. It's a buy. Estate bein' settled, and the widow wants cash. She can't keep it up on her insurance. She's goin' to marry again anyhow and live in Florida."

Elliot Ducroy was amused.

"Has she sent you an invitation to be an usher?" he asked. "You seem to know a lot about her."

"It's a swell buy," Irving insisted. He always ignored Ducroy's facetiousness concerning his own nose for news. "You can always get a bargain for cash and assume the mortgages."

"Mortgages? How many?"

"It's prob'ly plastered with 'em," said Irving. "These old places grow 'em like poison ivy. If you like, I'll get an option."

"Okay. I'll look at it. And I'm goin' to buy a car."

"You bought one. Like hell you bought one. That English bus."

"That's for her. Me, I want something for myself. I'm turning in the old Stutz."

"A coop you want?"

"Now don't say you've got a bargain!"

"Why not? A friend o' mine in Columbus Circle's got a demonstration model to dispose of. A de luxe coop."

"Why don't you buy it for yourself?"

"I'd rather have a taxi. When I pay off a taxi, I'm through. No insurance, no garage. Hell, what would I want with a car? To drive from here to New York?"

"Well, tell that flat-foot Louis of mine to bring in the bottle. I'll stand you a drink, Irving. Did you know Sydney Saxon's comin' up this evening to dinner? Did you know she's been a good friend of mine? She was on the job when I had that seizure. We were goin' to Cavoura's."

"Yeah. I know about her. They tell me she's doin' a script with Dryden Turneur. I saw something about it in *Script*."

"I guess *Script* got that from Dryden Turneur," said Elliot

Ducroy, biting his thumbnail. "I'm goin' to be fed up with this invalid stuff."

"Better take it easy," said Irving. He took the glass Louis offered and poured in plenty of soda water. "You'll have to take care of yourself, chief."

He made a slight gesture of salutation and drank. He was, Ducroy knew, a faithful soul, like Louis. Probably Terry was another. He had had a lot of visitors since it became known he had had a sudden attack, and they were all kind. But they all had their own affairs.

But Elliot Ducroy was discovering that inaction was not merely distasteful. It was impossible for him. He had always been a worker at high pressure who lived under the illusion that it would be heavenly not to have to work. He had honestly believed that if he only had the chance, he would "loaf and invite his soul," whatever the hell that might mean. He had not realized that the only life he knew was work at high pressure, almost twenty-four hours a day, that it was this aptitude and dynamic zest which distinguished him from the men who never got anywhere.

He waited a week and decided to resume the life and adventures of Gentleman Church. Louis wheeled in the dictaphone rented from an office supply house, and plugged it into the wall by the bed. Ducroy meditated sending for a secretary. It had always suited him to work alone at home however, and he plunged into dictation.

Louis would look in, gloomily, on occasion, forgetting that this unintelligible shouting into a long rubber tube was part of the day's work. He had only the most shadowy notion of how Elliot Ducroy earned his money. He knew it was in connection with motion pictures and involved sudden absences and equally sudden returns, with long spells of furious hammering on the typewriters in the study. The resumption of this work pleased Louis. He concluded that they would be going East after all.

Not immediately, however. When Elliot Ducroy was able to go out, it was rather cold and Dr. Seligman suggested either Palm Springs or San Diego.

"How about La Jolla?" said his patient.

"Sure. Don't work too hard. You put too great a nervous strain on yourself, Mr. Ducroy. You work 'all out,' as they say in England."

"Only way I know," he said sheepishly.

"That's all very fine, but as your physician, I'm telling you. Relax, if you know what I mean."

"I will. I do," he said.

He told Sydney Saxon what the doctor said.

"Now's the time," he said. "I'm to relax. I have to be in New York last day of the month. It's the sixteenth now. So we've got a week. I'll leave Louis here to pack. We can nip down to San Juan Capistrano to dinner, like I told you, and go on to La Jolla after. Or we can go direct."

She clapped her hands.

"I've been down there," she said. "I met a couple of fans. They're retired and live at La Jolla. They invited me down. You'll love it."

"How? You going to introduce me?"

"No. It's this way. I said how I'd love to live down there, and they said, 'We're going East for a month; why don't you use this house? We'd be proud, if you wrote one of your stories in our home.' "

He nodded. "That's California," he said. "My house is yours: take it. Real people."

"So they said I was to phone and the agent would let me have the key any time I want."

"Swell. Let's go."

"I can't tell you how lovely it is," she said. "The garden's on the edge of a cliff. And there's a sound, when you sit on the porch. . . . It's most ravishing! A sort of whisper. It's the surf, way down below the rocks. The house is a bungalow, simply buried in flowers."

They took the road through Corona and Escondido, through the hills, rather than the Coast route. Sydney Saxon drove her coupé, their two bags in the rumble.

"I wonder what Louis is thinking," she said, when they got clear of the city. "He's never taken to me."

"You don't need to worry about that," Ducroy said. He sat with the collar of a light overcoat turned up. "No need to worry at all. If you start wonderin' what people are thinkin' . . . Do we ever know, is what *I* wonder! Do I know what you're thinkin'? Or you what I'm thinkin'? I read a book once: *The Art of Thinking*."

"So did I," she said, smiling. "By a Frenchman, wasn't it?"

"It was about the time that other Frenchman pulled a fast one. His system was not to think but to talk to yourself. It was a riot for a while. Then it disappeared. Every day in every way we got worse and worse. Suppose it's all part of the entertainment business. People who know how to think can't transmit the knowledge to people without any brains. But you can always entertain the brainless. Take a look."

She saw the great beauty of the hills scarred by enormous signs and food and drink stands. She saw a building in the form of an ice-cream cone a hundred feet high. She saw another in the shape and color of an orange twenty feet in diameter. There were lubritoriums and automobile hostels. There were eateries and niteries, cabins, cabinettes, auto parks and hot-dog emporiums. And they were all brilliantly colored.

She saw all this and much more as she drove carefully in the thinning and thickening streams of traffic. The driving took her attention.

Elliot Ducroy sat silent for a while. Louis, he believed was a faithful seneschal and minded his own business bette than most. He was devoted to his employer's interests. He wa also devoted to Sonia. There was a gleam almost of living interest in the man's austere features when he was reminded of Sonia.

This, he thought to himself, was an experience. He had not intended to do anything so deliberate with Sydney. He had wanted—for the present—to keep their relationship somewhat more casual. The news of Perdita sailing for Paris had been an 'out,' as though Perdita desired their relations to be less rigid and conventional. He didn't suppose she thought of it at all that way. In fact he didn't know what went on in her head, except that she was fastidious and truthful in her conduct. She certainly hated the way many women in Hollywood accepted sexual intercourse as an indoor and outdoor sport or a game of musical chairs. He conceded that. She was superior to all of them, which was why he cherished a secret desire, once he was clear of Hollywood, to start all over again.

He suddenly realized the truth of what he had just said, about people thinking. Just look at what he was thinking, while Sydney was thinking—what? He looked at her profile, at the keen dark eyes fixed on the road, the strong hands lightly holding the wheel and the firmly modeled limbs with their small, neatly shod feet controlling the pedals.

He thought: it's nice to be taken care of. Too much introspection would make a mess of anything. He was going to enjoy himself. When the *Ile de France* came in he would be on the job again and carry on. He would take care of Perdita and Sonia. Just now he wanted to be taken care of.

"What about getting into this place?" he said, as they drove into La Jolla.

"I have the key," she said. "The agent mailed it to me, registered."

For a moment, as she stopped the car in front of a low dark frame house half hidden by trellis walls covered with vines, he was silent. It was extraordinarily secluded. A curve of the road and high walls hid them from other dwellings. It was now dark, the stars were very large and lively, and as

Sydney Saxon cut the engine and held her finger to her ear, he heard the faint sound she had mentioned. He could smell the flowers too. She settled against him and he put his arm around her.

It was a simple enough dwelling furnished in cedar and leather and with a good supply of books.

"She said she was a Rosicrucian," Sydney told him. "That's Mrs. Maybrick. He's a Theosophist."

"We'll have to take it up," he said. She went into the bedroom and shut the door. He lay in a deep chair and lit a cigarette.

Happiness, he decided, could only be achieved if you didn't think. He thrust out of his mind all problems involving responsibility. How else was he to relax? He could write that story "Where the Eagles Gather" when he got on the train with Louis. It was a strange thing, that the presence of Louis never interfered with his work. In fact it helped him, to see that austere lugubrious countenance.

But just now . . . He rose and went through a side porch to the rear of the house. There was a garden in which white statues stood at the edge of a pool. Beyond the summerhouse was a dense mass of foliage. As his eyes grew accustomed to the darkness he saw a path through it. He came out upon the edge of the cliff, where the starlight showed him a railing. He could see, far down below, the creaming foam among black rocks. He could hear, crescendo, the stealthy susurration of the water searching a passage. In front of him was the vague misty nothingness of stars and sea.

Then, as his match flared to light a fresh cigarette, he heard her voice calling him.

"I'm here," he said. "Can you find the way?" He struck another match and held it up in the murmurous, scented dark. It went out and he saw her white figure coming toward him. He opened his arms.

"You aren't in your birthday suit, are you?"

"Almost! Isn't it lovely and warm here? Listen. There's steps down to a swimming pool."

"All right. You wait. I'll go in, but not to swim. I'll wait a while."

"Of course."

He carried her back to the house and left her on the back porch. When he returned they sat for a little in the darkness. She had the talent for silence he so much appreciated at times. She permitted him to embrace her. Then they walked together in the darkness to the railed path which led down, zig-zag to the sea. He held his hand under her left breast as he guided her carefully downward. There was a small concrete platform over a pool that swirled and roiled as the surf broke into it over the rocks.

"This is great!" he said. She slid out of his arms into the water. He could see her white body against the blackness of the rocky pool. "Is it deep?"

She said it was not deep. He slid in, and they floated in each other's arms for a moment.

Next morning, while he slept, she made coffee. They heard a thump against the door and when she went to it she found the newspaper. There was also milk.

"That's some hospitality," he said. "I don't have fans like that. My fans want me to send them a photograph, signed, and a complete set of my works, if any. Failing that, a year's issues of a magazine containing my stuff. Listen, did it ever occur to you we have all the worry of bein' authors without any of the real veneration?"

"I don't know what you mean."

"Well, take that big British novelist we were supposed to meet at Cavoura's the night I cracked up. I met him later, at the Writers' Club. While I was talkin' to him I kept askin' myself, what's the difference between me and you? He sells his stuff to the mags, and it runs to a hundred thousand copies in book form. And the movies give him fifty grand for the talkin' and television rights. But that's not all there is to it. He gets articles written about him in the highbrow papers, about his art and his technique and his place in literature. That sort of thing. They say he's refused a title. And he'll probably be buried in Westminster Abbey, in the Poets' Corner."

"I still don't know what you mean," she said.

"Well, this. About a year ago the office bought one of his shorts. I'd call it a novelette. And they gave it to me to make a script. He's too big to do it. Well, it was lousy. It stank. You couldn't do a goddam thing with it! I had to scrap pretty near the whole thing and rewrite it. I made a good picture of it, no thanks to him. But will they bury me in Westminster Abbey? Answer, yes or no."

"No, I don't suppose so," she said. She was repressing a smile, almost a giggle. "It's a different thing . . ."

"That's my point," he said. "There's a difference. And we'll never change it. We're just hicks when it comes to litrachoor."

"I'm not worrying about it. Have some more coffee."

"I will. You see, we have to have sensation. What that Britisher called 'penny dreadful stuff.' He told me, over there a dime novel is a penny dreadful. Everybody has one sensational story in him."

"Like Dryden Turneur."

"Yes, like Dryden Turneur. Only he scared the lights out of the office. They reacted later. When you send in a script like that, childhood in a whore house, you make a certain effect. But you can only do it once. It isn't art. It's artifice. Or artfulness. I sometimes wonder if that's all it is anyway, no matter how good we are."

He lay silent, drinking the coffee. She leaned over and kissed him.

"Now," he said, "I'm not sayin' we've all got our feet in the trough. All I meant was, we're different. Did I tell you about my friend Piers Mallinson?"

She shook her head.

"I've heard of him. He's a poet. I've never read any of his stuff."

"It's not easy. But it has something. Couple of years ago I read some of it and I liked what I could understand. I went to see him. He lives in a shack on a cliff near San Luis Obispo. He was so thin you could see through him. I—well, I made him take a bit to carry on with. He's a sort of protégé of mine now. He's goin' to dedicate a book to me, if he ever finishes it. I'll be in the highbrow libraries! He says we're all a lot o' prostitutes in Hollywood!"

"What has he written?"

"A book of poetry called *Shining Vampyres.*"

"I've heard of it, but I'd forgotten. I read a poem of his in a magazine called *Sun Sacrifice.* It was horrible. About a priest cutting out the victim's heart on a Mayan pyramid, with an obsidian dagger. Of course it was all symbolical of something."

"All his stuff's symbolical. Just as well. But that Miss Linkweiler I used to have to coach me, she said he was important. Mallinson, he said this Caxton Derrick is important. You know, the one she . . ."

"What are you getting at?"

"I don't know what I'm gettin' at. I'm beginnin' to wonder if I know what it's all about."

"They'd all be glad enough to be in your place now," she said. She finished her coffee, pinched out her cigarette and slipped into bed again with a lithe movement.

"I'll say!" he said. "I'll say!"

V

SONIA LAY in her bed in her room in the new house and looked at everything. Her expression was that of a young and delightful fairy monarch who had reached the throne of her desires by using magic arts. Sonia had done all this, really. Now she lay in her bed, under the curved muslin canopy, looking out across the gardens to the beautiful sea, filled with a grave, sweet, sense of delight. They were all together again. Mummy and Elliot and Sonia, and Louis too. And there too was Hector, pretending to be asleep in his basket on the hooked rug in the corner. Sonia drew a deep breath and treated herself to a small inward smile. Outwardly there was only a brief rapid flutter of her long lashes.

It was now early summer, and they had been in the house which Elliot had christened Church Yard, for nearly a year. What changes those early months had made in the place! Sonia had watched the transformation of an eighteenth-century Colonial dwelling, with its shabby flaking paint and heavy beams, its curling shingles and warped porch floors, into a splendid mansion. She had seen rattly windows changed to lovely casements, and big old barns reclothed with white painted boards and fitted with handsome doors. There was a most lovely pigeon cote on a tall pole in the yard in front of the garage, full of cooing birds. The long drive in front had been graded and laid with blue stone, the old gate replaced with a new one of squared oak, and the architect had covered it with a lych roof such as they had in churchyards in England, where Mummy came from.

The architect had told Sonia those gates were used in the old days to rest the corpse under while they waited for the parson. Sonia used hers to protect her bicycle. It was one of her private thrills, as she came along the shore road, between the new stone wall and the shingle beach, to imagine a corpse resting beside the lych gate. A mysterious corpse, for it had no face, Sonia told herself. It rested on two trestles like those the carpenters used while working in the house, and it was in a box closely resembling the crate in which the enormous grandfather clock came from New York.

From where she lay in her chintz-hung bedroom Sonia could just see the roof of her own special possession, a complete little house with a tiny garden surrounded by a white picket fence. The brass door knocker was in the shape of a dragon fly, and the bright blue shutters of the windows were pierced, right and left, with pussies and puppies in silhouette. There was a chimney with a wooden puff of smoke trailing out of it. There was a kennel for Hector, which he never would use, and Sonia was proud of her tiny electric range, the telephone to her mother's room, and the simply perfect bed-sitting-room suite specially designed in maple by the architect. She liked the little shingle on her tiny lawn with the name "Sonia" in raised letters. It was all so satisfyingly complete, right up to the weathercock in the form of an old witch on a broom, atop of the rooftree. And because it was so complete Sonia had sometimes to make herself keep on loving it.

It was early yet, and apart from the knocking of Louis's feather duster against the bannisters, there was no sound indoors. Elliot did not get up very early, and Mummy in her own great beautiful west room, did not get up until noon. Sonia would go in and look at her and receive a mumbling response from a head buried under the clothes.

The sun was making a great shine over the sea now and Sonia lay watching the sky get hotter and hotter. Even Hector, yawning and snuffling and stretching and finally jumping on the bed to sniff in her ear, did not distract Sonia from her thoughts of the past few months. So Hector got down and lay quietly, waiting for getting-up time.

She had been horribly lonesome at that farm while Mummy lived in New York and Elliot stayed on in Hollywood making pictures. The terrible and implacable logic of a girl-child had been working on the complex destiny that began in a vast white hospital in Los Angeles and had carried her to a New England "farm" run by a corpulent, pop-eyed, ogress who worked incessantly at hooking rugs and scraping the paint off old pine cupboards, bullying her own two children with hoarse growls, and welcoming the customers in her antique shop with sudden, incredible smirks. The children at the small, uncomfortable school in the village had not been nice. On one occasion Sonia had smuggled a small dirty note into her weekly letter to her mother—*Mummy please take me away please Sonia*—which contrasted strangely with the sedate hypocrisy of the dictated words of her formal letter.

There had been a number of slight improvements after that and Perdita had descended upon the farm in a rented car, had taken Sonia into the village and bought her some picture postals. One of them had gone to Louis in Hollywood and one to Elliot Ducroy.

How she had longed for Louis, with whom she had held conversations (Louis contributing nods or expressive shrugs and glares) in the piercingly lovely kitchen in Elliot's house! Pushing her little bicycle up the steep canyon road to the green door beside the garage, a door that opened upon a flight of steps cut in the rock and led up, up, steeply, and curving, to Louis and his cookies. What happiness! A happiness that hung suspended in the bright air, like a jewel. A happiness that seemed dissociated from father, mother or any human relationships except old Louis. She thought of it now, and smiled.

Out of the haze of infancy came grotesque shapes to

haunt Sonia's loving imagination. Other children had parents, real parents who lived together with their babies and little boys and girls. They did not, for instance live in separate homes in California and hold long arguments at intervals that ended in slammed doors, or (even more mysteriously) softly closed doors, which the small Sonia was forbidden to open. Other girls had mummies who came to see them with exhausting regularity, who smelt of perfumes and rich clothing. They came with daddies to the summer camp to which Sonia had been taken that summer, with older sisters. They had aunties and uncles and cousins.

Sonia's Mummy needed looking after. Sonia had arrived at this conclusion by secret paths through the dense undergrowth of her own feelings. Sonia longed for relatives. She wanted to be like other girls in such matters. But with only her Mummy at hand, and with Elliot so far away, it was obvious that Sonia herself would have to make the most of what she had. And her Mummy needed looking after. The men who had occasionally come down in their cars bringing her mother to the farm were obviously useless. They wore berets, wide corduroy trousers and strange coats. They had hair down the sides of their faces and often wore rings and bracelets, like girls. Mummy didn't always smell nice, either.

Suddenly the world had changed from a dull gray to rainbow splendor. Mummy and Elliot, in a most enormous beautiful car, came down to Camp Lullaby (six hundred dollars for the season with horseback riding and dancing lessons extra) and took her with extreme speed to show her the new home. Sonia sat breathless between them as the great car, which Mummy said was "a six-liter Virago," shot like a bullet through Norbury, through Sutton Corners and along the sea front to a tangled garden in which stood an old, weathered house with several old red barns in the rear.

"Darling, we're going to live here," said Sonia's mother.

"All together, Mummy?"

Perdita exchanged a glance with her husband, pinched Sonia's nose and nodded.

"Oh, Mummy! It's a lovely house, isn't it?"

"Seventeen forty-six," said Elliot Ducroy solemnly. "That's pretty near two hundred years old, Sonia. The real-estate man says there was a house here before that, built in sixteen something. One of the early settlers, I guess. People named Penge. Same as that Miss Penge the real-estate man said sold antiques. We'll go and see her, get Sonia a real old New England bed and chairs, and so on."

Even Sonia could see Elliot was not in his usual glum mood when he was not working. She looked from one to the other with dawning happiness, and her mother suddenly put her arm around her as they sat in the red-leather tonneau of the Virago.

"Yes, an early settler," Elliot repeated, the words doing something to his imagination. Then he laughed, closed his eyes and shook his head. He would have to make a note of that, he told himself. A new Gentleman Church angle.

They got out and walked up the leaf-strewn paths to a rough shack erected around a monstrous affair with a pulley at the top. In the shack was a thumping, vibrating engine which hauled up a big block of iron on a rope over the pulley and let it drop. Elliot said they were deepening the artesian well. A contractor's truck and several cars stood around. A man in leather leggings, who carried a large roll of blueprints under his arm, came out to meet them. They then went into the house, talking.

This was the architect. Sonia wandered around while the grown-ups bent over the drawings laid out on a trestle bench in one of the downstairs rooms. Sonia was happy in a way she had never before experienced, and did not recognize it as happiness. It was almost a pain in her breast. An active black tomcat sprang away through the undergrowth in a series of long leaps as Sonia walked through the garden behind the house. The idea struck her that she would perhaps be allowed to have a dog. She would ask.

She heard her mother calling her and ran back to the house. Perdita was looking out of an upstairs window, beckoning. Sonia took two steps at a time up the staircase in her eagerness.

"Look," her mother said. They were in a large room at the northeast corner of the house. Down in the drive was the Virago and out beyond lay the blue Sound, asleep in the afternoon sun. Sonia saw a tug with a line of sand barges moving slowly out from the yellow bluffs near Port Jefferson. She saw a white steamer and several white-sailed yachts. It was almost too much. It was her first actual sight of a horizon apart from the vague brightness seen from Elliot's verandah up the canyon road. This was the sea! She held her lower lip firmly in her teeth to keep herself from being a baby.

"This is your room," said Perdita, and the architect looked smug and benign.

"Private bath for her ladyship too," said Elliot.

He opened a small dark room across the hall and made motions. The architect explained how he would make an annex between them, a sort of dressing room, and transform what was now a dusty hole into a young lady's bathroom, with old rose porcelain.

"And don't forget to brush your teeth while you're in there," said her mother. "You'll wake early, and see the sun rise," she added, bending down to Sonia's ear. "Mummy's on the other side, 'cause she likes to sleep in the morning."

It was an exciting day, and when they all drove back to Norbury the architect, still smug and benign, took Sonia along in his car, and they had dinner at the Inn. Sonia was suddenly tired and fell asleep almost at the table.

"Let's stay here for the night," said Elliot. The architect drove off after another conversation. By that time Sonia had been sound asleep and Elliot had picked her up and carried her up to bed. Sonia remembered that journey; the smell of an old New England inn blended with Elliot's cigarette; a whiff of food smells from a back staircase; the bump as she was dropped on a white bed; the shriek and roar of a train passing through Norbury.

She lay thinking of those days and the days that followed. It was the happiest time ever she thought, even though she could bring into focus only the special delights. And at the camp she had met her great friend Shiela Boldwin, whose parents were in Europe. Shiela's home was only a quarter of a mile away from Church Yard. It was near the yacht club. It was pretty hard to think of as a home because there was never anybody there except a short, dark Filipino gentleman who took care of the place. Shiela's parents were always away. They went to Maine in the summer and to Florida in the winter, and in between they went to Europe or to an apartment in New York.

One of the important things in Sonia's life now was her friendship with Shiela. When Shiela's parents learned about Sonia's parents rebuilding the old house on the shore road, they did not cease from traveling rapidly, by air if possible, to all parts of the world. They let Shiela stay with Sonia and the Filipino ran their house for the two children between camp and school. Shiela went to Harris, a school of enormous prestige at the other end of Connecticut, a school for the female offspring of people like the Boldwins. It was part of the curiously inverted relationship between Sonia and her mother since Sonia had turned ten, that she should instruct Perdita in the tremendous advantages offered by Harris, of which Perdita had never even heard the name. Girls from Harris matriculated brilliantly into Vassar (Perdita did have a vague notion of what Vassar was) and graduated multa cum laude into Park Avenue or the East Sixties, with places on the Sound, of which they were the chatelaines.

"Righto, we'll go and have a look at this wonderful school," Perdita had told her. And Elliot had agreed. Elliot was what Shiela called "a perfectly grand man," Shiela having picked up the phrase from an older girl. Shiela was at that time thirteen, and they were now both "at Harris."

Then there was the speedboat Elliot had bought. A marvelous experience, to sit in the uplifted bows of that rich, dark, powerful, plunging monster, while the exhausts of the twin engines gave out a deafening hullabaloo. The rush of wind on their faces, as Shiela said, was simply divine. It was hard to breathe, perched in the upward-slanting bows that swayed deliciously as the screws tore a wide gash in the Sound. Sonia had often shuddered with a deeply relished delight when she thought of it.

At that time, the time of the rebuilding of Church Yard into a modest country gentleman's estate; the time of the cars, the speedboat, the lovely toy house; and finally the time of the arrival of the expensively pedigreed Hector, Sonia felt that everything in the world was perfect. She lay in her bed now, thinking of that time and wondering confusedly why she was no longer quite so happy as she was then. There was a gravity in her small beautiful face, with its delightful short nose and the curiously changing color of the eyes which she had from her mother. It was the gravity of responsibility. Sonia felt she had to take care of her Mummy. The days of the beginning of Church Yard had been preceded by a peculiar period during which Mummy had been ill. She had been so ill that Sonia had been three weeks without any news of her. Then Elliot had come down and taken her to New York. They had gone to a house full of nurses and had found Mummy in a deck chair on the roof behind strong wire netting, so that it was like a cage. She had heard Mummy say in a low voice to Elliot, while looking at Sonia, "Why did you bring her to this place?" and Elliot had said, "I thought you'd like it, dear." He had put his arms around both of them and Mummy had smiled gently and said, "Don't."

Then Elliot had taken Sonia to see a musical show and had driven her back, very late at night, to Camp Lullaby.

Sonia knew perfectly well, now, what the trouble was. It seemed to her that in some way she could not fathom, she had always known it. Always, ever since she was able to remember, which was since she was four. Sounds of a hot dark place, with a blinding dazzle of sunlight outside; sounds of harshly grinding trains, of trolley cars roaring and banging past the end of the street; sounds of voices quarreling in the next room; sounds of Mummy crying at night. And now and again mysterious stretches of happiness on a yellow beach with Mummy quietly loving, were followed by difficult nights and mornings in which Mummy seemed another person altogether and did not smell nice.

It was not that Mummy was ever unkind. It was rather a going off, some distance away from Sonia and lying dead still, staring at the ceiling, while Sonia played on the floor. Once she had said, with her lovely smile and in her lovely voice while her eyes, that were the eyes of Sonia, seemed to change from brown to gray-green, "I wish you were old enough to take care of your drunken old mother."

So now she was taking care of her mother. At Harris, which was Episcopal, of course, and extremely formal in ideas, Sonia had come in contact with other girls who thought it nothing unusual to possess parents who didn't know how to behave. "You have to boss them!" shrilled one freckle-nosed girl, whose mother had a million dollars of her own and was honestly trying to drink herself to death. Sonia had no idea of bossing anybody. Hector was disobedient and she loved him. Sonia's idea was to be helpful. Mummy wasn't like those girls' mothers. She went along for weeks, sometimes months, just the loveliest mother ever, before she crashed. It seemed that being a grown-up was like riding a bicycle, Sonia surmised. They kept their equilibrium beautifully for just so long, and then—in the ditch!

Now, Sonia was uneasily aware there was something else. Coming back from Harris for the summer vacation, which for Harris was from the end of May to the end of September, there had drifted into Sonia's life a new care. That miraculously perfect solidarity of the three of them at the beginning was not there any more. Of course Harris was tops, and equally of course Shiela Boldwin was tops too. But it wasn't the same as having Mummy and Elliot all to herself, one on each side of her in the Virago, or in the speedboat. Sonia had a terrific passion for a family, for relatives. At school she invented them. She invented adventures in California in which her parents had been her partners and they were simply *screaming!* She invented relatives in England, aunts and barrister uncles, and a few more in California. It was easy to do this at Harris, though the house-mistress, who knew who paid Sonia's school bills, once remarked that "fiction seemed to run in that family."

Now that was over. It was useless to pretend to Shiela that Mummy and Elliot were really loving parents. Shiela knew all about parents who ran around separate. In fact Shiela had imparted to the troubled Sonia the thrilling news that her people were breaking up. "They're the best of friends," she explained; and indeed they had become even nicer to her than when they were merely living together.

Sonia was not Shiela, who had always had a home. Sonia, lying on her bed, looking around the lovely room and out into the garden with its background of great trees, was aware of the difference between her mother and the other girls' mothers. It was a difference so profound that it eluded all definition. As if she were some other sort of creature. Sonia had once said, "Oh, Mummy, you're an angel!" And Perdita had agreed. "A fallen angel, ducky," and kissed the top of Sonia's blonde head.

Now it was all over. Sonia had gone to stay with Shiela and when she came back her mother was in New York. Elliot had looked at her somberly at lunch when she asked, where was Mummy? There was a tense feeling in the air which made Sonia unhappy. Grown-ups had an extraordinary way of bringing on this tenseness, so that you felt as if something was going to explode.

"I don't know when she's coming back," Elliot said when Louis had gone into the pantry. "She may not come back at all! I expect she will, though. You play with Shiela. She'll come back all right."

"Can I stay with Shiela?"

"Sure. I'll be out to dinner. You'll be goin' to camp soon, I s'pose?"

"Oh, yes. But please, Elliot, I don't want to go to camp and not see Mummy. I have to take care of Mummy."

"Yeah. I know. Only she don't want to be taken care of. So she went to New York. But don't you worry. She'll come back."

Sonia said, in a shrill, piping voice, to hide her fear of blubbing, "Of course! I *hope* so."

Shiela was always saying, "Don't get watery, kid."

Elliot Ducroy, with an inscrutable, stern expression, pinched her cheek. He looked mad about something. He said, "You want Shiela to come and stay with you? It's only a quarter mile to her place. What's the idea? Lonesome at night?" He went on, as if to himself, "It's a fact, she ought to be with Sonia. What are we to do?"

He went away after lighting a cigarette, and Sonia could hear his typewriter rattling with fierce energy. She got Hector and went out. And suddenly, in the evening, there was Mummy in the station wagon. Elliot had brought her from the station.

"Hullo, ducky! Thought I was dead?" She turned to Elliot. "Sonia's in one of her disapproving moods. Look at her!" She gave Sonia a hug.

"Where you been, Mummy?"

"Where? On in New York. By request, ducky. This is the new system. What the eye doesn't see the heart can never grieve over. That's an old English proverb."

She was looking, not at Sonia but at her husband as she

said this. Her eyes, that seemed to change color as one watched them, regarded him attentively, without anger, without criticism, without even that opaque indifference that intelligent married women use to conceal their chagrin over their fate.

Elliot said, as he stood before the large stone fireplace he had had built in the central living room, a room which had been made by knocking three rooms into one, "You said that before."

He meant she had said it the first time he had made the suggestion that she go to New York and "get it over with," where he could not be a witness. Sonia had been at Harris at that time.

"That's right," she said, "I did."

She turned her head to look at Louis, who came in bearing two glasses of sherry and bitters on a tray. Sonia slipped out of her mother's arms, looking from one to the other, and ran off. The grandfather clock, which had come all the way from Madison Avenue, gave out a soft, muffled chirring, five strokes. Elliot Ducroy had once remarked that it was the most expensive sound he had ever heard.

"Did you see Irving, or Terry?" he asked. He drank half his sherry and put the glass on the mantel.

"You know I don't like her," Perdita said, sipping the sherry as though it were not very nice medicine. This sherry and bitters indeed was not a drink, not even an *apéritif*, for either of them. It was a symbol of compromise. Elliot Ducroy had read, or heard, that in England ladies did not drink in good society and big authors drank sherry. Which accounted, in his opinion, for the bum stories they wrote. Possibly, he had surmised to Perdita, who did not care a damn, sherry was good for novelists; but look at the English magazines!

On this occasion the symbol was accepted for what it was. He nodded understandingly.

"How should you? But she's good for Irving, and Irving's good for me, or us if you like. She doesn't fit into any classification that I know of. I admit that. I admit I like her. I know you don't."

"She makes me feel that I'm not married, and she is," said Perdita, sipping.

"I get you. In a way, perhaps . . . Hm." He dried up.

"Go on. Say it, Elliot. You think I'm no good. I spend your money and I'm no good. Yet, from my point of view I've been a good wife to you."

"Yes."

"Well, I said a good wife, not a good mistress. That's what you want, really. It's what you need, possibly. This," she went on, twiddling the wine glass and smiling at it, "is a damned polygamous country, my good man. Wives are like suits of clothes. You wear 'em, or not. You want 'em cleaned and pressed, ready to put on when you happen to fancy 'em. Or altered, what!"

"Now, now!" he said, smiling.

As though he had really warned her, as though he had blown a whistle as their conversation took a sudden dive into subterranean chambers, she pulled up and said, in another, more musical tone,

"This wine goes to one's head, doesn't it? We aren't quarreling, my dear. Let's not. Sonia doesn't like it."

"What are you driving at?" he said frowning. "What makes you think . . ."

She rose suddenly from the big chair by the low table, where she had been lying almost horizontal, her legs resting on the heavy brass and leather-upholstered club fender. She picked up her pocketbook, hat and gloves.

"Elliot," she said, in a matter-of-fact tone. "I don't think. I know! And I don't very much care."

vi

THAT HAD been the night before, and now Sonia, before she slipped out of bed and accompanied Hector downstairs to see Louis and have breakfast with him, lay looking around her room and out at the shining Sound, discovering, as she thought of all that had happened at Church Yard since they moved in, that there was a faint, transparent, yet perceptible specter in her mind, a disturbance of spirit rather than a defined shape of unhappiness. Out on the canyon road, in the foothills of Hollywood, the cure for such spectral uneasiness was conversation, as she called it, with Louis. "I had a conversation with Louis," she would tell her mother, and Perdita, putting down her magazine, would say, "I bet Louis never got a word in edgeways!"

It was obviously time for a conversation with Louis. Hector, giving up the idea of pretending sleep, left his basket and yawning, flexed his pedigreed, grotesquely bred limbs until his breastbone touched the rug. Like most pedigreed creatures he was completely incompetent, relapsing into fleas, worms and the wolfing of unspeakable garbage the moment he was given his freedom. Now, in the chaste perfection of his groomed and useless existence, deprived of the work for which his forebears had been scrupulously bred for centuries, screened and combed and sterilized into an animated toy, he watched Sonia with that alert concentration upon his own well-being which dogs have cunningly imposed upon their less intelligent proprietors as devotion.

Certainly he received devotion in return. Sonia lavished

upon Hector and Louis the affection which would have gone to Archie Pagett, who might have been willing to exchange it for the cyclonic battles he was experiencing with La Conchita, the ceaseless screaming recriminations of an illiterate and not-too-talented bitch in the City of Angels. Sonia knew nothing of her father except that he had been her father long ago. Her passion for relatives (to be like other girls) built him up into a handsome, glamorous phantom. Without deliberate help from Sonia the legend at Harris would have it that Sonia's mother had been a star of the now-dead silent screen, that Sonia's father was a White Russian who had fled to England after the revolution and changed his name, and finally Sonia herself was destined to go back to Hollywood.

It was a beautifully complete and harmonious legend, as plausible as it was inaccurate. Sonia had trouble, when the question was put to her by the other girls, in saying that it was not true. They assumed she had been drilled to deny such richly interesting details.

She knew nothing of her father; but in her affectionate nature the love that was his by right was given to Hector and Louis.

She opened the bedroom door, and Hector at once ran downstairs. The wide landing, the shining waxed boards and slender white painted balusters, the delicate old English prints against white panels and the dark chest of Pennsylvania walnut, were bathed in the morning sun from a high clear window. In her camel hair robe and bright scarlet mules, Sonia was transfigured by the sunlight into angelic brightness. Finger on lip she moved silently to her mother's door and knocked. It was not closed completely. Sonia opened it an inch and peeped into the dusky interior.

Looking down at the floor she whispered, "Mummy! Mumsy, darling!"

She waited for the usual faint sound of a movement from the bed, the almost imperceptible displacement of the air under the tester, the long inhalation as Perdita stretched her limbs and turned her head toward the door to mutter good-naturedly, "Ducky!"

This time there was silence. There was, Sonia knew, nobody there at all. She stood in the half-opened door and pressed her finger to her lower lip to stop it trembling. It was never any good to be watery, she knew. She stood again on the landing as the door on the other side opened and Elliot Ducroy came out part way. They gazed at each other, doubtfully, as though they had met in an enchanted wood. Elliot Ducroy rubbed his chin against his palm.

"'Lo, kid. Your mother went away in the car. 'S all right. She'll be back. You know. I *tried* to get her to stay. You goin' down to get breakfast? Ask Louis bring me some coffee. Coffee and grapefruit. Go on now. It's all *right*, I say! She'll be back."

He retreated and closed the door softly, solemn and silently thoughtful, as though going back into one of the trees in the enchanted forest, leaving the little girl to find her way alone.

Sonia descended the curved staircase, which had been copied from the original Penge homestead. She went slowly, pausing and sitting down, holding her blonde head in her hands. Then, quite briskly she sprang down several steps and scampered violently into the dining room.

The drooping shoulders of Louis, in an alpaca jacket, wearing a green baize apron, which he had refused to abandon in spite of Elliot Ducroy's sarcasms, were visible in a corner. He had spread newspapers—Louis had no other use for newspapers save to spread them under or over whatever he was doing—and he was polishing the arms, legs, stretchers and backs of the Chippendale chairs. There was a pleasant aroma of turpentine and wax in the air. Hector, tearing in from the kitchen, snuffed without enthusiasm the dark rags and oily bottles.

"Oh, good morning, Louis," Sonia said. "Is breakfast ready, please?"

"Chocolate's mos' ready." Louis had ultra-conservative

ideas about cooking things like cocoa and oatmeal. He rose slowly from stooping, looking at Sonia with an austere cadaverous solemnity that was on the point of breaking into an affectionate smile. It never quite broke, but it was there, and expressed an emotion that was otherwise inarticulate.

He washed his hands in the laundry beyond the kitchen and began to lay a meal in what Sonia called "our nook," a short extension of the kitchen, all windows with geraniums in boxes outside and with a table and benches for six, three on each side. Louis, who had become used to labor-saving appliances on the ships, now had every electrical contrivance on the market within reach. The gleam of duplex cupronickel sinks and drain boards ran along one side of the shining chamber. Crockery, china and glass stood on shelves, and a dozen saucepans, in diminishing sizes, hung over an electric range that seemed as valuable and as magnificent as some fabulous oversize music box.

With apparent legerdemain Louis produced orange juice, porridge, eggs, honey, toast, a large glass of milk for Sonia and a small one for himself on the outer corner. The chocolate was not quite perfect. Louis had a way of producing this provender as if out of a hat or from his sleeve, silently, with compressed lips and eloquent gloomy gaze fixed upon nowhere; yet obviously he was an artist who enjoyed practicing his art. Sometimes, to Sonia's secret delight, Louis would do tricks. He would discover imaginary defects in her plate or cup. He would pick it up and pretend to throw it out of the window, and it would bounce, being made of rubber, or he would almost drop a real plate and when he retrieved it from under the table it would be filled with cookies. He would pretend he had lost the pepper pot and would find it amazingly in the pocket of Sonia's robe. Casually he would lay a napkin on the table and under it, miraculously, Sonia would find a canary made of icing, or a goldfish of barley sugar. He could keep a paper butterfly in the air with a fan, making awful faces in the oriental manner, and would bring it to rest on Sonia's head. All the while his long horse face and grief-stricken expression would not change.

He kept this sort of thing for Sonia. Like many seagoing stewards, Louis had numerous talents which he used only in an emergency or for those whom he liked. Sonia and Shiela were the only witnesses of this side of his character. Louis, moving like a skilled lugubrious shade around the interior of Church Yard, or lying in his white iron bedstead in his room, as bare as a prison, over the garage, brooded over Sonia with secret indignation. The fairy child, who had trotted up the canyon road to have conversations with her friend, had become the companion of his dreams. The mother was there too, but there was no intimacy, even in dreams, with the woman who in actual life seemed unaware of his existence. She was there because of Sonia, and in his dreams he devised a life of patrician bliss for them with himself as a humble servitor.

So, when Elliot Ducroy had said to him, out on the canyon road, "Well, Gloomy Gus, we're going East pretty soon now. You'll see your little girl friend again," Louis experienced a secret happiness that was immediately soured, when he walked silently into the verandah one evening with a tray, setting it down silently and about to arrange without sound the cushions on the divan and the ash trays on a table. He saw the top of a woman's head, russet and glossy as a bird's wing, and two superb white arms whose interlocked hands lay behind the head along the chair back.

She was gazing, silent and motionless, toward the now invisible ocean, toward the tremendous sky that was green, orange and bronze, and would be, almost immediately, burnt amber and ocher, and then imperceptible as the lights of the city came on. She was waiting for Elliot Ducroy, who was changing his coat. When she became aware of the man in the white jacket she turned and looked him over with cool competence and shrewd animosity.

Louis had withdrawn then from the verandah, and into

himself, if it were possible, cherishing a misery that was almost physical. He heard Sydney Saxon say to Elliot Ducroy one evening with a chuckling contralto laugh, "That man of yours . . . !" The service door had swung to at that moment.

When the day came for them to board the train the danger he had imagined seemed to have vanished. Sydney Saxon had vanished too. Gone on location in Lower California, Elliot Ducroy said, as though he himself were pleased about it. Louis knew and resented, in a dark, inarticulate manner that seemed to be merely the obverse of his silent professional skill, the continual presence of Sydney Saxon. Elliot Ducroy knew also that Louis was right and it was a good thing the contract was finished and they were going East.

The first months in New York and at Church Yard had been incredibly agreeable to Louis. Church Yard was to him the pot of gold at the rainbow's end. To Louis the Californian conception of architecture and furniture did not appeal. Now, with the appearance of pine paneling, hardwood floors, and old furniture with a patina, he worked with an intense, staring absorption, caparisoned in the green baize apron he had worn when he worked in the West End of London, caressing with wax-impregnated cloth the limbs and arms of tables and chairs, of highboys and lowboys.

In his new kitchen Louis not only cooked and baked, but dreamed. He resisted Elliot Ducroy's suggestion that a cook be installed. Ducroy had in mind what he called "a couple," a man to work outdoors and his wife to cook. There was ample room for them in the reconstructed barns. Louis resisted. So Mr. Cagliari, the gardener, lived in Norbury and came and went in his own half-ton truck.

Louis would not hear of it. He became agitated, and got out, finally, the words "quit" and "women make trouble."

"Oh, all right. You want to be cock of the walk," Elliot Ducroy said. "We can use the club for a lot of people. It suits me too," he added to Perdita. "I work at home, you see. We can use the club."

The club had come into their lives when Mr. Ducroy's speedboat arrived. Most of the yacht club members owned yawls and dinghies. There were a dozen diesel yachts with real crews, and a fleet of outboard craft whose exhausts crackled and popped, making more noise than speed. The Ducroy speedboat made both, using incredible quantities of gasoline from the club's fueling jetty. The deafening uproar of its departure from the dock was like a salvo of quick-firing guns, and made the ice clink against the glasses in the bar.

It was this somewhat expensive craft which aroused Perdita's dormant sporting taste. And indeed, after the first few weeks as the squire of Church Yard, Elliot Ducroy discovered that his work was the most interesting and the most absorbing sport of all. The plain shack of brown shingles set away in the woods behind the barns, with an oil-heat studio stove, some pine shelves and tables, a typewriter on a block sawn from a fallen hickory tree, a chair and a camp bed, became the center of his world. It was, he told Sonia gravely, the power house. Here he spent his days and sometimes his nights, and Louis would bring over a meal with coffee in a thermos flask.

So the speedboat and the Virago became Perdita's and Sonia's, until Sonia went to school. Ducroy would merely go along to the club sometimes and sit in the bar a while, among the neighbors.

And among the neighbors he became aware that he was, in a sense, back among the producers and the executive moguls of Hollywood. He was a minnow among tritons. The difference between the moguls on the Coast and these was tone. They might not be individually so rich, though some of them were really rich; but they were able to assume something of the old-world stateliness and feudalism because the sources of their wealth were on deeper foundations and out of sight. They were, in fact, less theatrical about it, and their women more exclusive. They had been educated at famous schools and eastern colleges. They emphasized to Elliot Ducroy, whose year at Ann Arbor and graduation from an obscure business college meant nothing at all socially, the difference between earning money, making it, and having it. It was obvious that, to some of them, the fact that he had to work himself to get his money, instead of being an "executive," placed him in a special classification.

In course of time he made some friends among the less heavily-endowed club members, owners of yawls and cabin cruisers. They were younger and more Bohemian, and they would join parties to drink, bringing their own set—their women—with them and practically having their fun in private at the host's expense.

There was another thing. Elliot Ducroy was aware that a man like Irving, for instance, would not belong there. Which was strange, because gregariousness and the knack of mingling inoffensively with all men was almost a vice with Irving. What Elliot Ducroy pondered was that at the beginning his wife was accepted by these people more cordially than he, the already-famed creator of Gentleman Church. She was accepted by the men, that is, and some vague gestures were made by their women toward the incomprehensible, brilliant creature who knew nothing of their social background and cared less. The gestures grew vaguer as the speedboat devolved more and more into Perdita's ownership, and it became obvious that the men hung around, offering Perdita mechanical assistance, with ulterior motives.

The pursuit of beautiful women, however, is no longer carried on with fierce ardor. Any woman, beautiful or otherwise, is left alone almost as soon as she indicates that it is her desire. Elliot Ducroy, in his work, had been increasingly aware of the gulf apparently widening between conventional fiction patterns and the facts of daily life. Occasionally, in a flash of insight, he wondered whether it had not always been so, whether novelists were not all liars, and short-story writers damned liars.

The men who offered mechanical assistance when Perdita

was using the speedboat got nowhere. She might have been an overnight guest from Europe or a distant planet so far as intimacy with them went. The Lothario of the club, a young Wall Street man, told the group in his cabin cruiser one Saturday night that the trouble with Mrs. Ducroy was, she had never been what he called awakened. "Never met any man who had really awakened her."

"You been trying to sleep with her, I suppose," one of the women said.

"That's not the point!" the man insisted, amid hoots. "Don't you see what I mean?"

"Well, explain what you mean to her husband," said someone. "He ought to be let in on this."

"I shouldn't like to do that," said the host. "No, I shouldn't like to make the suggestion." A practical member of the party added, "No, and I shouldn't like to pay her gasoline bills either. That damned boat of hers uses twenty gallons an hour!"

To Sonia and Louis, all this was as if it had never existed. Louis, by some inherited European intuition, knew that Mrs. Ducroy paid no more attention to the men at the club, or those (and they were the same) who came to Church Yard for cocktails, than she did to himself. Not as much! There was something special in the smile she gave him which legitimized, as it were, his part in Sonia's world.

Now the boss had come East and was working furiously in his studio across the yard, Louis thought life was extremely good. Maintaining Church Yard's interior in a condition of almost fanatical perfection was an easy job to Louis, who was a natural-born domestic drudge. Only it was never drudgery to Louis, because he loved polishing silver and crystal and china.

He even loved the chores of the three bathrooms. In his green baize apron and huge knee-pads made of pieces of thick red carpet, he was a strange, grunting, wheezing animal burrowing away in corners in search of the last microscopic speck of dust. When visitors left liquor rings and smudges of canape on his furniture, or trod crackers and anchovies into the rugs, he blew out his cheeks and glared into space. He made no audible comment upon the local customs of leaving burning cigarettes where they could do most damage, and dropping the butts into highball glasses to disintegrate into foul, amber-stained sewage. To restore it all to immaculate beauty, moving without bustle or noise, save the faint hissing sound like an ostler working on a horse, was to him an enterprise of creative beauty and joy.

His was the artistry that concealed both the art and the artist. He leaned negligently by the breakfast nook, gazing solemnly down at Sonia and Hector. He might have been a casual visitor, save for the napkin over his shoulder, a magical napkin that would change, for Sonia, into a white rabbit with long ears, a bishop's miter, or even a pigeon in flight. He leaned there, listening to Sonia's remarks.

Sonia was telling him that there were some people living in that old house with the swing behind the hill.

"Swing?" Louis opened his eyes. Sonia nodded and finished her orange juice.

"I found it, once," she said. "An awfully long, high swing! And I went again, and somebody was there, moving in! There was a truck. So I didn't go close. Now there's people living in the house. Old people."

Louis moved his head slowly from side to side. He liked to hear Sonia talk about her adventures. He himself rarely went beyond the kitchen garden, where he had a radial clothes rack. Out there was the domain of the gardener, Mr. Cagliari, a Sardinian from Norbury, who came to the kitchen door for a drink of water and made amiable but incomprehensible remarks behind a thick black mustache with curled ends.

"Old people?"

Sonia nodded again. She was enjoying herself, building up a story about the swing that hung from the high horizontal limb of a tree she had seen near the house beyond the woods. A wide old swing it was, seen through a line of broken palings, and the shabby old house, with its dark rooftree sagging and its one thin chimney askew, had looked exactly as Sonia had imagined the residence of a witch, or perhaps a wizard, would be.

"Well, an old man. With a beard. The old woman was putting laundry on a clothesline."

Sonia put her finger to her lips.

"Yesterday," she said. "Yesterday afternoon, when Elliot went to Norbury to meet Mummy, I went there again! And there was nobody 'cept an old tomcat that Hector chased. It was all shut up."

"What you want to go there for?" growled Louis.

"Silly! It's a short cut to the beach. And it's an adventure. I'm going to write a story about a little girl who's locked up in the attic. The man doesn't know she's there and she can't make him hear. She cries and cries, but not loud enough. He thinks it's the cat and pays no attention!"

"You watch out! Maybe there'll be another liddle gel in that attic." Louis disliked Sonia becoming interested in anyone outside of her own proper sphere.

"It was the other old people who locked the attic door and forgot about her," Sonia said. "They were *terribly* old. I saw them once, when we came here to see this house. Mummy and Elliot were upstairs and I walked through the woods, and there they were, on the swing!"

"Swing?" Louis scowled. He was vague in his mind about this word. Swings had not played much part in his childhood in Antwerp.

Sonia gave a back-and-forth swaying motion to her body, very slow, to illustrate the strange scene she had witnessed through the trees.

"On the swings they were, side by side. Very old people. About ninety, I 'spect. It was a fairy tale."

"You tell Missiz Ducroy?"

Sonia's eyes were wide open as she nodded.

"Mummy said, 'If you start that! Trespassers will be prosecuted,' Mummy said. Then the gardener said Mrs. Mudge, she was dead 'n buried. And when I came back from Harris next time he said Mr. Mudge he was dead 'n buried too, and the Mudge Place was sold to a New Yorker, so I went to see, and there was the truck and the man with a beard. Daddy said he was a sailor, but he didn't look like a sailor. He looked like the doctor who came when I was sick in Hollywood. You know, with a beard."

Louis nodded gloomily, his lower lip thrust forward. He moved the cream jug nearer to Sonia. Like many stewards, he ate nearly all his meals standing up, like a horse. He took up now a dish of bran, which strongly resembled horse fodder, and began to eat it with a teaspoon, holding it close to his chin. As he munched he reflected that the boss and his missis, when he had brought the sherry and bitters the previous evening, had been holding themselves in. They had not looked at each other. Mrs. Ducroy had looked at him, Louis. Sonia had looked at her mother, and at Mr. Ducroy, before running out in a manner that Louis remembered well. When they were spatting in California Sonia would run out like that, and the memory of it seemed to produce a hollow feeling in his chest. He knew perfectly well that Mrs. Ducroy had left the house last night, driving the big Virago down the drive at sixty. And he knew Sonia knew it too.

All this conversation of Sonia's, he knew, was a trick to distract him from the immediate fact that they were both unhappy. All this about a swing and a man who looked like a doctor!

He heard Sonia laugh shrilly as if she were very excited.

"I wonder if he's a doctor and a sailor too!"

Louis nodded slowly, pulling the corners of his mouth down.

"Ship's doctor? Out 'ere? Off a yacht, maybe?"

Sonia clapped her hands, and Hector barked nervously. It

always upset him when he heard people talking of non-canine subjects.

"I'll ask Elliot. Elliot said he was retired. Now he'll open the attic and find that little girl who's been locked up there."

"Yeah. How'd a liddle gel live in an attig?" Louis was skeptical of all fiction.

"Oh, that's the story, Louis! The squirrels go along a branch and into the attic through a hole they've made in the roof, and they feed her on their store of nuts! 'Cause she used to feed them when she was free."

Louis made a vague sound, between a grunt and a sniff, as he finished his bran and went over to start the coffee dripper. Fantasy was not in his line. The only dream he had regularly frightened and delighted him. It was the sort of dream a man could never confide to a living soul. He imagined himself a steward on a passenger ship, which would be wrecked off an uninhabited island. Everyone except Sonia, who was a passenger, and himself, would be lost. He would swim ashore with her on his shoulders. Louis had elaborated a queer life for the two of them there. It was all extremely proper, and based on the fantastic assumption that Sonia never grew up to be a young woman. In his experience Louis had found that young women invariably brought trouble, and he sought to avoid this difficulty in various ways, which made it all the more impossible to confide in anybody.

He shook his head, disapproving of a little girl living on nuts. He thought it highly improbable that squirrels would give her any nuts fit to eat. Squirrels, so far as he had observed them, were not altruists. As he shook his head, the shadow of what had happened, the shadow they pretended was not there, fell between them. It fell across Sonia's face as he looked at her, and she sat, her thumb in her mouth, returning his look, her hazel-green eyes darkening to thrush-brown for an instant.

"Well, okay," he mumbled. He set down a cup of richly

creamed chocolate, and filled Sonia's cereal bowl from the double-cooker. "Okay. You find this better'n nuts, maybe."

Sonia nodded, at first absently and then with delightful, momentary decision, her smile like sunlight on her face to make Louis believe she loved her breakfast with him. Then she fell to work, her expression gently serious, while he contemplated her with solicitude. Suddenly she looked up, a finger raised to a shocked little face.

"Oh, *Louis!* I forgot! Will you please take Elliot some orange juice and coffee?"

"Okay," said Louis. He turned leisurely and put the hot coffee pot on a tray already set. He took orange juice and cream from the refrigerator. He moved without haste, yet with speed. He watched Sonia out of the corner of his eye as he folded a napkin intricately and it opened into an ecclesiastical cap, which he placed over the glass of orange juice. Then he laid his own service napkin solemnly, almost hieratically, over his shoulder with a gesture that delighted Sonia always, and took up the tray on one hand, the other arm akimbo. He marched to the service staircase with dignity while Sonia watched, smiling a little. They were both aware that this was his contribution to the great scheme, to pretend they were really happy in spite of what had happened.

The house was now perfectly still save for the faint hum of the refrigerator. Outside in the sunshine the pigeons cooed and Mr. Cagliari was mowing the grass with a power machine. Suddenly Sonia wiped her mouth with her paper napkin and slipped out of the nook, to Hector's great joy. It was a source of much of Hector's unhappiness that human beings could remain indoors doing nothing for intolerable stretches of empty time.

"Stay here now," she said shaking her finger at him, filling his soul with a sickening dread. It was incredible, the unpredictable character of humans.

Sonia drew her robe around her and ran up the service stairs so that she would not have to pass her mother's room.

She dressed quickly, deciding to brush her teeth later, in shorts and rubber-soled beach shoes. She dragged a comb through her hair once or twice and ran down again to the kitchen.

Hector led the way to the door, excitedly, yet with a touch of hauteur in his pose, not certain yet, so young he was, that his universe was adjusted with sufficient delicacy to respond to all his moods. Suppose, for instance, that Sonia should delude him with the prospect of a run and shut the door, and retire to read a book. This had happened more than once in his experience and he regretted it. Sonia had the makings of a really competent human, he felt, one worthy of a pedigreed dog. But she had some deplorable habits.

Across the paved yard and through a green door in the red brick wall that bounded the kitchen garden and formed a support for the greenhouses, Sonia followed the joyful Hector. She was recovering from the thoughts which had clouded her mind before breakfast. The fear, that Mummy *wouldn't* be taken care of, that Mummy didn't understand the terrific importance of staying with Elliot, was like a dread of meeting a specter, or of walking off into space over a cliff.

Of course Shiela Boldwin's parents didn't always stay together, but Sonia had found out from Shiela that that was absolutely different. Shiela's father had a girl friend and Shiela's mother was going to get a divorce and marry an aviator who had an autogyro and a Pussmoth two-seater.

Just now Sonia wanted to see Shiela very much, but she wouldn't be back for two or three days. She was visiting a tiresome aunt in New Jersey who wanted to adopt her to get her away from the bad influence of her parents. Shiela had no desire to go to New Jersey. She wanted to stay with her mother half the year and her father whenever she could. As a matter of fact Shiela thought her father's friend a perfectly grand person and her aunt simply terrible. Her mother had said, "For heaven's sake, Shiela, go and get it over with." So Shiela had gone from her mother's apartment in New York to the aunt's house in Elberon and wouldn't be back to go to camp for several days.

The walk through the woods always calmed Sonia. She loved the trees with a passion the fantastic foliage of Southern California had never awakened in her. Beyond the meadow, which had been graded and seeded to make a lawn, a bowling green, and a tennis court, with an oval swimming pool near the tidal brook that bounded the property, the high oaks, pines and hemlocks stood like columns in the shadow of their own verdure. The leaves of a hundred seasons had made a thick carpet of humus, and the small wild animals had made paths and runways toward the uncleared thickets of bayberry, sumach and wild cherry, with clumps of birch and young cedar. Here and there could be seen the droppings of deer that came down at night from their secret places in the hills.

Sonia loved to walk here. The golden brown carpet, with a pile six inches thick, was delicious. The squirrels would sit on a safe limb eating their breakfasts and watching her with the bright derisive glance of animals who had imposed successfully upon countless generations of sentimental human beings. As she pushed through, so that the house and also Elliot's low bungalow, where he worked, was hidden, Sonia knew that she would see, beyond the high trees that crowned the ridge, what Mr. Cagliari the gardener called "de Mudge Place."

It drew her because of that wondrous vision she had had when she first peered through the foliage, of two very old people swinging gently, their arms around each other, in the silent woods. Now they were dead, old Mr. and Mrs. Mudge, and a stranger, an Old Man of The Sea, was in their place. Would he swing too? Or would he let her use it sometimes? She thought of him as old because he had a beard, but she saw him moving about with great activity the day the truck was there, directing and helping, and uttering short sharp commands. There was a great deal of hammering going on for days, and men appeared on the roof of the barn laying new shingles. There had even been a scaffolding around the thin little chimney of the house, and men on ladders had gone up to rebuild it, making it less like a hobgoblin's chimney. One of the workmen had got on the swing and there had been laughter from the others. Sonia had not liked that. In some obscure way the swing for Sonia had come to be a symbol of a delightful world beyond her own, which was a nice world, of course, with Louis and Shiela and Mummy and Elliot; but the world beyond the ridge was the frontier of fairyland, where stories grew like flowers around a haunted cottage in the woods.

Sonia walked that way now and left Church Yard behind, while Hector carried out an exhaustive examination of certain holes in a large fallen tree, of which he had long entertained the gravest suspicions. The log lay like a tubular bridge across the bottom of a depression in the slope, where the last of Elliot Ducroy's trees, the boundary of his estate, stood extremely tall and formed a high, covered space clear of saplings on its hollow floor. Sonia liked to walk along the log to reach the final rise from which she could discern the house on the Mudge Place. There was, she noted, blue smoke spiraling from the chimney. There was also the faint sound of a whirring machine somewhere and the distant, muffled *tump tump* of a mallet.

Sonia, walking with exaggerated preoccupation, just in case someone might happen to see her, followed the line of surveyor's stakes northward to where the brook became the boundary. It wasn't much of a brook. A ditch, rather, which looked as if it might easily dry up in the heat of summer. It came from a spring and there was a pool the size of a basin, to which Hector repaired with the passion of his kind for genuine running water. It emptied into Long Brook, which emptied into the Sound.

It was a fancy of Sonia's that she was really two little girls. It was a fancy closely connected with her conviction that there was a little girl shut up in the attic of that haunted

Mudge Place. She never breathed a word to Shiela Boldwin about it because she knew absolutely, by intuition, what a crushing remark Shiela would make. No! This was her own secret, the existence of an outward Sonia, who was represented by that almost too complete toy guesthouse and her devotion to Shiela and Harris School, and another Sonia who was like the little girl in the attic of the Mudge house. So was she drawn there by a strange, delightful urge, as though she had another life to live, not as the heiress of Elliot Ducroy, the successful creator of Gentleman Church, but as a happy orphan whose only luxury was the high broad swing that hung from the great arm of a mighty white oak tree between the haunted house and the barn.

She followed the brook and Hector, greatly refreshed, tore on ahead to bark at a low-slung, badger-colored phantom which, quite in the tradition of phantoms, suddenly vanished. Sonia became excited too and ran up to the magical spot on the bank and found Hector lifting up his voice over a woodchuck's burrow. Sonia was suddenly gay. The weight of her responsibility seemed to be taken from her heart. She raced Hector to where the shore road crossed the outlet of the brook on a stone bridge. She was gay because she heard the horn of the Virago, the triple-note sound that came from the long, silver-plated trumpets of her mother's car. She clambered on to the road and ran along to the lych gate, which was open. Soon she saw the long, low machine, one door open, near the front of the house, and galloped up the drive. She blundered along, like a young foal, through the open house door under the deep porch and into the living room.

She saw Louis glowering at her from the stairs, the tray with its empty dishes and crumpled napkin in his hand. He shook his finger before his nose as he descended slowly, looking upward over his shoulder and making gestures with his head to indicate prudence on Sonia's part.

At the foot of the stairs Louis paused and contemplated the rug under his feet, listening to the voices upstairs. He shrugged and moved toward the pantry, when Perdita suddenly appeared, her face illuminated by the sunlight reflected from the polished landing. She leaned over the rail so that she could see Sonia, and smiled.

"All right, ducky. Come on up and see Mother. And Louis, bring me some coffee, please. Make some fresh."

Sonia and Hector darted up the stairs. Her mother, leaning over and smiling, submitted to a hug.

"Mummy!"

"Yes, I've come back. The Prodigal Mother has returned. I've been telling Elliot all about it. Know what Mummy's going to do? She's going to get a job and work!"

They walked in together, their arms entwined, to where Elliot Ducroy, who had finished shaving, was coming from his own room.

"I'll never agree to it!" he said quietly. "It's not necessary . . ."

"Yes, it is. Necessary to me."

"You haven't said what you mean by work," he pointed out.

"I'll go to an employment agency and take what I can."

"You know what those jobs pay?"

"Not an idea! Whatever it is, I'll take it." Perdita looked smilingly at Sonia.

Elliot Ducroy looked at them both. He had a sense of bafflement. She had come suddenly up the stairs as he rushed out at the sound of the horn, his face still soap-streaked, and she had announced what she called "a solution."

"Of what?" he said.

"Of us," she told him. "We won't squabble and fight, my dear. We'll gang our own gait, as the Scotch say, or as they say the Scotch say. I'll be on my own if you'll bear with my presence a few days."

"I can't let you do that!"

"Who says you can't? The thing is, we can't go on like this. . . ."

Elliot Ducroy took his breakfast tray and thrust it into the hands of Louis as he came to the door of the bedroom.

"Beat it," he said, and turned to his wife.

"I've done all this for nothing, then?" He made a gesture to indicate Church Yard.

"Yes, if you think you can keep me here and run across the river whenever you feel the urge. I don't want to go into that. I have my faults, but being bitched isn't one of them. . . ."

She turned her head to listen, while Elliot Ducroy stood looking out of the window at the lawn where Mr. Cagliari was moving back and forth on his power mower. Perdita went out on the landing and looked down the stairway at her daughter.

"You mean you'd leave me here, after I've . . . You'd leave me here alone?"

"I said . . . I suggested," she said quietly, her arms still around Sonia, who was extremely grave and still, "that we don't fight. I'm as much to blame as anybody. I don't want to be a millstone round anybody's neck. I won't mention the real reason I have to go now. I won't even make a melodramatic exit. I'll stay a few days. But I've got to make some sort of life of my own."

"Like you were doing in the Village?"

"Oh, no! Though for that matter there was nothing very terrible about what I was doing in the Village. I met a lot of interesting people. They were much more interesting than the people here. They weren't very rich or very sober, but, oh, they were infinitely more interesting than these people."

"I don't understand what you're planning to do," her husband said. He looked at her apprehensively. "You won't take Sonia away with you?"

Perdita looked at her daughter, who was clasping her arm in both hands.

"No. I'm not a lunatic. Sonia's going to camp and back to Harris. I'll take anything from you for Sonia. Besides, what I thought I'd do, I couldn't have her with me. . . ."

"What?"

"I'll tell you later. Sonia, my pet, go and see if Louis is making that coffee, please."

She thrust the child gently toward the door and closed it.

"It's just this: I can't be honest with myself if I stand in your way. From what I've heard it's an affair of quite long standing. I can believe you never wanted her to come here—no—but now she's come, I move out. Not like a tragedy queen—no—but out. It's better to have an amputation than die of a gangrene. I thought I could stand it, for Sonia's sake, but it's not possible. I feel as I used to feel at home with Father and Mother writing, writing, writing, all day. It does something to my nerves. Gives me the creeps."

"You mean I ought to write poems like that great friend of yours, Caxton Derrick?"

"Oh, no. You've always misunderstood that side of my character. It was simply that they were *persons*. They were themselves, not just machines for making money. They were idiotic, very often, and unconventional, and all that; but they were human. It wasn't what they did so much as what they were, themselves. I know you have a contempt for them; and they didn't think much of you. As a writer, I mean. And don't call him my 'great friend.' Not in that tone. There, there! See how impossible it all is! We start it all over again. To tell you the truth"—and she smiled gently, looking over her shoulder to make sure the door was still closed—"to tell you the truth, I think you're wise! Wiser than you were when you took pity on me. What did you think, then? That I could be bought, a nice piece of goods? Well, you're wiser now. She's probably just what you need in your life. She speaks your language. I gathered that, as it happens, in New York."

"Who from?" He turned on her with suspicion.

"Oh, Village gossip. Never mind now. If you'll only be a decent sport and take care of Sonia until I find my feet. . . ."

"I'll fix that. But I don't want you to do this. I think it's crazy. . . ."

"I'm not going to squabble. I'm going to make some sort of life of my own."

"It's not some other man, then?"

"You mean, some other man I'm in love with? No." She shook her head slowly, as though turning the possibilities over in her mind. Then she smiled. "I suppose it's natural for you to assume that. It's almost as if polygamy was in the air, over here! However, set your mind at rest about me, my dear. I don't believe I ever want to be in love again."

"I don't believe you've ever *been* in love," he said hoarsely. He was finishing his toilet and not looking at her.

"Well, perhaps not, in the Hollywood sense. Oh, *don't* let's quarrel! I'll be off, and you'll work all the harder, make all the more money; more, more, bigger, better, colossal!"

She laughed, held up her finger and went to open the door. She said through the opening.

"Thanks, ducky. Will you put it in Mummy's room? It's darling of you to bring it up for me."

She closed the door again and smiled at her husband, thinking of Sonia with the coffee tray.

Elliot Ducroy lit a cigarette and stood at the window looking out at his estate. He was perturbed because he was discovering that this news had no bad effect upon him in his mind. He was merely uneasy lest his wife planned to do something which would expose him to ridicule, commiseration, or possibly even upset his working routine. It seemed that she had no such idea. She was even leaving Sonia as a sort of guarantee. But he was perturbed. It did something to his pride to discover that she could be so composed and understanding about this decision, that she could quit him without any heroics or pangs. That she could, moreover, estimate the real value of his motives in building up this life around Church Yard, and regard with indulgence the fundamental drive of American existence.

"Well, it's for you to make a decision," he said, over his shoulder. "I still think you're crazy, though. I want you to stay as long as ever you want. Go and come just as you . . ."

The extension telephone at his bedside buzzed. He took it and listened. Then he said, his hand over the mouthpiece:

"The Inn wants to know if you're staying over. They may want the room."

"No. I'll get my things later."

When he had settled that she went on.

"I had to be by myself and away from here. I'm sorry. I ought to have told them."

"That's all right. I understand."

"I'll have my coffee and a bath."

"I'm going to work. Listen, why did you come back so early?"

"I had the idea I wanted to get it over. I wanted to have an understanding before you went out to your work."

"You going to stay here today?"

"I told you I wasn't going to do anything melodramatic. I only wanted an understanding, that you're quite free."

She paused and added, slowly, "Would you mind if I took out the speedboat? Give it a run some day soon?"

"Of course. It's yours. I'll give it to you. Take it. The same with the Virago. I want you to feel absolutely free."

There was a pause as she stood, looking over her shoulder, not at him but at a picture of Sonia, a water color done a couple of years ago. The thought passed through her mind, that he wanted her to be free in order to be free himself. And he was thinking that she would probably think that, though he was honestly not thinking it himself. And this was followed by another thought, that these complex misunderstandings only arose between men and women who tried to live together instead of living apart.

As the door closed quietly behind Perdita he had yet another thought, very unusual for him, for his mind had a coarse mesh and many subtleties slipped through unnoticed. It was, simply, that they were now in such a relationship that everything he might say or do made matters worse for himself in her mind. One would think he had actually imported Sydney Saxon into the neighborhood, and was paying her rent, whereas, in fact, he had not known of her coming, and would have preferred it had she gone to some other summer place to live. He couldn't order her to go away. Nobody could order Sydney Saxon about. She did what she wanted to do.

vii

As he went out to his work place among the trees he discovered, to his surprise, that he did not want it differently. If Perdita chose to believe that he had become infatuated with Sydney Saxon, he could not help it. The shoe in fact was on the other foot, to a certain extent. And that gave him a strange, complex thrill that was half sensual, half aesthetic. It appealed to his vanity as well as to his maleness. And Sydney herself had other qualities, which he knew had been stimulated by her extensive experience of men. They were none the less appealing on that account.

Elliot Ducroy was one of those men of ability who are naturally subordinate to a woman who suits them. It was a kind of psychical adolescence. They are, at any age, the juniors in a sex partnership. Their work, or art (as Elliot Ducroy called it without feeling he was exaggerating) came first in their thought. It was coming first in Ducroy's thoughts now. It was not for nothing that his work (or his art) was concerned with adventures, mysteries, crimes and characters in which love played practically no part at all. He felt, in that imaginary world of Gentleman Church and his sinister crew, more at ease than in playing up to Perdita's unformulated requirements as a knight-errant.

What were those requirements? he asked himself now. They were like a phantom barrier between them. They made him feel, no matter how generous he might be, no matter how he built up their life around her, or how grandiose his gestures, that he was just as far off as ever from capturing her imagination, from reaching the holy of holies of her indignant heart. Not even his devotion to Sonia could unlock the last few doorways that shut him out from her.

He closed the door to his shack to deaden the whir and sputter of Mr. Cagliari's operations and sat down to his typewriter. It was his habit to get a sizeable piece of work done before he got his mail from the box beside the lych gate out in front. Mail, to Elliot Ducroy, was rarely of immediate and pressing importance. The high-school boy in Tennessee who wanted advice about becoming a detective; the high-school girl who was collecting autographs; the publisher who wished to use a Gentleman Church story in a symposium of crime stories, without fee; the editor who wished to know what sort of Christmas dinner Elliot Ducroy liked, what books he would take to a desert island, what was his favorite drink, cruise, state, foreign country, sport, religion, philanthropy and color of tie, eyes and hair—all these could wait a while. So could the letters asking financial assistance for the writers, offering membership (twenty-five dollars a year subscription) in various societies, and appealing for help for Hindoo, Persian, Russian, Chinese and Syrian novelists in prison.

He had discovered that this stuff took up his time and lured his thoughts from his work. Even the thin, graceful writing of some obvious old maid, probably a shut-in, asking God to bless him and give him continued health to write more stories in *Quality* or *Unity* or whatever mag she took in, had a way of distracting him from the hard, grueling labor of constructing the close-knit, tightly-motivated short story on which his editors insisted. It had to read as if it had written itself, as if it had happened yesterday, and could be found in last night's newspaper. All the art had to be concealed, and it had to be written so that illiterates thought it was highbrow. What highbrows thought of it was immaterial. It might be incredible so long as it was plausible. There was, however, he knew, a conviction in the minds of most nonwriting people, that all a writer had to do was to have an idea. At least ninety percent of those readers were ready to send him an idea by return mail. It was, they insisted, an ideal plot for Gentleman Church. As a rule that was where they had got it, from one of Elliot Ducroy's stories.

He adjusted the old green celluloid eye shade (*What physical aids do you deem essential for doing your best work?*), and made a number of meaningless faces at the synopsis fastened to the pine wall just in front of him. Sometimes the inverted pyramid of his life, a pyramid whose volume was the life of a country gentleman with a fine estate, with investments and cash reserves, with a boat and cars and a horse for riding, with formidable credit both in business and in editorial faith in his future production—this pyramid sometimes became almost physically visible to him, balanced on its point, which was just behind the old celluloid eyeshade and the thin shell of his cranium. Everything rested upon that. His brain was a diminutive gyroscope upon whose incessant spinning on its axis at high speed depended the stability of the lives of Perdita and Sonia, of Louis and Irving. His was a business in which there was no "goodwill." It was a profession whose practise had no market value. He could not engage a brother practitioner to carry on while he took a vacation. Hell, no! He could not even have an assistant to train; nor could he bequeath it to a relative. Once he stopped working, so ephemeral was the product, the whole mechanism ran down, the pyramid fell on its side, and there would be only a little insurance.

That reminded him of Irving and Irving's friend in the insurance business. Irving was all for a big policy, but the medical examination had been unfavorable. Then, said Irving, what about an endowment? Or a trust fund? For his old age. For some reason Elliot Ducroy balked at paying out a large sum on the chance of receiving a monthly income when he was old. He did not feel he would ever be old in that sense. And since the fiasco of his investments and the peculiar results of taking title to acreage, he had resisted Irving's suggestion to lock up his money in anything. The letters from insurance agents did nothing to change his conviction that he would hold on to what he had and spend it himself. So, what with the heavy outlay and maintenance of his establishment, he had to keep on earning. He was like the mouse in the wheel, in a financial sense. He was going nowhere at high speed.

He sat in a pose which he had once described, to an inquiring interviewer, as based on that of "a bum on a park bench," and tried to concentrate. But he found his thoughts dangerously preoccupied with Sydney Saxon instead of the new episode in the apparently interminable career of Gentleman Church.

One of the penalties of inventing a popular character, he had found, was that the writer became a prisoner of his own creation. He, Elliot Ducroy, was handcuffed to Gentleman Church. He was known and valued, not because he was a great writer, with brilliant ideas like Shaw and Wells, for instance, but because he had invented a world-weary criminal titan whose simple outlines were now as popular and familiar to his public as Charlie Chan or Sherlock Holmes. A new story was not headlined as a new Elliot Ducroy yarn, but as a new Gentleman Church adventure. And if he tried, now, to do anything else but Gentlemen Church stories, the editors lifted their voices in anguish.

Well, he was doing just exactly what was wanted. He was in the middle of the fourth of a series of ten contracted for by *Unity*, a total of a hundred thousand words that would make a book. They would also make a picture, and Irving had an offer, including foreign and television rights, which was an improvement over anything received in the past.

He was doing it; but at present he was not feeling too good. For some reason the prospect of having Perdita go back to New York and Sonia go off to camp, while Sydney Saxon was in that house across the river which she had rented for the season, was not as attractive as it had seemed a few days ago. He was not acutely aware of it, but his moral sense was ever so slightly affronted by Sydney Saxon boldly coming right into the neighborhood. He wanted her; but he wanted even more to preserve the peculiar ethical ritual and formalities of his age and social order. When he was away from her, his work and a vague, grandiose dream of writing a novel that would electrify the public and set all the critics by their long donkey's ears, took precedence of Sydney Saxon's image. It was not that he forgot her, but her personality was like a magnetic field. It was mentally and sexually disturbing. She was very dynamic. He would have preferred to have her not quite so near, for his own sake as well as for what might be called the proprieties.

So he was uneasy and let himself go into what he called a tail spin. He was haunted at times by that idea, that his life was in unstable equilibrium and his knack of making money was a product of dark forces, so that as long as he lived he would be fighting something he could not see. He had a choice, it seemed, of wandering on by himself, a little frightened because he could not gain relief by writing what was true, or else letting a woman like Sydney Saxon take him and use him for her own emotional release.

The difficulty lay in his faintly prudish temperament, which was a little shocked by Sydney's experienced practise of the art of love. When he imagined himself losing his public and his money and deflated of his pride, he grew dizzy—went into one of his tail spins.

(What do you find to be the chief obstacle to concentration in your creative work, Mr. Ducroy?)

Staring out of the window, waiting for the mood to change, he saw Sonia, wearing shorts and a red beret, going through the woods with her dog. She was like a fairy, he thought; but dismissed the notion at once. She was much more like her own mother; there was nothing ethereal about either of them. Say, a dryad rather, or a young Atalanta. She would be a fine big wench at eighteen, going to college. Now he came to think of it, he knew precious little about what went on in that kid's head. She was having a life of her own, of course.

He frowned, concentrating on the unfamiliar problem. It did not concern him professionally, because he wrote, not about real people, but about the imaginary characters real people enjoyed reading about. But suppose you write about real people, he wondered, how do you find out what's inside *them?* Inside Gentleman Church and his underworld was nothing very much. Sawdust. They were characters moved by the plot. Sonia, however, was alive. Now . . .

(Do you draw on your own personal experiences for your incidents and characters, Mr. Ducroy?)

Sonia was alive, and Perdita too was alive, and in a mood like the present, when he could not get started, it seemed as though he himself were dead. It seemed as though he could no more get in communication with another sex and another generation than if he were actually walled up in a tomb of fiction, while they were out in the world. Sonia was dancing through the woods, which he owned but could not enjoy because he was everlastingly at work tunneling through the underworld of Gentleman Church. Sonia was a symbol. Where might she be going now? he mused.

He frowned again as he thought of that thick, strong, bearded chap to whom he had offered a lift in the station wagon one day, a chap with battered, travel-worn naval-reserve baggage. Walked into that old Mudge cottage with the air of a colonial governor taking over a frontier command. He seemed to keep very much to himself. It was probably due to inviting him to that cocktail party. He might have concluded from the absence of a hostess and the way a few of the company punished the drinks and acted like goats, that he, Elliot Ducroy, was some sort of rich playboy.

As a matter of fact, that fellow might be worth cultivating. He had given Elliot Ducroy the impression of intellectual solidity, of wisdom and integrity. Might invite him to dinner. Better still, make a few casual calls. What, for instance, would

Perdita think of him? You never knew what the English would think of each other! Out on the Coast you would introduce a couple of them and they would stand looking at each other like two dogs, neither friendly nor antagonistic, but on guard. Instead of striking hands and going into a huddle about Dear Old London, "Stands the Lord Warden where it did?" and all that, they remained stiff and formal, and maybe never got pally at all. This chap was even more of a problem, possibly. In a few years' time he might thaw. When he went away from that cocktail party, hat, gloves and a walking cane like a cudgel in his hand, it was what he didn't say that seemed important. It was as if he were so completely sure of himself he had no need to make explanations.

Elliot Ducroy went suddenly back to his typewriter and started to work. *(Do you wait for inspiration, Mr. Ducroy, or do you just have a schedule of production?)*

He started to work. He stared hard at the pale blue sheet of paper on which he had written, in clumsy block-print with a copy pencil, the stark outline of the second sequence of his fourth story, in which Gentleman Church, who has received a Spanish Prisoner letter from a mysterious senorita in Mexico City, impulsively takes the air-liner and uncovers a scheme of an international ring to rob a Russian branch bank by leaving a time bomb in a safe-deposit vault. He proceeds to bring his own gang on the scene, and when the bank is blown open, they kidnap the thieves and their booty.

The problem confronting the creator of this drama, as was usual with Elliot Ducroy, was to dispose of the beautiful senorita who had smuggled the letter out of her prison.

Gentleman Church was, by the rules of the game, immune to love. Ducroy, when asked by the interviewers, "if he ever intended to have his great character marry," had been tempted to explain that Gentleman Church was a eunuch. (There was a story right there, of course, but it would never be written.) The fact remained that it was technically impossible to bring sex into the Gentleman Church saga save as a minor digression and to pacify illustrators and circulation managers. There had to be a complication at the beginning, a complication growing out of the major conflict. How about a young, handsome special messenger, member of the Secretary of State's personal entourage, traveling on the same air-liner as Gentleman Church, whom that super-criminal had once aided substantially when they were both in Teheran on that business of the Persian crown sapphires?

(Your life must have been terribly romantic, Mr. Ducroy.)

It was nearly lunch time when he came up out of the travail of the first long draft. Somehow he did not feel at all well. He had a feeling which he described to himself as "lost." There was an aridity about his state of mind that made him imagine he was physically ill. That vague shadow at the back of his mind which he could never see but which he was always trying to exorcise, evoked a desire for sympathy. It made him want to shake the load of responsibility loose from his shoulders for a while. He envied those investment banker fellows at the club, who seemed to forget the office when they left Grand Central. They became hilarious in the club car, and swam and played tennis and badminton like boys from school.

He saw Louis come down the path, walking pigeon-toed, as he always did, carrying a covered tray. This was lunch, and on the tray was a heap of mail.

"Good egg," said his master. "You think of everything. Feed the prisoner and bring him his mail."

As a matter of fact Louis did not usually remember to get the mail. He was not much of a writer. When Ducroy took him into Norbury in the station wagon he had all his orders in his head and used no writing materials at all. He also manifested an almost maidenly bashfulness about going outside of the house. The trip down the bluestone drive to the lych gate, even though very few people passed along the road, was apparently a trial to Louis.

He came into the studio and, shifting the tray to the palm of one hand, proceeded to level off a space on a table near the window. Elliot Ducroy reflected, as he often did, that Louis was as good as a trained animal. There was no animosity in his silences, such as one so often detected in Asiatic races. There was a faint sound of his breath being expelled through gloomy lips, a sound like the beginning of an ostler's buzzing noise, but Louis was merely concentrating on his job.

Ducroy looked up from his mail to find Louis standing, his arms hanging, his napkin over his shoulder, gazing somberly out into the early summer sunshine.

"What's on your mind, Louis?"

Louis effected a curious contortion of his features to register a conspiratorial mood. He held his hand to his ear as though using the telephone.

"Yes?" said the other. "Who?" He was acquainted with the difficulty experienced in sponsoring a definite articulate statement. He saw him now waving a finger and rolling his eyes to indicate a far distance.

"Well?" Ducroy said. "Go on. Who was it? Who was the call for? You? Well?"

"New York," Louis said in a hollow tone.

"Oh! Well what was it? Did you get the message? It wasn't a telegram now?"

Louis shook his head. He put his hand into his trousers pocket and brought out a small piece of paper. It bore only a number, which Elliot Ducroy recognized. He took it and crumpled it before dropping it in the waste basket.

"All right," he said, sitting down to eat his lunch. "I'll take care of it."

Yes, he thought, as he watched the bowed form of Louis returning, pigeon-toed, through the trees, he would take care of it. He felt suddenly refreshed. He could complete the next-to-final draft of his story that afternoon, and then revision tomorrow would be simple. That idea of having Gentleman Church do a favor to this diplomatic chap in Persia would be a swell supporting sequence for the script. Hell! It was going to be a pippin after all. The old master's hand had not lost its cunning! He felt not only refreshed but powerful, and combative. His prudish prejudices appeared ridiculously obsolete in this new mood.

He knew Sydney Saxon had been in New York. Irving had made a long call one night about it. Irving had had one of his world-beating ideas and must have spent a couple of dollars in toll charges expounding it. And he had said he was seeing Sydney Saxon at her apartment. Now she was coming back to the country, and wanted Elliot Ducroy to call her.

He knew what that meant. Sydney Saxon had that magnetism which could act through a piece of crumpled, scratch-pad paper bearing nothing but her telephone number. For her the language of love was written in cipher, or cablese. Compared with the characters in her smoothly-flowing, interminable serials, she was inarticulate and illiterate. Elliot Ducroy did not analyze this paradoxical fact of her own character, but he had a dim notion that it might be due to her immense experience and curiosity. She had once been like the intense, romantic, idealistic young people in her stories, with their devotion to fidelity and virtue. She still believed in it for others, especially for the young. But for herself she could dispense with the pretenses and pretensions of love making, which were only useful to conceal the woman's lack of skill in the art.

He would call that number, but not until he had finished his day's work, by golly! The primary ethic of the craftsman, by which he could justify his search for the beauty of life, had a strong hold upon his mind at this time. It cleared his conscience and ministered to his professional pride, to finish a job of work.

Possibly, of course, Irving's world-beating idea was in her mind too. She might make it a reason for closer collaboration. She might have suggested it to Irving in the first place, with this personal end in view, of having Elliot Ducroy in collaboration.

Irving was doing a lot of press-agent stuff nowadays, creating what he liked to call "a build-up." Columnists made allusions to Elliot Ducroy being at some celebrated night club which he had never entered in his life. They told anecdotes about his career in Hollywood and quoted witty retorts which he had never made. They quoted fantastic sums paid for his film rights and other fantastic sums he had refused for film rights.

These plausible, inaccurate and even irrelevant items had the effect of bringing Elliot Ducroy's name to the attention of the millions who were not his 'fans.' It was useless to deny them. They were part of the build-up. Working like a beaver, out of sight and largely out of mind, Irving was preparing for yet larger campaigns. It amused Elliot Ducroy to accuse Irving of feathering his own nest, but he was flattered inwardly at the little man's immense faith in his client. Now he had Sydney Saxon too, and the knowledge that Irving was the means of bringing them together in a business deal was strangely attractive and thrilling. It was like that remark Sydney Saxon had made to Irving. She had told him he ought to urge Elliot Ducroy to write a novel. Because, she said, he wasn't using his full powers on that pulp junk. He was, she said, a genius. . . .

He rose now, wiping his mouth and dropping the napkin. Lighting a cigarette, he returned to the rear of the room. There was a door there, leading to a small platform overlooking the sudden dip in his land, a dip that had the brook at the bottom. It was a view. He could see the hills north of Norbury, their heights now crowned with foliage. It was one of his pleasures to share this with no one. He found in it refreshment and sometimes inspiration.

He stood for a moment looking at the horizon of verdure, and then he heard Sonia's clear little voice calling her dog. He saw the red beret among the trees and heard Hector's excited barks. Then the red spot vanished and he went in and closed the door.

Two hours later the intermittent rattle of his typewriter died down and ceased. For a long time he sat, his chin on his hands, his eyes staring at the pine wall. This was the worst moment of all in the fantastic process of creation—the moment when the whole thing seemed alternately splendid and spurious. It was the moment when the pyramid of his life shook a little, as though in an invisible current of icy wind.

The only thing to do was to put it all out of sight quickly, go out and lock the door. Perhaps, in the morning . . .

He lit a fresh cigarette and walked slowly through the trees. After all, and in spite of the upset at the beginning, he had had a good day. What a little thoroughbred Sonia was! Some kids would have gone into a squalling fit of hysterics on hearing a mother talk like that. Not Sonia. Sonia knew about her mother.

It was a most baffling problem. There were times when he forgot the kid's very existence—when she was away at school, for example—and yet her personality was a positive factor in his life. How was one to explain that the sound of her clear young voice, and the glimpse of her red beret flitting among the trees, could so resolve and co-ordinate his imagination that he captured an unexpected verve and lightness of touch in handling the finish of that story.

He paused to look at one of his tender extravagances, Sonia's miniature guesthouse. Already the interests of the Harris School, the influence of the slightly older and more sophisticated Shiela Boldwin, were superseding toys like that. But he did not regret it. He regretted nothing which proved his devotion to Perdita's child, and which showed up what he called Perdita's lack of reciprocity in devotion. He could become voicelessly rhetorical about her apparent inability to see that his conduct had been that of "a very perfect gentle knight," as someone had phrased it. He did not venture to utter this aloud. The expression on Irving's round face, when he heard the great Elliot Ducroy beginning to trumpet about what he paid for, had been humiliating. He hated to have Irving think of him as a sexual sorehead. But—wasn't it a fact that there were two sorts of women; those who made you feel you were in the very texture of their thoughts, and those who took everything as a matter of simple acquisition, like sponges absorbing their surrounding element?

He walked up the three low steps from the lawn to the terrace. He nodded to a couple of workmen who were erecting a steel-tube frame for an awning. Another hundred and fifty dollars, he remembered. The idea was to make a sort of outdoor room for the summer.

Indoors he saw Louis, who was now in a white jacket and moving with a subtle acceleration of pace.

"Anybody at home?" he said. Louis pointed through the living room to the front porch. "Goin' out?"

Elliot Ducroy went to the door and looked down at Sonia ordering Hector back into the house.

"Please, Elliot!" she said earnestly. "We don't want him because of Tobermory."

"Who's Tobermory?" he inquired. He saw Perdita's head turn so that she could see him from the driver's seat.

"Oh, he's a cat. We're going to see the old gentleman who owns him. He lives in that old cottage . . ." She waved her arm.

"And he's got an old cat? Okay. Give him my regards. I'm going to set for half an hour. I'll be out to dinner, I expect."

"All right." She did not look at him. He heard her say, as she leaned forward to release the handbrake of the Virago, "Give her my regards." And the car rolled with great swiftness and a crackle of flying chips, down the drive.

PART THREE

What Completed It

i

It looks like a good day," he said.

The man cranking the yacht-club pump nodded absently, his attention concentrated on Mr. Spenlove's boat, which he was fueling. Without being able to sort out his impressions, he was aware that "Glory Hole," like her name, was unconventional. The proportion of beam to length, the unusual angle of the hard chine, and the squat, safe-looking stern of her, registered sharply in the mind of a man who was constantly looking down upon yachts, launches and cabin cruisers in need of fuel. He nodded absently, chewing on his gum.

What Mr. Spenlove called a good day had begun, for him, before dawn, when he put a kit bag in his second-hand Ford coupé and drove along the Shore Road in the half-light to the yacht-club basin. The lighthouse was still sending out its slow, revolving beam.

At the turn of the road on the point he stopped the car and looked toward the sunrise. This was one of his private pleasures. The sun was coming, but not for a moment. The sea was as flat and hard as a cement floor. The horizon to the eastward was a hard black line. The sky above it was darker than at the zenith by reason of an immense mass of invisible vapor over Long Island, which the morning breeze was driving up the Sound.

He watched. The moment was at hand. The darkness had assumed, imperceptibly, a mysterious clarity, as if the beach, the rocks, the column of the lighthouse, and the surface of the sea, were all composed of a substance potentially luminous and semi-transparent. The illusion was completed by the sudden radiance that outlined a dense bank of cumulous cloud with flashes of sheet lightning, like distant gun fire. The flashes ceased; but there was the cloud bank outlined now by a thin line of silver. The flashes were then seen far away and less clearly. Now could be seen, like an apparition, the pre-dawn, the softening of contours, the stirring on the face of the sea.

This was the rare moment, to be enjoyed like a solitary prayer, and he sat watching, his engine silent, only the long pale beam from the lantern swinging above his head to remind him of humanity. He loved it even more than the line of light that ran swiftly along the low hills, the burst of color in the sky and the theatrical golden trackway across the sea.

The lantern of the lighthouse went dark as he started his engine and drove on. He could see the buildings sharply outlined against the hills across the estuary. Rabbits scampered across the road to sandy burrows. In the great Boldwin mansion was a blaze from the lights left burning in several rooms by a nervous Filipino houseman living alone.

He unlocked the gate to the yacht-club enclosure and drove in. He had been amused to find how quickly some of the fishing members had discovered the value of a dawn start. He saw one of them now, rowing out in a dinghy to an outboard motor craft at anchor. He saw him climb on board and begin the inevitable struggle with a cold two-cylinder engine not half big enough for its job. Mr. Spenlove, whose passion for fishing was always under control, smiled indulgently as he thought of the vigorous, healthy exercise enjoyed by outboard enthusiasts. He himself had a couple of heavy-duty storage batteries on his boat, to do his work for him.

He went on board "Glory Hole," which was moored to a buoy, near the jetty, and looked around the cabin. The whole boat, by reason of her beam and low freeboard, was deceptive. The cabin was large, and when the bunk was pulled out, you had a commodious bed place, he reflected. When the firm in New York wished to know what equipment he desired, because his blue prints showed no details, in the cabin space, he told them, "For an overnight run." So there was only a small Primus stove, a rack for a row of square thermos flasks, and a toilet. After a prolonged study of their catalogue he had thrown it aside. Only a millionaire could remain solvent once he was started on a spending spree for gadgets. This boat, he remarked, was a utility, an extension of his normal existence, and tungsten steel anchors, high-power searchlights, copper-nickel hot-water heaters, chromium handrails and two-way radios were not in his line.

She looked, he noted with satisfaction, businesslike. Her fittings were good quality bronze, painted black; the mattress and cushions were pneumatic and could be put away in a drawer when not in use. Even the portholes were painted. He had small use for the snobbery of scoured metal, for what was called "spit and polish."

He opened the hatch and started the semi-diesel engine, listening attentively to the soft, scuffling sound of the exhaust that harmonized perfectly with the blue-black sooty smoke puffing from the vent in the counter.

"She looks like a smoky commercial craft!" Perdita had said, with a relish she could always communicate to him. He remembered that conversation.

"I know she does. That's the way I want her to look. As little like a certain speed-craft as possible."

She had made a face at him.

"This," he told her, as though delivering a lecture, "is a functional vessel. That's the expression—functional. She's a means of crossing the water, a substitute for the old-fashioned miracles of the saints. They used stone drinking troughs and granite basins to sail the seas."

"Who did? What are you talking about?"

"The old saints. I told you they were once my favorite reading. They were so holy they could do anything. We are not holy, so we have to invent our own miracles. A granite boat is no more miraculous than an internal combustion engine, if you think the matter over."

"I dare say. I dare say. I'll admit your boat's damned comfortable. She's as steady as a barge."

"That's the design. And she does ten knots. What more do you want?"

"That Mr. Collins, who put the engine in, said more than ten."

"Did he? An optimist. Of course he took a pride in his job. I was surprised about it. He was a puzzle to me. I mean, about his wife. You saw Mrs. Collins once."

"Did I? Well, what's the puzzle?"

"You know they roomed with Mr. and Mrs. Cagliari? Your gardener?"

"Really?"

"Mrs. Cagliari is the bosom friend of Miss Penge. Bosom is right, if you've seen her. Mrs. Collins was a third. She refused the offer of a free room in my house. He would have accepted. She was terribly suspicious of me. She's a typical artisan's helpmeet. She'd lived all her life in Brooklyn, and the only possible change from Brooklyn for people like her is to move to Forest Hills. According to her ethic, when she knew who I was, a seaman, I was a renegade from married quarters in Forest Hills. I heard her say, out in the porch, 'What's he doing here, living all alone? Let's go and stay in that place we came through. I'll go crazy here.' She meant Sutton Corners. And Mr. Cagliari rents two rooms. What do you think of that, my girl? The three fates came together at last. Or perhaps we ought to call them the three witches. Out on Route Eleven, at the Spinning Wheel."

"How did you find out? And why didn't you tell me about it?"

"Collins gave me the tip. When we had a trial trip, you remember I told you I didn't want you to come? It was business. We gave "Glory Hole" a long run at normal full speed, a couple of bursts at all out and a run of above five miles at four knots. Collins was as pleased as if he had designed her himself. We had a bottle, and about six miles off the point we celebrated the end of our labors."

"Is that why you didn't want me?"

"Not exactly. I told you I'd never play tricks, my girl. I told you I'd play fair. Didn't I?"

"You did. You do. I'm sorry. Go on."

"We had the bottle. Collins turned out to be a lively article when he was lubricated. He'd impressed me as one of these suppressed radicals. You know, a thoroughly skilled man who had subconsciously absorbed a lot of radical ideas about the capitalist system and all that, and who regarded me, living in slothful ease, with calm contempt. He would do his job because it was his job; but don't expect him to be more than distantly civil. I was mistaken."

"He was always gone for the day when I arrived," Perdita said. "I came over once in the daytime, just to see the work going on. It was a holiday. I'd forgotten the Fourth of July."

"Independence Day! You wouldn't find Collins missing that. They'd gone to Brooklyn. Never was I more mistaken about a man. I told you that, to me, everyone except you wears a mask? Remember?"

She put her hand on his and laid her cheek against it. It was a gesture of pure emotion.

"Collins' radical standoffishness was a mask. I'd put those two down as a pair of workaday lovebirds. When we were having our third whiskey I discovered our friend Collins was Number One Iron Man. He bossed that mean, pretty little woman. He was proud of the clever way he managed to fool the outside world. She could put on all the swank she wanted for strangers. At home he had her where he wanted her. She hadn't any comeback, no, sir! She was goddam lucky to have a husband, yes, sir!"

"You shouldn't have let him talk," Perdita said, gravely. "It wasn't fair."

"Of course. But it was evidently bottled up in him under

pressure, and the whiskey released it. It was a relief. Some chance remark I made, about him being glad to get back to his own home, set him off. He bumbled on like a brook prattling over stones. A lot of it was unintelligible. What delighted me was the news that his Virginia—and you ought to have heard him *laugh* over that name for her!—would go out to the Spinning Wheel with Mrs. Cagliari and have tea with Miss Penge, talking gossip. Mrs. Cagliari has a car."

"I bet she has! And I bet they were discussing us, among others."

"Naturally, since they had such reliable sources of information. The excellent Cagliari, for one."

"And the excellent Collins, for another."

"Don't forget the excellent Miss Penge either. I had tea with her one day. She must have telephoned them to stay away when she knew I was coming. I bought these old things from her. It was an experience. She's quite a character."

"Old bitch!"

"What makes you say that?"

"Because! And I'm ashamed of you, letting that poor chump Collins split on his wife while he was tight!"

"I'm ashamed, too! I didn't do it by design, and I'm making you an accomplice by telling you. I even pretended not to hear, but he had the awful insistence and concentration of the drunk toward the end. Another thing, he didn't recall what he'd said afterward. He put on his mask again, a bit bent at the edges, of course, but still a mask, when he packed up to go home to Brooklyn. It was a tremendous experience for both of them. They will never be the same, never quite the same, after coming down here. They've had a glimpse of Arcady. They will always wonder what they missed."

"A matter of time, and you'll be telling me they owe you gratitude for a cure!"

"They're welcome. I wanted them to use my spare room. Mrs. Collins is the sort of woman I understand. At any rate the men I've worked with seem to marry that sort. I've seen so many of them."

"Not you! You'd never be caught. Not by the girls looking for free board and lodging for life."

"It isn't only that. It isn't only free board and lodging, my dear. It's safety from strange thoughts."

"Is it? Isn't it rather a matter of social position? *You've* never had to worry about who you are. You don't realize how important being somebody is to nobodies. They were much more comfortable with that fat Mrs. Cagliari than they'd ever be with you. Sisters under the skin."

"Miss Penge is a sister too. She has a sound taste in what she calls primitives. She was very arch about her news. 'I hear Mr. Ducroy's never at home now!' I said it was business. I said he was collaborating in a new serial. She cried out, a sort of 'Whoops! Sez you?' She didn't actually say that. It was a shrill whinny, like a horse. 'You born yistiddy? Business!' "

Perdita stretched out on the porch seat, nodding.

"I can imagine the whole scene. Did you inquire where she got her information?"

"I did. She roared. Everybody in Sutton Corners knew it, she said, except me."

There was a short silence. Mr. Spenlove knocked out his pipe and went into the house. This was the moment he had been waiting for since he had got his boat into the water and the Collins couple had gone home. It was late afternoon in late July. Sonia was at camp. He had been down to the yacht basin with Perdita to show her the cabin, and the various personal contrivances in which all boat builders delight. It was all marvelous, she said, if it didn't look so like a delivery truck. And so on. They had gone back to his house, not caring who saw them. The moment had come.

He came back with a tea tray and sat it beside her. He sat down to refill his pipe.

"It must be wonderful, for creatures like Mrs. Cagliari and

Miss Penge, to be natives," she said. "The natives are friendly! Like hell they are!"

She shook the teapot impatiently and then began to pour.

"It's their means of expression. I doubt if there's malice in it. Miss Penge enjoyed telling me about her friend, positively enjoyed it. Another native. She calls her Jenny."

"I know. She was a schoolteacher. Her name was Janice Jenney. Mr. Cagliari was one of her pupils in an Americanization class, and he married her. She told us the whole story when we came here. She's supposed to be a wonderful cook, and they wanted an engagement as a couple, but it meant getting rid of Louis. Nobody wanted to do that. She's a gabby wench. And big!"

"I've seen her. Like a Circassian odalisque. For a man like that swart gardener of yours she must have been a houri in an oriental paradise. Think of him, a Sardinian peasant, transported to a country where his teacher is a superb blonde of matchless plumpness, who permits him to use his newly acquired Americanism to make love to her, and who consents to be his bride. I was fascinated by Miss Penge's story of their love affair. She used to let them spoon in her parlor."

"Among all that antique stuff? One can't *move*!"

"You haven't had tea with her. Her parlor, behind those rooms crammed with antiques, is a museum piece. It's exactly as her ancestors would have had it. In a bleak way it is beautiful. There's all New England in it, except the Scarlet Letter. You ought to see it."

"Well, I don't want to. But may I interrupt?"

"You may."

"Let's talk about us. Just us. I'll begin."

"Yes."

"Let's go away."

"That's an order."

"In the boat."

"I have an idea. You've given me an idea. All right."

"And leave the natives to their cannibal feasts and savage customs!"

"All right. Cross over to that island we can see on the horizon."

She clapped her hands gently.

"Is that the idea you said I'd given you? Where shall we go?"

"Leave that to me. There will be no cannibals on that coast. No scribes and pharisees! The natives are friendly."

"How delightful! You always give me pleasure when I come to see you. Why haven't we thought of this before?"

"I was waiting for you. I went on with the boat. I said to myself: It's only a scow compared with that thing she tears about in, but it will have virtues of its own."

"Oh, my dear! Were you really thinking of me while making it? Never speak of it again. The speedboat's sold."

" 'Sonia' sold? You sold it?"

She stirred her tea meditatively.

"No. I turned it back to Elliot. I didn't want to have it on my conscience. He bought it originally for himself, you know. He thought he would like to have one. He's like a young boy in some ways. Wants a toy he finds he doesn't want. And yet he doesn't know *how* to play, really. He's a worker. He works all the time."

"Even over there?"

"Even over there. Even more over there. You mustn't misunderstand Elliot, my dear. He's in heaven now. He's working with her and in love with her. It's a great relief to him he doesn't have to pretend he loves me any more."

"Did he, at first? I've always had a doubt."

"As far as a writer can ever be in love with anyone but himself. Or herself. They live," she added pensively, "for their art. Elliot does, I know. It's a sort of desperation, like persons swimming to reach the shore before they drown. The only wife a writer needs is a hard-working concubine, who worships him, protects him, and brings him his slippers and hot toddy when he's tired. And keeps out of sight when he wants to have another woman for a change! Writers are born polygamists in this country. They'd like to keep harems. Lots of them do, from what I saw in Hollywood."

"You're free now," Mr. Spenlove said. "You can keep away from writers after this."

She waited a few moments before answering.

"Yes," she said. "It's an unusual situation. Elliot in some ways is not grown up. I suppose that's the secret of his marvelous skill in writing those adventure stories. He has no suspicion of you—or me. He has absolute trust in both of us. He thinks you're absolutely the best thing that could happen for me! He takes likings to people, and he liked you. He told me, when he first met you, how different you were from the people round here, how he liked your background."

"If we go away together, will it make any difference to his confidence in my sterling qualities?"

"He's certain you'd take care of me. You haven't quite understood, my dear. I have a character, too! He told you about the time I went to Paris with those people and took care of Caxton Derrick? Well, he's never had the slightest suspicion of me. He hates Derrick because he never met him and wouldn't understand him. Derrick, in spite of his failings, and his destroying himself, was grown up. When he was all right he spoke so beautifully! I don't mean just reading his poems aloud. That was marvelous. When you read them in a book they didn't do a thing to you. When *he* read them, it was superb music. You were carried away! And when he talked, he had a lovely, measured quiet tone that fascinated you."

"You mean he was a genius?"

She shrugged her shoulders. It seemed to him she had the loveliest shoulders in the world, and the hollow of her back was divine.

"Oh, Elliot's a genius too, according to Irving. So's *she*!" She nodded in the direction of the house across the river. "Now they are a team, the fireworks will be overwhelming.

Geniuses are a penny a quart nowadays. Derrick had something that brought out the maternal instinct. I don't think I have much of it, but he brought it out. Perhaps it's something else, and I'm mixing up the instincts!"

"It didn't seem in character, after what you'd said about writers."

"Caxton Derrick wasn't a writer in that sense," she said quietly. "He was a personality." She pitched her voice lower. "Like you. I don't mean there was any resemblance. Heavens, no! Just the reverse. You're exact opposites. I'd never fall in love with a man like Caxton Derrick the way I fell in love with you. I doubt if any woman ever did. I was speaking of individuality."

"Something in Elliot's voice made me suspect he hated Caxton Derrick on your account. It was as if he had a faint suspicion of *him*."

"I know he had. He used to nurse it like a baby. He didn't really believe it, but it helped him to justify this affair of his."

"So we can go away?"

"He'll hate it. It would upset all his plans. He wants to keep Church Yard going. As a matter of fact," she added, smiling, "he wants it there to come back to."

"And we ought to avoid anything that would spoil his happiness?"

"That's about the size of it," she said.

"Well," he said, "this beats cockfighting. What do you suggest?"

"Why, the boat. It's finished. Boats go in and out all day and half the night. We can go fishing. Wouldn't you like to take me fishing? We can troll."

"Very much. But is that a solution of our problem? To go fishing?"

"Well, if you mean Elliot, it isn't. Only a temporary expedient. I'm under a strain in that house, though. It's all his. It's in his name. I've promised not to walk out on him. Unless I go away with you, I can't help myself. There's no particular fun in being a kept woman, I can assure you."

"Ssh!"

"All right."

"Now let me get a word in edgeways."

Again she touched his arm and leaned her cheek against it.

"We'll do it," he said. "Tomorrow, early. Come down in fishing clothes. Tonight, when you come over to dinner, can you bring a bag? Just as if you were going to visit friends overnight?"

"What's the idea?"

"I'll tell you when we get outside. You sail under sealed orders."

"Aye, aye, sir!"

"It will be an adventure. It's rather a long shot for me because a man never knows whether the women he likes will like each other."

"Oh, we're going to see a woman?"

"And her husband, and possibly her son. Old friends of mine. She advised me to get married at once when she knew I was coming on shore to live."

"Did she make any suggestions?"

"Nothing constructive. The scheme didn't appeal to me."

"I don't wonder. I don't say there are no successful marriages, mind you."

"I didn't ask you for your opinion."

"I hope you told your friend that."

"She was thinking of my welfare, don't forget. She was afraid I'd be trapped by some designing creature, an unscrupulous female vampire who would bleed me white and leave me for dead. She likes me."

"She may like you, but she doesn't know much about you. She doesn't know the principal thing about you."

"That's quite possible. Well, will you come? Fishing? We may get some striped bass."

"I've been fishing for an invitation."

"A bold minx!"

"A brazen hussy! Aren't those old, pre-war expressions delightful? My Sonia calmly makes remarks that would have made brazen hussies in *my* childhood go into hysterics. They'd color up to their eyes! I'm not so very bold, really. I've been in a funk many a time. I was in a funk when I met you. I wanted to leave Elliot and hadn't the pluck to. I'd have had to accept support. I knew how wonderful I'd be, getting a job in New York! I might have gone and wangled something out of Irving. He'd do it—for Elliot's sake—so it would be the same thing. I was thinking, when I came in here that time: 'Oh, God, if I only had a thousand a year of my own!' "

"Instead of which, you found your life wasn't ended, after all. Only those without hope pine for a private, independent income, absolutely safe, tax-free, paid by mail every month. It was much better for you to do what you did."

"Well, it was your doing. You gave me the pluck to make the decision. I don't know why, but I made the decision that moment and told you. You, a perfect stranger!"

He got up and looked at the barometer.

"It looks as if it would be a good day tomorrow," he said. She rose and stood beside him, her hand on his shoulder. In the deep hush of the summer afternoon, in the half light of the awninged porch, they stood in silence for a moment.

"I hadn't the faintest idea of what was going to happen!" she cried. "I was in a perfect state of panic when I got back to the house. Then I thought, 'It's all right. He felt the same.' "

He did not speak. He seemed to be studying the barometer, but she knew he responded.

"Yes," she went on, "it's high, all right. Would you like to go out about twenty miles on the turnpike to dinner?"

"Why so far?"

"I'll tell you. I've a fancy to get away from the shore. We'll be on the water tomorrow. Do you remember that time we drove and drove, always on side roads, and we stopped and got out to walk? In a valley, in the evening?"

"I'll never forget it. I thought, almost, I was in the old country."

"Well, this place I'm thinking of is about four miles beyond where we had our walk. We can keep to the turnpike and turn left. I found it by accident, one day I was driving last year. I had lunch there. I was awfully wretched. I felt like a trapped animal. I had a lovely cage, and that car, and the boat, and plenty of food and clothes and pocket money, and I felt like a trapped animal. I had nothing of my own. All the people who came to the house were his friends. Everything was his. It had got me down."

"Yes," he said, quietly.

"This isn't a real roadhouse, you know. They have a farm, and sell eggs and poultry and vegetables at a stand on the turnpike. They send a lot of poultry to New York by truck and eggs by mail. They had a sign on the gate—just the one word 'meals.' I must have been almost the first customer. The next time I was there they had another sign—'rooms.' Very nice rooms too. They showed them to me. I think they are members of some sect. Don't ask me why. Just a feeling from talking to them. Would you like to go there with me? I'd like to be there with you, and be happy, where I was so miserable and alone. Then tomorrow we can go fishing in your boat. Didn't you say you were going to cruise across the Sound one of these days to visit that friend of yours? The one who advised you to get married and warned you against designing women? You could leave me at some place and go on to see her, couldn't you?"

"I have made arrangements about that," he said. "I didn't mean to tell you. I was on the phone last week. My friend wants me to come and see her. I warned her I was probably coming by sea as I had been building a boat."

"Did you warn her you had met me?"

"She inquired in a general way about how I was getting

along as regards living alone," he told her. "In fact she thought it quite likely I was married by now."

"Well, you can tell her the truth so far as I'm concerned. I don't want to meet anybody under false colors. If she is fond of you I shall like her. Anyway, we can go fishing. I shall love that."

So, watching the fueling of his boat, the next morning after that little pilgrimage to the farm, he had this tender memory of her in the old gray dwelling, where they ate marvelous fried chicken with their fingers and drank cider from blue mugs. With the coffee the host had bashfully exhibited a bottle of old apple brandy which he thought "had a good strength." It had, and Mr. Spenlove, haunted by the memory of a beautiful woman sodden and unconscious and foul with alcohol, poured two small portions and waved the rest away.

"I won't drink even this if you don't want me to," she had said humbly.

Does she know, he asked himself later, *how that hurts, and yet pleases me too?*

More than once he had protested when she had thrown responsibility upon him like that, as to what she was to do. "I gave up being a boss when I came ashore," he pointed out. But she said, "Please do. I like it." He retorted, "So do I! But is it *right*?"

"Oh, right! I dunno. I don't believe it matters whether it's *right.* If we both like it!" she added, smiling.

It was this sweet confusion in his mind, as to whether there might be a danger lurking for them in this relationship, whether it was a bloom that would wither overnight, as it were, which made her regard him attentively, sometimes, and say, in a whisper that was both shy and conspiratorial,

"You aren't sorry, are you?"

When he explained, and she said, "Tell me what to do and I'll do it," he would say, remorsefully, "You talk as if it was easy to give orders! You seem to think I really *want* to order you about; put you in a cage. I don't, as a matter of fact. Is that selfish of me?"

She said, "Very!" and took his arm. "My own idea," she assured him, "when I came to see you, was to give myself up . . ."

Now she was coming in at the yacht-club gate. She was in linen slacks and a sweater, her hands in her trouser pockets, her blue beret askew on her fair hair. He returned to Jerry Munzinger, chewing gum and working his pump crank rhythmically, as he put in the last ten gallons. He knew Perdita well enough now to be sure she would continue to walk toward him and would not expect him to stage a theatrical *entr'acte* of waving and grinning. "Acting at a distance," as he called it, was almost a national hobby.

He disliked such extroversions; yet how infectious it was! You found yourself making the stereotyped gestures, your face would crease and your teeth gleam as though a battery of ship news photographers were charging down upon you. You were hard at it, *manufacturing a mask for yourself*, like everybody else!

He heard her say warmly, "Good morning, Jerry." He saw Jerry's oafish response, a stiff thumb and finger briefly touching the brim of his old felt hat as he inclined his head slightly sideways. This was the last faint clumsy vestige of the medieval salutation, a knight in armor removing his helmet in the presence of a lady.

There was nothing knightly about Jerry Munzinger. He had a nice job, with plenty of pickings and gratuities. He was intuitively aware of a dozen subtle social gradations among the members, of which Mr. Spenlove had only vague and largely inaccurate information, and he kept his own counsel about what he saw and heard around the club. This was not loyalty, but longheaded New England caution. Nobody could ever say Jerry Munzinger had been blabbing about who was drunk on the cabin cruiser, "All Alone"; who was week-ending with the owner of the yacht, "Santa Ynez"; or why the dinghy of the "Pretty Polly" suddenly put ashore a lady guest who telephoned at once for a taxi. If the crews talked, that was their affair. Without going in for obsequiousness, Jerry had created for himself an aura of probity.

He finished with the pump and screwed home the brass plug in the foredeck of "Glory Hole." The name intrigued Jerry. It was a hell of a name; but he knew what the words meant and appreciated the use of them for a boat.

He also liked Mrs. Ducroy, whose speedboat had used so much fuel that he was likely to be short sometimes. He was aware of a lack of pretense about her, a complete obliviousness to what he described, in his mind and among his Norbury cronies, as "funny business." He saw a great deal of funny business at the yacht club. And when she said, standing easily on her long legs, her hands in her pockets, and her eyes smiling down at "Glory Hole," that she was going trolling for bass with Mr. Spenlove, Jerry Munzinger nodded and dismissed them from his thoughts. He considered them swell folks.

She stepped into the well abaft the cabin and coiled the line Jerry cast off from the dock. She heard the motor underfoot and felt the faint vibrations of the hull as they veered toward the fairway. *There's nothing romantic about it!* she said to herself. *Not in the usual sense of the word. Father and Mother would call it sordid, going to sea in a tub!*

She dropped down into the cabin and looked around. The settee was occupied by fishing tackle and a duffle bag containing groceries. There was also a carton of beer and another of mineral water. She set to work to transrer these to the icebox in the counter. The groceries went into a locker under the seat from which Mr. Spenlove was steering, in the small pilothouse ahead of the cabin. She could see his forearms, matted with dark hair, through the glass of the door, as he grasped the wheel. *Where is he going?* she asked herself, but without anxiety. She saw her bags under the folding cot. *Die's cast!*

she told herself firmly, and fell to work again, stacking the cans and cartons. It was marvelous to be with a person who did not hover over one, who was not everlastingly assuming a fake sexy proprietorship, who could give orders as if to a man, and leave one alone to do a job without any Sir Walter Raleigh rubbish!

They were passing the lighthouse. The engine had settled into a steady semi-diesel throb, very soft and muffled by the insulation beneath the thick hardwood floor of the well. She saw the flame of a match as he lit the first cigar of the day. The smoke blew away and she smelt the rich Havana fragrance of it. It was an integral part of his personality, that odor. It impregnated his clothes and beard with something masculine she could not define but admired enormously. The thought of it delighted her.

Clarence Price, the fertile author of scores of adventure stories for boys under the name of Norman Tower, and his wife, who wrote stories of adventuresses without ever having met any or having had any adventures, these exemplary toilers in the literary vineyard had never smoked.

Perdita's first husband, Archie Pagett, had always (it seemed to her now) had a cigarette in his mouth, almost from the first moment she set eyes on him at Marks Tey station. Always smoking and always sponging! Elliot had always been a chain smoker of cigarettes, but he was not the sponging sort.

The two men were so utterly different that even their ways of smoking cigarettes could not be confused, only contrasted. Archie had developed a jaunty air in Hollywood which impressed local residents enormously but merely made Perdita laugh, as she laughed when a star in the Brown Derby held a teacup with her little finger stuck out. Elliot drew very rapidly on a cigarette, inhaling gulps of smoke that shot from his nostrils in jets which never seemed to bother him. He worked, thought, and talked while this furious combustion went on in front of his face. It was an integral function of his existence, while with Archie it was like his Old School Tie, a piece of swank.

Against the white walls of the lighthouse buildings she could see a man smoking a pipe, watching "Glory Hole" going out to sea. As the estuary opened she saw the sun flashing on the line of windows in the Boldwin mansion. At their boat-house, across the street from the house, she could see the stern of their nineteen-foot Lightning class racing craft, which hadn't been in the water all season. Mrs. Boldwin had inherited a million dollars, and nobody had ever seen her look really happy. Now she, Perdita, had about forty-seven dollars of her own, and she was happier than she had ever been in her life.

She started the Primus and began to make coffee. She unhooked the table that let down over the bunk and laid the coarse linen cloth. She went out and sat down in one of the chairs aft and watched the shore. Beyond the trees rose the roof of Church Yard. She saw a milk delivery wagon moving swiftly along the Shore Road. It turned in at the lych gate.

The sea was perfectly flat, smooth and shiny, as though filmed with oil. Long streamers of curd-white foam lay on the steel-blue surface, like roads on an azure plain. *As if you could get out and walk on them!* she thought, smiling. They used to say, in the Sunday School, that you could do anything you wanted to do, if you only had complete faith. You could move mountains, for instance. She remembered asking Ludgate Hill if it would kindly move over to the Surrey side. Just for a start, as it were! She remembered also wondering, *could faith move things back again if they were better that way?* The answer invariably was, you haven't faith if you ask silly questions. But what was sillier than moving a mountain? What earthly good was it to move it? Now, walking on the water was an accomplishment of real use when one went to the seaside for a holiday. Imagine the sensation at Clacton-on-Sea, where Father invariably took the family in August, if Miss Perdita Price, staying at the Grand Hotel, was seen to be strolling across the water, carrying a parasol and a box of sandwiches, toward Harwich, and was nearly run down by the "Clacton Belle" when that vessel arrived from London Bridge! Perfectly easy, if you had faith! Did she believe that? Did Sonia accept such statements? Sonia would have to settle it for herself! Perdita sniffed and touched her nose slightly with her forefinger, a schoolgirl trick she still used on occasion to express a certain mood of decision. Perhaps, as the Boss said, she wasn't holy enough.

The water in the kettle was boiling. She went in to pour it over the coffee in the dripper. There was enough left to cover the eggs. She put them on, noted the time, and opened the door to the wheelhouse.

"I thought you'd gone to sleep," Mr. Spenlove said. "You've been very quiet in there."

"I've been getting breakfast and looking at the shore."

He made room for her to sit beside him. "Want to steer?" She shook her head.

"The eggs are boiling. Three and a half minutes, isn't it? Coffee's nearly ready."

The sound of the engine and propeller was muted to a faint murmur. She said something about this. He nodded.

"Insulation. I can see by the gauges how she's doing. I don't want to hear her. So I had heavy sound-proofing put in this deck here."

"The gauges, yes. I was wondering what all those clocks were. What's a tachometer? Oh, revs. Of course."

"Of the engine. Didn't you ever look at the instruments on the speedboat?"

"When you're doing forty, you don't look at anything, except where you're going."

"Noisy things. The only time I ever hated you was when I heard you roaring along. Remember? I said to myself, 'These restless Americans!' "

"And it was me! Serves you right, jumping to conclusions. It was a sort of relief for me, though, driving that boat. And there's another thing. I always wanted to have a look at that creature's house. The residence of my economic superior! It wasn't jealousy. Morbid curiosity, if you like. Unholy fascination! I was right up against something I'd heard about, read about, and even seen from a distance. I used to say to myself, 'Your husband has a mistress. He's in another woman's arms. And she's your economic superior!' That's a regular stock phrase in Mother's novelettes—'found him in another's arms!' It sounds funny in a novelette. It's not funny when you first find it out, first feel it in your mind and stomach! It's bloody!"

There was a faint tinkle from the cabin.

"The eggs! I'll take them out."

"I'll go another mile or so and stop the engine. You're right. It's bloody."

When she struck a spoon on a glass, he cut the engine and came into the cabin. The sea was, as they say, like glass. A faint, very long swell was now perceptible, on which the boat rose slightly and was depressed, so that the long, tan-colored bluffs by Port Jefferson changed their tints. Far away, a string of lighters followed an almost invisible tug, their movements so slow they seemed etched on the water as on a sheet of polished metal.

"It's going to be hot," she said. "Is it far to that woman you said you're fond of?"

He seemed to be calculating.

"About three inches!" he said. "You make a man say silly things. No. I would say it's about thirteen miles from here. We'll fish first. Trolling's a comfortable sport. When I said I was fond of her I meant just that: She's a person of position as well as wealth. One of my passengers. She invited me out to her place several times. The place we're going to now, unless you show the white feather and say you don't want to go."

"What's the idea? Are you showing me to her or her to me?"

"It isn't a matter of showing anybody to anybody. If I thought you'd be embarrassed I wouldn't go near the place.

She wrote she was coming over. They have a yacht, and Miss Penge once told me she'd sold antiques to them. Then she called up, one evening, and I said I was going on a cruise in this boat and might call on her. She was delighted, and began to inquire into my affairs."

"Cheek!"

"Not at all. I'd taken her into my confidence in the past. I haven't seen much of her lately because that's the way I am. I never have seen much of anybody, very intimately. That's what makes you something special."

"Hadn't you ever been in love before you met me?"

"Not intimately. You spoke of your mother's characters seeing their husbands in another's arms. In my case the only time that girl was ever in my arms was when she was dead."

"Oh! I'm sorry! Go on. Tell me. Not intimately?"

"She had been killed, accidentally, in some street fighting in Salonika. I was a young man at the time. I saw her fall and carried her into her house. I told this woman, Mrs. Colwell, about it. She's a fine person. But the rich—I mean the really rich—are not my meat. Even when I'm friends with them I'm really saying, all the time, you be damned! I'm on the defensive against something, I don't know what. Perhaps my own snobbishness. I don't suck up to them, as we used to say, at school. Keep them at a distance."

"You keep everybody at a distance," she said smiling down at the cloth.

"That's right," he said. "Except you."

"It wasn't a real love affair, then? You said, 'not intimately.'"

"It couldn't have been real. She was another man's mistress."

"It sounds fearfully romantic."

"*I* was fearfully romantic, in those days."

"You talk as if you'd given it up. I don't think so."

"I realize that now. When I left the sea I thought I was through, as Americans say. From what I'd seen of marriage among shipmates I didn't want *that!* I'd been thirty years with the Company. It seemed a century. There didn't seem anything to do except go into retirement and meditate. And I liked the idea of belonging to myself instead of an organization. Possessions never appealed to me as much as, ah, self-possession. I thought I'd have solitude for a change, after the fuss and feathers of a liner. It's quite a strain, you know, having a new set of faces six times a year. Even the crews change rapidly nowadays. A strain."

"I should say so! Well, you settled down, all snug, and —here we are! Are you sorry? I don't really mean that."

"It's not a question I could answer. It assumes you set a trap. It makes me out a victim, caught in the trap, struggling to escape. Whereas . . ."

"That's right. It's a custom, at home, for a man to say he's been caught. I suppose it is English humor."

"He is, as a rule!"

"While it's really myself that's caught in this case, and trying to escape."

She sat over her coffee, making little dabs with her spoon at a crease in the cloth, her head resting on her hand.

"Words don't seem to be any use," she said in a low tone. "They make you say what you don't really mean, half the time."

"I've noticed that too. Words seem largely ornamental. I suppose they were originally intended to express feelings we don't have any more. We lack a way of expressing sentiments without feeling ridiculous." He held out his cup for more coffee. "Our intelligence has grown so sharp we are afraid to expose ourselves to it. If we don't act like people in a fairy tale we are ashamed of not playing the game."

"I know. The lies I've told, just to square what I was doing with a fairy tale! Father and Mother believed them too. I told them Archie and I both had wonderful jobs in Hollywood. I was in a trance. I couldn't bear to have them think I'd made a ghastly mistake about Archie, and an even more ghastly mistake about myself."

He was drinking coffee from a cup held between his two hands, his elbows on the cloth. He looked at her keenly, shrewdly, silently, and with love.

"It's a fact," she said, looking straight at him. She fingered the heavy black strap of his wrist watch. "I thought I could be an actress in the films."

"You! You had hallucinations, then!"

"I know. I mean, I know it now. Elliot was honest enough about it to satisfy even my prejudices. So were the casting people. Well, that's all over. I don't know if I could get a job as a cleaning woman. They'd never believe anything was clean! Our family can only write, and some of us can't do that. I'm one of the unemployables of the Price clan. So is Archie, really. Which made it jolly awful to be married to him. He was *so* disappointed when he found he'd married a dumbbell who couldn't act and didn't screen! He believed in a fairy tale, too. In which he was Prince Charming. Words are always ornamental with Archie. He has no real thoughts to express. He's very correct. He doesn't have to conform to the crowd in Hollywood. That's the way he is, the way he always was. He's more at home there than in England, like that Romanoff who has forgotten his Russian."

She waited for him to make a comment, but he said nothing, and she went on to the end.

"So you see, I haven't been particularly bright. In fact I've been a damned fool where men were concerned. I told you, didn't I, about Caxton Derrick? I wasn't in love with him the way I'm in love with you. It was his personality that was so attractive. While you were with him nobody else mattered. He never flirted, you know. Now he's dead, people forget that. They try to make out he was a lady-killer and lived on women. In Paris, when I tried to get them to drop the charge of his stealing my things, you'd have thought I was an old lady keeping a gigolo! I knew that if he went to prison it would work on his mind and he would destroy himself. And it did. You must be thinking I haven't much sense! It's true. I haven't."

"What I was thinking was this: How do I compete with the men you've known? To me they all seem extraordinarily glamorous, by comparison."

"Who's looking for glamor? Who wants the stuff? What are you laughing at?"

"I was thinking of that girl friend of Elliot's script agent. Terry, they call her."

"The flesh-peddler's girl? I know her. She's decent. What makes you think of her?"

"Why, when I asked her if she'd ever met you, she said she had and then—'She's very glamorous,' she said."

"Meaning me? Well, that's always the way. She knows very little about me, so to her I'm glamorous. Am I to you?"

"Who wants the stuff? I've never had any occasion to use the words like 'glamor.' When Terry called you glamorous it struck me as an odd little bit of slang. She's not illiterate, but she has an extremely limited vocabulary. She was trying to convey an impression she had of you, of strangeness and loveliness and—I am guessing of course—breeding."

Perdita sat motionless for a moment, chin on hand, looking aft at the sunlit sea. Then she clattered the dishes together and half rose.

"Perhaps all that is glamor to her," she said, good-naturedly. "Are we going to stick here all the morning? Is your lady friend a mermaid? Will she climb in over the side? Or do we fish?"

"We fish. But further over, please. You wash the dishes and tidy up while I get her going. We'll move toward Eaton Point. Then we'll be handy for Smithtown Bay. The tide will serve about six-thirty. And we may get a striped bass in deep water."

"Is that where she lives?"

"Up Grampus Channel."

"Suppose she's not at home."

"What of it? We can sail away. We can leave a message. We can do as we please. That's the charm of the thing."

"Of what thing?"

"Of being with you. Do you know, except for an occasional spell when I've had a holiday, or been unemployed, I've never been able to do as I pleased? Even on those occasions, I was either in harness or expecting to be in harness. I had to watch my step, as they say here. We say, we have to watch out. I always watched out until I left the sea. Now I don't have to watch out in that sense. So that's the charm, or the novelty, of being with you."

He lifted the floor-boards and hooked them back to get down to the engine. She put the dishes in a wooden tub that stood in the little sink.

"You're the only man I ever heard of who would look at it that way," she said, going on with the dish washing. "Most men make a fetish of being regular and what they call moral. They *prefer* harness, as you call it, and they watch their steps, all right. They're damned funny when they don't quite know whether the girl is regular or not. They *reverence* women!"

"I don't," he said from under the deck.

"I know you don't, and I'm damn glad of it, my dear. One of the things I hate most about the men here is the way they combine reverence for women with the ethics of a tomcat. What are you laughing at?"

"Nothing. Nothing at all." He climbed out and let down the trap door. He was smiling as he made his way past her, holding his soiled hands away from her, and went into the wheelhouse. She heard the engine start. "There are tomcats in every country," he said, looking around with a quizzical expression. It was obvious that he was a completely happy man and that she was the cause of his happiness.

"Glory Hole" got under way. Looking over the stern as she emptied the tub, Perdita saw the smooth hump of the wake swell up abaft the squat counter. She saw the lighthouse and the roof of Church Yard in the middle distance. They were getting smaller. Louis was over there, hard at work, keeping the place spic and span. Louis was all that was necessary. But suppose she left for good? Suppose this plan of going to England, taking Sonia with them, materialized; would Louis stay on in that house, alone? Would Elliot be shocked out of his trance, and go back to live in his own place? Would he? And would he stay there alone?

The coast grew less distinct. The shore line opened out and she saw the far hills of Connecticut in the distance. The sun was hot. The breeze was pleasant. They must be doing all of ten knots, she thought.

She began to assemble the fishing rods.

She had never felt so secure in her life.

ii

And they're all so bare-faced about it!" Miss Penge exclaimed with a huge, sudden delight. "You never saw anything like it in your born days! I was fit to be tied, Jenney!"

She sat in her practically perfect pre-revolutionary parlor in her own old house, known as The Spinning Wheel, out on Route Eleven.

The door leading to the front part of the house, which was her shop, was open. Customers entering, supposing anyone did enter so early, would catch a glimpse of an antique paradise. They would have seen, on this occasion, the immense bust and broad features of Mrs. Ignazio Cagliari (the former Janice Jenney) seated in a pilgrim chair between a pine shell corner cupboard and the fireplace with its unique pineapple andirons and fretted brass fender. In front of Mrs. Cagliari's huge legs, which ended unexpectedly in small feet trimly shod, was a tea table on which the customer, now unashamedly staring, could behold the fine china brought home from the Orient by Miss Penge's legendary great-grandfather.

Miss Penge was seated, out of line of vision of any customer, on a fine Chippendale sofa behind the door. The reflections and changes of light in the numberless prismatic clusters of a rare candelabra over her head warned her of the entrance of strangers. But at the moment of her exclamation to her bosom friend, Janice Jenney, they were alone.

"Well!" Mrs. Cagliari said, looking demure and severe at

the same time. "Didn't I tell you it wouldn't last? Didn't I tell Ignatz he shouldn't count on that Church Yard job lasting any time? When that Mrs. Ducroy told me they weren't having a couple, I knew there was something fishy about the whole business."

"Oh, I wouldn't say that, Jenney!"

Miss Penge still called her friend by her maiden surname. Janice—after Janice Meredith in *The Prisoner of Trenton*—was too high-hat, she thought. All the local women who had known Mrs. Cagliari in school called her Jenney.

"Well, I would!" Mrs. Cagliari gave a New England drag to the vowels. She was expressing a profound conviction. When the Ducroys came to Norhaven and rebuilt that old Penge place, and hired Mr. Cagliari as outside man, it seemed that the one perfect thing for them to do was to take her on as cook-housekeeper, keeping that foreign feller as houseman. She and Mr. Cagliari could move in over the garage and they could rent their own place in the summer for five hundred dollars the season.

It had been perfect, as she saw it, and Mr. Ducroy's casual rejection of perfection had made a deep impression on Mrs. Cagliari. She was an artist with a cook stove, and she had all an artist's laziness, untidiness in operation, and passion for the ideal. It would have been ideal to live in that house, working in that superb kitchen, saving money, and listening in on those two people, who had captured her imagination.

"Well, you musta had somethin' more to go on than that."

Miss Penge glanced around her parlor. She too was an artist in her way. She had composed this room. When she had found the mahogany butler's desk and stood it against the east wall, so that the afternoon sun, shining through the century-old, violet-tinted panes, brought out the full glory of its patina, she had one of those moments of profound emotion that only a connoisseur could comprehend and share.

She glanced around her parlor and smiled. She was having a good season, and besides being an artist she was a business woman. Yesterday she had sold a sycamore and applewood highboy, with the maker's label and date (1730) in one of the drawers. She herself disliked both sycamore and applewood, and she had made a profit of a hundred and forty dollars. The same customer, a New Yorker, took away a chest-on-frame—another twenty dollars profit. So she could glance around with a sort of latent pride at her possessions, she could listen with half an ear to Jenney, and she could reconstruct in her memory the scene she had described to Jenney when they began tea.

There had been, she remembered, all four of them in the room when she arrived with the things Miss Saxon had bought. She had taken them over in her old station wagon, a regular mess of stuff the woman had taken a fancy to without knowing the first thing about what she was buying. Hadn't even known what the big arm was for on the writing windsor chair! And trying to jew you down all the while. Thought she'd get a signed Hitchcock chair for twenty dollars. And those girandoles! She thought seventy-five for the two was a hold-up, when they were practically unique and worth a hundred!

Miss Penge remembered the woman, in her absurdly young clothes, her hair like a schoolgirl's, short at the back and a strong dark red in color, while Mr. Ducroy, in a rogue shirt and a white beret hung about in the background, examining the china figurines and pressed glass. What a perfectly miraculous skin she had, that Miss Saxon! You had to hand it to her. She made all kinds of money, and she had Mr. Ducroy eating out of her hand. . . .

Well, the four of them are there, Miss Saxon, Mr. Ducroy, and those two from New York. To Miss Penge, who has had them in her shop (and kept a sharp eye on the man while he was handling things), they're more like a gangster and his moll than respectable people. Miss Saxon introduced him. "My friend, Mr. Irving," was it?, but not the other. Just "Uh-huh, this is Miss Uh-huh." Only one thing came clear—"My agent." Agents, it seemed went around with girls in shorts and halters, with house-jackets hardly covering their fannies, and wearing dark, white-rimmed sun glasses that might be for the sun, and again might act as a disguise.

One of the pieces, a cherrywood dresser, is too big for a woman, so she asks for help to unload it. Mr. Ducroy and Mr. Irving come down at once. The way that house is built, it has an awful narrow yard between wings in front of the garage, which is an excavation. Everything has to be carried up those stone stairs to the ground floor, and the *door . . !* My, it's not a yard wide. Tudor effect, with fake iron nails and the phoniest black iron bell pull you've ever seen. That dresser nearly gets stuck in her foolish entrance passage. She says she took that house " 'cause it's so antique-like!" I bet she thinks Tudor City's an antique!

That room, studio she calls it, it's like a barn! Or maybe a church. High! You could park a Ford in the fireplace, and the fire screen's like a monkey cage. That motion-picture feller who made away with himself sure had big ideas when it came to rooms. The window facing the river's one sheet o' plate glass, all of twelve feet by eight. Looks funny in a great place with a Tudor roof and sconces and a gallery at one end with a sort of an organ. They say she's payin' three hundred a month rent, unfurnished. I'd say there's half a dozen full-size orientals on that oak floor, lookin' like scatter rugs, it's so big. But with the doors so narrow she'll have to take that big window out and hoist the furniture with a derrick if she ever wants to furnish that studio, as she calls it, the way it ought to be. With a refectory table and all.

"That Mr. Irving is a case, Jenney!" Miss Penge was thinking aloud. She leaned forward and poured the tea into Mrs. Cagliari's cup. "A case, if I ever saw one. Believe it or not, he isn't *married* to that . . ."

"They never are!" Mrs. Cagliari said, staring, with pale blue eyes like convex stones, at her friend. She was a blonde, and she had an almost Circassian voluptuousness of contour.

She was inclined, now, to become slightly heavy since she never did any work. She was kept by Mr. Cagliari, in one sense, as in a harem of one, as though she were incapable of going anywhere without an escort of Janissaries and eunuchs.

He was a dark, diminutive, sinewy Latin with a natural genius for gardening, and produced marvelous grapes in his own yard as well as under glass. Janice Jenney had been his teacher in the Americanization class he attended to learn good English and acquire some knowledge of the Constitution. To have that magnificent creature for himself, in his own house, bearing his name, put an unbelievably perfect finish to his Americanization.

To him she was valuable and unique. It was impossible for Ignazio Cagliari to accept the Sutton Corners theory, that Janice Jenney had done very well for herself, the great, fat, lazy creature, when she married the little wop who owned his house and nine acres and who made around fifty dollars a week all season. Sure, she was a swell cook, and educated; but the only Americanizing she'd ever done in that class of hers was to Americanize Mr. Cagliari.

To him she was a dream woman. Her soft blonde blowsiness appealed to some Ottoman or Saracenic strain in his Sardinian blood, and fired him with the pride of possession, of conquest. He owned her, and refused to let her do any work, and he abased himself before her superior intelligence.

His jealous vigilance of her honor gave them both a deep, inarticulate pleasure. Sutton Corners had never suggested, in the most censorious moments, that Mrs. Cagliari was ever anything but a fanatically virtuous spouse. It was she who was censorious, and the modern girls, whose parents had been Americanized in Janice Jenney's class, disliked her for her outspoken criticisms of their behavior.

In her view, the people of whom Miss Penge spoke were not married at all, never were married in the sense that she was married to Mr. Cagliari. They constituted for her a separate class of human beings. They were *hetairai,* in her estimation, with their everlasting divorces and love nests; but she used a more modern colloquial phrase. For them she had the scorn of a faithful wife; but she was sometimes filled with regret. If she had only gotten that job at Church Yard, she would have been able to see them close at hand and confirm her theoretical suspicions. She had taken an instantaneous intuitive dislike to Mrs. Ducroy. *He* was all okay, maybe, until that creature got hold of him. But her . . !

"Ho!" said Miss Penge. She was enjoying herself. It pleased her to have Jenney say exactly what she herself believed. "Ho! You oughta seen 'em, Jenney. So lovin'! Mr. Irving, when we got the cherry dresser agin the wall, he says 'There, sweetness, what you think o' that?' And puts his arm around her and kisses her right before everybody. Barefaced!"

"Kissed who? Not Mrs. Saxon? Oh, you mean *her*? I'd say anything in pants could get to kissing *her*. Know what I think? I think it's all phooey about that Irving being an agent. He doesn't look like an agent to me. I think he's one o' these New York night-club entertainers who's been hired to bring his girl friend down, for a chaperone."

"She's some chaperone," Miss Penge said, but the way she said it implied that she thought there was a good deal in Jenney's theory. "Take it from me, it 'ud take more'n one chaperone to make those other two behave."

"What?" said Mrs. Cagliari. The blue prominent eyes became more stony than usual. "What? Did you see. . . ?"

Miss Penge did not reply immediately. She gazed introspectively at the carved McIntyre mantel, a minor work of the master, but very satisfying to its owner in its purity of design and perfection of workmanship. Miss Penge would rather have contemplated her parlor mantel than a Raphael cartoon.

The point was, she was thinking, what *had* she seen? The boys and girls on Norhaven beach were uninhibited enough. In the streets and stores of Norbury, girls in shorts and halters paraded all summer. Miss Penge was perfectly well aware of the cars parked at night or even in daylight among the trees on the edge of the dune or on the bluff above the shore. She had seen, with embarrassing clarity, the entirely unembarrassed love-making in the rumble seats of cars outlined by her huge headlights on Route Eleven. It was, she told herself, like she didn't know what, in a back yard . . .

In that imitation Tudor mansion of Sydney Saxon, the author of many love serials which Miss Penge really liked, the impression she had carried away was not the same. She was telling her Jenney of that Mr. Irving kissing his girl in front of everybody, including herself, and she was hinting that she witnessed appallingly amorous scenes between Sydney Saxon and Elliot Ducroy. That, she reflected, was because she was aware Jenney wouldn't understand anything else. Jenney wouldn't appreciate the fact that, up there, she, Miss Penge was actually—actually looking in on another world!

It seemed flat and unimpressive when she expressed it that way to herself. Jenney would simply inhale through her sharp short nose and say, "You sure were! *Under*world!"

She wouldn't get what Miss Penge meant at all. What Miss Penge felt, but could not quite explain, was that she had been aware of an entirely novel and not entirely unpleasant mental atmosphere. It was an extraordinary and even a shocking thing, and Jenney would never get it as long as she lived, but Miss Penge had a notion that she had experienced that sensation once before. And where, if you please? Why, when she was with that Mr. Spenlove, who lived in the old Mudge Place!

It was funny to realize, now, why she had felt so strange with that man. She had had other notions to begin with, and to ease her spirit she had kidded him along over the phone. It was easy over the phone. He had a voice that sounded as if he was laughing to himself at intervals. The way he would wait a spell, before answering . . .

She became aware of her Jenney looking hard at her,

waiting to hear what she had seen. She knew Jenney would be disappointed if she heard the truth, that what she had seen, in the gestures and glances and tones of voice, seemed perfectly natural to those people. They were not aware of anything unusual in their behavior. When Sydney Saxon said, in a casual tone, "Darling, give Miss Penge a cocktail. You'll have a cocktail, Miss Penge? They're not strong," she was not outraged at all. Mr. Ducroy didn't have one. He went and made them but when the Filipino brought them he didn't have one. He said he liked 'em all right, but they didn't like him. Matter of fact, that Mr. Irving was the only one besides herself who really *drank* one. Miss Penge was uneasily suspicious that he did it to keep her company. That girl friend of his didn't drink at all, he said. He pretended he had to drink for both of them, and he was getting arteriosclerosis of the liver, or some such nonsense, on her account. Miss Saxon, writing the check at a desk in the corner, had said, "You mean thrombosis of the brain, Irving. I've noticed it."

They were at ease with each other, in each other's minds. They were not keeping up appearances to each other. Like that Mr. Spenlove again! Was this the secret? Miss Penge took fright suddenly. She couldn't explain it to Jenney. She shrugged her shoulders.

The shop bell tinkled and Jenney's gaze was on the open parlor door. Miss Penge rose.

"Oh, I couldn't go into details," she said, under her breath. "After all, they're customers, Jenney. You can see for yourself . . ."

She moved briskly into the front room where a customer, as usual, was suddenly immobilized by the sight of so much furniture, glass, china, snuffers, candlemolds, Currier & Ives prints, miniatures, chandeliers, sconces, silver, pewter, Sheffield plate, coach-lamps, flax-wheels, toddy irons, curly-maple trenchers, rush stools, kneading troughs, bobbin wheels, noggins and towering grandfather clocks, all crowded into two connecting chambers. It seemed dangerous even to stand still amid such incredible quantities of bric-a-brac. There were visible more private shaving mugs, in a lofty black walnut wall cabinet from an old-time barber's shop, than most people had ever seen in their entire lives.

Mrs. Cagliari heard Miss Penge say penetratingly,

"Who? Well, s'pose I do! Who wants him?"

"A friend of his. Could I use your telephone, ma'am?" It was a soft resonant voice, with an unfamiliar cadence.

"Seems I heard he wasn't home just now. I'll see."

Miss Penge put her head inside the parlor door, winked tremendously at Mrs. Cagliari and said, loudly,

"Jenney, didn't you say Mr. Ducroy's not home just now?"

"That's right," Jenney said coolly. "He's visiting with friends."

Miss Penge turned toward the invisible stranger. "This lady's husband works for Mr. Ducroy. So, you see . . ."

There was a pause. The outer screen door was slapped shut firmly. Mrs. Cagliari, her hand on the radio knob, could see a tall presence close to Miss Penge, who stood in the doorway.

"Excuse me ma'am, it's important. I've come a long way to see my friend. He asked me to come and see him. If you let me use your phone, or call yourself if you'd ruther, and see if he's left a message for Piers Mallinson."

"Who?"

"Piers Mallinson, the poet, ma'am. From the Coast. From California. Would you allow me?"

"They's a call booth in Norbury," Miss Penge said in an unaccommodating tone. Mrs. Cagliari could see the stranger now, tall, terribly thin and shabby in his khaki trousers and blue denim jacket, like a workman. His face was not that of a workman. It was thin, hawk-faced, the brown features sharpened and the eyes deep-set in gray-fringed sockets. He had a fierce expression that was out of line with his quiet speech.

"Oh, well. . . . The phone's over there." Miss Penge felt

there was no real risk, with Jenney around. "This is a friend o' Mr. Ducroy's," she said to Mrs. Cagliari. "I tell him Mr. Ducroy's not at home just now, but he says maybe he's left a message."

Mrs. Cagliari moved with a quickness surprising in one of her bulk. She turned off the radio as she rose and the tall man, like a scarecrow, moved politely across the parlor. His deep-set eyes gleamed as he took in the furnishings, the carved mantel, the rag carpet's concentric colored circles, the wall clock and the prints from *Godey's Lady's Book.* The colored crystal chandelier was on a level with his head.

He fumbled with the telephone book. Miss Penge said, "It's on the card there. I'll get it for you."

She leaned over the shelf by the radio and dialed the number. The man sat, his hands on the chair arms, his gaze on the floor between them, as though lost in thought. There was a wait. The two women stared without expression at each other. Slowly the man's left hand drew a bag of makings from the breast pocket of his gray shirt. From the other pocket he brought cigarette paper. They watched his long brown fingers, like pointed claws, form a cigarette with unbelievable dexterity. He drew the string of the bag taut with his teeth and reached to his hip for a match which he produced, magically, alight.

"Yes? Church Yard? Hold it, please." Miss Penge handed the receiver to her guest and walked to the sofa, where she straightened the cushions.

The atmosphere had changed. Miss Penge felt it oppressive. She wondered if it would do to offer the man—he said he was a poet—some tea. He looked like a tramp. She walked into the front room with a new idea. She heard Jenney go to the kitchen. To get more hot water, maybe.

She looked out into the yard below her lawn, where cast-iron dogs, garden seats, fountains, sundials and a couple of old sleighs supported the giant red spinning wheel which was her business sign. She saw a very old touring car with a yellow brass radiator and gas headlights. The top was folded down and tied with cord. The rear was filled with amorphous bundles. The running board carried an oil container and what looked like a pup tent. The vertical windshield, in two sections, was broken at one corner. The flat narrow fenders were grotesque, like the starting crank and the bulb horn. The shiny flat leather cushions had rents, from which the stuffing was bulging.

Miss Penge put her hand to her mouth. It was almost in her line, that car, an antique. She knew those twenty-year-olds had marvelous stamina, but she had never realized a thing like that could cross the Rocky Mountains. She stared.

She heard the man talking without catching the words. That would be the houseman, the gloomy foreigner Mr. Cagliari had often mentioned. Not gloomy so much as taciturn. No conversation. Mr. Cagliari liked someone to practise his English on. According to him the houseman knew very little of that language and didn't want to use what he had. "Worka, worka, worka, alla time," was Mr. Cagliari's comment.

The tall stranger appeared in the parlor doorway.

"Was he home?" she inquired. She saw Jenney with the kettle.

"He was. He said he was goin' out at once, though. He said I was to come right along and stay in his house. He's got a man there, he says. I'm obliged to you, ma'am."

"It's no trouble. Will you have a cup o' tea? I didn't get your name."

"Mallinson. Piers Mallinson. A poet, ma'am. Thanks, a cup would do me good."

"That your car?"

"If you can call it a car, ma'am. It's all a poet can afford. It's not much for looks, but it has a good engine. No speed, but it gets along."

"You come from California, I see."

"From San Luis Obispo," he told her. His voice had

resonance and vigor, as though the very repetition of the sonorous Spanish name restored his western vitality.

"This gentleman's come from California, Jenney," Miss Penge said. He seated his long body in a rocker with his back to the light and contemplated the Puritan parlor. Miss Penge, a shade excited, poured out the fresh tea.

"You goin' to visit with Mr. Ducroy?"

"Well, maybe. I guess Mr. Ducroy was a bit surprised to know I was so close. He used to come to my place when he was in Hollywood. He'd extended an invitation to come and see him. He probably forgot all about it. He's a busy man these days. He as good as said, he'd forgot."

"You know Mrs. Ducroy?"

"Haven't that pleasure, ma'am. Mr. Ducroy was living on his own, a bachelor, when I first made his acquaintance."

"You in Hollywood too?"

"No, ma'am. . . ." The hawk-like features sharpened, and the deep eyes gleamed, and then he smiled gently. "I'm a poet. When you're in Hollywood you don't drive a 1922 model. Thank you." He took the cup she offered him. "No, thanks, ma'am. I drink it straight. You have a beautiful room here. This house . . ." He looked over his shoulder at the violet-tinted panes.

"Seventeen sixty-four," she said. "One of the Colonial salt boxes."

"So? The past is all around you here. My folks came from York State, but I'm a Native Son. Mr. Ducroy, he's been a wonderful friend to me. I was sorry when he came East. Yes, I was sorry."

"You thinkin' of settlin' here?"

"No, ma'am! I wouldn't feel I was alive for long if I was in these parts. I live"—he lifted his lean arm with a gesture simple and dramatic—"on a mountain, facing the Pacific. That's facing the future."

He drank his tea slowly, his mind sunk in deep thought.

"Well, I hope you enjoy your visit," Miss Penge said formally, not looking at him. She was somewhat confused at the notion of a man, practically in rags, with that terrible old car, sitting on a mountain facing the Pacific Ocean, and writing poetry. Miss Penge's ideas about poets were rudimentary. "Must ha' been lonesome, drivin' all that way by yourself."

"Ma'am, I'm never lonesome, as you call it." He set the cup down with care and smiled at the two women. They were aware of something queer about him. The word was Mrs. Cagliari's after he was gone. He was, she said, "queer." Miss Penge had a confused, fleeting impression, as he rose slowly, a tall, tanned Westerner, lean and with a native dignity, that he was in disguise, that he ought to be wearing chin whiskers and a tall stove-pipe hat and a shawl over his shoulders. A crazy notion!

He stood before them for a moment and then moved with his head bent, toward the shop. He turned and offered his hand.

"Thanks to you, ma'am, for the use of your telephone." His face creased into laughter. "And the tea. Does a man good. I'm frank to tell you ma'am, I couldn't use a call booth because I have no money. I was wondering whether I'd gas enough to make Mr. Ducroy's place, or whether I'd have to walk the rest of the way. I've had to stop and do chores quite a few times on the road. Folks are kind. To get money for gas."

"Why didn't you tell Mr. Ducroy you were in a jam?" Miss Penge said warmly.

"Well, ma'am, Mr. Ducroy's a busy man, and, as I told you, he's been a good friend to me. I've always made out. My needs are few. Good day to you, ma'am, and to you. . . ."

He made a vague, courteous gesture toward the large woman with the suspicious eyes, and strode across the grass to his ancient car. Miss Penge heard her friend come hurriedly to the window and saw her peer between the heavy molded glass goblets which stood on shelves there to catch the light. They both saw him turn and look long and keenly at the house, at the sleighs, and the great spinning wheel on the lawn flanked by red spotlight casings. Then he stooped in front of his car and cranked it.

"Not even a starter!" said Mrs. Cagliari in a whisper. Miss Penge nodded.

"You heard what he said. A nineteen-twenty-two model. See it shimmy? It's like you see in the comedies." She shook her head. The tall man, who had said he was a poet, Piers Mallinson the poet, clambered into the car and the contraption suddenly jerked forward and vanished behind the shrubs that lined Route Eleven. There remained only a faint cloud of blue vapor.

"Now what do you make of that?" Miss Penge said, aloud, but really to herself. "He's a Westerner. No money, not even for a phone call! Do you think that's a fact? He says Mr. Ducroy's a friend of his, and he's goin' there now. He'll meet that Mrs. Ducroy. What do you know about that, Jenney?"

"You sure you ought to let him call up? There's all kinds of transients on the roads this time of year. All you know, he's just a transient who's heard of Elliot Ducroy, and . . ."

Miss Penge shook her head vaguely. She was thinking of that crazy impression she had, when he sat so quietly, his long arms on the chair arms, his chin on his breast, waiting for her to put the call through. And that other crazy notion, that he had a stove-pipe hat and shawl stowed in his old car!

"No, Jenney," she said. "He's a honest-to-goodness friend of Mr. Ducroy, I'm ready to swear. I dunno about *her*. Says he's never met her. And what he'll think of what's goin' on . . . !"

"I should worry. I bet he's goin' to touch Mr. Ducroy for a loan."

"Oh, no, Jenney! You always think the worst of anybody you don't like. I . . . I got an idea that poet, he calls himself, is *some*body. Somebody important."

"With that car? And not even a nickel for a phone call? What makes you think so?"

"I dunno. There's plenty of *important* people don't make lots o' money, Jenney. You never heard about the man who did that sort o' thing first?"

She pointed to the Sheraton butler's desk.

"I got a book about him—Sheraton—somewheres," she went on. "He was queer too, but he made beautiful things, 's you can see."

"That was a long time ago," said Mrs. Cagliari. "Money's different now," she yawned. "I got to go," she said. Mr. Cagliari would be wanting his supper. She put her cigarettes in her bag, took out a piece of paper headed "Coming Attractions," and studied it. It was their regular night for driving into Norbury for a movie, when they took turns in standing treat.

In the Norbury Majestic, when the lights were down and the stars they adored blazed on the screen, the two women achieved a spiritual communion. They sat in the darkness side by side, as their forefathers did in the early days in the churches, and looked into heaven. It was heaven to them. They were disembodied, and so were happy. Like many modern women, they disliked the confusion and disorder of love on a lower plane. So they lived vicarious sex lives in the movies.

Mrs. Cagliari said, starting for the door, "There's a Gentleman Church short too."

iii

SAY it again!" she said.

"All of it?"

"No, not all of it. Begin where we are getting into Dorsetshire."

"We strike north from Abbotsbury after coming down the high road from Lyme Regis and Bridport, above Chesil Beach."

"And you show me a swannery in Abbotsbury."

"And a nunnery too. Then we go through Portisham to Dorchester. From there we have a choice of roads. We can go northwest to Salisbury and then east to Winchester or . . ."

"We'll do that. Isn't it ridiculous? I've never seen England except London and that corner of Suffolk near Brandeston Knights. Now I want to see it. How far's Winchester?"

"Well, we stopped off at Bath, and as near as I can figure we've done a mere hundred miles since the late breakfast you insisted on, and we've taken our time, and had tea in a thatched cottage at Combe Bissett—I think that was the name—so by the time we reach Winchester you will take one look at that hotel I spoke of, where I once spent a night when I was on a walking tour, and we'll go no further."

"Say it again, please," she urged him anxiously.

"Ye olde Hostel of God-Begot," he intoned with solemnity, and she sighed.

"It seems hardly possible," she mused. "It'll be awful for you if I find you made it up."

"No fear of that. It's there. It's been there four hundred years. You have breakfast in a bow window that lets you look right down the street. Just as well, because the room is so dark you can't see anything inside it. Black beams and rafters that shine. As if the place had been hewn out of an ebony cave! Each upstairs chamber is named after an English queen. Plantagenet for choice!"

She shivered with pleasure.

"The names are on the doors," he went on abstractedly, recapturing the mood of a time long past. "I was put in what they called the shepherd's room, being young and single. No bow window, but a lovely view of the stables and the cathedral. And a fine strong smell from the horses. That will be gone now."

"And then? After the God-Begot?"

"The Cotswolds. Steer due north until we can turn west for Wantage and on to Cirencester. I bicycled that way, and went trout fishing."

"When you were young?"

"When I was what we used to call an improver. I was out of my time as an apprentice."

"Were you happy in those days? But that's a foolish question."

"It's not an easy question to answer, my dear. What I am now didn't exist, then. I was a callow kid! I was afraid of girls, for instance."

"You!"

"Me. Not only that, I thought it would be a fine thing if I could arrange my life completely independent of women. I had that ambition. The only ones I knew at first hand were shopgirls, landladies and their daughters, and the girls you could pick up on the streets. I don't mean professionals, but girls of my own class. They were like me, looking for experiences. But at that time I had a bad case of mental measles. I was suffering from a rash of crude political notions."

"Socialism?"

"Yes. It was fashionable. We had a lot of rich soci England. In fact, unless you were rich you couldn't to be a socialist. I know I couldn't. It was a purely intel exercise, of course. I worked as a wage slave and enjo But it seemed to me that the sort of man I wanted would never take women seriously."

"You got over the measles all right."

"When I went to sea."

"That would settle the woman business. I had that when I first met you. You found another interest in life, so . . ."

"Well, you have time to think and to see life in persp tive. The things people fuss about on shore become important. You live your own life, not that of the herd. Th why so many men hate the sea. I liked it. I kept that sec for many years, that I liked it for reasons incomprehensib to those who hated, and who went to sea because they kne no other way of making a living. You know the saying—on fools and drunkards go to sea."

She laughed silently. She was lying back in the cockpit her shoulders against a cushion in the corner, while Mr. Spenlove, his arms around his knees, sat on the stern and kept a weather eye on the traffic. They were lying, almost motionless, under the afternoon sun, a couple of miles off Crane's Neck Point. A line of empty sand barges was coming up past Huntington Bay. Some yachts, their canvas dazzlingly white, were almost becalmed outside Setauket. Far away a high-speed cabin cruiser passed behind Stratford Shoal.

He heard her laugh and turned to look at her.

"I ought to make a good seaman, in that case," she said ruefully. "I'll bear it in mind, if all else fails! You *were* happy then?"

"Yes, I was. I knew what I wanted and I found I was able to get it. Can you believe that? I enjoyed every last detail of my life, even the really horrible work. Wait a bit. I didn't

enjoy going home and trying to fit into my place in a provincial town. I hated it."

"Where? You've never said."

"It didn't occur to me to mention it. It's a small place in Hampshire. Throxford, it's called. I'm the Hampshire wonder; I've often marveled that I could never work up any enthusiasm for going home. I used to stay in London, or Liverpool, if I hadn't a ship. And when I took service in a line running out of New Orleans, I liked that much better. No going home! I had a valid excuse for never going to that dreary place where I was born."

"I feel the same about where I was born," she said. "But I do want to see Brandeston Knights again."

"We're going there!" he said, strongly. He caught her ankle and pulled her toward him. She fell against him and enfolded him in her arms, his head against her breasts. The boat rocked slightly.

"That's right," she said, thickly, her breath coming suddenly fast. "We'll go there before we go to London. Can we?"

"Surely. Through Buckinghamshire. Aylesbury and then St. Albans. I was an apprentice when I was sent to Aylesbury on an outdoor job. A gentleman's estate. The gentleman was very rich and wanted electric light. We put in a plant for him. I lived there for several months."

"Didn't you have any adventures?"

"The beginning of one. The fair was on and we did the booths with some of the country girls. Mine was a very dark wench who wore nose glasses."

"Was she pretty?"

"It seems so, on looking back. I was young, about eighteen, and there was something intriguing about a girl with glasses. She was aggressive too, which suited my mood. And she had a French name. She was pure Buckinghamshire but her name was French. I can remember it was Autrand."

"How did that happen?"

"Hah! Romance! A French king was a refugee near by,

and one of his retainers, a seneschal, butler, major-domo or whatnot, must have had a romance with a local farmer's pretty daughter. This was their grandchild. She told me all about it. Her grandmother had been a maid at Hartswell Hall. That was where Louis the Eighteenth lived before Waterloo. She was a nice little thing, and if I had had more experience and enterprise, who knows what might have happened? She was romantic and so was I, but not in the same way. We used to sit in the big stable and coachhouse at the end of the yard in the Bull Inn. I thought I was being desperately unusual and romantic. French, you see."

Perdita stood up and looked down at him, smiling.

"You aren't going to take me to that place—what was the name again? Where you grew up?"

"No. Nor to the boardinghouse where I lived while I was an apprentice in London. There are some places one never wants to see again."

"Right. I'm that way about Hollywood. I served my apprenticeship there! What an apprenticeship! The longer I was there the more unskillful I became! In a town full of women earning fabulous salaries I became an economic inferior, almost a public charge! Sonia used to say, 'Mummy, what does a star do?' I would tell her 'She shines, ducky,' and she'd think that over. Of course, I'm prejudiced; but there isn't a village in Suffolk that isn't a million times prettier than Hollywood and hasn't more dignity and decent sense. And intelligence too, if you ask me. Elliot used to agree with me about Hollywood. 'Sure it stinks, and I'll blast it too, as soon as I've made mine.' That was his way of putting it. What a way to live! I'd rather be dead."

"That's what my shipmates used to say of going to sea. They'd as soon be dead. And so you can understand why I kept to myself the fact that I liked it. I became a man of mystery! No wife, no home port, no family, and he goes to sea when he could get a shore billet—I could have, you know. They knew I could. That's one thing you can't hide from your shipmates, intelligence. The natural thing for me to have done was to get a superintendent's job, go into the office, become an executive and live in Scotstoun Hill, Glasgow, or Bootle, Liverpool, or some place like that. As you so justly remark, I'd rather be dead."

"If you'd done that, I'd never have met you."

"If I had, you'd never have wanted to."

"That's true. It's very unusual to find anyone who has always done what he wanted."

She stood up, the prismatic binoculars to her eyes. The gesture revealed the sweet long curve of her thigh and flank, the hollow of her back and the firm thrust of her breasts, as she stood, her feet planted on a thwart.

"Those yachts are simply not moving at all," she said. "Becalmed."

She was in a state of complete happiness, so that the words were of no consequence. They needed no comment. The afternoon was drawing on. The line of sand barges was lost in the dazzle of the sun on the water. They were a long way off and would pass more than a mile to the northward. The tide was making. He had told her that there would be enough water in Grampus Channel, where Mrs. Colwell's place came down to the water, before seven. It was now half after five. He wanted to get in with a chance to get out at once if Mrs. Colwell were not at home.

She put the glasses on a cushion and stopped to look at the cabin clock.

"Would you like some tea?" she said doubtfully. He shook his head.

"Not today," he said. "Lower the table and . . ." He made a slight gesture to indicate pulling out the bed place.

The afternoon drowsed. A white excursion boat, with tiers of decks, like a heap of trays, and with two thin yellow funnels sharply raked, steamed eastward a mile away. The high-speed cruiser reappeared as it changed course for Port Jefferson. Either she was running out of fuel, Mr. Spenlove thought quietly, or the owner wanted to have dinner ashore. The hills on the mainland were purple and mauve-gray.

This, he thought to himself, was a life only a man who had been a sea-toiler and who had preserved his intelligence, could relish completely. Unaware of it, he had been preparing himself for this for years, he now understood. Almost he could conceive what men meant when they spoke of "being guided," or when they declared that they had been "led by the grace of God" to this or that felicitous consummation. Or the Victorian allusion to "meeting one's fate." It sounded mawkish and theatrical now, he reflected, but it was the phrase, not the experience, which dated. All over the world, for instance, young men were suffering the pangs of young love, just as he himself had suffered them thirty-odd years ago. The only difference was that, in those days, one had the seed and the tender flower, and then it withered. Now they had to nurse it along until it bore bitter fruit, and then they blamed society because it was bitter. Then, in middle age, dyspepsia—emotional dyspepsia.

He had a suspicion, moreover, that he was extraordinarily lucky because he had never exhausted himself, spiritually, as men like Elliot Ducroy, like that poet Caxton Derrick, and Sydney Saxon, exhausted themselves, in exploiting their personalities. The haggard, abstracted stare of Elliot Ducroy, when he forgot he was being observed, was that of a man in hell. There was that little woman who wrote murder stories, who had been a passenger once, whose mind seemed forever on the stretch with her mystery puzzles. And they were successful! What must it be for those uncounted thousands who spent their lives spinning words from their own entrails, and failing after all! They were the losers in the great lottery of letters, the anonymous swarm of magicians and clowns who made only a bare living, or no living at all. They had no secure status such as he had in his employment. Their patrons sucked them dry and flung them aside. They were at the beck and call of incalculable forces, and they had no chance to lead a civilized life.

Yes, he was fortunate in every way, and all without forfeiting what he valued most, his independence of mind and spirit. Perdita was the one perfect woman in the world, he believed, for sharing such a supreme experience. He watched her now, for a moment, before taking another look around. She had a genius for quick, silent obedience. Tell her to do this and that, she went at it and got it done. Whether she knew it or not, it was the right way with him. It astonished him that such a quality could be thrilling and an inspiration of passion. Yet it was. It had an almost corporeal shape, this attitude of hers, which he could handle and caress. All her qualities, indeed, had this solidity and shapeliness of spirit, so that you either loved her or hated her, he suspected.

The sun was declining toward the western mountains He was, he figured, five miles from the entrance of Grampus Channel, and it was about half a mile from there to the Colwell place. Plenty of time. He stood up and looked around the horizon. The yachts were farther away now. Probably a faint puff of air over there. The fast cruiser was gone inside. Plenty of water everywhere now. He could get out of Grampus Channel any time up to eleven o'clock.

He heard her speak in a muffled voice. She was pulling her sweater over her head.

"You coming in too?"

She had on a swim suit under her slacks. Kicking these off, she came out of the cabin quickly, a saffron-colored rubber cap on her head, her bronze-green eyes smiling.

"Just a second," he said. One of her straps was twisted and he passed his hand over her shoulder to straighten it. She stood perfectly still and straight, smiling and looking at the Long Island shore, as he did this, loving him in silence.

"Stay alongside," he warned. She stepped on to the seat, nodding.

"Your hands!" she said, as she stood making ready. "I never loved anyone to touch me before. Hurry up."

She went over the side cleanly and swam under water to the bow.

In a moment he made ready and followed her. The water was cool. He could never get used to the shock of it, having done nearly all his swimming in tropical seas. Not even a day of blazing sun could take the chill off these Sound waters.

When he reached the sharply raked stem she was swimming past the counter, which was like the roof of a house, a smooth slope on which the words *Glory Hole, Norhaven* gleamed white in the sunset. From the water his boat seemed a clumsy crate, he thought, as he swam aft. She was ideal for the purpose, though, and again he was astonished at the way he had been led by a blind fate. He had certainly not understood, when he drew the plans long ago, at sea, in his office on a cruise liner, that he was designing a boat for carrying off an Englishwoman, like Helen from Menelaus. He felt almost as though he had been mistaken about himself all his life, that he was not, after all, a strong forger of his own destiny, but the sport of a higher power.

He waited until she came into view, swimming idly on her back, and gave her a hail.

"All aboard," he said, and pulled himself over the gunwale.

As she came to the side he was waiting with a heavy towel-robe. He put it over her shoulders and she undid her swim suit and pushed it down to the grating, kicking it aside.

"That rubber cap suits you. What color d'you call it? Yellow?"

"If you like. Sulky saffron's the trade name."

"We used to call it gamboge," he told her. "Whatever it is, it suits you."

"Same color as my eyes," she said, toweling. "Excuse me," she dived into the cabin and closed the door.

"Your eyes may be mysterious, but they aren't yellow," he

called to her. "I've never made up my mind what they are. Sonia's are the same."

He wrung out her swim suit and spread it on the grating aft.

"They're yellow all right," she said, her back to him. "You're probably color-blind."

She sponged her body from a bucket of fresh water and began to dry herself. He went on working with his own towel, feeling extraordinarily elated. The sand barges were abeam now a couple of miles away, and only one other distant steamer was visible.

He saw her reaching over the bunk to draw the curtain of the scuttles, saw the long sweeping line of her back and loins and the enigmatic, female glance she gave him over her shoulder. He saw the glance change magically to the smile she reserved for him alone when she saw him, wearing the great towel like an Arab burnous, open the sliding cabin door.

"Oh, sir, you intrude on my privacy!" she said. She gave that delicious little chuckling laugh, a tiny, private sound. "Once aboard the lugger . . !"

"Here we are," he said. "It looks different from this side, naturally, but I know the house. And there are people on that boat. That's Setauket over there, I suppose."

He pointed to the left as he put the helm over.

"Your friends are swells," Perdita murmured. She saw a long façade of windows still reflecting the brightness of the western sky. The house looked down upon a succession of gardens with terraces, greenhouses, a tall steel windmill for pumping water, and a line of stables and garages with second stories obviously occupied by servants. Close at hand was a dock, with a formidable cabin cruiser tied up and on the after-deck of this a number of people were having cocktails.

"I told you," he said. She was standing at the entrance of the wheelhouse while he steered, at half speed, toward the dock. "And she has always had it. Her family, I mean. Had everything, I suppose. She has a sense of humor too, except about capitalism, and even about that she is tolerant. She lets me argue. Her son is an unabashed robber-baron, he told me. Always being investigated by the government!"

"Are you sure she has a sense of humor about people who call suddenly in a motorboat?" Perdita said doubtfully.

"I don't think she'll chuck us out," he said, smiling. "Have you been reading English novels about rich Americans? I thought you understood she was a friend of mine. Not just an acquaintance. A friend."

"Darling, I do! Is that *their* motorboat? Golly!"

"It is. Twin-screw diesel, with a crew of seven, my girl. That's what it is to have money. Making money is all very well, but having it is divine."

"Oh, dear, yes, I suppose so."

"Look," he said, as they drew nearer. "They have had the channel dredged. Doesn't it make you feel faint to think of the maintenance costs? I once told Mrs. Colwell that it was people like her who were bringing on the revolution. She was quite unimpressed. Rightly so. They survive all revolutions. . . . They get fat contracts to erect the barricades. I'll give them a toot. . . ."

He pressed his foot on the button, sounding three mellow notes on a horn he had installed.

The party under the awning looked up at the sound. Mr. Spenlove saw Perdita retreat into the cabin and close the sliding door. He knew that her clothes, a cashmere pullover and tweed skirt, were adequate, but he understood that she would be preoccupied until she met Mrs. Colwell. It was no disparagement of his own character that she could not be sure about such a person, just from his words.

There was Mrs. Colwell, however, in white linen, her fine vigorous features easily recognizable as she came to the rail with her son. Mr. Spenlove stopped his engine and leaned out of the side window of his tiny pilot house. He saw the flash of recognition in her expression, saw her speak to her son rapidly, and then they both waved.

"Mr. Spenlove!" she exclaimed. "You've actually come! I thought you didn't mean it. Are you coming to see us?"

"Coming aboard, madame, if we may lay alongside."

She leaned over to examine the craft.

"And is that thing the boat you told me about?"

"Be careful what you say! Yes, this is my new ship."

He was closing in on the glistening side of the "Agnes II," the cruiser that was almost a yacht, and young Colwell, in an amateur yachtsman's slacks and sweater, was lowering the teak and brass accommodation ladder. Mr. Spenlove took a boat hook from its rack on the cabin roof and drew alongside. He looked up.

"Anyone with you?" Mrs. Colwell said. He nodded, indicating the cabin.

"A particular friend," he said.

Mrs. Colwell looked extremely hard at Mr. Spenlove. He stepped on to the grating, shook hands with young Colwell, and made fast to a stanchion. As the boat lost way he stepped aboard of her again and opened the after cabin door.

"Ready?" he said. She came out at once and stepped up on the grating. Mr. Colwell looked astonished and delighted simultaneously. He shook hands, waved her up the ladder to his mother and immediately descended to inspect the boat.

"A smart craft," he told Mr. Spenlove. He made a face and winked. "Diesel?"

"Semi-diesel," Mr. Spenlove said, "if you are referring to the boat. I must go up and meet your mother."

He stepped briskly up the ladder.

"I'm terribly glad you came," Mrs. Colwell said. "I was afraid you'd forgotten all about us. We're having cocktails. Will you . . ? You remember Agnes? She's Mrs. Danford now. Clyde, this is Mr. Spenlove. I told you about him."

"How do you do? How do you do? Did you get the name? Mrs. Ducroy." Mr. Spenlove shook hands with Agnes Colwell.

"I'm simply astonished. Marriage certainly was the thing for you. I congratulate you both. Have you kept up your deck tennis, young woman?"

There were a couple of middle-aged guests who were introduced rapidly. Mr. and Mrs. Danford said they were going up to change.

"You'll stay to dinner?" Mrs. Colwell said.

"It looks as if we were arriving just for that," said Mr. Spenlove. "It was the tide, really. I wasn't sure about this channel. The chart says it has only eighteen inches at mean low tide."

"That's all it does have. We dredged here, of course. Well, it's delightful." Mrs. Colwell was obviously sincere. She looked from Mr. Spenlove to Perdita and back in a way that made him laugh outright. The white-coated steward brought his tray of cocktails to the table abaft the cabin skylight. The deep maroon cushions in the semicircular seat under the awning were amazingly comfortable. So were the wicker chairs. Mr. Spenlove was sufficiently carried away to wonder if this sort of thing were not a foretaste of heaven. He had never felt better in his life. He drank half a martini with relish.

"You seem to be doubtful of our reality," he said. "You think we are ghosts, coming in by water like this?"

"It certainly had a supernatural look at first." She glanced at Perdita, and seemed to be about to say something more. Then she smiled, as though deciding against it. "You must tell me all about yourselves," she said.

"All? I suppose you mean all about us, and how she"—he nodded towards Perdita—"happens to be here. All in good time. This is a most excellent dry martini."

"Won't you have one?" Mrs. Colwell was not drinking herself, but she leaned toward Perdita, who shook her head slightly.

"She doesn't drink these things," he said.

"A glass of sherry, then?"

"It doesn't matter," Perdita said, smiling. "Really, don't bother, please. Just ginger ale."

"We ought to open champagne," Mrs. Colwell said, "to celebrate Mr. Spenlove's visit on an occasion like this. Yes, we'll have a magnum."

"What's the occasion?" he inquired.

"Isn't it obvious?" Mrs. Colwell said. "Are you in the habit of sailing around Long Island Sound with girls? Is he?" she asked Perdita.

"Old habits are hard to break," Perdita said. "He told me he'd been sailing around the sea in liners with passengers. He said that was how he met you."

"So you just came along for the ride?"

Mrs. Colwell looked around. She saw her other guests walking ashore to go up to the house and waved to them. Mr. Spenlove accepted another martini. When the steward had retired out of earshot, he held up his hand to command attention.

"I wanted Perdita to meet you," he began.

"I don't blame you for that," she said. "Why have you been so long about it?"

"I was building the boat," he said. "It takes time to build a boat."

"You haven't burned any boats yet, you two, have you?" Mrs. Colwell smiled.

"We've discussed it," he told her. "Only today we discussed going back to England."

"For good?" Mrs. Colwell was shocked.

"I don't know about for good. A sentimental journey. She"—he nodded towards Perdita—"comes from Suffolk."

"I wasn't *born* there," Perdita explained. "My people live there. And it's only just inside Suffolk. Almost Essex. And a few miles to Hertfordshire."

"We are going to make a tour through the Old Country." Mr. Spenlove said. "I suppose that can be described as burning one's boats. Oh, no, not for good. New England has many merits."

"So I've heard. You might learn something from New Englanders, Mr. Spenlove. You have many merits, but being perfectly frank isn't one of them. I hope you have a marvelous time."

"We'll send you some picture post cards of the cathedrals," he said, enjoying her sharpness.

"Don't trouble. Are you getting married over there?"

"Are we?" he said. He looked at Perdita. "I'll be perfectly frank about that, Mrs. Colwell. We haven't discussed it at all. You'll have to put up with us as we are."

"I? Oh, I think you're extremely wise not to be precipitate. Heavens! I wasn't dreaming of hurrying matters."

"I'm very grateful," he said. "I had to clear that point up. We live in a New England community, Mrs. Colwell, and the curiosity of some of our fellow citizens seems wasted, to me. They would make brilliant careers for themselves in the F.B.I."

Mrs. Colwell smiled.

"You excite my curiosity, Mr. Spenlove. I'm not sure it's entirely unconscious on your part. You enjoy a scandal. You regard it as your due. I haven't forgotten the stories you told me." She looked at Perdita. "Does he tell you stories?" she said to Perdita, who nodded. "Stories about the love affairs of the men he has known? Not about his own love affairs, of course."

"Oh, yes, he does," Perdita said, and she nodded again to emphasize the statement. "He's told me a lot about girls he's known. In England, I mean, and when he was at sea, and, oh, all round."

"All round just describes it," Mrs. Colwell agreed. She was very pleased with everything. Seeing Mr. Spenlove had finished his martini, she rose. She took Perdita's arm.

"Shall we go up to the house?" she said, and then stopped.

Mr. Spenlove looked over the side to make sure his boat was secure.

"You'll stay?" she said, looking from one to the other. For some reason she seemed very much amused all at once. "You must stay. The tide will be running out tonight and you'd probably stick on the mud at the channel entrance." She led the way to the gangplank.

"We'll enjoy staying," Mr. Spenlove said. "It's something I've had in view ever since I got well settled at Norhaven."

"And you *are* settled? You like living in America?"

"Yes. But I don't fool myself. It is no joke being on the shelf. I mean, having no profession."

"You? You on the shelf? It seems to me you have an occupation!"

"Yes. I am always occupied. In fact I am busier now than I ever was in the old days, when I was in charge. But that isn't the same as being part of an organization, being *somebody,* in fact. I'm nobody now! It's a chastening experience. I know, now, why people belong to what they call 'society' when they haven't anything particular to do. It gives them some sort of standing, a reason for living."

"You're learning something about human nature," Mrs. Colwell said. "After all these years! Didn't I tell you you ought to be married if you came on shore?"

"You did. I mentioned it to Perdita here."

"A lovely name you have," Mrs. Colwell said to her.

"I've always disliked it," Perdita said. "I always wanted a name like Susan or Helen. Yes, he told me about you advising him. Do you think . . . Oh, well, I've never been keen on worrying too much about the future."

Mrs. Colwell stood stock still in the middle of the central garden and regarded her guests with severity. She said to Perdita: "But you can't keep that up. I know I'm terribly old-fashioned and you're terribly young, but you *can't* do that! What about, well, for instance, what about children?"

"I have a little daughter," Perdita said, "nearly fourteen.

I'm *much* older than you think! I've been married twice already."

"So she's an authority on the resources of matrimony," Mr. Spenlove pointed out. "In fact, if she was advertising for a position as a Voice of Experience, she has excellent testimonials. Would you like to hear some of them?"

He took Perdita's arm and felt her hand touch his linen jacket.

Mrs. Colwell seemed to meditate as she walked on.

"Plenty of time for that," she said. "I have some experience myself. All I meant was, you'll never get anywhere if you imagine you can defy convention. It's been tried too often."

"No question of that," Mr. Spenlove said briskly. "No defiances have been issued. All the same, it seems to me you strain at a gnat and swallow an entire herd of camels. You feel convention demands that you say these things, just for the record, perhaps? Come, come! Did you expect, when I turned up again, to find me conventional?"

"I'm not sure just what I expected, Mr. Spenlove. Perhaps just what you were on board ship. I expected you to come over, I think, and tell me some more of your stories. Unconventional stories, of course. I always enjoyed them. But this is a silly conversation."

She led the way on to the immense screened porch extending the width of the house. Mr. Colwell, Sr., in brown linen, rose from a chair in which he had been reading an evening paper.

"Greg told me," he said to his wife, and shook hands with Mr. Spenlove. He showed a sort of regal pleasure at meeting Perdita. "I hear," he added generally, "you've got a semi-diesel. How d'you find them?"

Mr. Spenlove told him. He was, he told himself, in high feather. He had a profound respect for Mrs. Colwell, not because she was rich, not even because she was not a snob, but because she was intelligent in a way only well-bred women can be intelligent. He knew he would have to run the gantlet of her criticism unless he announced his approaching nuptials. Once that was out of the way, they could all be happy again.

He saw Mrs. Colwell taking Perdita toward the stairs and accepted the old gentleman's polite indication of the powder-room in the main hall.

Ah, well! he thought, as he washed his hands and spruced up, *this is going to be an adventure.*

No concessions of any kind so far, he reflected. He had done what most of his countrymen found impossible. He had moved from one social stratum to another and he had made no concession. He had given no hostages to fortune. So far there had not been a single chink in his armor.

Now there was Perdita. Was she a hostage? Was his love for her, rather, going to bitch everything up? Was it?

He stood on the porch, waiting for the rest of the company, and watching the Norhaven lighthouse beam swinging across the Sound.

iv

AT BREAKFAST, which was early and strictly stag, because Mr. Colwell and his son commuted to New York, the older man spoke pessimistically of the situation in Europe. Mr. Spenlove listened without comment.

"One of our men in the London office was on the telephone yesterday," Mr. Colwell remarked. "He said he didn't see how it was possible to stop the Germans now. He said all the old ladies, and some of the younger ones too, are buying places in the west country. Funk holes, they call them. He has a place in the country, but it's in Essex. A couple of hours from Germany in a fast bomber."

Mr. Spenlove was lifting various covers on the side table, looking for liver and bacon.

"I suppose he means rich old ladies," he said. "I can't see some of the old ladies I used to know leaving Whitechapel, Bethnal Green and Battersea to live in the country. They'd rather die in London."

"Our man says they'll be shifted, if there's a declaration of war."

"They'll stream back," Mr. Spenlove insisted. He came to the table and sat down where he could look out upon the rock garden and enjoy a glimpse of the Sound. "I know the working classes," he went on. "There's a lot of chatter now about decentralization. When I was a young socialist in London we blamed the slums on the capitalists. It's too easy!"

"I thought you socialists believed in getting rid of the slum areas," young Mr. Colwell said.

"We did. I suppose, if I were still a socialist, I would now. But the people who live in what you call slums don't. That's an illusion of the well-to-do."

"You think it won't work, then?" the older man said. "What do you suggest? Or do you think there won't be a war?"

"I'm not in a prophetic mood just now," Mr. Spenlove said, going on with his breakfast. He watched the houseman bring in fresh coffee. "I've had a feeling for years, it will be all to do again because it was left unfinished last time."

"What do you mean, unfinished?" Mr. Colwell inquired, frowning at his plate.

"You'll see," Mr. Spenlove assured him.

"You don't mean that League of Nations business."

"Why not? If you don't have a League of Nations you will have another thirty years war on your hands."

Mr. Colwell shook his head.

"We'd never agree to the League of Nations," he said. He was a humane, civilized man, with a conviction that credit was a precious commodity.

"I know," Mr. Spenlove agreed sympathetically. "Think of some of the nations who are in it! No, I wasn't thinking of that. My idea, which I've kept to myself, was a new Holy Roman Empire in Europe. But it won't come in our time."

"I suppose not," Mr. Colwell agreed. "On the other hand, our man seems to think there won't be any war this year. My wife tells me you're going over, so I suppose you think so too. Going back for good?"

Mr. Spenlove did not answer at once. He was suddenly invited to express an opinion on a problem he had never honestly faced. He had evaded it by saying to himself, the Old Country would have to stew in her own juice now. The acid logic of his mind dissolved that base metal at once. He knew it was a spurious argument and did not accept it. The very thought of identifying himself with the aliens who crept into America and clung to her like barnacles on a hull, corrupting her social structure and remaining mentally inert all their days, was revolting to him. He had known so many of them in the past. He preferred—oh very much indeed!—the men who went home, on retirement, to England as by instinct, who had a definite emotion about America, even if it were an antagonistic emotion.

Was he going back for good? The possibilities of going back for good with Perdita and Sonia, taking up the immemorial life of his yeomen ancestors, the weavers, farmers, saddlers and coach builders from whose loins he was sprung, caught his imagination for a moment. How would it work out? he asked himself rapidly, and then looked up at Mr. Colwell and answered his question.

"That's on the knees of the gods," he said, gruffly. "I won't specify what gods. There's a faint touch of homesickness about our trip, I grant you."

Mr. Colwell Jr. seemed to find this amusing.

"You don't suffer from that complaint very often," he said. "I've heard you on the subject of England, talking to my mother. I wonder you have the nerve to ask for a visa!"

"You misunderstand the motives," Mr. Spenlove explained. "My criticisms of England include myself. It's from the head, while homesickness is from the heart. A matter of emotion."

"I didn't know you went in for emotion," the young man said. "Thought you'd left all that sort of thing behind you."

"You thought, you thought!" Mr. Spenlove glanced benevolently at the young capitalist. "What do you know about the short and simple annals of the poor? We have feelings as well as you. 'Hearts just as true and fair'—you know your Gilbert and Sullivan? I'm from Seven Dials, so to speak. I've lived in lodgings in Clerkenwell, anyhow. And just lately I've come to the conclusion I never gave England a chance to love me. I've been away from her practically ever since I was out of my apprenticeship. We may have an affair in our old age, after all!"

Mr. Colwell looked at his watch.

"Well, I have to congratulate you," young Mr. Colwell said agreeably. "She's tops."

"Who? England?"

"Oh, no. I don't mean England and you know it."

"Thanks. I agree with you."

Mr. Spenlove dropped his napkin and went out with the two men, father and son, to where the high, old, custom-built Pierce-Arrow touring car stood under the porte-cochere.

"Come and see us when you get back," old Mr. Colwell said, shaking hands. "You won't be able to stand it for very long. Spend half the year over there and half here. Make the best of both worlds."

Young Mr. Colwell made a vague remark about the income tax over there and got into the car.

"We'll be seeing you!" he said gaily.

Finishing his breakfast, Mr. Spenlove tried to analyze the motives that made people like the Colwells affect certain old-fashioned things and ideas. They had an English chauffeur, for instance, an ex-service man now as snug as a bug in a rug. They had an elderly housemaid with thick ankles and spectacles, from Scotland. They had a town car from France that looked like something in a museum. And in the country they used this antique Pierce-Arrow, which looked old enough to be without an accelerator.

What they were after, of course, he decided, was quality and character. Possibly that was why he himself appealed to them. It was an agreeable theory. He would discuss it with Perdita.

He wished to share everything with Perdita now. Since last night, when he watched her play billiards with young Mr. Colwell and beat him, he had been full of pride. He received the comments of Mrs. Colwell with outward calm, but inside he was delighted. He assured her that he had had no idea Perdita even knew how to play the game. She'd never mentioned billiards to him. Yet she was stunningly good at it. It was, she said, an inherited knack. Her father was very good. They had a table at Brandeston Knights, with argand lamps over it which threw shadows and gave you two cues, sometimes!

That was quality too, he decided. To have something and never mention it without real occasion. It was excellent quality.

That being so, he saw looming up a test of his own quality. He had, in an acute form, a sense of time. He had it even when thinking of Perdita. There was Sonia, in the background, becoming a woman. She might be only a very delightful athletic kid at an expensive camp, developing a quite unexpected passion for horseback riding and tennis, but she would be something else in no time at all now. At one time he had imagined Perdita wanted to be rid of her child. She had talked as if it would suit her if Elliot Ducroy took Sonia off her mother's hands. It turned out Perdita didn't quite mean that. She was matter-of-fact.

"You lose them no matter what you do, when they grow up. I'll be an old woman then. . . ."

His sense of time told him she would not be an old woman for many years yet, but she would be mature. She would not love another man if he fell down on the job. Yet she had always evaded the problem of marriage. She had been satirical about it.

Then what was he to do? He drank his second cup of coffee, gazing out across the gardens and the Sound. She was quite capable of going through purgatory again to keep her independence, which she had lost when she had married Elliot Ducroy on Sonia's account. Starve! She had an unknown side to her character, like the other side of the moon. He never saw it, but he knew it was there. It made her even more valuable to him, a connoisseur of character.

So what was he to do? It was repugnant to him to make an honest woman of her against her will. She herself had said it was making a dishonest woman of anybody, to make them enter modern matrimony! She had said half the women in Hollywood only used it as a publicity stunt and wouldn't dream of it if they couldn't get a divorce whenever they wanted it. It was, indeed, the idea of divorce which "stuck in her craw," as she had put it. She was not, she told him passionately, naturally promiscuous. . . .

Neither was he, he pointed out; but she did not, or would not, see the point. So he let it alone, and here they were; with their problem still unsolved. And they were going to England, and he at any rate was determined to have Sonia with them. Then in the late summer, or it would be autumn, in Brandeston Knights, in the deep English country, she might lose that fear of union which had so bedeviled her in the casual, pagan air of Hollywood. "So brainless!" she had strangely called it. He knew what she meant. They were like automatons. They lived their lives as they did their work in the studios. They had mental positions chalked out on the floor for them. They said "So sweet of you to come!" while they were thinking of something else. Even their absent-mindedness was secondhand, pilfered from Michael Arlen's Mayfair.

Now they must get back. He had to go to New York. He would lose no time, now the decision had been made. He must get passports and visas and reservations. And she must get Sonia from camp and buy her clothes for a voyage to England. It seemed that bringing Perdita over and showing her to Mrs. Colwell, acted as a precipitant, a catalytic agency, in his mind. There was only Perdita to convince.

He was about to light a cigar and go out for a stroll when Mrs. Colwell herself came in, followed by the houseman with a tray.

"Go on," she said, after inquiring how he had slept. "I don't mind cigars. From the way they smell I envy those South American ladies you told me of, who smoke them in preference to cigarettes. Did you have enough breakfast?"

He said he had eaten more than usual. He said he did not go in heavily for breakfast, but the liver and bacon . . . "Too good to pass up."

"I don't either," she said. "Coffee?"

"No more now. Someone's sleeping well this morning."

"At that age," Mrs. Colwell said, "all women should sleep till noon. Tell me, Mr. Spenlove, where did you find that lovely girl?"

"I didn't find her," he protested, smiling a little. "I received a call from her daughter. I must have made a hit with the daughter. She brought her mother to tea. Of course their place backs mine. I should say my few acres hide behind their estate."

"Who is the husband? I didn't quite . . ."

Mr. Spenlove told her.

"Oh. I've heard of *him,* of course. I see. Hm. I suppose he makes a great deal of money."

"More than enough. Spends it too, I fancy. It isn't a question of support. There's a *tertium quid.* An affinity."

"Of course. There always is."

"I mean a real affinity. He has become oblivious. She is as spectacularly successful as he is and they are collaborating."

"Collaborating in what? Sin?"

"If I wanted to, I could make a pun about that. . . ." he began.

"Well, make it, if it's a good pun."

"Some of our moralists hold there is no such thing as a good pun. I won't inflict it on you. Simply, they are writing fiction together. It will develop into one of the great romances of our era, like the Douglas Fairbanks-Mary Pickford union. Their agent is planning what he calls a supercolossal hook-up."

"It sounds impressive."

"Not nearly so impressive as when the agent sketches it. Never mind him. He's an amusing little parasite. They say parasites stimulate the organisms, on which they batten, to furious activity. I must say, my casual glimpses into that business have aroused my curiosity."

"She has left him, then?"

"He has left her. It is much more complicated than that, really. He is an idealist, I'm informed, and I believe it. An idealist in a queer, distorted sense. He sees no reason why he cannot have this marvelous, supercolossal hook-up, as it were, and yet find his wife by the fireside when he returns from his odyssey."

"You're making it up."

"No, I'm not. That's exactly how he expressed it to me. Not the exact words, but the exact idea."

"To you! He discusses it with you?"

"There again you miss the point. These things are always simplified in our minds. He seems to like me. He regards me as an elderly codger who can give his wife good advice, take care of her, in fact, and act *in loco parentis*."

"That's extraordinary!"

"No, it isn't. He has such a conviction of her honesty, he trusts her absolutely. He believes that even if she leaves him, as she will, that she does it on *his* account, not because she could ever love another man. You know, Mrs. Colwell, these successful beings get something done to them by their success. I can only describe it as a sort of emotional aphasia. They're all egocentric neurotics, in my opinion!"

"The word is exhibitionism, I think."

"It's a very inadequate word. I suppose their state corresponds to what the Bible calls 'possessed of evil spirits.' "

Mrs. Colwell nodded absently.

"Well, it did her no harm. I think she's a remarkable person."

"Oh come! Why?"

"Anyone who's able to get past your guard is remarkable, Mr. Spenlove," she said, drily. "Don't you think so?"

"Oh, of course! Of course! I didn't look at it that way, though. I was afraid you'd discovered something about her

I didn't know. It's possible. I had no idea, until last night, she knew one end of a billiard cue from the other. She's that kind of person."

"Then I'm right. She's remarkable. Are you going to marry her?"

"That's what I ask myself. Am I? I can't without her co-operation."

"A man of your character and personality!"

"A man of my character and personality is not able to do what you suggest. It would be an unwarrantable intrusion."

"Would it? Perhaps it would. It's none of my business, either."

"I understand all about that! Why do you suppose I brought her over here, if it wasn't to have your approval?"

"You have it. Only—marry her. She's a lovely girl."

He did not reply. He was seated by the window which was semicircular, while Mrs. Colwell drank her coffee. He made a sound of assent.

"I hope she doesn't sleep till noon today," he said, looking at the clock. "We hadn't much fishing yesterday. One bass and a bluefish too trivial to mention."

Mrs. Colwell glanced at him whimsically.

"Perhaps," she said, "you'll do better today. It's going to be hot. I wish you'd stay longer."

"Not under the circumstances," he said. "Now we have your opinion, there are a lot of things to be done at once. You know, I wasn't absolutely, irrevocably certain about my well-known sagacity, until I knew what you thought. I was prepared to hear you tell me I was making a perishing ass of myself, assuming an obligation."

"It's nice to feel one is of use to one's friends," she said. "What about the daughter? Tell me about her."

"Sonia? You'd like her. She's fourteen, nearly. Like her mother in eyes, and mouth, and so on. It sounds fantastic, and I wouldn't tell it to anyone but you, but I fell in love with Sonia! The day she came into my yard, pursuing her dog, who was chasing an old cat who lives in my barn, she was like a supernatural being. A dryad. It was almost a foregone conclusion when she brought her mother in the afternoon."

"That's a charming thing to say," Mrs. Colwell said. "You'll come back, and come to see me again, when you return?"

"We have several bridges to cross before we can call it a day," he said.

"You are enjoying the adventure?" she suggested. "I'm sure of it. It's taking years off your age."

"Am I? Is it? Sometimes I'm not absolutely sure I am an adventurer. I've managed to get my fun out of other men's misfortunes so far. But it seems on the cards, yes. It hasn't made me feel any older."

"No. Suppose I have breakfast sent up, since you want to get off?"

"I'd be grateful. She's probably tired. She was down at the dock yesterday before six. I'll walk down to the boat now and see what's to be done."

"Can we let you have anything? Tell the steward."

"Ice and fresh water. Nothing else, thanks."

He walked down through the gardens and sat for a while in a sort of arbor constructed of apple trees whose trunks and branches had been trained with such artifice they resembled metal tubes, while the apples hung like green globes, perfectly spherical. Super-arboriculture this, he thought. A mechanical Garden of Eden. He supposed the serpent would be made of flexible tubing. A loud speaker hidden overhead could be the Voice that . . .

He got up and went on down to the dock. He could never solve the problem of what Veblen called conspicuous waste. It never kept still long enough in his mind to let him come to a conclusion. Sell all that thou hast, if you have great possessions, and give to the poor. But sell to whom? It was a virtuous, if not a vicious, circle. What about the purchaser's soul and the poor? And what about the families of the mechanics and pomologists and tapestry designers, who go on relief when the rich cease to be their patrons? What about the drop in values when all that thou hast is flung on the market? Veblen never suggested any alternatives to conspicuous waste.

Some people might say the rich were not really, any longer, conspicuously wasteful. That old Pierce, with its indestructible leather upholstery and its dickey for a tiger, was almost fantastically thrifty. Quality was the object nowadays and quality implied character to appreciate it.

As he stepped on board the cruiser that was almost a yacht, and which was named "Agnes II," he found he had completed the circle of thought. Perhaps he had not the necessary mental equipment to solve economic problems. Perhaps, like Perdita, he was an economic inferior and should not try to judge his economic superiors.

He said good morning to the steward, who was talking to the engineer. He mentioned ice, for the bait locker.

"Not too small," he said, "or it melts so fast. Fifty pounds, about."

"I been lookin' at that job o' yours," the engineer said. "I used to work in that yard, over in Brooklyn, but we always had a thrust-bearin' in the layout."

"Just an idea of mine, to do without one," Mr. Spenlove said with exaggerated solemnity. He beckoned. "I'll show you."

They spent an agreeable half hour in each other's engine rooms. "Agnes II" had no "conspicuous waste" in her vitals, Mr. Spenlove noted, with a private smile. Her twin eight-cylinder diesels were like a couple of giant pachyderms in their stalls.

"Very nice," he told their keeper, "for you millionaires."

"Listen," the other man said earnestly. "She runs on nothin' at all. Ten gallons an hour, cruisin'. . . ."

"I grant you," said Mr. Spenlove. "Oh, I grant you! I was only kidding."

He was walking to and fro on the quarter deck with his

second cigar, when he saw Mrs. Colwell and her guest coming down from the house.

I swear, she's a marvelous wench! he said to himself. Merely thinking it sent a strong tremor through him, and he reflected, for the hundredth time, the narrow escape he had had, of going down hill to a lonely old age without ever experiencing passion at first hand. Love he had had, for years, a spirit wraith, and he had assuaged his body's hunger for the flesh. This was flesh and spirit, and now that he knew what it was he couldn't get enough of it!

He wanted to start homeward. The tide was on the run now. They could nip through Grampus Channel into clean water and have the trolls out in half an hour from stand by.

He went over to the gangway to meet them.

She was enjoying herself. She had that faculty, of being completely at home in this sort of environment. All the material richness of the Colwell life at St. James struck her as eminently right for them. Their background was comprehensible. It left her free to be herself, whereas that other life on the Coast had had her fighting back all the time because they were, as she once said to him, outsiders trying to be insiders. Because they lacked quality, he supposed.

Mrs. Colwell led the way into the after cabin. As Perdita followed her down the narrow curved companion, she looked up and smiled. Mrs. Colwell was out of sight as he stooped swiftly and gathered Perdita's face in his hands. With a quick movement she kissed them and descended. He followed carefully.

Mrs. Colwell stood facing them in the cabin. The morning sunlight flickered on the white ceiling through green curtains over the side-scuttles.

"I'm so glad you came," she said quickly. "I think you're doing a most sensible thing. Of course this is absolutely confidential."

She looked from one to the other.

"Absolutely—but what?" asked Mr. Spenlove.

"Being together," Mrs. Colwell said, catching her breath. "In a general way I wouldn't approve. . . . No, I couldn't possibly approve. But in your case, it's different."

She embraced them both impulsively.

"Come back and stay with us," she said. "Invite me to Norhaven. And have a wonderful time in England. Now you'd better be off while the tide is still. . . . John is bringing your things down."

They went up on deck again and down the accommodation ladder to "Glory Hole." Mrs. Colwell stood on the grating looking around the arrangements of the boat.

"Your own idea?" she said.

"A hobby for several years," he told her. "I drew the plans a dozen times. When I got hold of the Mudge Place I laid the keel. You ought to see her boat!" He nodded toward Perdita, who made a negative gesture.

"It's just for short runs," she said. "I've given up driving it. It's—it's sold."

"Twenty gallons an hour!"

Mrs. Colwell accepted this smilingly and waved her hand to bid them farewell. Perdita cast loose the painter and Mr. Spenlove, with an activity and energy which did not escape Mrs. Colwell's notice, climbed into the pilot house and began to back away in a semicircle. He looked up as he laid his cigar aside and met Mrs. Colwell's smile.

He gave her a grave salute, but his expression remained impenetrable. It committed him to nothing Mrs. Colwell could not figure out for herself.

Her expression, too, as the boat receded, was enigmatical. What she was thinking was, *How unfair time is to women, compared with men!*

She did not often permit this sort of thing in herself. It did no good, repining for the lost middle years of mature, vigorous living. She watched the girl coiling the line on the foredeck, watched her straighten up, her face flushed, her hands on her hips, as the boat headed down channel. She heard

Mr. Spenlove's melodious toot on his horn and the churn of the screw as he gathered speed. The girl gave her a last wave and disappeared into the cabin. Like a squat duck "Glory Hole" clove a blunt furrow in the water.

When they passed the channel buoys he set the course for Stratford Light Shoal. He was aware of her moving about in the cabin, stowing the bags and swatting some flies which had got in. He felt as if he had been away from her for ages. He knew, without asking her, that she felt the same. The sustained tremor of the engine seemed to get into his blood. The thrusting urgency of it took possession of his thoughts.

Suddenly she was beside him in the pilot house, her hair blowing in the breeze, her lovely long eyes reflecting the glitter from the water, her lips parted slightly. It was like her to come in and not speak, merely touching his shoulder with her own.

For a while he kept his eyes on the course. Once he raised his hand and pointed.

"Yachts racing at Greenwich," he said.

She didn't reply. That was not what either was thinking. The white triangles on the horizon were part of their happiness. The heat of the sun on the bright water was for their delight. Far away the blue hills beckoned them. For an hour or two they would be the only people in the world, a world of summer.

V

"THERE! That's the first flash," she said.

She nodded toward the Norhaven lighthouse. The sun was behind the hills and the light suddenly showed like a tiny jewel in the dusk. She was steering while he unjointed the rods and stowed the gear.

"I'll take her in a minute," he said. "Slow her down to sixty. There's no hurry."

"I feel funny coming back," she said.

"Take it easy. You are in my charge now. Oblige me by not feeling funny."

"Yes, but I'm not sure of myself."

"You are stronger than you try to make out. I think you're very strong, though I don't know"—he came in and sat beside her—"I don't know how you got that way."

"I don't understand you," she said.

"I don't see how you became what you are from the kid you must have been when you married that Archie Pagett of yours. How did you evolve into . . ?"

"I still don't understand. Evolve? It sounds as if I'd changed from something into something else."

"You have, I believe. I try to think what brought it about."

"Having Sonia for one thing. Did I tell you Sonia was Archie's choice for a name? Do you think it suitable?"

"Not very."

"It isn't. I had a bad time in the hospital in Los Angeles. She gave me a lot of grief. I don't see how any woman could help evolving in that place! Another thing that might help to change me from a bread-and-butter chit to what I am was starving. Doing without bread and butter."

"Starving?" She nodded without looking at him.

"I don't mean going short. I mean going faint because I hadn't money to buy food. I nearly went to heaven once, I was so dizzy and light in my head. Sonia was about four then. Oh, lor'!"

"A man always forgets that part of the business. Since I've known you I've come to the conclusion I've dodged a lot of things in the past."

"Oh, I wouldn't say 'dodged,' darling! You didn't dodge anything. One has these things happen or one doesn't. You've been loyal, I think."

"To what? To principle, I grant you. But to what else?"

"I'll tell you. You know you said that girl you were in love with, in Greece, or some such place . . . You were in love with her, weren't you? Yes, you take it now." She gave him the wheel.

"Yes, all right, what about her?"

"Well, you kept her memory all that time. That was loyal. But was she in love with you?"

"I don't know. Ah, well! She wasn't. I told you how it was, and she wasn't."

"And was any other girl in love with you?"

"I don't know. I never heard of one. If she was, I never knew it. What are you getting at?"

"There you are! I'm the first. That's what I was getting at. Because *I am!* More and more since yesterday. I'm a damned lucky girl. What do you think about that?"

"Can't tell you while I'm steering." He switched on his side lights. "We've got to face the facts of life now, though, my damned lucky girl. Do you want me to see Elliot and tell him we're going away?"

"Heavens, no! No necessity for that. What do you think I am? A funk? A cowardy, cowardy custard?"

"Stole her mother's mustard! No. But it is my job."

"Not anybody's job. Unless it makes you feel better. Are you going over to her house to tell him? I say, are you?"

She crept close to him in the deepening evening as they chugged softly into the river under the mild beam of the lighthouse lantern. The land was dark beneath the deep colors of the sunset. The red light at the yacht-club fuel jetty was his beacon, now that he was in the channel with the green gas buoy on the western point.

He kept his attention on the course, not wanting to look toward that other woman's house. He certainly didn't want the job of going there, and so he said, no, he wouldn't do that. She said, in a low tone.

"Well, what *are* you going to do?"

"Get you home first. If he's still over there, then we'll get Sonia and push off as soon as I can make the arrangements. I'll tell you what papers you have to bring to New York. I must go in tomorrow."

He could see the lights on the club verandah. He slowed down still more.

"I suppose you can depend on that man of yours to be on the job?"

"Louis? Good old Louis. Yes, he'll be there all right. I'll be sorry to lose Louis."

"I suppose it can't be helped. He wouldn't leave Elliot, would he?"

"He's not so keen about what's happened. He didn't like *me* at first. It was Sonia he took to. Later he seemed to tolerate me."

"I understand Louis perfectly. Well, I understand him in that respect. I don't know how your leaving would strike him. We can cross all those bridges when we come to them."

"Except the Bridge of Sighs! I believe I'm losing my nerve, my dear, now we're coming into port. Do you know what I was going to suggest? I was going to suggest we anchor near Church Yard, in Long Brook, and I could swim ashore.

So nobody would see me. What's the matter with me, do you suppose?"

"Don't worry. What we do is nobody's business. We'll just make fast and lock up. I'll bring up the stuff in the morning. And there's the car to take you along home. In the morning . . ."

Slowly "Glory Hole" moved into the dredged basin, behind the lighthouse to the dock. All around small pleasure craft lay tied up to buoys. The notion crossed his mind that it would be a neat trick, if he were not involved in this business himself, to cross the river farther up in the dusk and land Perdita at Sydney Saxon's boat house. Some women might do it, but not Perdita. He and she were at one in their attitude toward 'scenes.' It was the approaching 'scene' which was making her press close to him and talk about losing her nerve.

As they came gently to the end of the jetty he saw a group move along the club verandah and stand at the doors while one slender figure rippled down the steps and ran toward him. It was one of the club servants in uniform.

"Damn and blast!" he said. "Get into the cabin and stay there while I see what's up." He cut his engine and switched off the side lights.

She obeyed him. Stepping on to the jetty with his painter in his hand, Mr. Spenlove faced a youth out of breath with his run.

"Mr. Spenlove?"

"What?"

"Mrs. Ducroy—you seen her? We've a message for Mrs. Ducroy. It's important."

"All right. Make fast first. What is it? What's the important message?"

The young man made a sudden gesture of urgency. He gaped and swallowed.

"You better see the club secret'ry right away," he said, breathlessly. "You better!"

"All *right!* Mrs. Ducroy is coming ashore at once. Now run along, as you don't seem to know what the message is. Do you?"

"It's—it's Mr. Ducroy. . . ." the youth said. He thought a moment, and decided to make a run for it. He had news. She was here at last. She was about to be told. He hastened away to tell them she was coming.

The faint note of hysteria in his voice had reached Perdita readying herself in the cabin. She came out and he helped her on to the dock.

"You heard what he said?"

She nodded and they walked together toward the club house. Suddenly she took his arm and raised her chin a little. Her eyes were bright and hard with decision and a touch of panic.

"Now, now," he said.

He saw the club secretary come down the steps to meet them.

"What's wrong?" Mr. Spenlove said sharply.

The young man led them at once around to the back of the club where his office looked out on the parking lot. As he closed the door behind him he said, "There's been an accident!" he said. "Mr. Ducroy was swimming. . . ."

"Where was this? Here?"

The secretary coughed.

"At Miss Saxon's." He made a gesture in the direction of the river. "It was very warm and they went in swimming. He had an attack. . . ."

"Where is he now?" Perdita asked.

"At your house, Mrs. Ducroy. They tried to locate you. Jerry Munzinger said you were fishing. So we kept watch on the boats coming in."

"Did you get a doctor?"

"Of course. I understand there's a guest there."

"A guest?" Perdita looked at him. "You must be mistaken. I didn't expect any guest."

The secretary shrugged his shoulders.

"Miss Saxon said there was a guest."

"All right. I'll go." She stopped still suddenly. "A serious attack?"

"Very serious, Mrs. Ducroy. I was asked to warn you, to prepare you. . . ."

He looked at her with anxiety.

"He isn't dead, is he?"

The secretary nodded nervously. He was frowning in his distress. He made a gesture toward a chair, for her to sit down. He really wanted to sit down himself. Perdita turned and went toward the door without dramatics. For a moment she moved like an automaton, without fire or feeling. Mr. Spenlove had an impression that she was temporarily without consciousness, as though the higher centers of her brain were for an instant paralyzed. Then she came to life. She turned toward him gently but spoke to the secretary, who was also the manager.

"I see," she said. "Will you excuse us? It was awfully kind of you to . . ."

"Not at all," the secretary said.

"Of course I must go at once," she added. She looked at Mr. Spenlove for a moment, a glance of extraordinary intensity. During that moment, perhaps due to the lighting in the office, her eyes seemed black and opaque. It was a glance of supreme surrender and appeal.

He went to her and put his arm around her shoulders. He turned to the secretary.

"I'll take her home. Will you see my boat is berthed? I'll leave you the keys. I'll be down in the morning. Will you be so good?"

They walked across the parking space to his car in the early evening dusk. Once, in the smaller more intense darkness of the car, while he waited for the engine to get away, she held her hands to her face. He was careful to avoid anything in the shape of theatricals. From long habit at sea, he was conditioned to keep his head in a crisis, even in a crisis in which he could not, as it were, assume command. His philosophy was, if you can't be in charge of events, you can be in charge of yourself.

He drove down to the Shore Road, past the big Boldwin place, and thence along the half-mile stretch skirting the calm sea. He himself was outwardly calm, but in his mind was tumult. He was suddenly faced with a situation perfectly familiar as a common hazard of existence, but frightening as a personal issue.

To avoid entanglement with human folly had been his policy for so long, he could not immediately realize that period in his life was definitely over.

So he drove carefully and in silence, along to the lych-gate of Church Yard. Well, it was well named, he thought gravely as he started up the smooth, bluestone drive. A *lych-gate!* he said to himself. Did that tormented soul, frantically spinning melodramas out of his own entrails, know what they used to do with a lych-gate? Had he a mordant, ironic mind after all? He was gone now. Who would now give to the world those slick, smooth, entirely incredible fantasies?

He stopped behind a line of cars that led up to the front door.

"Now, do you want me to go in with you?" he said. He held her arm firmly, halting her movement to get out. She turned to him and put her arms around him.

"It's going to be awful, but I don't see how I can bring you into it. But, will you come round tomorrow? I'm going to telephone to the camp for them to bring Sonia back."

"Why not let me go and get her? It's only sixty miles."

"Would you? It's dear of you. Yes, it would be better."

"Because I want Sonia as well as you," he said, stroking her cheek.

"I love you so much!"

"You'll have people there. By the way, he said there was a guest. Any idea who it is?"

"Not the faintest. I say, will you come in, just for a minute? You've every right. And help me through the first shock."

"All right."

"You don't suppose . . . I say, you don't suppose *she's* here, do you?"

"I'll go in and see. Yes, I'll go."

He got out of the car in spite of her holding his hand, and closed the door quietly. He walked past the Ducroy station wagon, the doctor's coupé and the Norbury ambulance. There was also, slewed to one side and partly in the shrubbery, a very old car with a California license plate. He stepped lightly up to the entrance. Through the screen he saw someone extended in a deep chair, a long thin figure of a man. He tapped lightly and opened the screen door.

The figure in the chair unwound itself and reared up, astonishingly tall and thin. It came forward, wearing yellow-white slacks, an old striped undervest, and a khaki jacket that hung on his shoulders, Mr. Spenlove thought, like a bosun's shirt on a capstan bar. And the lean bronzed features that loomed out of the dusk above the deep-shaded floor lamp across the room were startling. The cavernous eye sockets made Mr. Spenlove think of death as something present in person.

Is this the guest? he asked himself with a sort of internal shout. *Is this the guest who has come to Church Yard?*

He pulled himself together and assumed an expression suitable to the occasion. He explained that Mrs. Ducroy was in the car.

"My name's Spenlove. I live back of here," he said.

"Mine's Mallinson, Piers Mallinson, the poet," said the scarecrow. "I come for a visit with my friend, Elliot Ducroy. I used to know him in California."

He began to tell Mr. Spenlove how he had arrived at Norbury and had been told over the telephone to make himself at home and had come to the house the night before, finding Mr. Ducroy away visiting with neighbors. The houseman had remembered him from a visit he had made to Hollywood, and took care of him.

"Anybody else here? Anybody from the house where Mr. Ducroy was when he was taken ill?"

"Not now. Matter of fact, Mr. Ducroy phoned when I arrived, and said he was sendin' a car over to get me, to go to that house. That was just before it happened. Nobody here now except the doctor and a couple of nurses from the hospital at Norbury."

"Well, I'll bring her in," Mr. Spenlove said. "You know her, of course."

"No, sir. Mr. Ducroy wasn't married when I was visiting with him."

"Well, you'll know her now. Better go fetch the doctor. She'll wish to see him."

She was coming toward him as he opened the door. He held her to him closely for a moment.

"I've seen the guest. It's a man named Mallinson."

"I know him. I mean I know about him. I'll explain some other time. I know about him. Yes?"

"He's bringing the doctor down."

"You mean there's hope?"

"I don't mean anything. I fancy he has waited to see you. Shall I go now? Will you be all right? You know . . ."

"Please! Oh, how do you do!"

The doctor, an elderly, gray-faced person with a sagging abdomen and pale eyes behind gold-rimmed nose glasses, was coming down the curving staircase with the tall visitor. Together, as by an unspoken suggestion, they went into the living room with the doctor, leaving Piers Mallinson, the poet, in the hall.

"This is Mr. Spenlove, Doctor. A friend of—of ours. What was it? The stroke, I mean. Was it . . ?" She touched her breast.

"Angina," the old gentleman said. "I had a consultation with Dr. Shelton at the hospital. He came to Miss Saxon's.

He's a heart specialist. Best man in the state. We had a consultation. Angina pectoris."

"He's had one or two attacks before," she said.

"He told me about his heart," Mr. Spenlove added. "So did a woman who knew him." He looked at Perdita. "That Terry Florence," he explained. "He took very little liquor," he went on to the doctor. "That was how I knew of it. He explained he avoided liquor on account of it."

"He ought to have avoided violent exercise too," the doctor grumbled. "Dove off Miss Saxon's float. Been working all day in a hot room. It's been hot today," he added. He took out a yellow silk handkerchief and wiped his glasses.

"Then it was drowning?" Perdita asked fully.

"Nope. He got to the stage all right and was pullin' himself up and fell back. Somebody saw him and grabbed him. Got him into the house and sent for me."

"Too late, I understand."

"I thought there was a chance at first. Can't always tell with the coronary art'ries. Dr. Shelton came over soon as he heard what 'twas, and we had a consultation. Overexertion. Must have forgot the warnin' he had in Hollywood. Miss Saxon told us he had an attack out there. Fell down at the telephone."

"I know about that," Perdita said, looking down at the rug. She was standing by the window looking out into the darkened woods. "I was in Paris."

She turned suddenly.

"I'll go up with you," she said to the old doctor. Then as Mr. Spenlove moved toward the door, she said, "I don't think I'll stay here tonight. Will you take me to the Inn later?"

"I'll be back about eight-thirty," he said.

He saw her appeal in her eyes, to keep this business, this infernal business, on a formal basis. He made a bow to include them both and as he went out he heard her tell the doctor who he was, and how he was going to get her daughter from camp next day. How he had been so kind as to bring her up from the club. She had been out sailing. . . .

On the way out he saw the guest in a porch chair in the unlighted alcove. Mr. Spenlove heard him speak and halted. He went toward him.

"Maybe I'd better get along," Mr. Mallinson said in a low tone, leaning forward.

"I think you'd better see her first," Mr. Spenlove said earnestly. "She's going to the hotel at Norbury, the Inn we call it. She might appreciate it if you stayed here for the present. I'll be back later. I'd stick around if I were you."

"Suits me. Mighty good of you to suggest it, sir, mighty good!"

"Don't mention it. See you later."

As he turned into his own narrow entry and drove up to the cottage, Mr. Spenlove suddenly realized he was in need of a stimulant. He unlocked his house and turned on the lights, and experienced another need. It was a shocking thing, he realized, but it was the truth, that he wanted Perdita there, now, in his house. It was a sudden overpowering realization that his scheme of things, cunningly contrived over the years to keep him safe from the disintegrating forces of society, had itself disintegrated.

He poured himself a double whiskey and water and sat down in the dark porch to take stock. There was a hoarse sound at the screen door. He rose to open it.

"You too, eh!" he muttered. Tobermory thrust a lean, hard body against him. Here was another individualist who had discovered that it was better to give an occasional hostage to fortune. It wasn't, he reflected with a dour smile, as he went out to give the old warrior his evening chop—it wasn't merely "cupboard love" as they stupidly called it. Else why, after he had been fed, and sometimes when he might have gone off on his own affairs, would the old bandit crouch close to the boat or the bench and watch the tools moving through drowsing green slits, making the deep rumbling of utter cat's peace in his throat?

It was a strange sensation, he thought, when he went back to his drink, to find oneself a different person entirely from the imagined perfection. He still assumed that being an intellectual hermit was perfection, though why? Why? The hermits he had read about had not been admirable save through the art of writers who had not been hermits. Was it a fallacy on his part to think he could live in Arcady without being an Arcadian? Wasn't he introducing the harsh customs of Sparta into that happy land? In Arcady one worshipped Pan and Diana.

What would Mrs. Colwell say to this happening to him? Would she make her old-time comment, that adventures are to the unadventurous. It had seemed so in his own case. He had chosen a humdrum profession and tried to make a humdrum person of himself, and he had had romance, and had experienced adventures of which a man like Elliot Ducroy, who made a huge income writing romantic adventures, had no experience at all.

Now the great adventure of all had come to Elliot Ducroy. Must have been a shock to the woman. What would she do now? There was a certain irony in the fact that she suddenly ceased to exist so far as Church Yard was concerned. She couldn't even send a condolence or call like a neighbor. She might be Elliot Ducroy's professional collaborator, but if Terry Florence was to be believed she had had no intention of marrying him if he got a divorce.

He was finishing his drink when the telephone rang. On the table, as he listened, he noticed a scrawling note in Mrs. Sankey's hand, on a three-cornered piece of wrapping paper. There had been a call for him, she wrote, and gave the number.

He listened. It was, the voice said, the girl he had met in New York with Mr. Ducroy. Terry Florence? he suggested. Yes, the voice said, speaking from Sydney Saxon's. She had called him that morning. Elliot Ducroy had asked her to call him. The cleaning woman had said he was out in his boat, fishing. What did Mr. Ducroy want? he inquired. The voice became agitated.

"Don't you know what's *happened?*" it said shrilly. He waited an instant.

"Well?" he said quietly.

He heard the voice speaking to someone in the room in a low excited tone. Then:

"He wanted to know if his wife was at your place. He wanted her to meet a guest he had coming, so . . ."

"Yes. Is Mr. Ducroy there?"

"Mr. Ducroy had a stroke. He had to be taken home. We had a doctor. Haven't you had any news? Have you seen Mrs. Ducroy? She ought to be informed. They said she was with you yesterday. They said at the yacht club you'd seen her. . . . We were afraid she wasn't in a fit . . ."

He waited a moment and, as she did not continue, he said, very quietly, "She's at home. I'm going there in an hour. I'm going to get her daughter from camp tomorrow."

"Oh! Then you *knew!* Why didn't you say so, Mr. Spenlove?" The voice was flat and cold.

"I knew he was at Sydney Saxon's all this time," he pointed out, still very quietly.

He heard the receiver put back gently at the other end. So that was that. Obviously they were anxious to find out something about Perdita over there. Terry would naturally get the job of telephoning all over the place. He could hear her tell Sydney Saxon she'd met that friend of theirs who lived near by, Mr. Spenlove. Should she call him?

He wondered what had decided Terry to accept the Ducroy-Saxon collaboration? Probably anything Irving wanted suited her. She was one of those girls who take sides, and Ducroy's side was Irving's, and so it was her side too. Ducroy was the big log; the plank which was Irving was close to it as it floated, and Terry was the chip that adhered to both of them by natural attraction of mass for small fragments. Sumptuous visits to expensive country places would be important to Terry until Irving could afford to spend more money. Until he got organized, as she had put it.

Mr. Spenlove frowned and walked back to the porch. He frowned because he still held a grudge against that girl. She was a type he disliked without being able to justify his aversion. Common-law wife!

He found his thoughts pulled up short. Damn and blast! Why, if he gave way to Perdita's ideas, that was exactly what *she* would be. It became clear in a flash that no matter how either of them drew back from marriage, he couldn't have that. Too sticky!

This revelation, for some reason, gave him courage and a fresh desire to see Perdita again, immediately. It might be shocking, but the fact was, he could not remember that upstairs Elliot Ducroy was lying in the house his energies had created, lying with a ruptured coronary artery. He could remember nothing but what she had been to him, what she meant for him, and what he now desired. That was possession, and it meant Sonia too, her child, his first friend in the new world of Arcady!

VI

THERE was a small branch post office at Sutton Corners. It had been his custom to call for his occasional mail. Now he had a lock box. As a rule he went to it when picking up Mrs. Sankey, who would meet him there in the morning.

The post office was a drab, inconspicuous place, around the corner from the rest of the stores. It was very narrow and shabby. Of the three windows inside only one was commonly used, and the desk was a narrow shelf.

As he unlocked his box Mr. Spenlove was aware of someone behind him, standing very close, as though desiring to reach a box in his vicinity. He drew out his mail, which was small, and moved to one side without looking behind him. But the person behind moved up alongside of him and so he turned to confront the little man he knew as Irving.

"Hello," Mr. Spenlove said. He shook hands. "Glad to see you. . . ."

Irving was attired for the country. He wore Mexican huaraches of woven snake skin, green corduroy trousers and a polo shirt of dark blue which exposed his abnormally hairy chest. Seen above this ensemble, his circular features and circular dark glasses, with tremendous celluloid frames, were fantastic until you realized that every beach resort was crowded with New Yorkers exactly like him.

Irving was quite unaware of anything bizarre in his attire. It was he who went over Mr. Spenlove's old linen suit and conventional haberdashery as though he had met a freak.

To Irving a man who did not follow the trend, as he called it, was a freak. America was called a free country because there were so many freaks, he insisted.

He had never believed any of the stuff he had heard from Ducroy about the man with the beard who lived alone in a shack and did so because he liked it. It was of no consequence and wasn't any of his troubles, but he had not believed it. Now, staying as he was at Sydney Saxon's, it transpired there was something in it. Terry had called him up. Terry said it was true. He lived there all right. And here he was, in the post office, getting his mail.

He had not believed it because his instinct had warned him that Mr. Spenlove was not to be sneezed at. Consequently what was he doing down there, buried in a shack in the woods?

Once the ice had been broken and Terry had consented to come down with him to stay at Sydney Saxon's new place, Irving had become curious. He had wanted Terry to drive him over to investigate. Irving did not drive. Terry, for some reason of her own, had not wanted to do this. Ducroy, for some reason of *his* own, had shied away from visiting Mr. Spenlove.

It had made Irving more convinced than ever that Mr. Spenlove had a mystery attached to him.

"Hello. Glad to see you," Mr. Spenlove said. He looked over his shoulder at the elaborate get-up of the little man and watched him unlock a mail box. "You living here now?"

Irving shook his head. He kept his face turned toward Mr. Spenlove as he closed the box and then stood close up to speak. Mr. Spenlove could see the mail was for Sydney Saxon. Irving showed it to him.

"We're guests there," he said.

"I know you are," Mr. Spenlove said. "Your girl called me up last night."

"Did she? Did she tellya about Elliot?"

"She did. It was kind of her, but I knew about it. Did I mention it? The Ducroys are neighbors of mine."

"I know. Terry told me. I metya in New York. Remember?"

"Very well. Are you staying long?"

"I'm his agent. There's a lotta business to settle now."

"Of course. Well, don't let me keep you. I have an engagement."

He looked down at the keen, acute, anxious, overwise little face at his shoulder.

"An engagement with Mr. Ducroy's daughter," he added gravely.

Irving followed Mr. Spenlove out of the porch like a spaniel.

"Say, I didn't get that," he said. Mr. Spenlove saw a station wagon at the curb. It contained several dogs of expensive breeds, mostly ears and lolling tongues. In the driver's seat, a bright scarf tied around her head, and reading a morning paper, was Terry Florence. She looked up and waved to him with a hand holding a cigarette.

"Didn't get what? His step-daughter, if you want to be particular. Didn't you know Mrs. Ducroy had a daughter?"

"Oh, sure. A kid. I seen her out on the Coast. It was the way you said it. An engagement. You going to the fun'ral?"

"I'd have thought you knew things like that, Mr. Irving."

"Well, for Gawd's sake! You were a friend of his. He used to talk a lot about you, Mr. Spenlove. My best friend, he talked about you."

"Did he? Favorably, I hope?"

Mr. Spenlove stood on the low stoop outside the shabby post office, out of the way of the people coming and going. He made no attempt to follow Irving's obvious desire for him to go up to the station wagon to meet Terry Florence. Irving held out the hand which was holding the mail and tried to propel Mr. Spenlove gently with the other. He met with resistance.

"I dunno what you mean by favorably," he said, suddenly

desisting, and looking down at his fabulous footwear. "He said you were not so crazy. Terry said we ought to ask you over. I wanted to come and see ya, but she said nix to that."

"That was my loss, Mr. Irving. Perhaps some other time . . ."

He began to move, but Irving followed him.

"Listen," he said in a low tone, "you could render assistance, maybe, bein' a friend of Elliot Ducroy. I guess you knew how things were, over where we're stayin'. Terry says she told you."

"She did, yes. I didn't ask her, but she told me. He's been practically a permanent guest."

"Well, it's this way. I'm his agent. I got an option on all work up to the end of the year, and naturally I gotta get somebody to carry on."

"Carry on?"

"Sure! Under the Gentleman Church contract. He's left a lotta stories we can use, with some pointin' up, and so on."

"Well, who's stopping you? I'm not clear what it is you want me to do. I don't know anything about Gentleman Church."

"No, but you see, it's this way. I got serial, second serial, motion picture, television and translation rights all in my contract, but she owns whatever's in his desk, as it were. Get that?"

"She? Who's she? You mean Mrs. Ducroy?"

"Cert'nly. 'S why I wanted to see ya."

"I think you'd better see her lawyer. Look here, I have an engagement. You'll excuse me now, won't you?" He walked on to his car.

"She ain't got a lawyer," Irving said earnestly. His round black eyes were brilliant behind the sunglasses. "She said so when I phoned."

"Perhaps she thought you were intruding."

"I was. I gotta intrude, in his interest. It's a responsibility, bein' agent of a big man like Mr. Ducroy. I gotta have power of attorney now, see?"

"I still think you're confusing me with some other fellow," Mr. Spenlove said. He laid his hand on the door of his car, from which Mrs. Sankey suddenly looked out, militant, suspicious, red-haired, and with an air of suppressing a mysterious indignation with the world.

"No," said Irving, taking in Mrs. Sankey rapidly. "Oh, no. It's a delicate situation. She won't have anythin' to do with anybody who's a friend of . . ." He indicated the letters he held in his hand well out of Mrs. Sankey's range. "See what I mean? And I'm her agent too, for scripts. This puts me on a spot. So as you know Mrs. Ducroy intimately, so Terry says, you could put it to her, see?"

"I can tell her you want an accounting," Mr. Spenlove said, without enthusiasm.

"Sure, I do. I had power of attorney, from him, but only in his lifetime and for six months, renewable. You make her understand that. Nobody knows the Gentleman Church account like I do. I built it up. Jesus, I *made* him, Mr. Spenlove! But it's up to her now. This is important, Mr. Spenlove. I got a conference in New York tomorrow with a producer. New series of shorts . . . She'll have to give me . . ."

"Well, suppose you come over and see me. I'm going now. See you later."

He got in beside Mrs. Sankey and started the car. Irving was obviously concerned about what had happened. From a position of delightful prosperity, thoroughly deserved, of course, as the confidential man of business of a phenomenally successful writer, he was suddenly transformed into an outsider, dependent upon a woman whom he could not understand and whom he suspected of hating both him and his girl because of what they knew about her. Irving probably was aware that the law of diminishing returns applied with particular emphasis to the Good Samaritan business. They had been extraordinarily tactful and kind to Elliot Ducroy's wife because she was his wife. Their tact and kindness, however, had been exercised in a situation which excluded appreciation.

"You hear about Mr. Ducroy at the big place?" Mrs. Sankey said suddenly, with an expression of bitter resignation on her reddish features. It was as though she felt that Mrs. Ducroy had all the luck. "Got cramp while he was in swimmin'."

Mr. Spenlove nodded gravely.

"Think she'll keep that place on, now she's a widow?"

"Why don't you ask her, Mrs. Sankey? I would, if I were you."

Mrs. Sankey sniffed and said no more. Mr. Spenlove happened to be a much better employer than she cared to admit. He paid her more and gave her less trouble (now he had a car) than any of her other employers. She knew more about him than he suspected. There was plenty of gossip at Sutton Corners about the Mudge Place. Mrs. Sankey could let sleeping dogs lie better than most, but she knew from experience that women like Mrs. Ducroy didn't go into no convents when their husbands died, and she herself didn't want to lose a good position. The note of annoyance in Mr. Spenlove's voice made her feel that it was an uncommonly good position.

As they reached the cottage Mr. Spenlove touched her on the shoulder.

"I expect to go to England for a few weeks, Mrs. Sankey," he said, and followed her out. She stood stock still, frowning. He knew by now that it would take perhaps ten seconds for the idea, of him going to England, to reach her intelligence. He closed the door, examined his letters, and then looked up at her and added:

"How would you like to take care of this place while I'm away?"

He did not wait for an answer, but went in at once to make ready for his trip to Camp Lullaby, which was in the lake region beyond Torrington.

Last night, while he was taking Perdita to the Inn, she had

suddenly begun talking very fast and eloquently of Sonia and their life in Los Angeles. It was as though she had changed into someone else while he had been away changing his clothes and having a Scotch and soda. He had mentioned this to her, casually and off his guard.

"Scotch and soda? Yes, I had one too. I had a Scotch and soda, with Mr. Mallinson." She made a jumble of the name, he noticed, and was silent for a moment. She remained silent too, only throwing herself back in the seat and looking out of the window with a sort of lunatic eagerness that almost frightened him.

He thought to himself: *She's under a strain. She's had a shade too much. I'll leave her alone.*

He was not sure, afterward, whether he had been wise or not. She said, suddenly, and like a child pouting:

"What you cross about? What 've I done?"

He was approaching Norbury just then and he was watching the traffic. His heart was like lead at the moment. A cross draft gave him an inkling of how many drinks she had had. He supposed that fool of a poet had fallen into the trap as easy as easy! He would like to kill all the poets in the world just then, and all the damned, sanctimonious people who could take care of themselves, and who would look down their noses if they saw her now.

Well, he thought, *here's something I can't delegate.*

He drove into the Inn parking lot and stopped at the side door which led to a service stairway behind the lounge. More than one guest had come down that back stair silently while interested parties had ascended to visit his room by the impressive front staircase.

He got out and found the waiter who had often served him at dinner. He put a five-dollar bill in the man's hand, which closed on it automatically. Then he explained the situation.

The news about Mr. Ducroy had already reached them, the man said. Well, Mrs. Ducroy had been under a terrible strain, so. . . .

They had her out and up the stairs in two-twos, he reflected grimly. He wrote her name in the hotel register, which was on a table on the upstairs landing instead of in the office. Then he descended to the office to give some explicit instructions, which were accepted by the landlady with an understanding nod. To her it was a very simple situation.

In his then condition of mind it had not occurred to Mr. Spenlove that roadhouses knew a lot more about such matters than a retired seaman. It did not occur to him then, though he saw it later, that the landlady had precisely the same problems as the steward of a liner and was patronized by the same people.

As he drove home, he tried to co-ordinate his thoughts. The trouble lay, he believed, in his being unable to take care of her, in his position as a fortuitous element in her life. Of course, everything since she came to America had that quality of chance; but surely the manner in which he had reached his present status was the very essence of chance. He had no standing at all in the world of Elliot Ducroy, the successful producer of mass entertainment.

Nor would the shadowy Norman Tower and his literary spouse, Vivienne Vavasour, Perdita's parents, who were producing mass fiction in the depths of the English country, accept him as an equal. They were embedded in a social fabric which was showing a lot of cracks, but that did not mean it was falling down—yet, he hoped.

The only thing to do was to assume full ownership of her, because it was obvious that unless he did, she would destroy herself. As he thought that over this morning he found that the problem was an adventure and he wanted to embark on it, even if it involved him in unexpected situations. His heart was no longer like lead. He knew, and he was preoccupied with this delicious thought, when Irving suddenly accosted him at the post office, that he had an ally in Sonia.

He told Mrs. Sankey she would have to walk or catch a ride home as he would not be back until dinner time.

She looked at him for a moment. Mrs. Sankey did not make a habit of meeting anyone's eye. He remembered suddenly what he had asked her, to look after the place if he went to England.

"Would you take it on, Mrs. Sankey?"

"Couldn't live here," she said, abruptly, going on with the kitchen cleaning.

"You could keep an eye on it. Keep it clean and give it an airing. Lock it up, of course. And feed the cat. He's used to getting his grub now. Why couldn't you live here, Mrs. Sankey?"

She gave him what was almost a leer. Outside, the faint sound of Old Jim, sawing a log for the slowly mounting pile of firewood, could be heard. She gave a sensuous shudder.

"I'd be seein' ghosts!" she said.

"Would you? Well, I'll get Old Jim to keep an eye on the place. Think he'd stay sober?"

"Not when his time comes," she said, sweeping past with her paraphernalia into the parlor. Her voice sounded like a sybil's, full of foreboding and a gloomy relish for disaster.

"You've got something there, Mrs. Sankey," he said gravely, putting cigars in his pocket and taking the key from the corner cupboard. He spoke amiably. "There's some beer in the ice box. Help yourself. Mind *you* don't fly off the handle and get tight."

"Me?" She turned on him from the chair she was moving. "I'd throw all the hard likker in the world into the sea!" she cried, with a sudden return to the mood of her peasant ancestors. "It's never been anythin' but a curse to me!"

"I said beer, Mrs. Sankey." Mr. Spenlove was impressed in spite of his mild correction. Mrs. Sankey had the problem in an acute form, of course. Old Jim was a saint compared with Mr. Sankey, who had reached the point of complete inebriation. Old Jim, if not a saint, was intuitively a gentleman in his cups. He would have hobnobbed with three-bottle men a hundred years ago in Virginia. It was not a curse to Old Jim.

He rose to his real bacchanalian stature when he fell under the table, which was about once a month.

"Beer?" Mrs. Sankey subsided and went on with her work. "If it was only beer!" she mumbled.

"Well, leave the key under the mat," he said. It occurred to him that he did not want Mrs. Sankey's job. He wouldn't be in her shoes, he thought. He went out to the car. He hoped for no more interruptions.

But it was his luck, when he stopped in Sutton Corners for gas, to draw up behind Sydney Saxon's station wagon with Terry Florence at the wheel. She was alone. She saw him in the rear-vision mirror and got out at once.

There was something disarming about Terry in shorts, with a bright handkerchief over her brown bob tied with a knot under her chin. Her arms and legs, not very tanned as yet, resembled a nice child's still in elementary school, and when she took off her sunglasses she seemed about eleven, at the most. The bashful expression she cultivated was more pronounced now than when she was in her own apartment. Mr. Spenlove almost expected her to put her finger in her mouth. He wondered why he was so instinctively distrustful of her. He ordered ten gallons of gas.

"Why didn't you come and speak to me this morning?" she said, reproachfully. Now was the time for her to put her finger to her lip and a tear to start, he told himself.

"I was in a hurry," he said. "I had a woman waiting, the woman who cleans my place."

"That's not the reason. Irving is upset."

"What's upset him?"

She came around and got in beside him while the gas was going in.

"The way you spoke to him! It's the best friend he's ever had in his life who's gone. He thought you'd understand. You know, Irving's scared of you!"

"Scared of me? I don't believe it."

"He was from the first. So was I, as a matter of fact. We felt you didn't believe in us."

"Believe in you?"

"In Elliot, too."

"I didn't think anything about it!" he exclaimed.

"Yes, you did. You took her side! I was sure of that at once. She ruined his life, and now, just as he was going to get his freedom and be really happy, he . . ."

He paid the attendant and moved his car away from the pump.

"And you blame my bad influence?"

"Elliot said he was sure his wife had changed lately. He said she was going to get a divorce."

"Didn't he want a divorce? He gave me the impression he didn't. You gave me that impression too."

"I know. Because *then* it was impossible. Mrs. Saxon had kept her divorce out of the papers. We didn't know how she had changed. Irving thought he was going to have a tough time persuading her to collaborate with Elliot. I didn't think it was a good idea at all."

"You said so. It seems to have worked."

"It was an inspiration! Irving and her literary agent have got the highest price ever known for the serial they were working on. She had got Elliot to consent to get a divorce too. We were celebrating only yesterday. It was going to be perfect. Now it's all washed up."

"Due to my sinister influence, of course."

"Oh, *please* don't be so cynical! Irving is worried because he is afraid Mrs. Ducroy will crab the game."

"How?"

She looked at him gravely.

"You think there aren't plenty agents want to jump Irving's claim? Irving's smart, but he hasn't the flash of these New York agents. They have a smooth line. It would be just our luck, after Irving had built up this connection, to be gypped out of it. Anybody could make a fortune out of Gentleman Church *now*! See what I mean?"

"I'm in a hurry, Terry, but I see what you mean. What makes you think I can use my influence in your favor?"

"Elliot said she takes your advice in everything now. Said you had more influence over her than anybody he knew. Said she trusted you because you were English, same as she is. Elliot said she *quoted* you."

"Why didn't you bring Irving over to my place when he asked you to?"

"I told you. Because I was scared of you after that talk we had in New York. It kept coming back to me. I'd been spilling it all to you, thinking you were Elliot's friend, and maybe I'd done Irving some harm."

"You'd better come over and see me," he said. She opened the door.

"You've no idea how bad Irving felt this morning. He thought you were against him. He gets very nervous and starts telling people how good he is when he ought to keep quiet. Mr. Spenlove, he *loved* Elliot! He doesn't know what he'll do now."

"I see. It may surprise you, but Mrs. Ducroy and I have never discussed this. I told her I'd met you. Do you know what she said?"

Terry got out, stood by the door and looked at him. She had replaced her sunglasses and became suddenly adult and sophisticated in appearance.

"I know she never liked me," she said.

"She said you were decent. Know what she meant? It's a special kind of praise, but it's praise all right. I agree with her."

"You do? I thought you were on her side. Didn't I tell you she never liked me?"

"Perhaps we'll never understand each other about that," he said and closed the door sharply. "Perhaps we'd better not argue about it. Mrs. Ducroy, I mean."

Terry Florence stood staring blankly, incomprehensibly in at the window of the car. He could not see her eyes, only a gleam like shuttered sunlight on a brown pool in a dark forest.

"My God, Mr. Spenlove! You aren't *interested* in her, are you?" She put her hand to her mouth, and stared across the highway. The flash of sunlight on the windshields of passing cars was reflected in her sunglasses.

"We've been dumb!" she said, as if to herself.

She went away, gracefully and clean of limb, like some abnormally healthy and wholesome child bred to take prizes at a physical culture school. Several men watched her climb into the station wagon.

Mr. Spenlove, as she turned into the road that led over the river to Sydney Saxon's Tudor chateau on the bluff, nodded agreement. He reflected sourly that possibly his appearance was against him. There was also his unfortunate habit of letting the other person talk. Listening was not a virtue here, he reflected. Those who were betrayed into loquacity suddenly become alarmed and suspect sinister trickery, whereas he had merely omitted to unbosom himself to them.

At sea, of course, he had talked to receptive audiences, who accepted his stories as part of the relaxation of a sea voyage, an agreeable substitute for professional organizers of get-together clubs and snappy travelogue lecturers. At sea, what he said had no bearing on the lives of the listeners, whom he knew only as agreeable beings in comfortable circumstances and who vanished after a few weeks of innocuous traveling.

He had discovered, when he came ashore, that it was he who was now an abstraction, a casual stranger without roots, regarded with tolerance because he was solvent and with curiosity because he took long walks on the shore and lived alone. It was the living alone that had caused Mrs. Sankey, who was not introspective, and who would rather be beaten with rods than experience a solitary existence, to mention the seeing of ghosts.

Gradually, as he became known by sight, and especially

since the Norbury *Times-Echo* had carried an item about "Glory Hole" which was spelled wrongly, and its owner, whose name became Spenlore, a former sea captain, he was aware of a change in himself. It was not that he prized solitude any less, but that he understood it better. Silence was only valuable if what you said, when you did talk, mattered to some other human being.

It was a warm day again and he wished, for once, that he had overcome his conservative reluctance and had bought a faster car. Today he wanted to go fast. He wanted to flash up these Connecticut hills and float marvelously, swiftly, as though air-borne, through the townships. Cars passed him and he experienced a new emotion, of mortification. There was no logic in it. He had inveighed with irrefutable sagacity against Perdita's occasional eighty miles an hour in the Virago and she had accepted the reproof meekly, dropping to sixty-five just to please him. Now he felt that if he had it, he would do sixty himself.

This was a symbol of the change going on, undoubtedly a form of rejuvenation. The fact of his immense seniority in his job at sea, because he had come into the company so long ago as a result of a merging of financial interests, had imposed upon Mr. Spenlove a patriarchal role. He had been there before any of them. Even the executives on shore could no longer recall when "old Spenlove" had not been in the employ. The ships he had originally served in had been scrapped years ago, like many of his early contemporaries. Drink, women, homesickness for their native countries, had disbanded them. They had cherished fantastic illusions, some of them, that they could become rich in America. They had gone into business for themselves and had failed. Only old Romaine, over on Second Avenue, was making a sound living out of his restaurant serving "Park Avenue Meals at Second Avenue Prices." He must go and see Romaine some time. . . .

Driving, at something under fifty, into the Connecticut hills, Mr. Spenlove saw how he had become conditioned, as they say, to being a sort of oldest inhabitant in his profession. When he retired, after thirty years in which the Maracaibo Mail Line was merged into the Yucatan Line, being finally engulfed in the Afro-Iberian Mail S.S. Company, he was, figuratively speaking, in the eyes of the modern staff, a museum piece, a prehistoric monster who had bucketted around the Caribbean in small steamers bought second hand from Scandinavians who could no longer afford their extravagant coal bills.

It had had its inevitable effect upon him. He had become used to regarding himself as a veteran among men who had been boys in school while he was gaining his first laurels in the company as a man who could keep a worn-out triple-expansion engine going without major repairs. The feeling that he was "on the shelf" as he called it, had hardened around his mentality like a shell and immobilized his emotions.

Perdita had broken the shell, and now he was beginning to move again with ease. This trip, to fetch Sonia home, not only took him away from Norhaven while they took Elliot Ducroy's body to the mortuary in Norbury. It gave him an excuse to keep away from Perdita until she was herself again. He was also strangely eager to avoid further contact with that tall, gaunt visitor who called himself Piers Mallinson, the poet. Mr. Spenlove was instinctively distrustful of a man who paraded poetry as a profession. He was not convinced that a poet was indispensable at Church Yard at this moment.

Once beyond Torrington and on the right road, he began to think of Sonia. In any case her life would run parallel with his for a few years. His passion for loveliness had been on a strict regimen for many years at sea, fed on the austere grandeur of lonely waters and mountains seen from afar. The virginal loveliness of youth, as Sonia had it, just on the point of adolescence, was like wine to him. There was also her character, which had a firm grain and a strength he could feel when she was with her mother. He found himself depending on that strength already, to aid him with Perdita.

The dirt road he was following, past a state forest with lofty green hills beyond, took a wide sweep around a stand of tall timber and then forked. To the right he saw a cypress board on which was painted "To Camp Lullaby." He had made good time in spite of his old car.

There were other cypress boards along the way and presently he met a private bus with the same legend on its doors and a number of extremely brown girls inside. He stopped abreast of it and made inquiries of the chauffeur. One of the girls called out in a shrill voice, "Sonia Pagett's going home. She had a phone call from her mother."

"That's all right," Mr. Spenlove told her. "I'm the messenger. Sonia's coming home with me."

He went on and soon, among the trees, he saw log cabins. He saw archery targets, very brilliant, set up in a row on a grassy sward. He saw barbecues and tennis courts and, presently, a lake with canoes and yawls and diving boards in front of a boathouse. He saw a rustic amphitheatre with rough seats, where two girls, almost nude, danced silently with veils made of long pieces of cheesecloth while an older woman, in shorts and a turtle neck sweater, stood by a portable radio perched on a tree stump, which served as an altar. As he proceeded he beheld tents in which more girls lay on cot-beds, enjoying a siesta after lunch. And then the track led on to a large building where cars were parked in a semicircle and another bus, exactly like the one he had met, stood empty by the steps leading to the central door.

A modern nunnery, he supposed, as he parked and locked his car. *Get thee to a nunnery!* How much tragedy was due to the lack of this sort of thing? he wondered. Ophelia, for instance, and the Wuthering Heights woman?

He went into a wide dark hall. A sign showed him the office and a young woman with gray hair and an appearance of extreme competence came forward to greet him. He told her who he was.

"Mrs. Ducroy phoned this morning," she said, nodding.

"She said you were coming for Sonia. Won't you sit down and wait? She'll be right down. She's changing."

"Did her mother tell you . . ?"

"Yes. She asked our advice about telling Sonia at once."

"What was your advice? This is rather out of my line. I'd be glad to have a suggestion. I don't fancy a hundred-mile trip under false pretenses. Sonia is intelligent."

"I told her. I said her father–stepfather that is–had had an accident, and was not expected to recover."

"That's true. He isn't."

"That's the impression in her mind at present. You can go on from there. The Hartford paper has just come and there's something about Mr. Ducroy. Just a brief mention. Of course, Sonia wouldn't read the paper, but we have held it up until she's gone, so nobody will tell her."

"You have a nice place here."

"It's a good camp. The girls are really happy."

"Did Mrs. Ducroy say anything about Sonia coming back?"

"She said she might have to leave, at any time. I suppose Mrs. Ducroy's position is bound to be, well, changed, now."

"She's going to England. She's English, you know."

"Is she? I heard she was in Hollywood. She's very lovely. And is Sonia going with her?"

"Naturally. Sonia could come back here next week, let's say, for a few days. After this funeral business."

"I understand. We'll be sorry to lose Sonia. This is her second year at Lullaby and she has a lot of chums from Harris here. Harris is an excellent school."

"Sonia told me she liked it. She's a good kid."

"Very good. Fine spirit."

She moved off, obviously eager to be back in her office.

"I'll send her right out," she said smiling professionally. Mr. Spenlove bowed and sat down in a large chair in front of a prodigious stone fireplace. He took a magazine from the table.

There it was, one of the featured stories in the magazine: "Gentleman Church Goes Home." That was prophetic, Mr.

Spenlove thought. He looked at the colored illustration fronting the first page. The famous master criminal was in a hay field confronting a beautiful country girl with her hand on the neck of a very large and noble dog.

Mr. Spenlove laid it down and pondered the situation. The quick nervous sentences, the rush of action, the staccato dialogue, the incessant allusion to forceful qualities and virile antagonisms—all this brought the now-dead writer before him in imagination. It was a strange thing that such a man, who could fill the leisure moments of millions with harmless amusement, should have been so unsuccessful in achieving enduring happiness for himself. Stranger still that, now he was gone, Irving would find someone else to carry on. Elliot Ducroy might be in his grave. Gentleman Church would live on.

He took the magazine up again and in doing so his eye caught another brilliantly colored cover. In large type in a white patch were the words *Sydney Saxon's Splendid New Serial, "Flapper's Harvest," Begins in This Issue.*

It seemed to him, in his inexperience, that it was only the other day he had seen the same legend on some other magazine with another serial by the same writer. What incredible industry! He had heard of Alexander Dumas, who kept a stable of hack writers toiling on his masterpieces. Elliot Ducroy had once revealed to him that a celebrated cartoonist, now long dead, was still appearing every day in a hundred newspapers, the jokes and drawings coming from a factory run by the original artist's wife. Was this immortality?

He glanced at "Flapper's Harvest." The idea of producing at this speed made him feel faint after his experiences with his scrap log. He was not sure that writing should not be left to professionals.

He put the magazine down and waited. It was a dizzy experience, impinging upon the lives of people who had the marvelous gift of feeding the hungry minds of the great public. The "gaping public," Elliot Ducroy had called it, with a sort of angry affection. A marvelous gift! Mr. Spenlove remembered that little woman passenger, Nora Cavanagh, who was a devoted wife and mother, who wrote stories of horrible crimes among international crooks and foreign nobility. Her nearest personal contact with the law was a parking ticket, yet she wrote of Scotland Yard as if she had played as a child in its corridors.

The only thing that bothered him, as he thought admiringly of the extraordinary ability of these people, was the effect of such temperaments upon their families. They were very like prima donnas, he thought, and one had to make allowances. Caxton Derrick, the great poet, and Sydney Saxon, the prolific spinner of love stories, were probably brother and sister under their skins. The difference was one of industry and it was the industry that Mr. Spenlove found so dismaying. He forgot that he had been pretty industrious himself for a good many years.

These magnificent young virgins, living lives of cleverly adjusted happiness in Camp Lullaby, would read these stories of crime, and love, and even lust, and would rise refreshed to go in for more calisthenics and dramatics and athletics. What was the answer to that? Frankly, he didn't know, and with Sonia coming into his life, he wished very much to know.

He was continuing this line of thought when a young lady in a tweed coat, yellow shantung skirt, silk stockings and white shoes appeared on the landing over his head. Her face seemed vaguely familiar. As she came downstairs holding a small hat and a pocketbook he saw that it was Sonia, dressed for the street.

He was astonished to realize that he had imagined it was Perdita. He had never seen Perdita in the child so plainly before.

Sonia came up to him quickly, a sudden charming smile of welcome on her deliciously small features. For a magical instant she was close to him and seemed to utter a faint sigh of pleasure. The gray-haired young lady came out of the office. Another girl, in camp clothes, was carrying Sonia's suitcase out to the car. Mr. Spenlove heard the gray-haired young lady murmur something to Sonia, whose eyes were on the girl with the suitcase. He bowed to the director and followed the two children to the car.

"This is Shiela," Sonia said. "Shiela Boldwin, my friend."

The other girl put down the suitcase beside the car and gave Mr. Spenlove a firm handshake, a precise, businesslike salutation. She immediately dropped his hand and stood looking at him. She had a broad freckled face with gray eyes and firm mouth. She was slightly bigger than Sonia; her breasts were more fully developed, and her manner more authoritative. Sonia was obviously the follower, Shiela the leader.

"She'll be back," he told Shiela, who looked straight at him without speaking. Sonia said suddenly, putting out a hand: "Good-bye!"

Shiela suddenly broke her pose and hugged Sonia, quickly, strongly, like a boy hugging a chum after a fine feat. Sonia responded vigorously.

"Skip it, kid."

Sonia got into the car, the suitcase was shoved in behind and they started.

Sonia did not speak for a long time. Once or twice she waved a hand to girls she saw in tents or walking on the forest paths. Then, as they reached the main road, she subsided and looked ahead.

There was an odd air of maturity about her. She seemed older. Mr. Spenlove had never seen her save in the play suits and shorts of her life at home. Now she was elegant and possessed an unexpected gravity and dignity.

"What about Hector?" he asked her. "I expected him to come too."

"He's at the vet's," she said. "He picked up something in the woods."

There was another silence, yet it was not unpleasant. Sonia sat, ever so slightly, nearer to him than if he had been a stranger, and she had a sympathetic personality. It was, he supposed, the germ of Perdita's thrilling magnetism. Possibly, too, the not-so-wonderful Archie Pagett may have contributed something to Sonia's charm.

"What about lunch? Did you have any?" he inquired. She nodded, waiting politely to hear if he had eaten. He said, not since breakfast. Suppose they stopped somewhere. She could have a cola while he had sandwiches and beer. She nodded gravely.

As the car pulled up at a roadside restaurant she leaned towards him.

"Is Mummy all right?"

His heart gave a queer jump. He realized with a pang, both painful and pleasurable, that he and Sonia were confronting a job of work. The way she said the words "all right" told him that Sonia was aware of this.

"Quite all right," he said. He was noting that she made this inquiry first.

"I'm awfully glad. I wanted to ask you, but I couldn't at camp, and we're not supposed to talk much to anyone driving a car."

"Quite right. Now we'll have a snack."

"Is Mummy worrying about Elliot? Did it happen at Church Yard?"

"No, not at Church Yard."

"Then he was at the other place."

"What other place?"

"That house where Sydney Saxon lives."

"What do you know about Sydney Saxon?" he asked. They were both out of the car now. Sonia stood beside him, her white cotton gloves and pocketbook in her hands. Mr. Spenlove locked the car.

She said, "Mummy's been upset. She said she was going to leave Elliot. Shiela told me. . . . Shiela heard. . . ."

She looked down at the graveled parking place and poked a pebble with her white shoe.

"You like Shiela?"

"She's my bestest friend!"

"Oho. I thought I was going to be a friend."

"Oh, you are! And Louis! Have you seen Louis?"

"No. But I think he's on the job. Your mother told me only yesterday morning that Louis was on the job. You see, your mother and I were out fishing in my new boat when Elliot had this accident. He was swimming."

"Mummy told me. Have you finished your boat? Oh, and how is Tobermory?"

"He prospers. You know, the wicked always prosper. I'm sorry Hector is out of luck."

"It was his own fault. He's so disobedient."

"It was his disobedience that introduced us, don't you remember? And that introduced your mother too. You introduced her."

"I know," Sonia said. She walked into the restaurant as though her heeled shoes were unfamiliar. Once or twice her ankles turned on the pebbles of the drive.

They sat down in a room empty of customers but full of tables with check tablecloths. The bar was vacant. A waitress came and took their order.

"If anything happens to Elliot you will have to take care of your mother."

"Oh, yes, of course."

"Do you want to go back to that school?"

"Harris? Of course. To graduate."

"Your mother gave me the impression, Sonia, that if anything happened, she might go to England, and of course she'd want you to go too. Wouldn't you like that? See your grandparents?"

"Oh!" The idea of England was evidently novel and vague to Sonia. Her beautiful, enigmatic eyes, changing in color, expressed a sort of virginal skepticism of the reality of any existence so far away from Camp Lullaby.

"Well, would you? I practically promised to inquire and see how you felt about it."

"Is Elliot at Church Yard?" she asked suddenly.

"Not now. He's at the hospital, I expect."

She had her fingers on the cloth in front of her, and she raised her eyes from them to look across the table at him with her clear, trustful, interrogating glance.

It reminded him of her aversion to being "psyched" as she called it, and his secret consternation at discovering such notions in the head of one so young.

Now he suspected a shadow of doubt in her thoughts as to the exact state of affairs at home. Moment by moment she was adjusting herself to the world outside Camp Lullaby. The image of Shiela Boldwin, who represented for her the ultimate perfection as she knew it, was retreating to make room for the idea of life without Church Yard as a setting, without Elliot (who had sent her to Harris and who paid all the bills), without even Louis.

"I see," she said, and looked down at the tablecloth again. She was demure in her acceptance of what the immediate future might hold for her. Possibly, he thought, she had the instinctive confidence of youth and sex that she would be guarded and cherished. Possibly she had already an intuition of his part in the business.

He began to tell her about the fishing, about the visit to his great friend, Mrs. Colwell, on the Sound, practically opposite Church Yard, and the return to hear the news of the accident. It was really easy to tell her the exact truth except the final fact of fatality. She knew, and he recalled how she had told him in the spring, of Elliot Ducroy's occasional heart trouble. She nodded gravely.

"Elliot works terribly, terribly hard!" she said in her high little voice, which sometimes got out of control. "Writing, writing! Was he any better this morning?"

"I didn't hear. I don't think so, to tell you the truth, Sonia. I really don't think he will recover. Do you know a man named Irving?"

She moved her hands to make room for the glass and bottle the waitress set before her.

"That's Elliot's agent for his picture contracts," she said clearly. "Of course I used to see him sometimes, when we lived in Hollywood."

"Well, he's in Norbury now, staying over there, you know. . . . He spoke to me this morning and he had no news. So . . . Well, if I were you Sonia, I'd wait till you see your mother. She'll know."

"I'm pretty certain it's terribly serious," she said earnestly. "About Elliot, I mean. Mummy wouldn't have sent for me if she hadn't felt it was serious."

There was a sort of magic in that word "serious," he told himself. He realized he had repeated it twice, as she had. It was a refuge. He hated prevarication. He was unconsciously attempting to thrust it from between them.

He thought, as he ate his sandwich and drank his beer, *I must have Sonia with me if I marry her mother.* It was suddenly and completely apparent to him that Perdita had no chance to stand out against the two of them. Sonia was too grown up to be fooled by any common-law-wife fakery.

"Don't forget," he said, as he paid the check and they went out to the car. "If your mother goes to England you must go along to take care of her."

"Of course I'll go with Mummy," she said.

"I was thinking of going over too," he said, as they got into the car.

"Oh!" She looked at him with beautiful, unfathomable eyes. She clapped her hands softly so that he lost his heart to her over again. "Oh, couldn't we go together?"

"We might. Ask your mother. Think she'd like it?"

He started the engine and let in the clutch.

"I'm pretty sure she would!" Sonia said. As the car gathered speed and headed westward she gave a quick, gasping laugh. It was as if she had gained a glimpse of the golden future as the sun shone in her eyes, and she repeated her words.

"I'm absolutely *sure* she would!" she exclaimed.

vii

HE WAS upstairs packing, preparing to go to New York, when he saw the huge old Locomobile. He remembered the car as belonging to Miss Penge.

He was not surprised. He had seen her at the funeral service in Norbury sitting with Mr. and Mrs. Cagliari. He had seen her catch sight of him and immediately converse with Mrs. Cagliari, who at once stared across the aisle at him. Two whacking big females, with the wiry, diminutive, sunburned Mr. Cagliari only partially visible between them. They reminded Mr. Spenlove, most unfairly, of two wardresses.

The sight of the big old car, with Miss Penge preparing to get out, brought back the experiences of that forenoon in a sacred edifice. He had remained completely aloof from the cortege, which had surprised him by the number of black frock coats and top hats. He had not realized so many men still had them in this country, he told himself. The honorary pallbearers walked in couples behind the paid mortuarians who actually carried the casket. They were, the Norbury *Times-Echo* said, representatives of art and literature. Editors, publishers and illustrators were there, to do an office for the dead before they hurried back to serve the living. They looked like mutes, Mr. Spenlove thought, with their expressionless faces, funereal garb and the gray gloves supplied by the undertaker's assistant.

He had remained completely aloof. When Sonia had seen her mother in a black dress, she had stood stock still for a moment and then had put her arms about Perdita gently and without speaking. Then she had walked gravely out of the room to find her friend Louis.

Perdita had said, "I suppose you're disgusted. I wanted to shoot myself this morning."

He took her by the arm and led her into the garden. She stood on the terrace dressed in black, beautifully tall and full of splendid vigorous life. It was almost as if, without her knowing it, the death of Elliot Ducroy had bequeathed his vitality, which he no longer could use, to her.

She stood with hands clasped in front of her bosom, regarding watchfully, even sternly, the flags of the terrace on which she stood, as though she was on her guard against the love in his heart, and her own emotions.

For a moment he had wanted to shake her, to tell her that it was a custom only popular in certain savage tribes, for a widow to immolate herself. He knew that was a weakness of his, to disparage feminine exaggerations. Instead, on this occasion he was patient.

"Wouldn't it be better, under the circumstances, if I stayed away until the officials have departed? Until you've got back to normal?" he said.

"If you like. Yes, it would be better."

"It looks rather as if I were leaving you in the lurch just when you need support. I'm risking that."

She walked down into the garden, where Mr. Cagliari was to be seen, bent double, beneath a huge Mexican hat of straw.

"I thought you'd come to say good-bye," she said, not looking toward him at all. "When you came in with Sonia just now there was something in your expression that made me certain I'd earned your contempt. I couldn't bear that. It was lovely of you to bring Sonia. Coals of fire, in fact."

He looked at her, thunderstruck.

"I never dreamed that what has happened was going to do *this* to you," he said. "You sound as if you'd gone off your head! Have you?"

"Have I? No, I don't think so."

"You can't treat me like this! Do you think you can? Of course, it's possible. Yes, on second thought, it's possible!" he said, in a voice she could hardly recognize.

She had been looking away into the woods beyond which his house stood, when he started abruptly for the front of the house, to reach his car. He walked with swift determination. For a moment she stood watching him as though in a trance. As he pushed through the shrubbery and vanished around the corner of the building she turned and hurried into the house. The eyes of Louis and Sonia watched her as she went out on the front porch.

He was lifting out Sonia's suitcase when she caught up with him. He put the suitcase on the steps, and started to get into his car. He had been tired by his drive and the strain of the past twenty-four hours. And now he was furious.

She ran around to the other side of the car and got in beside him.

"If you go now you take me too!" she said in a low tone.

The words broke the tension between them.

"Do you mean that?" he said, smiling faintly.

"Yes," she said, clutching his arm. "Yes, yes, yes! I won't let you go! It was the contempt I couldn't bear. Forgive me. Yes, I mean it! So much!"

"No contempt," he said abruptly. "There was no contempt. Do you know, I am a believer in forgiveness! Charity, if you like. We're both talking nonsense."

For a moment, her hand on his arm, they sat silent. The immense difficulty of bridging the gap between two personalities overwhelmed him for a moment.

"Now," he had said at last, "I'll tell you. I'll come and see you–and Sonia–after it's all over."

"Don't go away! I want to feel you're there. Don't leave us!"

"I'll be there. I'll go to the funeral too. One of the fellow townsmen. Yes, I'll be just a fellow townsman. Have you had a bad time today?"

"I've had a hell of a time. People coming and phoning all

the time. I had this dress sent over from Norbury with a woman to do some fitting. She's here now, making me some widow's weeds. And I'm out here in your car behaving like a lunatic. Well, I was a good wife to him as long as he wanted a wife. That was a long time ago, before he made so much money."

"Have you seen Mr. Irving, the agent? You ought to, you know. He is very upset."

"Not yet. Elliot trusted him. I can't attend to business yet. I don't *want* to!"

"You should have a competent lawyer. I know a man in New York—he advised me about this place of mine, got it for me, in fact—he'll know a good firm. Mr. Merry would know a good man."

"Couldn't I leave all that to you?"

"No, you couldn't! The moment anyone in Norhaven heard that they'd say that I was after your money. Sinister influence of mysterious stranger on wealthy widow."

She pressed his arm again.

"How do we know I'm wealthy."

"I'm assuming there's something in Irving's anxiety. He has bank books to show you. And contracts. And in addition to that, he told me he is going to find a ghost to go on writing the Gentleman Church series. It will be"—he paused—"a voice from the tomb."

"I know about that," she said. "Elliot said once that Gentleman Church was a property. I suppose that's what he meant."

"It's an extraordinary thing to me," Mr. Spenlove said. "I know the dyer's hand becomes subdued to what he works in, but the idea of the hand going on working after the dyer's dead . . . Hm."

She gave a hysterical giggle.

"I said I was behaving like a lunatic. I'm a scandal. The woman who's fitting me is outraged. She thinks I ought to be lying down in a darkened room, weeping. What I feel, my dear, isn't grief, but confusion. I'm so puzzled over my own emotions. You see, he was so horribly in love with her! It was painful to think of when you knew. It's she who ought to be measured for these weeds. . . ."

She held back a laugh that became a choking convulsive sound. He stopped her.

"Go," he said quietly. "Go now. Sonia has been splendid. Sonia will take care of you. My dear!"

He pressed her arm and pushed her out gently.

"I'll be there all the time," he said.

"That's a promise!" she said.

So he had gone to the obsequies, sitting well back, but not so far back that Miss Penge, who knew everybody in that part of the church and nodded to them all, did not notice him and told Mrs. Cagliari, who looked at him almost at once.

There too, in a respectable dark suit, was the tall Piers Mallinson, the poet, half visible behind a pillar, his head sunk upon a clawlike hand. Mr. Spenlove thought with pride of the fact that Perdita was able to accept Mr. Mallinson instead of asking him abruptly to leave. Louis, she said, had made him comfortable. He had come all the way from the Coast in good faith. He had, Perdita said, a small pension which Elliot had paid him monthly.

"You know, darling," she said, "Elliot was splendid in some ways. Much more splendid than I am. He's been keeping up the payments to his first wife ever since her second husband lost his job with some truck firm. I found the papers in his safe in the studio."

"Did you know he had made a trust fund for Sonia?" Mr. Spenlove asked. She looked at him. He nodded gravely.

"One day last spring he took me to New York in his car, and he told me about it. He saw a lawyer, I suppose. He said you weren't to know because you'd misunderstand his motives. So she'd be sure to go to college."

"I didn't know that, dear. All I had was his word that he

would always take care of Sonia. Well, I said he was splendid in some ways. I'm glad you didn't tell me about it before."

He remembered that conversation, now that Miss Penge was coming up to the porch, looking around shrewdly and yet with some timidity. He heard Mrs. Sankey clumping through to answer the bell he had fixed outside the screen door.

He remembered it because, on that occasion, Perdita had simply walked through the woods, to see him. When she had come to the old boundary stone wall she had found Mr. Cagliari and Old Jim, one on each side, having a chat. She had walked straight up to them, not being the type to make pretenses to employees, or to turn back. She had stepped over the wall where it was displaced and walked on, to his house. It had been agreed between them that Mr. Cagliari would mention it when he got home that evening, and that Mrs. Cagliari would mention it too.

And here was Miss Penge, he thought, come to spy out the land. Making, as the local phrase so crisply put it, a check-up. He put on his coat and went down to see what she wanted.

He had made his arrangements with Mrs. Sankey to keep an eye on the place. He had not wanted to close it up. He had suggested to Perdita that Piers Mallinson, the poet, might live in it until he was ready to go back to the Coast. The tall hawk-faced scarecrow had not accepted the offer. He had announced that he would die in the East. When the closing of Church Yard approached he rode into Sutton Corners on Mr. Cagliari's covered truck and took a room at that gentleman's house for a while. His own old car had disintegrated. The local garage had offered him five dollars for it for scrap.

As he went downstairs Mr. Spenlove looked at his watch. He had about an hour to finish his packing and lock up, leaving Mrs. Sankey to put the key under the mat. The barn was already secured and his boat was hauled up.

He held open the door for Miss Penge. She came in smiling. She was dressed with unusual smartness. New shoes and thinner stockings than she usually wore, and her hair had been rearranged, so that she seemed, if not younger, less virtuous. He shook hands as he thought of this, and the gleam in his dark, ironical eyes, under the up-thrusting gray brows, daunted her a little.

"Miss Penge, this is a pleasure! I thought you'd forgotten me."

She sat down on the porch seat. The door of the house was closed and the shade of the window giving on to the porch was down, to keep out the afternoon sun.

"Thought you'd forgotten me," she said briskly. "Thought you'd never recognized me at the funeral service."

"It was the hat," he said, smiling. "A hat does change a woman's appearance. You're looking extremely well. How's business?"

"Very good. That reminds me. You got any spare cash?"

Mr. Spenlove was startled. That, he thought, is New England. They come to the point.

"On the premises, you mean?" His thoughts went to the leather case upstairs, with its thick roll of traveler's checks and cash money, its sheaf of passports, and steamship papers.

Miss Penge waved the idea away.

"Shucks, no. There's a party died suddenly over by Totoket, an old friend o' mine. We used to go to auctions together up in New Hampshire and Massachusetts. She was a widow. She died suddenly. The whole of her stock's for sale at about half what it's worth. I took an option on the lot. I've got to take it up this week. Ye see, they know I'm one of her oldest friends, and her nieces, who've inherited, are goin' to live in the house, so they want a quick sale."

Mr. Spenlove said he supposed Miss Penge had private reasons for confiding in him her business problems.

"Thought you'd like to go in on it," she said. "It's a mite too big for me to handle alone, but you'd turn your money over in six months and make a good profit. There's some curly maple stuff I been after for years. I know just who'll drive right out to buy it. Your friend Mrs. Colwell give me an order for a butterfly table I couldn't fill, and it's there out at Totoket, waitin' for me to pick it up."

"What are they asking, Miss Penge?"

"Twenty-five hundred for the lot, take it away yourself. That's what I called to see you about. I didn't care to use the telephone. Nobody knows about it yet."

"I don't know anything about the antique business, except in a very general way, Miss Penge."

"You couldn't lose your money. You'd make twenty-five per-cent in six months. Guess you wouldn't beat that on Wall Street."

"It's a speculation," he said gravely.

"Sure. But you got something you can *see,* and it always sells above what I'm gettin' it for."

"Twelve hundred and fifty dollars?"

She nodded.

"You must be a mind reader," he said. "Let's have a beer. There's a couple of bottles in the ice box. We can drink on it."

He made his voice sound as casual as possible. Miss Penge, sitting on the swing porch seat, had her back to the house that Mrs. Sankey was setting in order for his departure. Miss Penge was not sure whether Mr. Spenlove had agreed to her suggestion. He was surely a cool customer. But he evidently didn't realize that it was *because* he knew very little about the antique business, and wasn't likely to take advantage of what she was telling him, that she was making the proposition.

He came back with the beer, the last contents of the ice-box. Mrs. Sankey was carrying off the rest of the perishables when she went home this afternoon. He handed Miss Penge a glass and held up his own.

"The best of luck in your adventure," he said.

"You mean to say you'll go in with me? I'll git Lawyer Sturgis to draw the papers. You'll not regret it, I can say that. I'll take up my option at once."

"You attend to it. I'm going to New York to see a friend of mine."

Miss Penge sipped her beer and nodded, smiling.

"I guess you'll find it a bit lonesome here now your neighbors are goin' away. Mr. Cagliari says she's goin' to see her folks in England."

He looked at her gravely from his chair in the far corner of the porch, took a drink of beer and nodded before setting it down.

"Possibly. Would you take a check now and give me a receipt? It happens I sold an investment and it brought me considerably more than I actually needed. So I've the money there in the bank."

Miss Penge nodded. She understood such things. She was also a businesswoman, and never refused money. He got up and went into the house. The Armenian rug had been rolled up and put away, but he hoped she would not notice that. He went upstairs and took out his checkbook, tore a receipt form from a block and went downstairs again. He invited her in to sit at a table and offered her a fountain pen.

"You can leave the papers with Mr. Sturgis," he said.

"I'll have a catalogue printed," she said. "I got an invent'ry of the stock." She put down the pen and took up the check. Mr. Spenlove blotted the receipt and folded it.

Miss Penge was a little excited when she resumed her seat on the porch. She drank some more of the beer.

"I hope you don't think I come over just to do business," she said.

"Didn't you?" he said, smiling in the way that had confused her so when she first met him.

"Why, no!" she said. "Thought maybe you'd be over to visit again, some time. Now you got a car. Guess you find a car a convenience."

"That's right," he said, nodding. He hoped she wouldn't stay too long. She smiled with a certain archness. "So is a boat."

"I heard you'd fixed your boat. You go fishin'?"

"I was over to Long Island not long ago. Just before Mr. Ducroy died. In fact I was visiting Mrs. Colwell."

"You were? That's brought some changes, I guess, him dyin' like that. They say it was only a matter o' months and she was goin' to get a divorce. Waitin' for a residence qualification, I guess."

"Who?"

"Why, Mrs. Ducroy. Do you know, Mr. Spenlove, when I delivered some antiques I'd sold to that other woman, he was *livin'* there, and she was callin' him 'darling.' Yes, sir!" Miss Penge sat up straight. "None o' my business, of course, and money's got no smell. But when this happened, and he was taken home *dead*, I said to my friend Mrs. Cagliari, 'Jenney' I said, 'those things never last. She'll give up her lease, you see.' And she will too. And Mrs. Ducroy's goin' to England. See what I mean? They come and they go. I've seen a lot of 'em here, come and go."

"Mrs. Ducroy is only paying a visit to her parents, I believe," he said quietly. He looked at his watch again.

"Maybe so, but she'll never live here alone, after what's happened."

He folded his arms and seemed to meditate this, his eyes on the floor between them.

"I think," Miss Penge went on rapidly, an unusual brilliance in her glance, "I think we ought to set an example. Most Norbury people live here all their lives, and they live with their lawful partners too."

"Are you thinking of getting a lawful partner?" he inquired.

Miss Penge gave a loud laugh. She looked around at the door to see if it was closed.

"Oh, me?" she said. "It's not because I haven't had an offer." And she laughed again.

"You have? And it wasn't good enough?"

"D' you ever meet that Mr. Mallinson, a friend o' Mr. Ducroy's?"

"Why, yes. A poet, he said he was. You mean to say . . ."

She nodded, still laughing.

"He called at my place the day before it happened. Come all the way from California to visit Mr. Ducroy. He spoke on the telephone to him from my place. He's been roomin' at Jenney's, Mrs. Cagliari, since the funeral."

"I know. Mrs. Ducroy asked me—as a favor—to go and fetch her little daughter from camp. It was Sonia, the daughter, who introduced me to her mother. I met this chap when I got back, I think it was. He was at the funeral. A poet, he said he was."

"That's what he said when he called at my place," Miss Penge said. She was becoming extremely animated and confidential. "He had the most terrible old jalopy you ever saw in your life, and he come all the way from some place in the California mountains, to visit his friend."

"His patron, I'd call it. Mr. Ducroy admired his poetry. He is very poor, so Mr. Ducroy gave him an allowance. Mrs. Ducroy is going to keep it up for another year."

"I'll say he didn't make much money!" Miss Penge exclaimed. "He hadn't a nickel for a phone call! I can't say I'm surprised. I wouldn't say that po'try of his was so hot."

"You've read him? I'd never heard of him. I was going to . . ."

"No, I ain't read it," Miss Penge admitted. "He recited some. Sounded like he was makin' an oration, but there's nothin' patriotic about it."

She rubbed her nose quickly, as if to assist her powers of elucidation. Mr. Spenlove's expression sharpened. He said, in a tone of surprise,

"Recited? What did he recite? Was it, as you might say, in the nature of a serenade, Miss Penge?"

Mr. Spenlove made a gesture of playing a guitar under a window.

Miss Penge gave a loud derisive laugh, but she was not outraged by the suggestion.

"Took me a while to get it straight," she said, rubbing her nose again and then taking out a compact. "Seems he wrote it as a sort of farewell to his friend, and was goin' to recite it at the grave."

"Didn't he know it was going to be a cremation?"

"Can't say. Anyhow, there he was, with a poem he'd wrote in the house, right on the spot, and he couldn't use it. There wasn't any ceremony at the cremation. Never is, they tell me. So when he come out with Jenney to see me, he stood up in my parlor and recites what he calls 'Shapes of Flame.' Said shapes of flame were motion pictures and Mr. Ducroy, he was good at makin' 'em. I'll say he was, too. Jenney and I always took in Gentleman Church features and shorts at Norbury."

Mr. Spenlove sat looking at her.

"So what happened? Don't keep me in suspense, Miss Penge. Did *he* make you an offer?"

"I told him he was crazy," she said. "His old car folded up. You should have seen it. It was an antique. It folded up, and he got five dollars for it."

"Mrs. Sankey told me. She knows the man who bought it. These things get around."

"Well, so-o," Miss Penge went on, "he hikes out to my place one day. I had clients there and I ain't sure they didn't think he was my hired man, only he sits down on a garden seat and waits till I'm through."

She paused and seemed to recall the scene with strong feelings, but with a relish for the telling of it. Mr. Spenlove had a sudden dizzy vision of a life spent in close, unbreakable contact with that strong, New England voice, that harsh, benevolent, yet implacable personality, so sensitive to the beauty and charm of a hundred-year-old bedstead, so entirely unimaginative as to the forces that made a man want to have a bed and put a woman in it. She loved *things*, he suspected, listening to her strong voice, toned down to keep Mrs. Sankey from hearing.

"Most extraordinary," he murmured. "What has happened once can happen again, Miss Penge."

"That's what I always say," she declared, "I told him he was crazy."

"How did he imagine . . ?" Mr. Spenlove's voice failed.

"Why, I was friendly!" she said in a shocked voice. "You got to hand it to Mr. Mallinson, he's a gentleman. He'd been over to Mrs. Saxon's, you see. Mr. Ducroy, almost the very last thing he did that day, was to send Mrs. Saxon's houseman over in the station wagon to fetch Mr. Mallinson. So he was there when they got the poor feller into the house after the attack. Then he rode in the ambulance back to Church Yard. I must say that's a lesson," Miss Penge said abruptly.

"What's a lesson?"

"Why, callin' that place Church Yard, and buildin' that old covered gate to it," she exclaimed loudly. It didn't matter whether Mrs. Sankey heard that. She continued, in a lower tone.

"Well, of course, I don't suppose Mrs. Ducroy figured she wanted him around all the time, so he's been roomin' with Jenney. I heard Mrs. Ducroy fixed it, as he hasn't a cent. So he'd been goin' up to Mrs. Saxon's to talk about Mr. Ducroy, I guess. Mrs. Saxon's had a few people there, though he said she worked all day just the same as before. I must say I like her stories, don't you, Mr. Spenlove? All the characters are so clear and she nearly always has a good plot, and not gloomy at the conclusion."

"I must try them," he said. Once again he glanced at his wrist watch. *After all,* he thought, *I must not rush this. In a sense this is my last day in this life. My last day in Arcady. It is Arcady she is living in, only she wouldn't know it under that name.*

Aloud he said, "I must try them, Miss Penge."

"Well, I was sayin'," she continued, settling herself with a sensuous movement of her shoulders. He thought *I don't wonder she couldn't telephone me!* "As I was sayin', Mr. Mallinson was up there quite a lot for a day or two. There was Mr. Ducroy's agent and his—wife, I s'pose you'd call her."

"Common-law wife," Mr. Spenlove said, nodding. "I know her. She was here with her common-law husband. Do they have common-law husbands, Miss Penge?"

"Can't say. Well, they went back to New York, and all the other guests quit except one. A young man from Hollywood who's makin' a picture of one of her books. He's just a boy, Mr. Mallinson said. Mr. Mallinson said he was a dude. Said he was actin' like's if he was in charge o' the place. And I seen him myself in the station wagon in Norbury. You'd sure say he owned that bus."

"Just a boy?" Mr. Spenlove said, frowning. He was thinking of the stories Terry had told him in her penthouse in Greenwich Village.

"They say he worked with her in Hollywood," Miss Penge said primly. "Mr. Mallinson said he understood he was something in Hollywood. He said it was pretty plain to see what he is over there." She made a gesture toward the river.

Mr. Spenlove made a sudden convulsive shift of his person in his chair and Miss Penge looked at him with a shrug and a smile.

"See what I mean?" she said, as if sympathizing. "Mr. Mallinson said he couldn't stand that."

She opened her pocketbook and looked into it. She took out a clipping torn from a New York picture tabloid and handed it over to Mr. Spenlove.

He read it quickly and handed it back. It was part of a Broadway column called "You're Tellin' Me!" and it said:

Latest from Nutmeg State is, Wonder Boy of Hollywood, Dryden Turneur, who wowed 'em on the Coast before he was dry behind the ears, is making a smash hit with Sydney Saxon's new love-'em-and-leave-'em opus, I Would Be Thine.

Mr. Spenlove handed it back with care. He had no comment to make. It was another brief and not very illuminating glimpse into that world which Perdita had spoken of. She had called it names and wanted to be away from it.

"So-o . . ." Miss Penge said, replacing the clipping in her pocketbook. "Looks like Mr. Mallinson was right. He came and told me all about it."

"I suppose Mrs. Saxon doesn't want her own story gloomy at the conclusion," he said. "I suppose she thinks the clouds have silver linings even in real life."

"Oh, she sure does! And don't you, Mr. Spenlove? I think it's such a mistake to let tragedies get you down."

"Mr. Mallinson had the same idea, too."

"Oh, him! I was goin' to tell you and I forgot all about it. He comes to see me and tells me all about him bein' a Native Son and I tells him about my folks goin' to California. . . . Forty-niners, you see, and how they come back. Leastways some of 'em, my folks, did, and bought the house I own now and two hundred acres on Route Eleven. So then he says, 'Why don't you come back to God's Country with me and be Mrs. Mallinson?' 'Why,' I says, 'and leave Norbury?' He says, 'Sell this place and come to the great West, where nature is divine!' "

Mr. Spenlove sat looking keenly at Miss Penge, and smiling. He was thinking how like the Old England New England was becoming, how conservative and reluctant to move and explore. He himself had been a regular Columbus compared with Miss Penge!

"Of course you couldn't do that," he said.

"I'd say not! I told him he was crazy. He hasn't a cent. Look at Eddie Guest. He writes swell poems every day and makes good money. I asked Mr. Mallinson why he couldn't do the same and stand on his own feet."

"He wouldn't do that," Mr. Spenlove said. "He might be a good husband, easily managed. . . ." he suggested maliciously.

"That's not my idea at all," Miss Penge said. She began speaking a little faster and her eyes were increasingly bright. "I told him that's not my idea at all. I told him marriage is a partnership, and it's best for each of 'em to have a bit o' property, to make a regular partnership of it. Don't you agree that's the best way, Mr. Spenlove?"

"I've no doubt that's about the size of it," he said, smiling. He looked at his watch again. Only a few minutes more, and he would leave this wonderful world, this little Arcady in a fold of the Connecticut hills.

"Well, then," Miss Penge said, in a lower tone. "You can see what I mean! I don't mind admittin', Mr. Spenlove, I used that bit o' business, takin' an option on that Totoket stock, as a sort of lead. I thought to meself, this is as good an opportunity as ever to offer Mr. Spenlove a partnership. Seein' you'd nothin' to do and maybe had the cash . . ."

There was a silence. There was, for a moment, no sound at all. Mr. Spenlove did not fall down dead, nor did he spring up and run into the house, as Miss Penge more than half expected him to. She had done the most adventurous thing in her life and she was healthily desperate, a novel and stimulating sensation.

The very reason why she enjoyed Sydney Saxon's love stories and the romances of the film was because she was afraid of that sort of thing in her own life. Here, she had conceived, was a happiness she could handle, as she put it. The more she had thought of it the more perfect it appeared. Its perfection had made her laugh good-naturedly at Piers Mallinson, the poet, and her assertion that he was crazy had no sting in it.

The afternoon sunlight lay in long bars of gold athwart the tops of the trees outside, the shadows were lengthening across the yard. Under the great elm the swing, with bright new hemp ropes, swung ever so gently in the breeze. Flies buzzed above the hood of the long old car, and the air shimmered over its radiator.

"A partnership?" he said, at last, faintly. "A purely financial one, of course."

"Why, of course?" she muttered, and looked at the toe of her bright new shoe.

He began, "I'm afraid . . ." and stopped short. He sat up listening. So did Miss Penge.

"Someone comin'," she said. After all, he thought smiling, what made her think he would never have any other visitors? His hermitlike appearance? His infernal self-possession? The sound was coming nearer. Miss Penge stood up slowly.

"Guess I'd better move my car," she said frowning.

"Don't trouble," he said. "Since I moved that wall back there's plenty of room. Ah!"

He did not dare look at Miss Penge as the Virago suddenly thrust its immense nose and headlights past the shrubs of his driveway and swung into view. He stood at the door looking down at Perdita, in a close black hat and suit, with Sonia at her side in rust brown. The car stopped beyond the Locomobile, which seemed no longer very large but unimaginably obsolete.

The occupants sat quietly, smiling at him. The rear of the tonneau was full of coats and hand baggage. The large trunk at the back had new yellow leather straps.

He kept his back to Miss Penge and went down into the yard. He went up to Perdita.

"Miss Penge has been making a call," he said in a low tone, indicating the lady's car. "I'll excuse myself and we can start. I've made all arrangements with . . ."

He moved away, looking at both of them. Perdita got out. They met Miss Penge coming hurriedly down from the porch.

"How do you do, Miss Penge? Have you met my daughter?"

Mr. Spenlove slipped into the house.

"I'm going now," he said, out back.

Mrs. Sankey, resting in an old rocker, passed the back of her hand across her moist brow and then wiped it on her apron to shake hands. All the orders and final words had been uttered. She said she hoped he'd have a good time.

"I'll write you," he said. "You have my box key. Read the mail if you like! Good-bye!"

He hurried upstairs, closed his two suitcases and his attache case and carried them down to the car. He found Miss Penge already sitting behind the huge steering wheel of the car she had bought for a song. Her robust figure seemed to be built into the vehicle. Perdita was saying:

"I'll back up and let you go out."

Miss Penge said shortly:

"No, you go on out."

"Good-bye, Miss Penge," Mr. Spenlove said. He offered his hand. He had put his baggage in the Virago. "Mrs. Ducroy is giving me a lift."

He left it at that, seeing her stare stonily at the new steamer labels on his baggage. Slowly he got in beside Sonia, who made room for him with a welcoming little wriggle that meant a great deal to Miss Penge, who noticed it.

Slowly the Virago moved back, its enormous dual-valve engine sighing with an almost voluptuous ecstasy, as if it too were full of virile pleasure at returning to the land of its birth.

Mr. Spenlove gave his Panama hat a light tap to settle it, extended his right arm behind Sonia, and raised the other in a grave gesture of farewell to Miss Penge. The car suddenly went forward down the drive.

"Now go slow," he said, and Perdita nodded, keeping her eyes on the road. She knew what he meant, that it would hurt the feelings of Miss Penge if they flew away out of sight immediately.

They went slowly toward Sutton Corners. In the rear-vision mirrors they saw the lumbering vehicle of a past age, with its large wheels and solemn façade, following them. They saw Miss Penge turn into the gas station.

"That's that," said Perdita, smiling. "Please, can I go now?"

"Go on," he said, looking down amiably at Sonia, as if amused at his new role of commander. "Full speed ahead. That is indeed that!"

"What did she want, dear?" Perdita asked.

"I can tell you what she got," he said. And told her.

Perdita whistled. He said quickly, "It's a perfectly good investment. She knows all there is to know about furniture. Yes, I was lucky. I got off cheap."

"Cheap? I don't understand."

"Some day I'll tell you. Some day when we have got out of Arcady."

Sonia looked up at him, her nose wrinkling in inquiry. She was very happy. She had everybody she loved, except Hector and Shiela. Poor Hector couldn't get into England on account of the quarantine laws. Shiela was going to Maine to a hunting camp. Louis, however, was in New York, with heavy baggage. Louis would be on the ship with them. But–Arcady?

Perdita laughed. Evidently, Sonia thought, it was a grown-up allusion. The car sped through Norbury and fled along the pike to where they turned into the Parkway. They would leave the car at the dock to be shipped and have time for dinner and a show before going on board. A musical show, Sonia suggested. They sailed in the small hours.

"Is this too fast?" said Perdita. She gave him the old magical glance from those lovely eyes that changed color as he looked at them.

"No!" he said loudly. "Go faster! Full away!"

As the car began really to move he added, calmly:

"Go as fast as you like!"